HALF
IN
SHADOW

ALSO BY GEMMA LIVIERO

HALF
IN
SHADOW

A Novel

GEMMA LIVIERO

LAKE UNION
PUBLISHING

Published by Lake Union Publishing, Seattle

www.apub.com

Amazon, the Amazon logo, and Lake Union Publishing are trademarks of Amazon.com, Inc., or its affiliates.

ISBN-13: 9781542026963
ISBN-10: 1542026962

Cover design by Kathleen Lynch/Black Kat Design

Printed in the United States of America

HALF
IN
SHADOW

LONDON

1938

PROLOGUE

ELEANOR

My father was executed for the crime of desertion. This is declared in a letter from the War Office and confirmed by an office bearer at the bottom, unapologetic and seemingly supportive with a signature that is bold and decisive, and overbearingly underlined. This record that my mother keeps in a box in her bottom drawer, hidden beneath other papers, is one of the few links I have to Arthur Shine.

This year I turned twenty-three. I was six years old when I first learned his name. The gulf between those two events had been sparsely filled with assumptions about my absent father. The answers my mother gave me were vague and short, but as children, and sometimes as adults, we accept the simple explanations we hear from those we trust. Though there were things unsaid that suggested my father wasn't welcome in our house, even in death.

There are no photographs of Arthur on display. I have been to the houses of others who lost their fathers, brothers, and sons in the Great War and all of them were enshrined in some way: in display cases, on mantelshelves, enlarged and featured in entranceways, sometimes with medals, certificates, and war memorabilia. A helmet, a final letter framed, a woollen coat lovingly preserved, a spoil from battle, or bottled foreign soil.

From what I gleaned, my father's desertion had led to the death and massacre of many of his own men in France, in the autumn of 1915. The description I have of his crime and service is lacking, along with other details of his life that might allow one to draw their own conclusions or understanding. One crime in isolation seems a most extraordinary, if not terrible, thing. But what of the pieces that make up the whole? What of the life that came before?

What happened to his parents? I asked many years earlier when my mother, Harriet, was tending the rose beds that lined the sunny terrace, her golden strands of hair, in amongst the white, shining brilliantly in the sun.

Whose? she asked.

My father's.

She stopped digging and turned to look up at me, eyebrows raised, seemingly stunned by the question at first.

I never knew them, she said, her expression then fixed and pleasant, and paper thin: a veneer to hide a pain I had not considered until then. Though her life began with wealth and privilege, the latter years had not been as kind to my mother.

They died before I met your father, she said, turning back to the blooms and clipping needlessly at foliage that had already been trimmed.

I know that already, Mum, I said.

He comes from a line of miners, an only child.

She paused.

There isn't really much else, she said, ending further intrusion to a period of her life she had closed the door to.

I was fourteen at the time, and it wasn't that I particularly wanted to know at all; it was that others had started to ask me about my missing parent: curious adults, teachers, friends, always about fathers, where they were born. The titles of men seemed more significant to some.

The rest of the conversation I've forgotten because, like everything with my mother, any further querying would not have led me far.

However, I do remember her gloves blackened with soil as she then proceeded to dig with her trowel more fiercely, and realising that I had driven her to memories she had no desire to revisit.

Halfway through the war, my mother's comfortable circumstances left her when my grandfather's British textiles were no longer productive or competitive with those from American businesses and his country residence had to be sold. The allowance my mother had been receiving from her father's money dwindled to the point where she was forced to apply for a war pension, only to be rejected. Widows of deserters did not receive the same benefits as others who had served. And by the time this pension rule was reversed, my mother was too ashamed to then make a claim. That much I had learned about Arthur and our situation by the time she died, as well as from other comments that would float about a room when her distant relatives were visiting, as if such words were insignificant, or as if I were considered too much of a dullard to absorb their true meanings. *Lucky she has her mother's lineage . . . Poor Harriet, having to carry such baggage . . .*

At the funeral earlier today, I read out the eulogy I had spent days preparing. Mum was a good woman who ultimately carved her own way in tumultuous times, who created a home for her only child, and who had nursed each of her parents in their final months of illness. She rarely missed a Sunday service, was particularly kind to children, and loved me. I could say all these things from my heart, and I loved her, too. I just couldn't tell you what she thought about things, what her hopes were, or whether she was ever truly content.

"Come and stay sometime," said my mother's cousin, who fared better in postwar industry. But they are only words that people say to allow them to escape present company.

"Your mother sounds like she was a lovely woman," said a dark-headed stranger with a French accent and a walking stick. I had seen him there at the back of the church in a light-grey suit that matched the silver streaks just above his ears. He was tall and smiled the whole time I spoke, which caused me to falter distractedly at one point. At the end of the service, as people milled about with sandwiches and tea, he approached me.

"I am very sorry about your mother. I never knew her, but it was a great honour to serve with your father during the war," he said, handing me a calling card and a small package wrapped in brown paper and tied with string. "Please feel free to contact me, but only when you're ready, and if you wish to of course."

It was the first time I had heard something good about my father, and with so many questions I wasn't sure where to start. But before I had a chance to ask him, I was interrupted by others stopping to wish me well, and by the time they departed, the stranger had disappeared.

After the service, attended by Harriet's acquaintances and relatives I barely know, I am relieved to be home. I grieve properly, noisily, after being so busy with the arrangements and various duties that surround a death. I hold a photo of my mother as a young woman, lamenting the short time we'd had together and how little I know about her early life.

Outside, her garden is coming alive in spring, a burst of lime-green buds and a bickering pair of wrens, the heads of her fruit trees tilting eagerly toward the sun. I can see her there, too, if I shut my eyes. Without a doubt I will miss her.

I stare at the calling card, with a name I don't recognise, rolling it between my fingers idly while I try to remember if Mum ever mentioned him. Then I open the package to discover photographs of my father in civilian clothes, letters, and photographs of other people and places I have never heard of. I am temporarily transfixed by the handsome dark-haired man that I am connected to by birth, having never seen his image so clearly before. There is only one small photograph my mother had kept in a bureau, taken so poorly that most of Arthur's features can't be distinguished.

I sift through the items several times and gain a sense of the history I'd been shielded from. I feel sad, angry, happy, and finally a sense of belonging, a second coming-of-age, as if, through these puzzle pieces, I am finally put together. I see my father for the first time, and also myself in the hard lines of his jaw, the tightly clenched mouth with its sense of determination.

Then with a shaky hand, I open the letter personally addressed to me, and tears fall as I read the words, as I try not to judge my deceivers, as I find out my story has been based around a lie.

LOUVAIN, BELGIUM

August 1914

1. BROKEN TREATY

Yves is dead and Gisela has turned to stone. She has a photo in her hand that she isn't looking at. Instead she stares at the face of the baroque clock. It ticks louder since Yves has died, demanding attention in the house that is now filled with whispers. Sounds have died with Yves: doors slamming, running steps, minor pointless words and arguments, the bustle of a thirteen-year-old boy and a frustrated mother.

Josephine has prepared the eggs. She is the first to sit down at the table. She peels away pieces of cracked shell, dips a teaspoon into the yolk, and rubs the back of the scoop in a patch of sprinkled salt. She watches her mother stand up from the armchair and walk to the table mechanically. Her father enters the room and does the same, his black suspenders drooping at the sides of his trousers. The tears Josephine has swallowed have formed a glutinous lump in the back of her throat, constructing a barricade against the food.

It is different in the house, as if they are too small for it, the house vast, rooms empty, people scattered. The walls now papered with tragedy, the outlook from every window bleak, and the air thick with disbelief.

Where is Eugène? No one asks. Though it was always asked before the previous week. He was hard to tie down, in and out of the house at all hours. Now they know he is a fixture in his bedroom, angry and plotting, and talking to himself, cursing the Boche.

Yves had run. *Why did he run?* Josephine tries to remember the moments before he did: firecrackers, shouts, screams, her hand shading her eyes at the sight of a giant balloon in the sky. When she'd looked down, he was lying still on the road, a tiny, dark hole growing larger on his back. He was gone, head turned on its side, eyes open, one arm curled around the top of his head. His small body in the position he would lie in bed. It was a stray bullet, said the men with pointed hats, without regret. They had to be careful. There were franc-tireurs around every corner.

Yves had stopped holding Josephine's hand. She missed his soft, hot, sometimes sticky grip. He had been at the age of wanting to stand on his own two feet, his toe on the first step toward manhood. Still wary of it: much hesitation, such a long way to climb. In the days before his death, he would reach for her hand when he wasn't thinking, then draw it back again when he became aware. He infuriated her but fascinated her also: clever, funny, serious, and angry in the space of a day.

We have to keep going, Gisela, Maurice said. The night before, Josephine had heard her parents talking in the bedroom below hers, catching only snatches of their conversation.

What about Josephine? said her mother. *Like Yves, she may never get the chance . . .*

Chance of what? Josephine wondered. Of love, most likely, of marriage, of children: her mother losing hope for a normal life for her family under occupation.

On Josephine's birthday at the beginning of the year, Gisela leaned forward with a damp cloth to wipe a stain from her daughter's blouse.

You are a new woman today, she said.

I was a new woman yesterday also, said Josephine.

You have a smart mouth sometimes, but it is no good for an unmarried girl of your age. Think before you speak; then maybe you will find a husband.

Happy birthday, Mouse! Xavier said to stop Josephine from responding, to prevent a quarrel.

Maman says I am an old maid.

Twenty-three? He scoffed. *She doesn't mean a lot of what she says. She is goading you into marriage. You are still young. You are still of childbearing age.*

Josephine pulled a face. *Now you sound like Maman.*

Xavier laughed softly.

He had been joking of course. He has always been the one who understands.

Xavier is a parent's gift. He had trained to be a doctor and is now a priest, living and tutoring at the university. He is the oldest of four, then Eugène, then Josephine, then Yves, who was a mistake, a timing error as Gisela had called his conception, because she always says exactly what is on her mind. Not like her father, whose thoughts are often directed into his coffee cup initially, and any words then distributed with care.

Her parents get up from the table and back to what they were doing before. Yves is gone, and it seems he has taken them as well.

Josephine sinks beneath the bedcovers and listens to the darkness. Hobnailed boots scrape the cobbles, trolleys clatter, horses trot, and cannonade rumbles low in the distance. Voices somewhere, conversations in German, raised and joyful. They have won this round. A single shot sounds from somewhere in the town, and Josephine flinches. The smell of scorched earth and sweat catches on the breeze and contaminates her room.

Carry on! said the invaders. A few people were killed, and things can continue the same. Though much has changed. People aren't stupid. Posters are placed on public buildings, demanding order and threatening execution if there is any attempt to resist, even word of it. Rumour has it that women are being raped in villages, children killed. Rumours are like clay, they are told, and shaped by the people who tell them. *Get on with your day. There is nothing to see here,* they say.

Yves's bed lies abandoned under shifting moonlight. She stares at his sheets, imagines a shape there. She had crept over to his bed earlier to lay her cheek against his pillow so she could keep him with her during the day.

Why did you let go of his hand, Josephine? The first question asked by Eugène.

She puts her head under the pillow, on a patch of tears that have not yet dried, to smother the whimpers of her mother and the pacifying words of her father below. Also beneath her in another bedroom, Eugène paces the floor, drops something heavy, curses at whatever it is.

She has stepped through what happened over and over, and still there is no answer to Eugène's question.

⬤

Josephine had woken up, watched the light inch toward Yves's head to catch the lighter strands of his hair and spin them into gold. He raised his head to view her, hair kneaded into knots on the side he slept on.

"Did you hear the bombs?" she asked.

"No."

He rubbed his fists into eyes that were stuck with sleep.

She checked that Papa's old camera was still on the floor beside the bed, that Eugène hadn't squirrelled it away during the night, since they shared the use of it. Maurice had promised to purchase one of the newer ones, lighter to carry, for Josephine's personal and business use, now that her interest in her photography had begun to outgrow her mother's scepticism about her daughter's career choice.

"Yves," Josephine said. "You snore like Eugène, but worse. More like a grunting hog."

He broke into a smile, poked out his tongue. She jumped up, then straddled him and tickled him until he screamed, and below them Eugène threw something at the ceiling, woken up like an angry bear, often sleeping late. It was not unusual for him to be awake for much of the night, painting or drawing or pacing with insomnia. It was the reason Yves had moved to her attic room. Eugène was difficult to live with sometimes.

Highly strung, Maurice would say about their middle son. *Sensitive,* Gisela would counter.

Yves had been small for his age, most in his class a head taller. He never ran with the other boys down to the creek. He would come straight home, and Gisela would put his head over steam.

"He has my lungs unfortunately," said Gisela, looking at him, brows together.

Josephine dressed and followed the smell of burnt sugar and butter down to the kitchen.

"Where's your brother?"

Josephine refused to provide answers her mother already knew. She knew, for instance, that she had to call twice for Yves. That he had likely moved to the desk in their bedroom to continue painting his miniature wooden fleet of ships.

"Yves!" Gisela yelled up to him from the bottom of the staircase.

"Good morning, Papa," said Josephine, and she reached down to kiss him on the bald spot at the front of his head between tufts of hair that pointed in various directions. His ink-stained fingers reached around her head to hold her there a moment longer. He was tall and stooped, with the long legs of a stork and a smile connected to his heart. She had worked for him for several years at the newspaper he'd started with money saved from the age of fifteen.

"But what about the treaty, what about our neutrality?" said Gisela fiercely, responding to some earlier conversation back at the table. "Is that definite? Will they fight us? Are they coming?"

Eugène and Maurice were not arguing, as they usually were, about the Walloons and Flanders, where Gisela was born, and who was better and who should do what, her brother always driving the argument deeper, always passionate. Maurice defending the Flemish, and Eugène for the South. Talk that was boring to Josephine.

"Gisela, you need to remain calm," said Maurice. "The king is sending a force to guard at Liège. If Germany wants to come through Belgium, then they will not get far. They will have to turn back and re-enter France directly across their own border, not creep in the back door like rats. Besides, Gisela, the Germans have been our friends. They will not harm us. I am in contact with them regularly. We have cousins there, remember. They would not support this. No one wants a war with Belgium."

Gisela dropped her shoulders. She was not so easily convinced.

"Now, my love," said Papa, "everything will be fine. Josephine, you are coming with me early today. You need to order more ink and sweep the floor. Then if there is time, you can take your photographs and develop them in the darkroom."

"It is no work for a girl," said Gisela, moving toward Josephine with a comb to plait her hair as if she were a child. "Do you want dirty hands all the time, ink under your nails, and the smell of chemicals always on your skin like your father?"

"Yes, I do," said Josephine, wincing. Her mother was hard with the comb, scraping the top of Josephine's ears as if grating cheese.

"Our daughter is good at the work," said Maurice, "and I haven't found anyone who does it half as quick."

That afternoon, Josephine looked sceptically at the sky. Tiny spots of rain dotted the lens of the camera fixed on top of the tripod. She had only minutes more. No time to search for birds to photograph. She had collected seven different kinds so far, though not all images completely successful, and more to find to complete the bird album that she would give her father for Christmas, which Eugène would help colourise. She was still to find her father's favourite, the waxwings with their black bandit masks and pale, rust-coloured head feathers combed back like a thick head of hair, tips of tail feathers dipped in yellow paint.

That day she settled for a horse grazing beside a curly-headed tree in front of a farmhouse with a darkly hollowed space for a door in the shape of a mouth surprised, and the sky thick with twists of grey wool behind it. Beyond the house, steeple-shaped roofs that would likely appear blurred. She looked with her eye first, then through the viewfinder, suddenly critical of the angle, which did not feature enough of the horse, not enough contrast of light and shade.

She released the shutter bulb, folded the camera back into its box, and placed it with the adjustable tripod into the front basket on the bicycle. She tied up the bottom of her skirt into knots at her knees and rode the narrow track between the grainfields, her arm brushing against the ripened stalks leaning toward her with the breeze. She raced against the rain cloud that sat above her right shoulder. At the crest of a low ridge, she could just see the roof of her house wedged between others, with three floors and narrow arched windows and ornate architraves, built from red bricks and grey stone. Into the town square, pigeons scattered, and she jumped off the bike to walk through the busy market.

There was a flurry beside the stalls as people came out to watch the last of the Belgian soldiers marching east to their forts at Liège. People packed into cafés, saying their goodbyes to their sons, and Belgian flags flew from churches and public buildings. A horseman had dismounted next to a soldier with rows of brass buttons on his coat of navy blue. The soldier was handing the man a certificate before taking the reins to lead the animal away.

Josephine weaved between the conversations. A cobbler was debating with a shopkeeper about the state of impending war. Many were worried that supplies and trading with Germany would halt, that there could be a shortage of produce. That it would cripple the economy. Some were saying that Belgium should let the Germans through to

France, that they didn't want any trouble. Though the cobbler, vexed and red-faced, disagreed. Some said war will never happen, Belgium wants no part of war, and others said their men must enlist in the army to fight.

Eugène did not look up when she entered their house then exited through the back door, deftly pulling linen into a washing basket to beat the heavy daubs of spitting grey.

Josephine put the basket down inside and leaned over Eugène's shoulder to see what he was furiously scratching on his drawing pad. He had drawn a picture of an eagle and a rooster thickly, with red and black pencils, the rooster more powerful with its wings spread wide and the eagle cowering behind a rock. She disliked the small artwork, dark and foreboding.

On a wall hung his watercolour called *Dames Blanches*, which he won a prize for. The women in the art piece are spirits according to folklore, and Eugène depicted them all beautiful and partially clothed. Eugène's painting of a mermaid in the legend of the sunken city of Saeftinghe was also on display. There are houses of gold in the picture, and a woman with a long, shimmering fish tail lies in chains as a prisoner. Josephine had stared at that painting often and tried to imagine what Eugène sees inside his head, which must be wondrous and mysterious, even dangerous, and murderous sometimes. She found him dislikeable at times, but also too interesting to ignore.

"It is very impressive," she said, even though she didn't much like the dark topics he chose. "But why only the cock for Wallonia and not the lion for Flanders, too?"

"Why don't you go and do something else and stop bothering me with questions?" he said, focused on the tip of his pencil.

"Is that for the academy?"

"No," he said, still not lifting his eyes. "It is something Papa will print on leaflets to send out to everyone to prepare."

"Prepare for what?"

18

"War."

"What war?" she said.

He looked up at her this time with his large eyes with lids that drooped slightly at his temples. His unruly dark hair, his clothes crumpled as if he had slept in them.

"Are you that stupid?" he said. "Maybe you should read things other than your seedy little novels."

She froze. It seemed her secret was more known than she thought. The book Josephine read in private, the pages as new as the first time she read them, was *Les Liaisons Dangereuses*. She was that hapless ingénue, sadistically seduced and deceived. Emotion ran through Josephine's body in vivid colours, red with rage and blue with despair. She was also the Présidente de Tourvel, demented and tortured by the heartless Vicomte de Valmont, who broke her will and cast her love to the earth for the favour of another, equally as detestable as himself. After Yves fell asleep, she would read by candlelight, to keep her room as dim as possible, with just the steeply pitched ceiling leaning in to spy. Each time there was a sound from her parents' bedroom, she had pushed the wick into the wax with the tip of a knife to extinguish the flame without smoke. Her mother had the nose of a hound.

"Do you not listen? Do you not read the articles that are prepared at the newspaper? Where you spend most of your time?"

She did, sometimes, though most of her time was spent in the darkroom, developing photographs that line her room. There were better things to do and read, and talk of war was dull. There was also word that all such talk would come to nothing.

She ignored him and folded the washing. She was tired of his insults, of his moods.

"Mousey!" he said over and over until she looked up to see his clown-like smile. "Don't be grumpy with me!"

She threw a piece of clothing at his face, and he caught it before it knocked his open jar of pencils from the table.

"You're an ass!" she said before attempting to leave the room, his foot out in front of her suddenly so that she tripped. He laughed at her as she stumbled, but his grin was cut short when she retaliated with a kick to his leg. She ran up the stairs two at a time to escape. The competition between them was both friendly and fierce.

A week later, she was woken by shouts, and explosions that were edging closer, that shook her bed.

"The Germans have broken through our forts!" someone called from outside.

Josephine stood at her bedroom window, pulled up the sleeves of her nightdress, and rubbed at her forearms, nervously watching people scurry and shout to warn others. A trail of smoke and metal had infiltrated their house, and the windows rattled from distant rumbling. She could see red and yellow lights flying through the stars. People were running through the streets. Only when the bells were sounded did Yves wake.

"Stay here!" she told him.

In the next room her parents' bed was empty, and the panic that she had managed to hold back reached deeply inside her chest to grip it with two fists. On the floor below, Eugène had left his bed, and the floorboards shook as his giant feet thudded down the stairs.

Stepping onto the cold tiles on the bottom floor, she saw at once her parents and Eugène at the front window, merged into one dark shape that was silhouetted against the brilliant swirls of coloured fireworks in the sky.

"Get dressed, Eugène! Quickly!" said Maurice, switching on the light. "We must go and check on Xavier. Bring him here if we can."

Josephine felt the rush of air as Eugène passed her to leap back up the stairway.

"I want to go, too!" said Josephine.

"No!"

Maurice had pulled a pair of ink-splattered trousers from the dirty linen basket over his nightshirt and unhooked his coat from beside the door.

Gisela stood with fingers dug deeply into her upper arms as if she were chilled, shoulders trembling.

"Maman?"

"The Germans! They are coming en masse! I was told that most are just boys," said Gisela. "Why do they send boys to war? What is it that they are teaching them over there?"

"Gisela, they aren't boys, and they aren't innocent," said Maurice. "They are the same as men if they carry a gun."

Gisela collapsed on a chair nearby.

School had been cancelled after word came that Germans were sweeping toward Louvain. Eugène had gone to speak to his friends, to learn what was happening. Their father was at work, printing details about the event. Gisela was gone to buy food. Josephine had to stay home with Yves.

The sound of a baby crying drew them both to the window. Outside, a woman was weeping as she walked past. She had a sack tied to her back, a baby strapped to the front of her, and she carried bags in her hands.

"We have to bring her in!" said Yves, moving toward the door.

"No," said Josephine. "Papa said we must not leave the house for any reason."

But Yves had opened the front door.

"There are our soldiers!" Yves had said, pointing excitedly. "I want to see them!"

Josephine was suddenly curious also as she stepped beside him.

"All right. But stay close to me."

She took hold of his hand as they entered the confusion of the street full of people, but by then the woman with the baby had disappeared behind the group. They appeared frightened, some of them breaking into a run.

"It's over!" Belgian soldiers shouted as they ran past. "Louvain is done for."

She had briefly looked in the direction they were running and was about to pull Yves back inside. Then she had seen something strange above them. She released his hand and lifted both her hands to shade her eyes from the flashes of light in the sky.

"What do they mean?" Yves said.

"Get off the street!" someone yelled.

Josephine turned her head to see what everyone was running from. Around a corner at the bottom of their street, men in grey came by the dozen, firing warnings.

Yves had startled, run forward. A shot was fired into the crowd, toward the Belgian soldiers.

Now Yves is dead.

2. THE PURGE

Germans have been occupying the town of Louvain and told its inhabitants that everything will remain the same. That is not true. There are curfews, and roundups of suspected Allied sympathisers and those hiding Belgian soldiers. Postal and telegraphic services have stopped. The milk cart no longer comes down the street. The bakers, laundrymen, and vegetable sellers have had to give up their cart horses. The sounds of daily chatter have been shut away.

The Descharmes family has an empty coop with a scattering of feathers, and a shiny dust-free circle on the mantelshelf from where a silver dish was taken. The enemy has swarmed the town like flies, posted notices threatening execution, and taken things that don't belong to them. Precious things: copper pots, silver spoons, money, tobacco, and livestock. They have plundered the cellars. Even people who they deem dangerous have been taken.

Talk of rape, murder, and pillage continues from people who were forced to leave their burning villages. Women are fearful, and men look for ways to join the fight against this regime.

Josephine walks quickly through the near-emptied streets where people are now fearful to go. A labourer, permanently tilted at the waist from his work, stands beside a horse and cart filled with wood. He is pushed roughly in the chest by a German soldier, and the horse disconnected from the cart and taken.

"I heard about your brother," says a friend of her parents as he passes. "There's too many stories." He proceeds to tell her another one, and Josephine finds an excuse to get away. She doesn't want to talk about Yves, to compare the horrors. It is too early, too painful. He has only just been buried.

Entering the kitchen, Josephine can see her brothers arguing in the rear courtyard. Eugène, high and intense, gesticulating, Xavier, low and muffled and secretive, his speech more likely filled with information that is useful, practical, and logical. Next to the sink there are potatoes, partially washed; a mortar with the remains of crushed pepper; the peeling knife on the floor; and the vinegary smell of her mother still lingering. A kettle has burned dry on the stove. She turns it off. It is not like her mother. She rubs a finger across the sill beside the pot of dying chrysanthemums, leaving a pathway through the fine layer of white dust. These small things unsettle her: her mother gone abruptly from the kitchen, tasks incomplete, washing still sitting wet in a basket, drops of water across the floor, pavers not swept. Her routine interrupted by the death of her son.

Gisela cannot be consoled. Her father's hands tremble. Josephine has seen him stop talking in the middle of a sentence, distracted by another thought, or as if there is no point to continuing.

I can't go on, Gisela said after the burial, eyes permanently red, her hair loose, an oily stain on her dress. People in their house as fragile as eggshells. Josephine can't bear it.

I should be dead, not Yves, said Josephine to her father.

Don't say such nonsense, said Maurice. *Don't let your mother hear such words!* Josephine sobbing against his chest. His hands lightly on her back as if she were too hot to touch now. Tainted.

They've had no time to adjust to the death. Soldiers pour in. Rules are changed.

Josephine wants her mother back, the controlling one. She wants the worries they had before.

Josephine pushes open the back door, which squeaks her arrival, and two faces turn suddenly: Eugène, wild curls, tall, features sharp, head bent forward as if he were always whispering in someone's ear; and Xavier, hair cut short, his expression softer, edges more rounded. Xavier doesn't wear his collar and robe. Gisela has begged him not to for now. The occupiers scowl at the sight of priests, at practising Catholics, at their songs and statues.

"What are you doing home from work?" Eugène says this like an accusation, the skin around his eyes rubbed pink, fingernails jagged. Yesterday, he had broken all his pencils in anger. No one cared. Gisela had looked away. Maurice had left the room.

"There is no work," says Josephine. "The Germans have shut down the printing and sent the staff home. Papa is no longer to distribute the newspaper. He is livid. He has gone to speak to the governor-general about it."

"See?" he shouts at Xavier. "It is just a matter of time. Xav, you and the churches will be next if we don't do something, if we don't plan now."

"Shh! Calm down! We will deal with this in some way. We have to make sure Papa is all right." Turning toward her, Xavier says, "Did they harm you?"

"No. I wasn't there when the Germans came," says Josephine. "Someone told me when I arrived. Where's Maman?"

"She has gone to stand in line for groceries before they are all gone."

The previous day she had come home with half a loaf of bread, several eggs, and a few potatoes. She had stood in line for two hours just for that.

Josephine bites the tip of her thumb in place of the nail she has bitten down.

"What is it that you are planning, Gène?" she says. Signs are placed around the town by the Germans who have taken over Louvain, warning that the townspeople are now their prisoners, threatening the execution of franc-tireurs, anyone with a gun, anyone thinking about taking the battle into the civilian population.

"Taxes, money from the banks, silver, copper, sugar, coffee, even potatoes, and now it is men," says Eugène to Xavier, ignoring Josephine's question. "They are taking our friends, sending them away on trains, anyone they suspect of conspiracy. They are censoring our speech, our news. They are deciding what we can know, what we read. They have set whole villages on fire! They are not our friends."

Eugène is right, though she doesn't voice this out loud, for fear of throwing fuel on the fire he ignites.

"We should wait," says Xavier calmly, hands in pockets, staring at paper that is torn into tiny pieces on the ground. He has a head that makes rational sense of everything.

All week the Descharmes family has been adjusting to news that changes daily, the news that Maurice collects for the newspaper that has given them little time to grieve. Everything they plan to print must be approved, and much of it censored to make it favourable to Germans.

The newspaper, a small version earlier in the week, had been printed and added secretly to the back of prayer sheets also produced at Maurice's shop, with information on the deaths and destruction they have learned from those who have had to flee their villages. The publication was to be distributed by churchgoers. Someone from the German administration got hold of a copy, or someone had passed it to him, a Belgian, perhaps one more aligned with Germany. It is a problem now to trust people. Some are out to protect themselves. Maurice had then received a visit, a warning, and today was asked to shut the doors. The Germans do not want to report certain news. They don't want him to write about the sickening bloodbath in Liège, about bombs falling from giant balloons in the sky, causing craters in the ground, buildings being burned down and whole villages on fire, and fugitives who have flooded their town on bicycles and wagons overflowing with possessions.

"You should know," says Xavier to his sister, "that civilians are preparing to arm themselves. Gène wants me to store the guns at the church and hand them out to the parishioners."

"No, you mustn't!" Josephine says, suddenly afraid for her brother. "Gène, don't ask this of him!" Mistakes are made, like the one she made with Yves. Things happen that aren't supposed to. People die from guns.

"Be quiet, Mouse!" says Eugène. "Stay out of this. You've done enough!"

It is like she has no voice, not anymore, not since Yves is one week cold in the ground.

"We will all need to be armed. It is inevitable," says Eugène.

Xavier shakes his head, his voice a little stronger.

"Gène! You have read the notices. They will punish us . . . execute us, if there is any retaliation, anything hostile."

Josephine has rarely seen Xavier without composure. His face is reddened, sweat trickling from his temples.

"What if France is conquered?" says Eugène, arms above his head as if the conquering will include the sky as well. "What if this is permanent?"

He runs his fingers through his thick mane and places one hand on his hip. Seconds pass, an age it seems, and a crow on the fence caws them to hurry.

"Xavier," he says, his voice gentler, tears in his eyes. "This is our only chance to prepare. You must see that! We will only fight if they shoot first. I can promise you. If they take our people and kill them indiscriminately, if they break into homes to steal. We must raise our own hell and then Belgian soldiers, British, and French will finish them off. We are not alone."

Xavier shakes his head and walks toward the house. His shoulders suggest he has acquiesced to a certain degree though the twist of his mouth means he is unconvinced. He is against violence.

"You are an artist, Eugène. Stick to that," Xavier says over his shoulder.

"I am a Belgian and a brother first," he calls after. "Remember Yves."

"I do, but more death isn't the answer."

Xavier sees his sister's frown, lips quivering.

"Don't worry about Eugène, what he says to you," he says, hands on her shoulders when they are alone inside. "He is like that, says whatever is in his head. Most times he doesn't mean it. It wasn't your fault about Yves. Don't ever think like that. When you do, remember this moment. Remember me telling you to stop punishing yourself."

"I didn't know . . . ," she says, tears flooding his shirt. She should have drawn him off the street straightaway. But the balloon in the sky, an ivory wingless bird, was distracting, strange, and beautiful the way it burst out through the clouds, then continued to glide. "It is killing Maman."

"I've been to the chemist, and she now has medicine that will calm her nerves. She needs time to adjust. We must keep reminding her that Yves is in heaven now and we will see him again."

"Run!" someone shouts from the darkness.

Bullets tap incessantly and people scream. Josephine's eyes are watering from the smoke. The town of Louvain glows red, orange, and white against the night. Windows explode from grenades, sending shards of glass into the street, and roofs sink and building walls crumble, releasing clouds of grey smoke that rush at Josephine as she weaves her way homeward. Onions spill across her path from a cart that has toppled amongst other strewn items: wooden shoes, hats, and bodies bloodied.

Several German soldiers ahead punch their way through a window and climb over broken glass. Josephine turns left and right then left again, then stops to see more destruction up and down the street under a shower of building dust. Another explosion, and part of a church spire shudders then falls sideways.

Josephine feels something rush from behind and past her ear. A piece of the stone has sheared across her cheek, and she reaches for her face to feel a sticky clump forming.

Ahead, the farrier is sitting on the road. Someone is bent to speak to him. Someone else in the next street is calling for help. She has never felt so alone amidst the noise and destruction that comes from all directions. She whimpers, mouths a short prayer, and squeezes back tears, before another round of bullets forces her to flee again.

Josephine is seconds from her house when a man falls in front of her. She jumps back at first, unsure if she should pass him. He is listless, but alive, eyes toward her. There is a large patch of red on the front of his shirt, and his hand taps blindly on his chest to find the source of whatever has put him on the ground. She walks to crouch beside him, to touch the other hand that reaches out to her for help. The sound of another gunshot and the man is still, blood bursting out from a second wound, this time to his head, and Josephine covers her own instinctively.

When she looks up, an enemy soldier is pointing his gun at her. He is so close she can see the whites of his eyes, the angry exhaustion in the lines around his mouth. His face is covered in powdered debris, and he turns the tip of the gun toward another street, indicating with a nod in the direction she must leave. There is no sense of malice, just a resolution that this carnage, this killing must be done, which seems more chilling, more terrifying to Josephine. But before she runs, more rifle fire sounds, and the same German soldier crumples on the road, taking a hit to the leg. *An eye for an eye.* This is what is happening, violence supposedly to stop violence, she thinks, somewhere in the mass of confusion that crowds her head.

She turns back to the Belgian twisted on the ground, touches his arm, though it is more for her than him, an apology of some kind that she couldn't do more.

Rushing through the front door, she finds her mother sobbing at the table. Gisela jumps up excitedly to cradle her daughter's face, to then place her wet cheek against hers, the relief more obvious by the way Gisela's grip is fierce and needy. She separates them finally.

"You're injured! Come!" she says, leading her daughter to the sink.

She soaks a piece of linen, then cleans away the blood, dashes around to find the iodine. "It is only surface. There is nothing to worry about." The last sentence is more to convince herself.

"Your skirt!" Gisela says, and Josephine looks down to see the stranger's blood on the front of it.

"It's not my blood."

Gisela shakes her head sadly.

"Did you see your papa, your brothers anywhere?" she asks. They had woken to the terror. Maurice had gone to see what was happening and never returned, Josephine to find Xavier at the university before abandoning the mission. Eugène had been absent since early that morning.

"No."

"How many dead?"

"Many."

Gisela's expression shifts between disbelief, fear, and sorrow as Josephine describes the outrage.

"Do you know why the sudden shootings?"

"No," Josephine says. She thinks of the guns, of Eugène's promise, hoping it has nothing to do with her brothers.

There are more sounds closer now, heavy-footed steps and pounding on doors. The women run to the front window to see that the elderly Cadranels next door are being dragged from their house and led away.

"What threat are they?" says Gisela, not expecting a response. Soldiers exit the house also carrying silverware and bags of food. Gisela closes the curtain.

"Quickly, Josephine! You must run and hide the jewels."

Someone bangs on the front door, and both women jump.

"Maman?" says Josephine, unsure if she should leave her.

"Go! I will handle them."

Josephine lifts her skirt and commences up the stairs two at a time.

"Who is here?" one soldier shouts. "Names!"

"My daughter and I," Gisela calls through a seam in the wood. "We are harmless. We have no weapons."

Josephine's legs feel like lead as she listens to them kick at the door, bust apart the lock, and smash things angrily to assert their dominance. She picks up the box with her mother's jewels and rushes across the landing to Eugène's bedroom. It is easier to climb down from, where she can't be seen from the street. She can hear heavy steps on the stairs, foreign shouts. She throws the box into the rear courtyard below as the bedroom door slams back against the wall. A soldier enters, pointing his gun.

She raises her hands, and he points toward the door to instruct her back downstairs. She is shaking uncontrollably, her feet frozen to the floor. She jumps when he yells at her to move again, making herself thinner to pass him. She is unable to look at his face.

In the living room downstairs, the other soldier is ransacking the cupboards. They have pushed over the clock, scattered chairs, and attacked the fabric sofas with their bayonets.

"What are you looking for?" asks Gisela.

"Guns."

"Then you are wasting your time," says Gisela tersely.

The one who has followed Josephine down the stairs asks them their names, for their papers, and Gisela opens a drawer nearby. Her mother appears calm as she hands the German some documents. The other soldier exits the door to inspect the rear of the property, while the first soldier briefly examines their identity papers and thrusts them back at her. Moments later, the second soldier has returned with a handful of Gisela's jewels from the box that has smashed onto the pavers. He shovels the jewels into his pocket as they both exit through the broken front door.

"Boche!" Maman hisses in their wake. "We will wait for your father and brothers, then leave the town, go west toward my sister's house."

Eugène eyes the broken door as he rushes into the house.

"What happened?" he says breathlessly, examining the rest of the damage.

"German thieves," says Gisela.

He stands at the table, hands flat on its surface to catch back his breath.

"Maman," he says, taking the glass of water that his mother passes him. "They have taken the priests somewhere."

"What are you talking about?"

"The priests . . . They believe they are agitators, the ones who have incited the city to fire at the soldiers, handing out rifles to civilians."

"That is ridiculous. Xavier an agitator . . ." Terror and outrage flash across Gisela's face while she turns to look at the blood on Josephine's dress again. "Where is he now?"

Josephine opens her mouth to ask about the guns, about the conversation, but stops herself. Gisela can't know.

"They have taken them to the town barracks. Someone said they saw several priests being loaded into trucks near the train station. I do not know if Xavier is one of them, Maman. I'm sorry."

Gisela stumbles as she steps forward, her hands crossed against her heart, and her children rush to help her to a chair.

"Maman, are you all right?" asks Josephine, kneeling beside her. "Is it your heart?"

"Only that is beyond repair," she whimpers, head in her hands.

"I will find Papa," says Josephine, standing. "I will learn the truth about the priests, where they have been taken."

"Do not leave!" commands Eugène, who springs toward her to grip her arm.

But she won't be told what to do. Not anymore. The rules are changed. The Germans said so. She yanks her arm away from his grip and spills out through the doorway and back into the madness that has infected the streets. People are leaving, running with bags, and dragging children and elderly relatives, arms overflowing with items they value.

"There's Boche down that street," says one. "Go a different way!"

She takes the long way circling back to the printing house. The door of the building is open. Paper litters the floor, shredded and pieces burned. The printing press has been vandalised, the art plates smashed, furniture broken, her darkroom and chemicals spread around the floor. But worse are the drops of blood that lead to the door.

Her father is gone, but where? Outside the streets are emptying, and random shots are fired somewhere in the distance. Only that morning they were at the market and stall owners were giving their food away for nothing so Germans couldn't take it.

One old woman leans against a wall, eyes staring upward to the stars, her dress ridden up to reveal her knees, but no sign of injury. As Josephine bends down to offer help, the woman falls sideways, lifeless, purple tongue tipping out of her mouth. Josephine looks around for someone to help, though there are other bodies, too. *Where to start?*

"Get off the street!" yells a woman from a window nearby. She is waving her arms. "There are more coming this way."

"I'm looking for my papa, the printer!"

"Maurice! I have seen him. He left with several men. Several Boche."

"Did you see where?"

"In that direction," she says, pointing toward the train station.

Something whizzes above her head, and Josephine looks up and around in confusion. When she looks back at the window, the woman has been hit, slumped forward over the sill.

A whistle shrieks, and she hears commands in German. Belgian civilians spill out from another route toward her.

"Go back," they yell. "Run to the forests."

She follows the group toward the lamplights of the Saint Albert Bridge, but drawing closer sees that it is manned by German soldiers, several of whom lean over the balustrade to search for something. They have not yet seen an older man and two young women crouching and hiding beneath them on the embankment beneath the bridge.

Someone grabs her elbow, and the word "hurry" is sounded in her ear. She is swept up into the panic and rushes with him. Others merge with them part of the way as they run past the entrance to the bridge.

"This way," a male stranger urges when Josephine drops back slightly. Several others join the group, some with suitcases under their arms.

"Where are you going?" she asks, pulling up her skirt in front of her to stop from tripping.

"We must go to the forest first," says the same man, waving every-one forward.

"But they have my father, my brother!"

The man falls in beside her.

"If they are caught, it is too late," he says, scanning the soldiers on the bridge, several of whom glance their way. "You need to save yourself."

Josephine turns back to learn that the people beneath the bridge have been spotted. The soldiers on the bridge begin firing below them.

She is suddenly yanked to a stop by the stranger, fingers digging hard into the soft flesh of her upper arm, and forcibly pulled off the pathway to crouch behind the dark corner of a building. Soldiers are coming from the other way. They begin firing on those who have not had time to hide or turn back. She spies several Belgians crumple to the ground nearby, while the rest run for safety. Soldiers on the bridge also fire in their direction to catch the stragglers. The group she was with has completely dispersed, and it is just the two of them.

"Keep your head down or you will lose it," says the man, the side of his heavily lined, sun-browned face against hers.

They listen to a young woman pleading from below the bridge.

Josephine is trembling, her mouth open, and she fights an impulse to flee. Her companion appears to sense this and holds her tighter.

"Stay," he whispers.

The plea from the bridge is drowned out by more gunfire, and Josephine flinches and raises her arms to cover her head. She doesn't dare look.

The man curses under his breath and releases her. He wipes the back of his arm against his sweaty forehead.

"Was your father taken?"

"Yes, this morning from his work."

"Then there is nothing you can do," he says.

"I told Maman I would find him and my brother, a priest."

The man wears the same hesitant, vacant look that most people wear when they hear about Yves.

"I can't leave," says Josephine.

Tears fill her eyes, and she sits on the ground with her face on her knees, arms around her legs.

"Come with me," he says, gently pulling her to stand. "We will have to go a different way now anyway. We'll pass the train station and see if your papa and brother are there. That's where they are assembling people to take to prison."

The pair weaves between buildings until they reach the train lines that they follow into the rail yard. They step carefully alongside a building before crouching down in the shadows to spy on a large group of men assembled. Many, with their hands on their heads and rifles pointing at their backs, are herded into cattle trucks.

Three other people have joined the pair: a woman, a boy younger than Yves, and a small boy of three or four that the woman carries. The youngest boy is whimpering.

"Keep him quiet!" hisses the man, the woman then pulling the child toward her breast. Josephine knows the woman from the fruit stall.

The detainees are barked at and separated: one group sent to sit on the ground in a brightly lit pen guarded by soldiers with guns, and the others, hands bound behind them, sent to board the trucks. Josephine wonders if her father is already inside.

One Belgian is kicked to stand, then led with five other men to the wall of a building. They are spaced several feet apart, their hands tied behind their backs. One of them is praying loudly with his eyes closed.

Josephine scans the men. She recognises Pietr, her father's apprentice, and puts her hand over her mouth to catch a gasp.

"Do you see your father?" the stranger asks.

She shakes her head, and he looks behind him furtively, for soldiers that may come in from elsewhere.

Six German soldiers point their rifles at the prisoners against the wall.

"*Schießen!*" shouts the commander of the Germans.

Rifles explode as men collapse, some on top of each other. Josephine is overcome and turns to retch.

"They are brutes," says her companion, whose gnarled hand rests gently on her shoulder.

Josephine can hardly breathe, her chest swelling with terror to crush her lungs.

"Why are they executing people?" asks the other woman, arms wrapped protectively around her sons.

"Anyone carrying a gun, or anyone found to have a gun in their house, is being arrested or killed. All firearms were to be handed over."

Josephine is feeling light-headed and regains her crouching position to view more men rising and ordered toward the place of execution. Her father is not amongst this group, either.

"We need to go," he says to both the women. He looks around him impatiently now. Josephine is not ready to leave, not until she knows for certain.

The pleading and crying of the men who are being rounded up for execution is grating on her, and she covers her ears and waits for more shots to pass. When she opens her eyes, her father is against the wall. He is not pleading or crying. He stares at the shooters, willing them, she thinks. Her father, who has never owned a gun, who has never posed a threat to anyone, is about to be slaughtered.

The man tugs at Josephine's arm to leave, then follows her gaze.

"Is that him? Your father?"

She draws back a breath and holds it, stopping herself from crying out. Josephine stands up to let her father see her, to know he isn't alone, but the stranger pulls her back down again. She turns toward him, closes her eyes, then opens them again, wider, to focus only on him.

"You must carry on his memory," he says gently.

The man releases Josephine and takes the small child from the woman to help her. The other three follow, leaving the sounds of more gunshots behind them.

Josephine flinches as if the bullets have entered her own heart. Her legs feel like rubber as she forces them to move, tears streaming.

Josephine is half-asleep, half-awake. Random crackles of rifle fire outside entwine her memories and dreams.

In her mind she is at the table at home, her father absently reaching to squeeze her mother's hand while he listens to her speak, turning to smile at Yves, then at her. But that is not real life. Josephine opens her eyes. Real life is bare arms against a gravelled floor, below a broken window in a partially destroyed, abandoned barn.

She raises her head slightly, eyes sticky and puffed from crying throughout the night, from listening to her town burn in the distance, the shouts and cries of people fleeing. Her feet are bare. Sometime during the escape, she lost her shoes. Her rescuer, who introduced himself as Romain, is near a window with his pistol.

She makes a scraping sound with her foot as she rises, and Romain turns sharply toward her. She can view him better now, in the early light of day. He is small and wiry and used to hard work. He is perhaps younger than he looks.

Josephine brushes off the dust and tiny fragments of rock that are stuck to her arm.

"I have to get back to the town," she says, moving to stand beside him at the window.

"It is your funeral if you do," he says distantly, watching parts of the town still burning. "We have all lost people, but we can't do anything about it. My wife hopefully has gone north with my youngest son, across the border, as instructed. I am heading there, too, but I do not know about my other sons and brothers. I do not know where any of them are."

The coldness in his tone makes her feel hopeless.

"We need to cross the Dutch border. It is our only chance. We must leave now!"

"But my family . . ."

"You have to hope they have already left the town unharmed."

She thinks of the ones who haven't and feels tiny needle pricks of tears in the corners of her eyes.

Colette, the other woman, is waking; her children curled up on either side of her.

"My mother, my brothers . . . they are somewhere here," says Josephine. "I have to find them."

"People are fleeing," he says. "They have probably gone north, too."

She ponders his words as she examines the morning through cracked glass. Pear trees stretch in rows toward the river, where ripples play tug-of-war with the breeze, and the dewy grass glistens like it is any other day. But beyond that Josephine recoils at the sight of plumes of smoke slithering menacingly between Gothic spires and rooftops that burned through the night.

The other woman sits up, her children stirring also. The smaller of her two children whimpered like a puppy for much of the night. Colette wears the same look as Josephine, she imagines, dazed, not sure if the world she went to sleep in is the same one she has just woken up to, if she dreamed some of it.

Colette had already explained the previous evening, as they sat in the dark and waited and listened to the last prison truck depart, that her husband was killed in the fighting at Liège, and about the stray bullet that caught her elderly father as he walked to the front of the house to inspect the commotion. A naphtha bomb had been thrown through her window, curtains soon covered in flames that spread quickly throughout the house. The Germans were vicious, enraged further by those who refused to comply with their orders.

Romain has filled up a pot of water from the pump near the front door. The older boy uncurls, a wet patch on the front of his shorts, and sits up to look immediately for his mother, who has moved away.

"We should leave before everyone awakens," Romain says, returning and taking a mouthful of water before passing the pot to Josephine. "The Germans will have sore heads today. They celebrated into the night." He takes a map from his bag, crouches, and unfolds it across the floor.

Josephine passes the water to Colette, who has crouched down to study the map also. Josephine sees the name of the village west of Louvain, where her mother suggested they go.

"I believe the soldiers are heading west," says Romain, pointing, "so we go north this way."

He folds the map, placing it inside his shirt pocket as he steps outside.

"I won't be going with you," says Josephine, joining him.

Suddenly there is a single loud shriek from the smallest child, who has just woken up frightened.

Romain turns toward the sound, then back to movement several fields away.

"Germans are coming!" he says.

Josephine can see uniformed men in the distance, who have likely heard the child.

"We need to leave," says Romain.

"We should just stay here," says the woman as she emerges outside with the child on her hip, bouncing him soothingly. "We have done nothing wrong."

"Neither did many of the people they executed," says Romain. "Do you want to risk it?"

Colette frowns down at her other son, whose hand is twisting nervously in the folds of her skirt.

"We have to hurry!" Romain says, and Colette agrees to let him carry the small boy again. They depart swiftly, veering west of Louvain, cutting through fields of golden wheat toward the forest beyond. Germans are closing the gap behind them, their voices clearer.

Shouts for them to stop force the group to sprint the final metres to the trees. A warning shot rings out, and Colette wails fearfully. Josephine looks back to see the other woman has become confused and frightened, losing ground as she turns to run in a different direction, dragging her son behind her.

"Hurry!" says Romain, and Josephine runs as fast as her legs will carry her, weaving through the conifers, until they reach the other side of the small forest, then crossing a clearing toward a short, grassy rise. Once over the other side, they stop to catch their breath, Josephine's lungs burning. They have lost sight of the mother with her child, her youngest now stupefied and submissive in Romain's arms. In front of them, a farmhouse is smouldering, its thatched roof almost gone, and a cart, full of scraps and waste, sits disabled, missing two of its wheels. They crawl into the tight space underneath it, Josephine first, pulling the child toward her, followed by Romain, his gun readied in his hand.

They wait, huddled together, listening to the distant sounds of soldiers shouting. The boy gazes at Josephine's face, thumb in his mouth and channels of dried tears down his muddied cheeks. She strokes his head and whispers in his ear that his mother is coming and prays silently that he will not cry or scream again. They can hear Colette crying from somewhere nearby, begging for mercy for her son, and telling the Germans that she must find her other son.

"Should we take the boy to her?" asks Josephine, torn about the separation.

"Have you lost your mind? Do you want to go to prison, too, and this child? Or be executed?"

Tears cloud Josephine's vision as they wait for gunshots that don't come, only voices and whimpers that fade toward Louvain. They climb out from under the cart.

"What will happen to them?" she says, placing the child beside her feet. "What do we do with him?"

"I don't know," he says, his mind already elsewhere.

The child is distracted by something on the ground, and he rubs at the dirt with his chubby hands.

"We will have to take him with us," says Romain. "We have no choice. He is safest over the border for now."

They walk in the direction Romain had chosen from the map, looking back occasionally, the odour of smoke and waste still in their nostrils, and follow the track until it forks. Romain, the child on his hip resting his head sleepily on his shoulder, turns to see why Josephine has suddenly stopped.

"I can't go with you," she says. "I have to find my family. I am sure they are here still."

He nods and continues walking.

"Thank you," she says to his back.

Without turning, Romain puts up a hand in acknowledgement, and the child raises his head to blankly watch her over his rescuer's shoulder. Josephine turns in the direction of a squeaking wagon in the distance. A bullock pulls its load of small children, a cage of chickens, blankets, pots, a wooden crate stuffed full of items, a woven basket full of clothes, and a dog walking beside them, tied with rope to the side of the wagon.

"Are you from Louvain?" she asks the man, who is dragging his feet as if they were made from lead, his wife beside him. Flaps of rubbed skin hang like turkey wattles beneath his eyes.

"No. We went there after Aerschot, thinking it would be safer. But it's as bad there as it was in our town. They have set whole villages on fire across the east."

"Is there anyone still in Louvain? Did you see?"

"I don't know. Many are leaving. That's all I saw. Many have lost their homes."

"And the soldiers? They are still there?"

He nods.

"I hope they rot in hell," he says. "Don't go back. They are burning down the churches, the university, and set fire to art pieces and ancient manuscripts."

"Do you know about the priests?"

"No, but I heard some were sent away."

He shakes his head and tells her that the invaders have massacred many from his town also, children, too, and even the burgomaster's son who was only fifteen.

They part ways, the family continuing in the same direction as Romain.

The chateau sits on the rise that falls to a narrow stream on one side, and beyond are forest firs that tumble northward. The structure was built with white bricks and quoined with blue, with rows of pointed arched windows, Romanesque vaulted ceilings, and ornate iron fireplaces.

They were here as children in the summers sometimes, with many other visitors, too, filling every corner of the house. As children they would slide along the polished wooden floors in the hallway to the piano room at the end, where they were shooed away by fussing adults. Her aunt had since died, the cousins gone to Antwerp and abroad to earn a living.

Josephine is wondering if the key is still hidden in the same place when she sees Eugène exit the front door. He pauses to watch her, perhaps making certain who it is, then runs to swoop her up in his arms. He has never been so pleased to see her.

She gasps, then sobs, unable yet to speak.

"Maman has been crying since last night," he says. "We thought we had lost you, too. Come in! Come in!"

Gisela grips onto her daughter's arms, when she is barely through the doorway.

"I knew you would come," she says. "I knew you would remember that we talked about coming here."

"It is not safe here, but I couldn't get Maman to leave," says Eugène. "She wanted to wait for you."

"We are staying here until Maurice comes," says Gisela. "Xavier knows to come here, too."

It is all too much, their ignorance, her knowledge. Josephine searches for words that don't come, that get drowned in her tears. Gisela sees them anyway, steps back, and turns from the truth.

"Maman . . . ," she says, her voice breaking. "Papa is dead, and some of the priests taken elsewhere. I didn't find out whether Xavier is one of them."

Eugène stares as if he were struck across the head, and Gisela's legs give way from under her.

"Maman!" They rush to catch her and help her to the sofa.

"Oh, my poor boys," she says. "My poor, poor boys." She emits such a mournful cry that it twists Josephine's insides until they ache. The children sit at either side of her, arms around her supportively, but neither of them able to find words of solace or hope. It will take more than words to heal.

"Did he suffer? Your papa?" Gisela says when she is finally able to talk.

Josephine shakes her head, afraid to hear her own voice. The wrong word or inference could send Gisela deeper.

Josephine peers through the curtains to stare into the dark fields, a shallow valley, and a sprinkling of dull house lights in the distance under a moonless sky. To the south and the east, several villages glow yellow from the trail of fire the Germans leave behind them. At the rear of the property, there is a stretch of lawn toward a forest to the north. The smell of smoke sticks to their clothes and hair.

The family has spent much of the day keeping watch by the front windows, speculating about the future, and listening to the distant firings and rattles of wagons, cars, carriages, and bicycles on pathways to the towns in the west. Eugène and Gisela had carried pillowcases filled with clothes and items from Louvain.

As night creeps into the room, Josephine draws closed the heavy brocade curtains and Eugène strikes a match to light the wall lamp. Gisela has fallen asleep, exhausted from grieving, in one of the upstairs bedrooms.

"You're shaking," says Eugène. "Are you cold?"

"No," says Josephine, perched at the edge of the couch, her arms folded tightly around her.

"Don't be frightened!"

"It's not fear," she says. "It's something bigger."

"It is shock. I feel it, too," Eugène says quietly. "We can't stay here long. This house is away from the main route to Brussels, but we sit here exposed and unprotected. Sooner or later the Boche will find us."

"Towns and cities offer little protection, either," says Josephine. She remembers the bodies in the streets of Louvain. "I will check on Maman."

Gisela lies curled under a crocheted blanket of multicoloured squares. Even in sleep, she is not at peace, her face contorted with bad dreams, mumbling.

"We will get through this, Maman," Josephine whispers to her dreams. "We will find Xavier." For Josephine's entire life, her mother had been the centre of their family, and a barrier against the world and all its terrors. Now Josephine must be strong for Gisela.

In the kitchen cupboards, the siblings find a tin of preserved peas and the remains of oats, which they devour, leaving Gisela's portion for when she wakes. They light candles they have also found, since most of the lamps are out of oil and there is no electricity.

"Where do they take prisoners?" asks Josephine.

"To Germany," says Eugène. "To prison camps. The Marquettes think they are like large animal pens. I hope that's not true."

"You saw the Marquettes?"

"The family passed us in their old carriage and offered us a lift to Brussels, but Maman wanted to come here. She knew you'd come."

"You despised the Marquettes, their wealth, the number of servants they employed. They were pompous, you said."

"We have some common ground," he says. "They have lost their house, too, and everything in it . . . We should get some sleep. I am too tired. I have not slept for days."

"Should we return to Louvain, see what has happened?"

"The house is gone," says Eugène.

"But we can rebuild there. Louvain is our home."

She cannot imagine being anywhere else, and without her father and brothers.

"I think that eventually when things calm down, we will go back, but for now we must start somewhere else," says Eugène.

"In Brussels?"

"We will see what the situation is like there, if the city still stands, then decide. It is where we might learn more about what is happening, if Belgians will continue to fight. Someone told me on the way here that the king is in Antwerp, or somewhere safe. The Belgian army will not surrender easily there regardless. But the reprisals on citizens have been bad. They are being rounded up everywhere."

"Did Belgians fire first, Gène? Did you help start this? I have to know."

"Whatever you think of me, whatever our differences in the past, I would not have put Maman or any of you in danger. The Boche are blaming what happened on us, of course. What else would they say? All I do know is that they have been looking for excuses for more blood, to take everything from us now."

"What about the guns you were hiding?"

"They lie unused, buried deep below the rubble."

"They are executing any they think are franc-tireurs. Did you know that?"

He nods.

"Did you see them shoot Papa?" he asks tiredly.

"Yes . . . No. I couldn't look."

The candle flickers as he stands to retrieve it.

"I will make sure they pay for this."

"Gène, it is not the time to talk of revenge."

"But it is, Josephine!" There is mania in his widened eyes, fleeting, before he closes them briefly and sighs. "But I am too tired to feel any more rage at this moment."

He passes the candle to Josephine.

"Find a room. I will check all the windows and doors and come up and find one, too." As she turns away he touches her shoulder to stop. "Josephine, you showed real courage trying to find Papa and Xavier. They would be so proud of you. I am proud of you."

The affection and feelings she has for Xavier and Yves were never the same for Eugène. She softens toward him now that he has shed a layer of arrogance, the pair now merged with loss.

Josephine is in one of the big beds on the top floor. She is restless, kicking away her bedcovers, then growing cold and pulling them back on; dozing, then waking often with tears to find her nightmares are real. It is only hours until dawn. The sounds of the shootings replay inside her head, the look on her father's face, his last moments. How hopeless he must have felt.

The windows shudder at a sudden wind, and Josephine sits up in bed. It is confusing, the dark, in a large bed in a room she wouldn't recognise in daylight. There are sounds and whispers, a heavy object is bumped downstairs, and its contents rattle in protest.

She climbs out of bed, still in the grimed and torn clothing she was wearing the previous day, and peers through the curtains. Voices sound in the distance, though she can't see anyone in the grounds below. She treads quietly downstairs and can smell metal and the stench of something that has been left to rot in the sun. She follows the smells to the end of the hallway.

Someone in the kitchen is opening a drawer.

"Gène," she whispers, and the noise stops abruptly.

When there is no response, she is suddenly wary and steps hastily back toward the stairs. Someone thuds the floor behind her, and when she is halfway turned to see who it is, an arm reaches fast around her middle, her arms restrained against her body, and a hand is pressed over her mouth. Muffled grunts replace her screams into the hand clamped tightly, and she squirms and pushes against the assailant to free herself.

Dragged backward into the sitting room, she kicks out frantically, her foot landing on nothing but air as she bites down hard on his flesh. He pulls away, and she screams loudly then until the intruder lands a punch to the side of her jaw. He grabs her shoulders and throws her roughly onto the sofa. As she starts to scramble away, he pins her down with his heavy body.

"Stop!" he says in German. "Or I will kill you."

He has one hand around her neck, the other hand lifting the rifle strap over his head and placing the weapon on the floor beside them. He fiddles further inside a pocket in the jacket he wears, searching for something.

"Are you alone?"

She nods her head.

"If you're lying, I will shoot you and anyone else who enters." The stench of sweat and alcohol oozes through the pores of his skin.

With his free hand he shines a small torch in her face, then retreats back on his knees, the light roaming over her body to examine his catch. In the shadow of the light, his eyes look like dark wells or black holes to hell. He puts down the torch while he retrieves something else clumsily from the side of his trousers.

German voices close by outside stop him briefly.

"Quiet, and no harm," he says, his speech slurred.

Josephine nods again. He has trouble undoing the front of his pants. While he is looking away, she knees him in the crotch and then rolls off the sofa to claw across the floorboards. He grabs the back of her skirt to catch her, his pistol clattering across the wood, then forces her over onto her back again. Once more, he is on top of her, the full weight of him, making her struggle for breath. She pushes at his face as he pulls her skirt up her legs, and he slaps her several times, blood on her tongue and pain in her nose. She is no match for him, and she whimpers as he begins to thrust against her, almost tearing through her underclothes, fuelled with alcohol, anger, and lust.

Then suddenly he lifts himself up on his knees, her mother's screams now piercing the air as she hits at the back of him with her fists. He reaches for his rifle on the floor nearby and, backward over his shoulder, slams her with the butt of it.

There is a burst of fire from somewhere else, and pieces of ceiling plaster rain on top of them, and half a dozen Germans stride into the room, filling the house with light from their portable lamps. Someone yells at the soldier who is still on his knees above Josephine, fumbling his penis back into his pants, and a young German captain enters also. Josephine counts four or five soldiers inside and the sounds of more outside.

Gisela has rushed quickly to her daughter's side to check for harm. With the back of her hand, Josephine wipes the blood from her mouth. Eugène has arrived also.

"Stay where you are!" the captain shouts in French.

He walks over to the drunken soldier, who rises sheepishly in front of him. Once he is standing, he sways slightly, his eyes averted, head down.

"What were you doing here?" the captain asks in German. He appears to know him. "There were no orders to enter. Why aren't you on the way to Brussels?"

"I was looking for food," the soldier answers, glancing around him, his eyes unable to fix steadily on anything. Food was doubtfully the motivation. More like searching for treasures.

The captain slaps the soldier across the face, then takes his rifle. Josephine can clearly see the members of this group, the men averting their eyes, disgusted by what has happened.

"Take the fool away and lock him up when you get to the city!" he commands to other soldiers, who lead the drunk man away. The captain takes a handkerchief from inside his coat pocket and hands it to Josephine. He wears a finely cut uniform of grey. She is reluctant to take the offering at first, and then she reaches tentatively. Gisela beats her to it, then dabs the cloth gently at the blood dripping from her daughter's nose and the side of her mouth.

"I must dampen it," says Gisela, who has a bump and bruise on her forehead that she seems unaware of. She leaves, boldly pushing past the other soldiers, and one of them follows to keep an eye on her. The captain reaches down to take Josephine's hand to help her up.

"Leave her!" says Eugène, stepping forward to be near his sister.

The captain withdraws his hand, and Eugène bends near to place a protective arm around her shoulders and help her onto the sofa. Josephine is suddenly worried that her brother might do something that will see them killed. He is rash and more so when he is angry.

"Is this your house?" the captain asks Josephine in French. He has seen that some of the furniture is still covered with sheets.

"What does it matter?" says Eugène, answering for her, and the captain regards him without expression.

"It belongs to my cousins," Josephine says, "who are presently living elsewhere."

The German official turns his attention once more to her, his chin raised slightly, with a penetrating gaze that compounds her sense of foreboding and the trembling in her body.

"Where are you from?"

"Louvain."

Josephine can feel that Eugène is resisting the urge to say something further, his foot restless on the floor, and she is relieved that Gisela has returned to distract him. With the dampened handkerchief, her mother sponges Josephine's wounds. She winces slightly from the contact.

"You need one for yourself, madame," says the captain.

"Your soldiers have taken everything from us," says Gisela suddenly. "Our house is gone. My husband was executed. One son dead. Only thirteen. Another son, a priest, gone also. And now one of your barbarians has tried to force himself on my daughter. Haven't you done enough? This is not war, it is rape. It is theft. It is murder!"

The young captain turns to contemplate Gisela, then glances at Eugène and then back to Josephine.

"That soldier was wrong," he says, seemingly unaffected by her mother's outpouring. "He will be reprimanded. We neither encourage nor accept such treatment of women."

"Tell the others who did not receive the edicts," says Eugène. "Have you not heard? Have you not seen?"

Eugène sounds spiteful, and Josephine can see now, behind his back, the drunken soldier's pistol that he had picked up, perhaps in the instant before the soldiers ran into the room. She is fearful of further violence and wants the soldiers gone.

Several Germans have returned with oranges and tins of food and are directed by their captain to place them on the coffee table in front of the Descharmes family.

"I apologise for the soldier," he says. "It won't be tolerated, as I said. He will be punished."

The recent events have made it hard to trust these men, but Josephine mumbles a thank-you if only to protect Eugène, to clear away the combustible air that sits around him.

"You should go to Brussels," says the captain. "There is no disturbance there. The city is calm."

He nods his goodbye, then looks at each of them in turn before departing abruptly, his steps even and slight. He is down the front stairs, and Eugène rushes to the window to report they are leaving on horses.

Josephine touches her stinging mouth where her lip has been split, her fingers then gently stroking the tender flesh around her neck. She stands to walk stiffly, because of the bruising to her groin. From the window, she watches the captain climb his mount and gallop immediately west until he fades into the darkness.

"You should not have thanked murderers and rapists," Eugène says coldly, and disappears to check the doors.

"How badly are you hurt?" says Gisela, who has moved to be close to Josephine.

"Maman, he . . . He did not . . . Please don't worry," she says, turning to view the lines on her mother's face deepening.

Gisela caresses her daughter's cheek with one unsteady hand.

"You're shivering, my poor darling. I will get my shawl."

"Maman, take care of the injury to your head. I will be fine."

Josephine does not wish her to know that she is sore and nauseated, that she can still feel the repugnant intruder's fumbling hands, still smell his sour breath, that she fights to remain in control of her emotions for the sake of her mother, already laden with distress.

"He must have climbed in through the basement window," says Eugène, returning. "The latch is damaged."

"You look a mess," he says, calming down a little. "Your nose . . . Is it broken?"

"I don't know. I don't think so."

"We must get out of this house," says Eugène, examining the pistol the drunken soldier has forgotten about. "We are easy prey."

"Brussels then," says Gisela. "We won't die here." Some fearlessness in her voice that Josephine hasn't heard in days.

LONDON

1914

3. TELEGRAM

Father!

Arthur wakes suddenly into the violet-grey dawn that coats his bedroom. His heart is pounding from something he has seen in a dream, sweat trickling down his chest as if he stood too close to the fire he witnessed inside his head. He turns to look at his wife, silent and still on the bed beside him except for the faint rise and fall of her shape. Her gold hair tied up neatly for bed has loosened during the night, and tendrils escape across the white linen. He pauses his own loud breaths to search for sounds, voices, a reason perhaps that he was torn from sleep. His eyes dart around the room, no doors open, no sounds on the floor below. Harriet's glass bottles on her dressing table remain in neat rows, nothing disturbed, nobody.

Arthur sits up slowly on the edge of the bed, scratches his head thoughtfully, then reaches one hand behind him to fan the nightshirt that has stuck to his back. He closes his eyes and retrieves the images from a heavy night of dreams: the sight of men running from buildings on fire, terrified faces burning into ash, and his son there amongst it; his call in the midst of madness, which forced him to wake. The nightmares come often, though not like this, not so vivid that it forces him to briefly ponder what is real and what is not.

His terraced house sits perched on the high side of the road above the roofs of others and facing stretches of dairy pastures, from where the gentle sounds of lowing can be heard at night. From his bedroom window, strained through beads of dew and the barren fan of an oak tree, a crown of gold peers over ribbons of rose and blue, colours that offer Arthur shades of hope after such a troubled sleep.

Arthur reaches for his pocket watch on the nightstand and adjusts his slippers to his feet. He creeps across the bedroom rug and turns the doorknob, which makes a faint clicking sound. It stirs Harriet to shift her body, rearrange her legs, and rub her cheek softly against the pillow until she is once more still.

Gently closing the bedroom door behind him, he whispers his son's name, the sound travelling down the hallway and dissolving into nothingness. It is a kind of madness, he thinks, a desire for something he knows isn't there. Then the wait in the silence, the hope for a response, fragile and fruitless before finally a conclusion, an explanation, that he is not fully awake yet, not yet over the dream.

He has always been a man of hope and expectation, unlike Harriet, who thinks about neither, who carries on as though life itself is a necessary task of the here and now. Despite the contradiction, they have stayed married for twenty-one years.

He pads down the oaken hallway, a creak in the places he steps, a faint screeching in the distance from the machines in the factories starting up, and intermittent scratching inside the attic where the pigeons nest. On the landing he sounds his son's name again. Just to hear it, to make Jack seem within reach. As Arthur arrives at the bottom of the stairs, the large clock in the entranceway chimes softly as if in response.

In the library, Arthur switches on the newly installed, ornate brass wall sconce that instantly washes the room in an artificial sunlight. He can never get over it, get used to it even, such abruptness of light from dark. It is something that bothers him. When he was a child, the warmth of a candle or a lantern brought the family closer, around a table, away from the shadows. But these new lights scatter people like mice, drive them to other rooms to hide and separate. Machines now in the streets that prevent human contact and deter conversation. These things, new conveniences, he thinks will change people. The future more hurried, more complex; the one his son, Jack, will have to navigate.

He turns on the oil heater, switches off the light again, reclines in the reading chair, and watches the rising sun lick the dew from the apple trees and fill the room with day.

Sometime later, when he pours his second cup of tea, Harriet enters in a dressing gown of navy velvet.

"Where is Mary?" she says, her hair now free around her shoulders that are slumped as if there were nothing in the kitchen to look forward to, such posture aging her beyond her forty years.

"She's not arrived yet."

"Damn that girl!" she says.

"Perhaps we don't need her as much." Arthur has lost two of his workers, signed up to war, and business is quiet. Money is dwindling.

Harriet makes a grunting sound to disagree.

"Who will do the cleaning? Besides, she needs the money. We are doing her a favour."

He understands his wife. She has come from a comfortable beginning and a grander house than this one. She has not known what it is to go without. She married beneath her.

"I'll make you some tea," says Arthur, who stands, expecting to serve it to her in the morning room.

"Stay sitting. It's fine," she says, waving him away. "I've grown to quite like the task."

She has changed a little since war began only three months earlier. She is becoming less bothered by people's ineptness. She has even begun to feel sorry for Mary, their housekeeper, whose favourite nephew has been sent to war also. They have found something in common.

He follows her anyway and squeezes past her between the stovetop and the table, to open the back door. Just outside is the laundry where Pippin sleeps. The cocker spaniel pays no attention to his bad hind legs and scampers toward Arthur for a scratch behind the ears. Once satisfied the dog collapses on the kitchen floor and moves his tail back and forth, dusting the floor with gratitude, pleased to be close to them. Arthur empties a brown bag of dog biscuits into his bowl, then moves to sit across from Harriet.

There is a letter from Jack on the table that arrived a week ago. He has read it several times, Harriet possibly more while he was gone to work. He pulls it toward him to retrieve it from its envelope while she fiddles about the sink and places the kettle on their new stove. He had been impressed by the letter, never realising his boy could write with such depth. He'd shown no aptitude for it earlier.

A knock on the door pauses their tasks, and they both rise to enter the hallway that leads to the front door. A person outside in a hat, a ghostly shape behind the glass of the door, and Arthur thinks again about his dream.

"It could be Jack," says Harriet, though she sounds unconvinced. The mention of his son's name, and Arthur feels something stir in the pit of his stomach, where bad feelings and uncertainty can sometimes fester.

Harriet looks to Arthur, who forces himself toward the door. *Why? Why am I so afraid?* His son was planning on leave. Why does his throat feel so thick that he can hardly swallow?

A man in uniform carries a small folded piece of paper.

"Arthur!" Harriet calls out behind him. She remains near the kitchen doorway, though he can still feel her anxious breaths against his neck. He can sense her panic. Arthur takes the piece of paper, stares at it sceptically as if he might return it.

"I'm sorry," says the man. *No, a boy,* thinks Arthur, not much older than Jack. Arthur has lost the ability to speak, cannot think of anything to say, cannot even part his lips.

He has heard about these slips from Mary, who talks a lot, whose art of conversation remains the same in any company, be they gentry or the working classes. She has told stories of the young men who bring telegrams at any time of the day with news from the Front, Harriet listening without comment, willing her to stop.

They are in an awful state, the Wallaces. Their son was blown to bits and now without legs and a hand. It is dreadful business . . . There won't be any joy this Christmas with our boys abroad. What is it without them?

Arthur thinks he nods to the boy, who turns to leave, though he can't remember. He can't say for sure how long he was there in the doorway, if there were other words spoken from the point of opening the door to closing it again. The moment is already becoming blurred, as if warding off the truth, as if postponing will lessen the blow.

It is Harriet's face that he will unlikely forget. He can see already the anguish, blame, and hostility she feels in that moment. Her reactions and accusations, in most cases groundless, have cut him deeply at times. They remind him that he is flawed, that they were not born equal, something society has told him since birth.

Did I push him? He reflects and will no doubt say it over and over in the days to come. He sent Jack to military college to knock some sense into him. He had been a troublemaker at school, unable to find himself. Suspended from one college and placed into Sandhurst through Harriet's connections.

In times of anger Arthur had used lowborn phrases that Jack has quoted back to him many times, confirming that one cannot fully undo what station they are born into. Small things carry through the chain. Hence, he strived to change it, strived to make Jack a better, stronger man.

Father, I don't want to join the military. I want to be a teacher perhaps.

You should feel honoured to be here. This will be good for you, Jack. You lack self-discipline.

Who says?

Your teachers, your mother, and I.

Mother doesn't care. She wants me home.

She spoils you . . . Look, it isn't easy, these years. There can be distractions. Lord knows I had them.

If this is a lecture on what you went through as a child, about the opportunities you didn't have, spare it. I'll find my own way.

Arthur finds Harriet returned to the kitchen, doubled over, hands across her stomach as if some food doesn't agree with her. She sinks to the floor on her knees, bumping the table and knocking a teacup that smashes on the floor. A sound, guttural, barbarous, escapes her. He goes to reach for her, but she shouts at him, vile words that spill out in rapids. She hates him, she says. Yet he understands. Things between them had been close to brimming over for years.

Sometimes it is easier to navigate the passage of bereavement by pointing fingers at others to make sense of something that way, to find another cause. It has been Harriet's way throughout the marriage. *A strange match,* said a college friend at the wedding, and yet Arthur didn't think of those words again until some years later when their differences became starkly apparent. Unlike Harriet, he has always carried blame, been accountable. Fixed a situation quickly to turn her mood.

He picks her up and she resists, pushing him away and tearing the telegram in two, attempting to erase the brutal truth. She will worsen. He knows that from experience. He will need to call the doctor. She had been hysterical before, throwing things when she didn't get his attention early on in their marriage. Hated being ignored, forgotten, especially when he was working long hours. This time is different. He can't fix things, the loneliness. He can't fix death. Their son is dead.

⇒

Letter from Jack Shine to his parents, 20 October 1914

Dear Mother and Father,
This letter will probably come as a shock to you. I have been a terrible correspondent with just a postcard here and there telling you nothing, and my heart has been heavy lately because of that. I've had time to think on things, situations I've found myself in, that have given me

new perspective. An appreciation for things, small things, I didn't see before.

I hope by now you have forgiven me for leaving without saying goodbye at least. I should have come to see you first, but I knew it would upset you. Father, don't worry too much about me. I think I have finally achieved the independence you dearly wished me to have.

We left on trains to much fanfare from the crowds. A military band played and people clapped and I thought we were doing something important. Not necessarily for patriotism and adventure. But for France also, our friends and enemies over centuries and to end the spilling of blood that we have suffered. We are as one.

We are waiting in a forest near [blacked out] just south of [blacked out]. We were told to go hard, and we did for days, and we have finally driven the Germans back a way, though it is temporary they say, their forces growing stronger. We did not let them capture Paris, and I am proud to say I was part of that successful campaign. I have never forgotten our holiday there, and I fought to protect it for selfish reasons also. I do not want to be learning to speak German the next time I go. French was hard enough for me to master.

If I have been an errant son, now is the time to say sorry. Now in the midst of chaos with bullets whizzing over my head on any given day, my mind is clearer than it has ever been. Being here without comforts and seeing others who will never experience those again, those petty complaints seem so juvenile and selfish. If anything, being away from England has taught me to appreciate life, especially the one you gave me. Henceforth, I will take responsibility for my decisions. And I do. Father, you once said that I need to grow up, that I should learn how to be a man, take responsibility. I think you will see a change; I think this at least will show how I've changed.

I wish I could paint you a picture of glory, like in the stories of war I read growing up. The truth about war is that it is dismal and dirty, so don't expect my letters to be sprinkled with the scent of violets but dotted with muddy fingerprints. Perhaps Father should read them first, though I believe, Mother, you are strong enough to take it and you would want to know everything.

France is beautiful at any time of day. Fields of flowers and soft rolling hills and rustic villages and their quaint bartering and commerce practices that haven't altered in hundreds of years. I vow to come back here when it is all over, perhaps find a French wife. I know that will shock you, Mother, for you, no doubt, are already plotting other ideas for me.

I have made many friends, though I hesitate to put that in writing. I worry the people I name will not be here tomorrow. It is like that here. Friendship is fragile and momentary oftentimes. People come into my life, offer me something of theirs, and then they can vanish beside me in battle, leaving behind a tune they whistled or a humorous phrase, which might stay with me. And I wonder who decided that their life was so meaningless to cut them down so cruelly.

I wish I didn't sound so morbid, but it is dark and cold, and I am tired and hungry. The rum here warms us a little, but the tinned stew is tasteless, and the bed I am on right now is made from straw and riddled with fleas.

I can hear the shelling even now in the distance. Every so often the ground shudders and I duck automatically, expecting something to fall on my head, the ceiling to cave in.

Our lieutenant says we are moving out tomorrow. We will reinforce another group back from fighting "fiercer than ours," he said, though I can't see how it could be. If there are shellings and snipers and mines, it is probably the same. Though you taught me to bite my tongue, and I am trying harder with that. The consequences for such bravado are more serious here.

A soldier I befriended has gifted me something from his home. Private Charlie Penney from another division was at our rendezvous, and we struck up a conversation and swapped addresses. Our groups are moving out together tomorrow. But I won't do too much more of that, I think. Much better to lightly befriend all so the baton of camaraderie can be passed along more swiftly when one drops off.

We took some prisoners, too. Pale-faced lads with little to say but several with a sense of humour at least. They were bewildered like the rest of us. Being this close to the enemy, my eyes had the chance to wander curiously over the faces of the men who had, till then, been seen as one giant beast to slay, not these pallid human scales that have fallen from its back. We are human all of us. We have nothing to fear when we face each other without our armour, when we stare into the eyes of our supposed enemy.

I have been told I have a week's leave at Christmas already. Some of the lads are going to Paris, but I will be home hopefully. Perhaps to make up for the past.

Give Pippin a hug.

Your loving and dutiful son,

Jack

4. MOURNING

Arthur and Harriet have received many visitors, strangers, some of them, messages of condolence, and food that will be hardly picked at before it is thrown away. Arthur prefers to work and forget about what has happened, to confine it to a moment, the blurry face of the boy at the door. Perhaps it is his subconscious guarding him from ever truly seeing that visit with clarity, boxed up carefully, stored to the back behind more agreeable reflections. If he were to see the messenger's face clearly, perhaps the reality of loss would be more profound. But for now the boy is gone, the door is closed, he can cope, he can see a window to the side instead, always open, the light and wind rushing in, clearing the air, and he has somewhere he can escape if need be.

Harriet, however, is grieving. Sometimes it is too much. It fills up the room with such intensity that he feels like he is drowning in her tears. He loves her and has loved her ever since he first saw her as a girl of seventeen. Those mannerisms that make her unique, that he used to love, seem foreign now. He has watched her change, blossom into beauty, and now to shrink into something else. She takes an opiate, something that calms her, though it doesn't completely eradicate the grief. Tears still escape, the wanting to talk about everything, anything, labour on the letter Jack wrote and Arthur himself, his shortcomings, possible decisions that changed the course of Jack's life. At moments when it is too much, Arthur wishes she would disappear.

Harriet's blame has now turned silent, a look that gives nothing away, an absence from the rooms they share, which is worse than words in a way. It frightens him. He doesn't know her.

Most nights, he attempts to justify things in the bottom of a whiskey glass. It is a form of self-therapy to speculate that Jack would have found his end early anyway. A boy with a restless heart ends up in crime, in more devious pursuits. The military seemed the lesser of evils. More importantly, it seemed the only option.

"She will be all right soon, Arthur," says his mother-in-law, Alice, warmly enough, though he never much cared for her. She was originally against the marriage and then, he felt, tolerated it for her daughter's sake. "She takes disappointment poorly. Since she was a girl."

It is an understatement. He has spent years trying to avoid disappointing Harriet, keeping her happy. His restraint and overindulgence at times had saved their marriage early, he thinks. Then came Jack, and suddenly he was the gleaming link in a chain that had already begun to tarnish.

He watches Harriet through the glass panel at the top of the door to the drawing room, her face turned away to the window. There is nothing he can say that will give her comfort. He is perhaps dispensable now, and she has grown silent toward him. An accusation she wears without the use of words. She touches the fine strands of hair at her temple, smooths them back from her forehead, though it is more a habit, the touching of her head, the stroking of it. It is distinctly her. It is a characteristic, one of many that he fell in love with.

"I will take care of her," says Alice. "She needs some separation at the moment."

Quite what Alice means he isn't sure. She has always been possessive of Harriet.

"She needs me," she says.

"I need her," he replies, and Alice looks away as if she knows this but can do nothing about it, or perhaps doesn't want to.

Alice follows him to the front door as he takes his coat from the hook, climbs into it, and puts his hat on.

"Will you make sure Mary cleans out Jack's room today?" he says. "Clothes are needed by the poor."

"It's too soon," says Alice, who rarely agrees with anything he says.

After his leave of absence, it is time to return to work. Arthur catches the Underground to Temple and climbs the stairs. He buys a newspaper, and a small boy who can read the quality of his coat follows him a short way before Arthur stops to give him a coin. The little boy nods and scurries away back to the top of the stairs to wait for more.

Arthur watches him briefly, admires his persistence, then briskly finishes the short walk to his office that overlooks the Thames.

"I'm truly sorry about Jack, sir," says his clerk, awkwardly, seemingly unsure if he should say more. There is nothing more to say. Arthur thanks him for taking care of things, then nods the boy away. Then it is work that fills only half a day, and he sends the clerk home. He puts his pen down, straightens his books and papers on the desk, and sits back in the chair. At least he can think better here, without Harriet. He pictures the day they saw Jack off to military college, a rare moment of eagerness from the boy, then a frown once he saw the pessimism set in the lines around his father's mouth, lips pressed tightly together, preventing the release of words of disappointment, spoken too many times before. Arthur knew Jack was hoping for encouragement and pleasantries, seeking some kind of recognition, which his father couldn't give. Not then. Jack needed to grow strong, show some discipline. He needed to prove himself. He had been thrown out of school for larking; he had been in trouble with police also for rowdiness and disrupting the public. Finding a commonality had been difficult for both father and son, and yet they were threads of the same cloth. Arthur can sense that now. He can feel Jack's presence everywhere he looks. This connection to a child that nothing can break, not nature, not distance, not even death.

He had made enquiries by telephone, learned of the battle Jack was killed in, and roughly where he had died. He had learned that some had been sent home in a bad way, that perhaps it was for the best he was killed, the wounds, dependence, and suffering worse in the long run for a soldier and his family.

He phones the War Office to enquire about the soldier mentioned in Jack's letter and hears papers shuffling. "Yes, he was sent back to the military hospital."

Arthur returns to his accounting, fastidiously, focused. He had started off small, a loan from his father-in-law, and he had grown the business. But now there are fewer clients on his books. He needn't have hurried back. Businesses are closing, many men gone to war.

And then Arthur is home again, the day come and gone so quickly, whole hours missing, he thinks. What was he doing for much of it? He can't say.

Mary has put a plate of food under his nose in the kitchen, away from the dining room, where the other women are. Separated now, he thinks, or he is banished perhaps.

"I've cleaned up a bit," Mary says hesitantly. "Harriet asked not to give all of his things away. Not Jack's favourite toys he had as a boy. If you don't mind me saying, it is probably better for Mrs. Shine to keep such things."

"Of course," says Arthur. "Just most of his clothes to take then. People need them."

"Yes," says Mary. "You're truly kind. I understand. I will take them to the Red Cross. There are children who need them at the orphanage, and his recent clothing I thought I would take to the hospital for the soldiers."

"Thank you, Mary," he says, waiting for her to leave so he can eat in peace, but a thought strikes him.

"Is that the Royal Hospital?"

"Yes, sir."

He pauses.

"Thank you," he says.

In the drawing room after dinner, he stretches back in his armchair and pours himself a drink from the tray beside him, then another one until the voices in his head are muffled, until his mind stops venturing too far from practical concerns.

Harriet enters and sits opposite on the sofa, and he is surprised. She is not usually up this late. She spends much time in bed. The doctor's account is growing.

"Where's your mother?"

"She's gone to bed," Harriet says, eyes glazed. Her hair is pinned up differently, coifed by her mother, formally, something Harriet would hate. But the life she knew has left her, and she is filling it with trivialities, or rather Alice is, to keep her mind off her sorrows. The disdain she'd been powdering across her face is missing at least, the medicine dulling some of her scorn toward him.

"I'm sorry, Harriet," he says. "I'm sorry we have lost our son."

"It's not your fault. It's the fault of those who started all this violence."

He wonders if she means it in her heart or whether it's the drugs. They are different words from days ago.

"I know you loved the boy, our boy, Artie. I know that. You work hard. I just wish . . ."

"What do you wish?"

"I just wish we could have had longer with him."

Arthur moves to sit beside her on the sofa and reaches for her hand.

"Don't," she says, drawing it away.

"Please tell me what I can do—"

"Nothing, Artie," she says firmly. "There is nothing you can do now."

He feels remorseful and useless.

"Harriet, I wish I could have changed things. Prevented him from going."

"Perhaps you could have, perhaps you couldn't. We'll never know."

She looks at him then clear eyed, and he feels the same twinge of newness in his heart that he had at twenty. She is still as vivid now as she was then. Pretty olive-green eyes, soft curls of gold. It is this return to such sweetness, and forgiveness, that makes him feel guilty of everything she said prior. As if her understanding is undeserved.

"Harriet, I love you."

Unexpectedly, she puts her hand on his cheek.

"I know," she says. "But I'm not sure I can get through this. I'm not sure I can let him go. He looks so like you . . ."

She leaves him again, alone. He has lost her, he ruminates. They seem broken and irreparable, though he won't fully admit that out loud. He can barely admit it to himself.

He will take the spare room.

He climbs the stairs to the attic bedroom.

In the morning, the window is covered in frost, which means Mary will have already put coal in the hearth in Harriet's morning room, let Pippin in, and put tea in the pot. He climbs into trousers and braces and puts on his coat, follows his usual morning routine, and tries to forget his dream, once more filled with fire and Jack's voice somewhere within it.

Downstairs, he drinks his tea in silence, eats some toast. Mary is gone somewhere in the house, perhaps to collect the linen.

It is a new day, a new chapter. He will be strong for Harriet. He will seek out new clients, perhaps look at foreign interests and the business of war that is becoming more profitable. They will start again as a family. He will sell the small parcel of land he bought for Jack's future and donate to hospitals in his honour.

As he is leaving, there is a pile of clothes near the door, neatly washed and pressed. And next to Arthur's tall Wellingtons is a smaller pair of boots. Jack's, when he was eight or nine. They are marked and scratched, with a small hole on the toe of one where he dropped a lit match. Arthur stops to look at them, remembers the small feet inside. He remembers the large teeth and the gap and the chip on the edge of his tooth, the touch of his hand on his father's knee as they crouched down to search for winkles on the rocks by the sea, the feeling of love for a child who trusted him implicitly. He finds he needs air, the hall too boxed.

He steps out onto the ground covered in a fall of sleet, and an early morning drizzle to prepare the day bland. He has forgotten his umbrella, but he is scarcely aware of that as he steps surely along the pavement, eyes ahead, seeing into the past. The boy is sixteen, evicted from school, standing with his hands behind him, frightened, waiting for his father to react. Arthur remembers the anger he felt at the time, which stopped him from seeing the feelings of his son, his suffering, his fears, humiliation. He sees that now, as if the winds have blown open the windows that had shut away his thoughts. He can see his son's face, clearly, the desire to please, the disappointment in himself. The barriers of life and work placed between them that so often block the other things, the simple wants children can see, and adults can't. *Why did I not see him?* He loved him. But it wasn't enough. Why now can he see him? See his fears. Why not back then? They sent him to war. He was barely a man.

Arthur feels a pain in his chest crushing him, his legs are suddenly too frail to walk on, and he falls on his knees, arms full of lead, then a feeling of numbness, and one hand gripping the front of his shirt as the rain grows heavier, mockingly, having waited for him to be so exposed. He has forgotten his hat, too. He does not know how far he has walked, if he was even heading in the direction of the station. All he can see is

Jack's chipped tooth and his small hand and his life that went too fast. He crumples to the ground, face to the sky.

"Jack," he whispers.

Father, he hears again, louder as if his mouth is close to Arthur's ear.

He is aware of people surrounding him, whispering.

Someone rummages in his pocket.

"Don't take that," says the voice of an older boy. "It's his wallet. We should call for a doctor."

Fumbling in his coat continues, and then those hands are gone, and someone comes near.

"Away with you," someone shouts, and claps, someone maternal sounding, and running steps that fade away.

"Are you all right, sir?" says a woman. A hand clasps around his wrist, then she instructs someone behind her to call for an ambulance.

Arthur looks up at the small opening between the clouds, at the brilliant white light that strains to reach him through the grey. He knows now. He can see the boy at the door. Short, freckled, in uniform. His eyes, tilted downward, regretful. The messenger bows his head, says he is sorry, holds out the letter in one white, darkly freckled hand. It is overwhelming, this surge of truth, this moment of pain now memorialised in the small break in the clouds.

He knows what pain is, why it is better to shield from it. The loss of a child, a son, their son. He understands better now, the magnitude of it. He had let his son go. He, Arthur Shine, had sent his son to an early grave.

5. A RECKONING

He was taken to the hospital, oblivious to the happenings around him. He was given foul-smelling medicine. The doctor had been back several times to check on him, examinations, bright lights, questions he couldn't answer. Alice came to see him to tell him everything would be all right, unconvincingly, patting him on the arm, eager to leave, he felt. His clerk, Lewis, popped in briefly, too, a nice lad with a modest personality that Arthur was more drawn to. Not the effusive, ambitious kind of worker who says all the right things but doesn't necessarily mean them. That shows up late with the prize for the best excuse. Lewis tells him he has made sure all the work is up to date. He wants to say something more, Arthur can tell by the way he presses his lips together and searches the air around him for the right words. But Arthur is tired, and he closes his eyes, and when he opens them again, no one is there.

Where is Harriet?

Someone puts something in his arm, a sting, and he is sleeping, dreaming, not of fire but of life when Jack was small, walking across the common, teaching Pippin to heel and fetch, Jack laughing, chasing the pup around in circles. Arthur couldn't keep up. This makes him cry in his sleep so deep he has only vague snatches of it, only enough to remember why his cheeks are wet.

It is bright in the ward, lots of noises and movements and tinny sounds of bedpans and instruments and rattling carts and clattering and the smell of cooked lamb in gravy, rosemary and onions, and ammonia. He is thinking clearer today. He must organise a memorial plaque for Jack.

He watches the doctor. A large man that towers over the bed, with tiny spectacles. Big, meaty arms and fleshy fingers.

He sits beside Arthur, listens to his chest through a stethoscope, then pats the patient's arm with a measure of force behind it.

"Mr. Shine," says the doctor. "May we talk?"

"Yes, of course," says Arthur. His head isn't clear.

Arthur has forgotten something, he thinks. A birthday? Something he was meant to do. He has lost all sense of time. There is a sort of suspended feeling in a hospital bed that is therapeutic. Life as he knows it has just stopped, the one that holds much pain, this one very little.

"We have done all the necessary inspections, and your heart is working perfectly. We suspected the worst. What we can conclude is that you suffered a breakdown, brought on from stress or panic, or bad news. A likely case in this instance."

The doctor pauses, waits to see what Arthur might say of this, though he can't think of anything appropriate: anything that would either validate or invalidate the statement. He likes living moment by moment, like perhaps Jack or Harriet, not distracted by the past or the future. He wonders briefly what Alice has said about him.

"Sometimes it happens to the best of men, Arthur. Sometimes the mind can only handle so much bad news . . . I'm sorry about your son."

Jack.

The name he sounds to himself, feelings about him softened, better memories, happy ones, with drugs. It is wrong, he thinks. Him being here, coddled. It's not the person he is.

"I believe you are now well enough to go home."

Arthur nods.

"Yes, yes, I must."

Jack in the ground. Harriet at home. She needs me.

"If you would like, we can prescribe something for the coming weeks."

Arthur shakes his head. He wants to feel the pain again, share some of Jack's. The pain will keep them close.

"Very well, old chap. Don't be so hard on yourself. If you can, tell yourself that your son is a hero. He did what many wouldn't do. And perhaps because of him and others like him, things will be back to normal."

Normal. What is that? The word seems to float around in his mind as an abstract concept.

"Anyway, you should be pleased to know you are in great shape for forty-three and no heart issues."

Arthur flickers a smile and nods, and the doctor considers him a moment, seemingly searching his thoughts, unravelling the tangles.

"If you don't mind me saying this, time will pass. You've had a shock. Dwell, if you have to dwell on something, on the good things not the bad."

Arthur picks up a newspaper on the way home. He had been in the hospital for several days, but it feels like weeks. He catches a bus and flicks through the pages, reads the personal messages of support for "their boys" at the Front. In the back there are small advertisements taken out by people appealing for information on their missing sons. Perhaps that is worse, he thinks. False hope and waiting. Various reports suggest the war will not end soon. They anticipate it could stretch out for a year at least, that no side will back down in the meantime. Certainly not the British.

He steps off the bus at an earlier station to make the walk longer. He feels his cheek is smooth. The nurse at the hospital cleaned him up.

Have you fresh for your return! she had said, smiling, efficient, kindly.

Arthur closes the front door behind him and picks up the scattering of letters on the floor beneath the mail slot. He places these and the newspaper on the hall table, then notices the clothes by the door are gone, as well as the boots. He remembers now what he meant to do: to tell Mary not to donate the boots. He looks at the space on the floor, slows his breathing as the doctor had shown him. Distracts himself with other thoughts so as not to think of the boots being gone, the disappointment.

"Mary!" he calls, his voice echoing along the front hall and off the high ceilings, then regrets the noise. Harriet might be sleeping.

Pippin is not there to greet him at the back door. Another memory. Jack running into the dining room and Mary apologizing for Jack's enthusiasm, after Arthur had spent long hours at work. Bending down to study the boy, to see how much he had changed during the day.

What have you been doing?

Pippi caught a bird.

Pip . . . pin.

Pip . . . ping. He caught a bird.

Oh well, these things happen. He is only doing what comes naturally. He is a hunting dog, you know. The dog of kings and queens.

Jack looked at Pippin, absorbing this, then back at his father, who was elevated then for gifting him such a prize.

Piece by piece, information had been fed to his young mind; the same mind now blown to bits on a foreign battlefield. Arthur feels his chest tighten at the thought, commencing to breathe deeply, and pacing around the centre bench.

Dwell, if you have to dwell on something, on the good things not the bad, he repeats to himself.

He should have said yes to the medication. Self-medicate like Harriet. Perhaps she is handling it better after all.

Arthur feels the need to speak to her now, pick up whatever fragments he can from their marriage and put it back together. He will look after her. Spend fewer hours at the office. Their expenses lowered in recent years, less entertaining, no fees for Jack.

In the kitchen there is a loaf sitting in the bread bin that is rock hard, and the air in the house is icy. He turns on the oil heater, then steps upstairs to knock on the door of the marital suite. No answer. The bed is made, hearth empty. Harriet's glass bottles are gone, and so are half her clothes.

He sits on the edge of the bed, remembering something Alice said at the hospital when his mind was drowsy.

She needs a change, fewer reminders. You understand, don't you, Arthur. She is quite ill. Better for both of you.

Was he such a bad husband? A little distant sometimes, unable to say exactly what he felt. Confined. Restricted. It's what he'd been taught by his own father. That didn't make him bad. Everything fell to him. An expectation to provide. And now he is punished for something. *What?* God knows perhaps. Though Arthur is unlikely to get any straight answers there.

He will go to the local vicar perhaps. Talk to someone. He must talk to someone.

He re-enters the kitchen. Sees the note from Mary pinned to the wall beside the pantry that he missed when he entered earlier.

Harriet has gone away. Please send for me when you return. I have Pippin with me. Will bring him back. Mary

Arthur is relieved, at least about Pippin. Pippin is Jack's dog. He should be here in this house where the smells of Jack would comfort him.

Inside the library he pulls out a piece of paper from the bureau and writes a letter to Harriet to wish her well, sending his love and asking when she might come home. He needs her home. Together they can get through this. Though he doesn't write the last sentences. It sounds needy and he has never been needy.

The practice mail has been redirected to his home address. There is a letter from his clerk, saying that work is drying up, customers gone elsewhere, and he has decided to resign, something he tried to do at the hospital visit but couldn't, seeing how miserable Arthur was. The boy has signed up for war.

Arthur steps out again, coat and umbrella this time. It is blustery. He boards a train for a London hospital, and for most of the journey pictures the soldiers as his son described, wonders if they are cold today, if they have enough warm blankets, enough food.

At the hospital, he asks to see a soldier by the name of Private Charlie Penney, hopes he is still there. Then a moment of excitement as Arthur is directed to a particular ward.

The soldier wears a bandage around his eyes. His face, on one side, and down his neck is disfigured by burns. The skin on his arms is clear and strangely unmarked. All the firepower directed to his head. Arthur's not sure whether the soldier is asleep or awake, face toward the opposite wall, unmoving.

He pulls up a chair, and the patient turns toward him.

"Who's there?"

"Ah, hello . . . Private Penney?"

"Yes."

"My name is Arthur Shine—"

"Jack's father."

Arthur feels a fluttering in his chest.

"Yes, yes, Jack's father . . . What is wrong with you, if you don't mind me asking?"

"Took a blast, lost one of my eyes completely. A piece of shrapnel. They think the other one will improve."

"How long are you here, have they said?"

"Hard to say. I'm hoping to be sent home soon."

"Where is that?"

"Penarth, originally, where my mam lives, but many years in London more recently. Can't stay here anymore. Not like this."

A father without a son, he thinks, a son without a father.

"Well, if I can make your stay any more . . . comfortable," he says, hoping it is the right word. "If I can bring you anything."

"Thank you. I'm not sure what you could do. Be my eyes perhaps, tell me what the room looks like, honestly. Not a sanitised version from the nurses, as kindly as they are. And while you're at it, describe them, too."

Charlie smiles. Even white teeth.

Arthur looks around the room.

"The metal beds, some of them rusty," he describes, "old, pulled out from storage, not prepared for the volume of injured, I imagine. The paint on the walls like curls of butter, removing itself over years, and the trees outside that are barren of leaves. It's very dull today, no sun, even duller in here. A sort of white light and lots of shade across the ward. Can't think what . . . Oh, the nurses. Hmm . . . Mostly young. The one who showed me here, fairish hair, green eyes, I think, or light in colour, though I might be getting them confused . . . The one here now, small, efficient, shapely, busy in a hopping, birdlike sort of way. Lovely smile, the men watch her leave with longing."

"I guessed right about her then," Charlie says, smiling wider this time.

"Now tell me," says the private. "What have you come for? With no disrespect, Mr. Shine, I imagine it wasn't only to check on my welfare."

"My son mentioned you by name in a letter. You served with him."

"Yes. We spent some time together. He was the sort of person one wants at their back."

The flutter in Arthur's chest has turned into an ache.

"You gave him something," says Arthur. "He didn't say what that was."

"It was a shell from home, from part of the collection I'd started as a child. I brought several of them with me for luck."

There is silence. Arthur swallows, then takes a deep breath.

"Did you see . . . did you see what happened to him?"

Charlie turns his head slightly, as if toward a window that has the best view of a past event.

"We were in different units but the same battle. The last time I saw Jack he was running. His line was farther forward. We could see many of the men gunned down, and some were thrown into the air . . . bodies . . . pieces of . . . No one would have made it out of there. I lasted less than a minute in the fray. It was over quickly."

"Did you see . . . just before, I mean?"

There is silence that seems to go for many moments, enough for Arthur to hear the conversation between two nurses, instructions for more pans and antiseptic.

"If you're asking me," says Charlie, "whether I believe he survived, the answer is no. He didn't. He was there one second and then an explosion and then another one and he was gone. It was fast."

Arthur nods to himself. It is the answer he was expecting, though he'd be lying if he said he hadn't carried a sliver of hope.

"He is dead, Mr. Shine. There is no other way to tell you."

It is a cold, hard reality to have it driven home by someone who was there. But it's what he came for. A simple truth. Someone to end the hope.

"He did speak of home," says the private. "He told me briefly . . . We don't get a lot of time unless we're in the same unit, but he was talkative."

Arthur smiles downward at his hands gripping and ungripping in his lap.

"We swapped addresses on the off chance that we lived. He said he wanted to travel. We both had visions of travelling to India."

There is further conversation about his family, why he joined the army; then it is time for his sponge bath and a changing of bed sheets. Arthur wishes the patient a fast recovery. Charlie wishes his visitor peace.

Arthur stops at a café on the way home and orders a pork pie, mashed potatoes with gravy, and a pint of ale, then watches the people from the window before something catches his eye: a poster on a door across the street, a call to arms. Men are needed.

He will attempt to make things right, pay for whatever mistakes he might have made. He can draw from Jack's courage and continue the battle for him.

He eats only half the food, downs the ale quickly, and pays and nods his thanks to the barman, then straight down to the station to check the train times to take him to the sign-on office.

He is certain now that Harriet will approve, certain that she will think it right, he counters, when he at first had argued a different response from her. It might actually bring them closer.

Yes, he can make things right, he tells himself again. Jack's death will not be for nothing. Jack was changed. Arthur can change for the better.

Though what better is, he still isn't sure.

6. TO THE FRONT

He is on the train to the Front after weeks of training. He is kitted with a government-issued hat and uniform, boots, puttees, rifle and bayonet, ammunition, and water bottle, tin cup, spoon, knife, as well as toiletries and dressings. He now has the freedom to kill his enemy with a rifle or stab them in the torso with a bayonet. He also knows the difference between an incendiary bomb—fire starters useful for sabotage and diversion during covert night operations—a grenade, and a mortar shell that can gouge yards out of the earth's crust and splinter as many men as possible with metal shards. He is told something about the Germans, how they fight, a very strange-sounding "trench warfare," what to do, say, rules, commands. He understands the ranks, too, who does what.

Men with your skills are needed, said the recruiting sergeant. *You can apply for a commission, a corporal perhaps. You have had some military training during school.*

It was a long time ago.

Still, lieutenants and corporals are in short supply at the moment.

Arthur didn't think to ask why.

No. I'm quite happy to serve as a private.

Your son was a corporal. One of the youngest.

Yes, sir. Just a rank for me.

Very well, he said, completely miffed.

Arthur had phoned Harriet at her parents' country residence. She sounded better on the phone, though distant. She was still on medication, and "Mummy" was taking care of her. It grated on him. If she'd stayed, he would have taken care of her.

But it has worked out for the best, he tells himself. Either way he has to fall on his sword to please Harriet.

Why are you signing up? said Harriet.

To help win the war. To finish it.

Do you think you will make the difference?

He wanted to say something, feeling sudden anger. She had given up on him, on them, on herself. She had left without seeing him first. She has confined herself to grief. At least he was doing something for it. He wanted her to say that she loves him, that she will miss him.

Will you be there when I return? he asked.

There was a pause.

Artie, you can write to me any time.

Their conversation seemed so flat and irrelevant. He could sense the rope that moored her to him unwinding, that she was about to drift away. He wanted to tell her this, describe his fears. He wanted to ask her, When did he become so irrelevant?

Very well, I'll write then, he said, in the voice that suggested he was taking a holiday.

He was about to hang up.

Harriet, please try to reduce the medication. Time will ease things. I am certain of this.

There was silence.

I'm not taking anything now. I do feel better and the doctor here is wonderful. I see.

Artie, there's . . . Heavy, deep breaths.

Harriet?

I wish you the very best. Goodbye, Arthur.

From the train window he can see meadows spotted with manure, and farms and people in boots, and women in scarves, and bell towers. There is a smell of freshly churned earth as he steps onto the station platform and is ushered into a lorry that will take him to the field tents near the front line. Along the journey, he has heard about the casualties, the failures, and the successes. He is warned again about writing home, not saying too much, and about the French girls, too. They are off limits. There is an order to things in the army that he likes. He has always worked well with structure. When he commented to someone on the train who was returning to the Front from leave, the soldier had laughed at the comment.

"Well, you can kiss structure goodbye when you're out in the battlefield. It's as untidy as it gets out there, all out for oneself."

They were amiable enough, these men, many of whom are younger than Arthur, the new recruits, ambitious, eager. He feels a fatherly concern for these strangers, boys, not yet men some of them, as if he should be telling them something, for there is much of life they are yet to experience. Not that he feels a sense of superiority as such, but that he wants them to know about the things they can look forward to, and things to look out for. Then he thinks otherwise, when he thinks where he sits in that moment, when he remembers where his own experiences have led.

He does not talk about Jack. It is not something he can raise suddenly. It would be like beginning a sentence from its middle. Such personal information built upon long conversation and released at a time when other more pressing subjects have been exhausted. He does not want their sympathy. He despises pity to the point of saying nothing much of the time, to avoid any questions altogether. It is his nature, the same one Harriet originally desired of him: his steadiness, his lack of showmanship that her own father possessed, which annoyed her once, though not anymore apparently. They had entertained; however, it was often woven with business or with her family: parents, cousins, uncles. Such frightful bores; he wondered how Harriet was born so different and he understood why she was so keen to break away. She was much like Jack: restless, charming, wanting to live life the way she chose it, and without so much dependence on systems and structure. Something that was not possible in any society. Sooner or later necessity fills an open mind to drive out any philosophical dreams.

War is fetid. It is not filled with medals and smart Bond Street uniforms and badges and hearty meals cooked over campfires outside cosy, dry tents. Where men on quieter days bond by sharing their futures under a starry sky. He learns this quickly. Waiting to be sent in as a reinforcement, he sees the mangled bodies brought in from the field, carried through the new trench lines dug deeply to fight a war that seems from the outset unwinnable by either side. The strategy of running at each other is simply a game of numbers, and an acceptance that many will die, and you may or may not be one of them.

Residents from the local village who are unfortunate enough to be only miles from the front line come out to wave handkerchiefs at the soldiers heading in, the children running parallel to the street, pointing and clapping, sending them off to battle, the wind turning their colourful coats into sails, their cheeks red, boots worn and caked with mud, their enthusiasm joyous to most, though half the men are more seasoned to what lies ahead, thinking only of the finish line, in fact some not even that far.

Arthur considers the villagers, worse off than the soldiers in many ways, carving out their existence amongst buildings that have been shelled or pocked with bullet holes. The church tower broken, a jumble of bricks and pieces of sculptured stone, and the lush grass fields that once fed cattle in vast numbers are filled with the remains of exploded shells and the remnants of soldiers these have strewn.

Why are the villagers still here? asked Arthur.

It's their homes, some of which have been in the family for centuries, said the sergeant, a ruddy-cheeked man with a gruff manner that belied a gentler side. *They refuse to cower or give up everything they have worked for. Until they have to. They are all good people here. Have not met any that didn't want to help us with something.*

Arthur wants to fight for them also, decides there is even greater purpose.

Once at the foothills of battle, the soldiers wait in ankle-deep rain-water that has turned the trench into a murky, stinking swamp.

"We sleep here?" asks Arthur to the next man, trying to hide the disappointment in his tone, so the question comes out as slightly desperate.

"Apparently," says another.

The rain pours in sheets over days, his coat and boots drenched, and then it is time for battle. He looks from face to face of the other soldiers along the line, on his first day going over, to gain a sense of how he should feel, if the weakness he feels, if the desire to run, is the same for others, with the sound of death above them. Someone is weeping just up the line, and the men move about restlessly in response until someone yells for him to stop.

Arthur asks the soldier next to him to swap so he can stand near the boy who appears panic stricken. The soldier doesn't need to be asked again.

"What's your name?" he asks the young soldier.

"Leon," he says, trembling, eyes sunken into dark pools, rubbed constantly into his head.

"It's my first time over, too," says Arthur.

"It's my second."

A sudden realisation floods his thoughts. The boy doesn't fear the unknown, he knows already what he should fear, and something about this threatens to tear whatever resolve Arthur thought he had.

The whinnying of a horse in distress distracts him. Forgetting for a moment the purpose, the terror beyond it, someone climbs up the parapet to learn the source, and to also learn his fate: to see firsthand the thunderous, murderous creature that vibrates through the trench as if it has been angrily stirred from slumber. The soldier reports what he sees: a frantic horse breaking away and zigzagging awkwardly in front of the trench line toward the field of fire, dragging a wagon on its side now empty of ammunition, and a hapless soldier running behind it futilely stabbing at the reins for release with a bayonet before both are shot up by the enemy, the soldier falling instantly; the horse, screaming in pain, is shot quickly by another who is watching from elsewhere.

Curiosity gets the better of several others, Arthur, too. They climb up to see. Shells screech across the lake of mud that leads to a slight ridge, and he watches soldiers of the first line run directly into an unseen enemy hiding behind it. Many scatter before reaching this first obstacle, as explosions force diversions and break the chain of men, some vanishing before his eyes. In the distance the skies are lit with fire from a village burning in the north.

Hands pull at his coat, and someone else shouts, *"Get down, you bloody idiots!"* though it is barely audible under the clatter.

Water funnels from soldiers' hats to fall on the backs of already saturated yellow-brown woollen coats that do little now to block the cold. Arthur's feet ache from being wet for several days, and now immersed in trenches held up by sandbags and timber bracing that buckles under the pressure so that slimy white-grey mud slides inward. His trembling from the cold is followed by a sudden yearning for his childhood home, conjuring images of his mother waiting for him on their doorstep, anxiously sometimes, that he didn't see till now. Waking up to the sounds of her stirring the embers in the grate and the smell of bacon blistering on the iron. Reserved in her affections but caring, working hard to keep him fed and warm. This vision of his once simple life stirs his heart, reminds him what is important, but also, what he might not know again.

"Soldiers!" shouts his lieutenant, who is walking up the line behind him, taking him away from his morbid reflections that threaten to disarm him before he has begun.

"Eyes up, head down, remember, focus!" he shouts, with his voice that has its own low rumbling timbre, only just audible above the noise. "Don't look to either side or behind. Eyes ahead on the finishing line! Look for gaps, watch the craters! If men fall in front of you, keep running."

The order is given and soldiers hoist themselves over the top and dodge the craters and puddles, pummel the tufts of grass still left, and crush the fragments of dead soldiers' belongings from earlier battles deeper into the mud, where they will likely be preserved indefinitely, then onward to rage against an enemy who is waiting on orders to do the same. It is a curious thing how fear can abruptly leave one in these instances, and courage takes over.

Arthur runs forward into the chaos, no longer aware of the danger as he fires on the enemy deep within the smoke and haze of rain as it hits the ground. These lunar fields lay waste to countless men. They'd not had time to forge a cohesive team with the dead piling high, fired upon by hidden armaments beyond a plateau to the north. Several Germans run out from the smoke and are gunned down immediately before they have time to raise their firearms for the first time.

It is disorder on a mass scale, the groups now broken up, and Arthur takes a defensive position this time, crouching behind a low stone fence. They had made some progress and more dead Germans than English to account for, to step over, if the result were measured in bodies in these first attempts. The men continue across the earth, slipping on the mud and hurdling over bodies, some clumped together to form a mass of gore from exploding shells. The whirring, whistling of shells and crackling of rifles, sending bullets whizzing in all directions, fuse into masses of smoke that disintegrate in the walls of water that surround them.

Arthur takes check of his platoon's position. His sergeant is somewhere missing, though he can see Leon farther forward, relieved that survival had ridden above his fear; but there are still yards and hours to fill. Then suddenly Leon is pounded full of bullets, part of his face blown away. Arthur runs forward firing, doesn't look, can't look at the dead boy, thinks of his son, imagines him falling, and this powers him on, raging at the fire and machines that callously scythe men down with ease.

With nowhere to run and numbers down, they are ordered to retreat, both sides with heavy losses. And somehow with less than half the men, they are back in their rabbit holes, shivering and shocked by what they just witnessed. The captain comes to tell them to hang in there. There is another day of it. And no one is talking, their faces muddy, their teeth chattering. Bodies are ferried along the line by stretcher bearers who have reaped the dead. There is some kind of truce, as the Germans are doing the same, and it seems strangely civilised, this dirty war, until a rogue German bullet strikes a bearer climbing upward, who then falls back in the pit. Like soldier ants, a crowd of men descends upon the body to drag it off the boards, clumped with others, to clear the way for other bearers coming through. The rest continue as if this interruption is normal, simple as a tap on the shoulder, a call for more water. It is seamless, this machine that is the army, that doesn't back down, that moves bodies in and parts of them out.

"Bloody Huns!" says another. "They couldn't give us this one to collect the dead."

The bearers aren't going out anymore today. Too risky. Arthur searches the faces of those injured that are carried past him, some so hideous that he can only bear to glance until he sees the fair head of

Leon, the bottom of his jaw missing, one eye open, blue, the other beneath the pulp.

He touches the arm of the bearer, who appears disgruntled by the interruption.

"He's dead, is he?" says Arthur.

The soldier looks at Arthur as if he has lost his mind. He is new to this much death; stunned by it, he thinks.

"What do you think?" says the bearer, unstopping.

Arthur mouths a prayer. He had not been religious prior to Jack's death, but since then he has thought about mortality, questions his own, questions the hereafter. He believes in it. He must.

Then more rifle fire spasmodically as the same sniper uses dead Englishmen for target practice, and the Allies retaliate. A flare goes up, several random shots, and then it is silent and dark, clouds obscuring the moon, and low gas lights dot the inside of the trench walls as men try to sleep. Arthur has the first night's luxury of a dugout purely by the luck of lower-than-usual numbers returned to base, a winning ticket, and he lies under eight feet of dirt, stretched out, a blessing also, and falls into a slumber that feels only partway real.

Then in following days they are stuck, unable to go forward, the firing more violent now, the gouging of bodies continuing. Nowhere is life more raw, more personal and primal, than on a battleground face to face. Then it is something that forces men to rage against men they would in other circumstances, in a different time, greet with a nod or a wave or a handshake.

And then after days, after the initial shock of going over, of becoming slightly injured from bullets, he was "seasoned."

BRUSSELS

1915

7. HOTEL MÉTROPOLE

For over six months the Descharmes family has been living in the city of Brussels. But for a tiny scrap in the corner, where the country meets the sea, Belgium is under German occupation.

They arrived with their pillowcases carrying the few belongings Gisela and Eugène had grabbed frantically when they departed Louvain. The family had stood in a long line to register their names at the new German administration in the town hall. Their savings at the Banque Nationale had been taken, and they brought with them little money except for that which Maurice had kept in his office drawer. Donations of coffee, butter, and bread were offered, and after a night of no sleep with others on a factory floor, they were allotted a house that had been vacated, squeezed in with several other families and one bathroom to share.

Some weeks later, Eugène encountered Anja, whom he had known at the art academy. Anja's mother had died years earlier from illness. Her father had gone to war, and her grandparents immigrated to England as the first rumour of German invasion had spread. Anja gambled to stay, to look after their interests in Brussels, to take care of her grandparents' property.

Anja knew people in the city, and haggled with a property manager until a price was agreed for a furnished house in Cureghem. The family who had lived there had vanished. Josephine wondered whether the owners were even aware that someone was living there, whether the manager of various properties in the area had found war to be opportune.

"We will all have to find work," said Gisela after they had settled into the house. "Otherwise, we cannot continue to afford this place."

"There are some wealthy people here still, despite the looting from the Germans," said Anja. "I can get you their names, and you could deliver letters to them to arrange an introduction for your lacework. There are also couturiers.

"And you, what did you do?" she asked Josephine.

"I worked for my papa in printing."

"Have you worked in a restaurant or hotel before?"

Josephine shook her head.

"I might be able to get you work as a waitress," Anja said. "Benôit Fallières, a restaurant manager, is always looking for new girls. I work there, too, at the Hotel Métropole."

Gisela gripped Anja's hand. "Oh, thank you. I'm sure that anything will be helpful."

"There is something you need to know," she said, looking at Gisela first then to Josephine. "Aside from the manager, you would be working mostly for Germans who took over the hotel. The owner had no choice since there will be no more tourists, and since . . . they have no choice anyway."

"Oh no!" said Gisela. "She cannot work there. We will work for Belgians only."

"Madame," said Anja. "Germans pay well and there are tips."

"Maman," said Eugène. "It is not like we have a choice with anything. We need the money. Papa would agree if he were here. He was business minded always."

Gisela shook her head in disagreement and closed her eyes. The mention of Maurice had strewn misery across her face once more.

"Maman, I will do what I have to so we can survive this even if it means serving Germans," said Josephine.

Gisela pulled out her handkerchief to dab at the tears beginning to form.

"It is better than begging, Maman," said Eugène.

"And what will you do?" asked Gisela of Eugène. "We can't just send your sister out into danger."

"I will find work. I will find something."

Josephine's footsteps crump evenly across the snow, and starkly against the silence of the city under martial law. She passes a German guard as she enters the Place De Brouckère, with her hands in the pockets of her coat, eyes downward and chin lowered to sink beneath her woollen scarf to avoid his eyes. There is currently a curfew for some misdeed that someone committed and therefore the Belgians are collectively guilty. She is becoming a little tired of atoning for someone else's supposed misdeed.

A medieval shadow has been cast across the city, as people live in fear of saying the wrong thing, of crossing paths with angry soldiers, of cruel and oppressive laws. Crops have been taken for the German army while the Belgians grow hungry. Parents and wives are being deported to prisons because of the crimes of their young sons and husbands who have fled across the border to fight, children left behind to live on the charity of others. Or the wives left with children they can't afford to feed. Singing Belgium's national anthem, any form of patriotism, is a grave offence.

Stationed in busier areas across Brussels are guards in spear hats that many citizens privately mock behind their doors, and their long jackets with too many brass buttons that flicker haughtily at passersby. They are there to protect the citizens, say the German authorities. But it is a lie they all play along with. The guards are constantly on the lookout for Belgian dissatisfaction. They regularly parade through the streets and organise speeches, and people pretend to be pleased, some even clapping.

Those who are continually missing from events are noted.

On civic buildings the flags fly black, white, and red. They are no longer to fly the Belgian flag or sing their songs in public, nor their Catholic hymns, unless they are quietly sung within the church walls. German soldiers have a problem with Catholics, too. Churches are breeding grounds for franc-tireurs, those civilians who might take it upon themselves to create an army, those who preach dissent.

Near the central fountain Josephine sees a woman standing in front of a guard, one hand holding something behind her back and the other hand gripped tightly to the hand of a small child, the mother's knuckles white with fear. It is not unusual for civilians to be stopped and questioned, and bags routinely searched.

He is asking her something, and the woman doesn't understand, and at first Josephine thinks to walk on. *It is not my issue.* But she can't help herself. She speaks German and the woman does not.

"Excuse me," Josephine says to the guard. "I can help."

He looks her up and down, a look that takes her back to the night of the attempted rape, and she shudders inwardly. At first displeased by the interruption, he then nods and watches Josephine closely, perhaps to see that she is not deceiving him.

"He wants to check the basket for guns," Josephine tells her in French. "He is looking for people who are smuggling items in and out of the town. He is also checking whether you are taking food and clothes to Allied soldiers somewhere hidden in the city."

There is no exact intelligence on the number, only that some have been caught crossing the border to Holland, and they are rounding up any found participating in such a crime.

"I am not stupid!" she says. "As if I would be doing such a thing. I do not wish to die!"

Josephine turns to the guard, who is repeating his request.

"You need to show him what is in your basket. He says he does not want to harm you. He does not want to take anything from you if it is legal."

"But he will when he sees it. It is a big, fat chunk of ham that was given to me as a gift from my employer."

Josephine hesitates because she knows food is desired. They have taken food from people before, raided farmers' stores and barns. Everyone must contribute.

"You will have to show him," says Josephine. "You have no choice." She looks to the little girl, who is staring at the guard, chin on chest and eyes raised to him fearfully.

The mother pinches her lips together and releases the child briefly to pull her light shawl around her modestly, and Josephine suspects she is remembering the stories of atrocities committed against women and wary he might attempt the same offence. She holds the basket forward for him to open and inspect.

He pulls aside the linen cover, inspects, then nods and takes a step back and says a few words in German.

"He is allowing you to walk on. He doesn't want your ham."

"He will probably want it next time."

The woman cannot bring herself to say thank you. She is about to leave when the guard's attention turns to the little girl. He bends down to her to say some broken French to suggest she is pretty, turning back to Josephine to reaffirm. She nods and forces a smile, something Gisela has told her to do more often since she wears much of her honesty in her expressions.

The guard picks up the child and places her on his hip, an act that has caught both women nervously off guard. From his pocket he pulls out a sweet, wrapped in coloured paper, to hand to her. She takes it, her eyes examining the object before returning to the face of the man distrustfully.

"I have a daughter this age, too!" says the guard, and Josephine translates it for the girl and her mother.

"Then it is better if he went home to care for her," says the woman.

Josephine sneaks a look at the guard, who does not appear to understand the barb, though she is never too sure. Germans are good at masking their thoughts. The woman is playing a dangerous game.

The guard bounces the child up and down a little until eventually she releases a smile, though she has sensed some dissatisfaction on her mother's face, which alters her mood. The little girl begins to whimper again.

It won't seem to end, this spectacle. Josephine is due to commence work, but she is anxious about leaving the woman and child and offending the sentry. The guard has begun a German song to soothe the child, who has stopped whimpering but cannot manage a smile. The girl is finally handed back, burrowing her face into her mother's neck, the sweet still gripped in her hand. The guard is wearing this rejection well, and for reasons Josephine can't explain, she feels a fraction of pity for him.

"Please tell the woman she has a lovely daughter and wish her a pleasant day." The German is smiling at the mother, who is still unable to force a smile herself as Josephine relays the comment.

"Please tell him to burn in hell," she says.

"She says she wishes you a pleasant day also," says Josephine.

There is something slightly changed about his expression. They must never be taken for fools.

Josephine is pleased to leave and steps quickly toward the hotel, her eyes lifting to the gilt bronze of Saint Michael, who always gives her a moment of strength before she begins her work. There is an elderly couple sitting on the steps of the fountain. Most days the woman raises one twisted hand to wave and the man lifts his hat toward her. These small interactions give her courage as well.

Josephine straightens her skirt as she hurries the final steps to the entrance of the hotel and tucks in the strands of hair that have slipped outside her cap. She enters the hotel, where everything glistens: the polished teak, the shards of light through the ceilinged lead glass, the crystal chandeliers, the coloured glass windows, the gilded décor, and the exquisite marble columns that shine like mirrors.

"Good morning," says Benôit, at the front desk of the hotel that is now almost exclusively housing German officers. Benôit is stout and stiff at his post, and what remains of his hair is slicked back, his moustache neatly twisted and fashionable. Tiny dark chest hairs escape over the top of his collar, and he wears a permanent shadow around his jawline, like pencil shavings smudged, that grows darker by the end of the day. His pleasant nature, Josephine has discovered, is mostly for show in the front rooms. In the back room and the large kitchen, he drives the staff hard, and is not so easily forgiving if they are careless or forgetful. She has proven herself, but other girls hired to serve the German soldiers and shine the silverware have been fired for the smallest of service crimes: a shaky hand, an error on the order book, a smear on a spoon. It does not do well to upset an officer.

"You are in the main café today, mademoiselle. There is a group of eight there for lunch. And you will also serve the cigar lounge."

She nods and walks to the back room to check the service book, to check for any messages or special orders. Lieutenant Bentz, who lives in the hotel and is a regular at the restaurant, for example, is allergic to shellfish and therefore his food cannot be contaminated. To injure or offend an officer is a serious offence. Benôit told her a story before her interview, perhaps to check that she was serious about the job, to scare her away if she was faint of heart when situated close to Germans. One woman, he told her, who spilt boiling tea on an officer's lap, was sent away to prison at Liège for forty days. She was accused of doing that deliberately, though Benôit said she was very clumsy. Her time in prison made her so ill she is unfit for any work now.

Josephine had passed the interview with Benôit in his little office that is stuffy and filled with cigar smoke.

———

"Have you worked in such employment before, Mademoiselle Descharmes?"

"No. But I am diligent, I learn fast, and I enjoy food."

He laughed, and she blushed and inwardly called herself juvenile. She was remembering Anja's instructions to show an appreciation for the industry and the business.

"Anja says you speak German."

"Yes, very well, better than Dutch."

Benôit did not seem impressed and continued to write in his notebook, then asked several questions in German to test her.

"What are your parents' occupations?"

It was evident Anja had told him little, and Benôit had noticed her pause.

"What happened to your family?"

He heard Josephine's story, writing down everything, his expression remaining impassive when he learned of Yves, though once when her voice had broken slightly recalling her father's execution, he raised his eyes. When she had finished, he put down the pencil.

"My dear. I cannot give you enough consolation for what you have been through. Nothing I say will make up for that, or any hollow apologies on behalf of others. I am manager of the restaurant only, that is all, and I am making the most of the situation like many other Belgians. But I will give you some advice. You must draw a line between what was and what is. Only then can you leave the past in some context and allow yourself to make the best of what you have now. It is hard, I know, for you have not yet lived the years that I have to know that life is rarely ever perfect in any given moment and that things can go from good to bad to good again in the time it used to take me to kick Madame Picot's, my previous neighbour's, dog when it urinated on my front door. It is a life nevertheless and you still have choices. Time has a way of reckoning. If you do your job, you will get your money, and from there you can buy things. That is what you must focus on. I might also tell you that the German officers tip well, so make the most of it, take everything you can. Few will get that opportunity."

It was hard advice she had not thought of, bogged down in angst and loss.

"You will have four days of work, paid two francs a day. It may not seem a lot, especially with the cost of things now, but it is more than any other job you will find in the city for a woman without the experience required here. The hours are long, and on some of your free days, you will have to cover other people's shifts.

"You start tomorrow morning, at eight o'clock sharp. You will be taught to take orders, to serve, to be civil and cunning. How does that sound?"

He winked and stood up, and it was Josephine's cue to stand, too.

"Bonsoir, Mademoiselle Descharmes!"

He bowed and Josephine retreated from the office, stepping more purposefully and confidently than when she first arrived.

8. CIRCUMSTANCES

Anja is already there at work. She sees Josephine from across the room and gives her a secret wave; she is careful and discreet with everything she does. She walks toward an elderly gentleman having breakfast alone, a Fleming who is in tight with the Germans. There are a few, both Walloon and Flemish, who seem comfortable with the new Belgium.

Back in the kitchen, the two girls collect several plates to serve. As they commence to leave, Anja leans in to speak quietly.

"Did you hear?" she says. "They have imprisoned the chemist Monsieur Théry at Saint-Gilles for withholding medicines and keeping them for Belgians only. And there is something else he has been doing, though we have no details yet . . .

"They caught a man guiding several Allied soldiers to the Dutch border. He was executed on the spot. It is not recorded anywhere in their news. He was not imprisoned and received no trial."

"Who was he?"

Anja pauses as they near the dining room entrance. She looks ahead at the room full of German officers.

"Just a farmer," she says, turning to examine Josephine's expression to see if she is as horrified as she. "A good man. He left behind seven children."

"How do you know this?"

Anja looks back toward the restaurant clientele, then down at the plates they carry, checking they have them all and that nothing is out of order. There is roast beef, beets, and beans soaked in mushroom sauce, the smell of which makes Josephine's mouth water. Perhaps there will be German leftovers, those that can't be reused the following day.

"I hear people talking!" she says. "You should listen also. Don't speak of anything I tell you." Josephine follows her into the room.

The restaurant is situated in a long hall with lead glass lights and a high, coffered ceiling, panelled walls, an opulent glass chandelier, marble floors, and large planters with palm trees in the corners. The easy chairs have plush cushioned backs, and tabletops are set with bright-white tablecloths and silverware. There is an intoxicating fusion of smells in the room, of roasting meat, herbs and spices, cologne, and polish.

The girls separate and go to different tables. The officers, some in differently shaded uniforms, turn toward her as she approaches. Though she is their focus at the moment, she is to remain invisible when she can. She wills her hands to remain steady. She has almost mastered the skill of hiding her nerves.

Only look at them to match their faces to their orders. Otherwise don't look at them unless they ask a question or engage in conversation, said Benôit during training.

The officers are discussing something intensely, but pause as Josephine approaches and while she is serving. It is a sign that the information is sensitive and likely about a military operation or some law that is to be imposed, a piece of news that will affect the lives of Belgians. The people she serves are pleasant or arrogant or condescending. Sometimes they say something personal: a complaint about the food, a compliment about her appearance, a comment about the size of the meal, too big or too small. Some are more important than others. Some have come for social events, and others are there to discuss matters of business, papers from their briefcases on the table. And then there are those officers who talk privately, watching out that no one is listening. Josephine is mostly uninteresting to all of them and prefers it that way.

But she also serves some of the Belgian elites who appear comfortable amongst the Germans, who might profit them in some way. For many others, however, businesses have closed, machines taken from factories and sent to Germany without reparation.

She has managed to learn some things that she takes home to her family. Battles have been mentioned. Talk about raising taxes to buy better food, to bring in German services, to find more horses, workers.

Gisela examines her daughter after she returns home, inspects the small white scar on her cheek. Her mother is worried about illness and scurvy. They have food, but they do not have access to all items. Last week there was no butter available. The Belgian newspapers were stopped upon occupation, and only those approved by the German administration are now sold, with censored news. They are isolated, and the world outside grows distant and dim.

The light from the small, ornate lamp burnishes warmth across the dull burgundy walls and the chipped and darkly aged wood of the dining table. It appears that few of the furnishings in the room have been changed in over forty years, and a gentle hand remains in the yellowing lace tablecloth and the frames of pressed flowers that hang around the walls.

Gisela is pacing while she waits for Eugène to come home. He disappears often and is vague about where he goes, but there are other, greater concerns for their mother.

"Did you hear?" says Eugène when he enters that evening. He takes off his hat and walks straight to the fireplace to warm his hands. There is a bite to the air tonight, and Benôit has given each of the staff some coal left over, smiling like a cat, since it seems the "Germans have an oversupply" (though not really), and the warmer weather is on the way.

Eugène sees that Gisela is quiet, that she has other things on her mind.

"What is it, Maman?"

"Come sit," says Josephine to Eugène, putting a plate of cabbage and ham, which has already gone cold, at his place setting.

"Maman?" he says, sitting down, watching her as he does and waiting for her to reply. "Is everything all right?"

"Oh," she says, putting her hand to her forehead. "I'm having trouble remembering things. There is so much bad news. I'm not sure exactly what they wanted, what they said."

"Who?"

"There were officers from the German General Government who came today to ask that you report to the administration," says Josephine, repeating what she had just been told by her mother, who is still clearly distressed about it. "They are calling for those still unemployed to sign up to work in the German factories."

Eugène laughs with a tinge of scorn, plucks something absently from his teeth. He has a faint beard around his face, angry frown lines, and pursed lips that have become a permanent feature, hair unruly as usual, more so, in fact, and unwashed clothes.

"They will have to wait. I told you I have something already. I perform deliveries for people, friends of Anja."

"Who are these friends?"

"Farmers, businesses. What does it matter who? It is work for now until I can find something better."

Josephine knows Eugène is not telling the whole truth, since he is angry about being questioned, and none of his wages ever come home. She suspects he is staying with Anja, that they are lovers.

"We have already heard how the government is rounding up men and sending them on cattle trucks and trains to Germany to work in their factories in conditions not fit for fleas," he says. "I will not go. I will die before that happens."

"Stop it, Eugène!" says Gisela. "I've lost enough sons. Enough of such talk!"

Eugène continues eating, while appearing to fight back more he wants to say. He sees the newspaper on the table, drops his utensils, and opens it up, his food forgotten. He traces his fingers down the columns.

"Nothing about the Belgians who are executed!" he says. "See how clever they are to keep things out of the paper, to only report the news they want us to know. They want people to remain ignorant. It's how they control us, and how they make us beg for everything, thankful for anything. The executions of civilians are illegal. Breaking the agreement of neutrality is illegal. Slaughtering innocent people is illegal. But still some think that Germany is acting within the code of war. None of that is mentioned here! It is all *merde*!" He slams down the paper.

"Things will get better," says Gisela pointlessly, as she always does, though she doesn't believe it herself; it is merely to pacify her son. Attempt to anyway. It makes no difference when Eugène is in this mood, when he is obsessed.

"I heard from someone that *La Libre Belgique* is printing again in secret. I will find one and bring it home. Some in our group have brought copies of Dutch and French newspapers from England. We need to know exactly what they are doing so the people here know the truth."

"Anyway, Gène, you should know that Maman told them you had a job without knowing anything you do, to cover for you." She has put herself in danger if Eugène is lying about everything. "They told her that anyone who changes occupation must report it also. They are expecting you within the week."

Gisela scratches nervously at the back of her hands, a habit she has developed only recently. Josephine is worried that the death of her father and Yves, and Xavier missing, has driven her mother to dark places sometimes that she can't express. More and more it seems to Josephine that their fates rest with her, that she is the only one thinking clearly most of the time.

It is her father's voice she has trained herself to hear when the light first touches the walls, always when she is weakest, when she feels a sense of hopelessness, that this day will be no better than the one before. *Get up, get dressed, my angel.*

It is Eugène's birthday soon, and she has bought him some paper and drawing pencils. If she can get him to draw and paint again, perhaps he will calm, not go without food, not disappear.

"Josephine!"

Benôit has drawn Josephine's attention. She had been staring out the window of the restaurant, only briefly but long enough to be caught.

"Don't dream of freedom, my dear. It is too early for that. Get to work. It will be very busy today. Full house. If there are no patrons, then go fetch the milk and ready the jugs, wipe down the tables, help wash the crockery. Don't be idle."

The tables become full. Today there is a particularly important general from Berlin who will be staying at the hotel. She has become accustomed to the emblems on their coats. At the general's table there are Belgian businessmen and several other senior officers she hasn't seen before.

Josephine attempts to write down the general's order first, but he speaks too fast and becomes frustrated when Josephine politely asks him to repeat his request. He makes her nervous, more than some.

Benôit has seen immediately, eyes in the back of his head, and comes to the table to intervene. "I'm sorry, General, is there a problem?"

"You need to recruit smarter girls."

"Of course," says Benôit. "We will certainly look into the matter. Perhaps I will personally take your order."

Josephine stares at her order pad.

"Pfft," says the general, who begins to talk about something else, to waste everyone's time.

Someone else has politely addressed the general and asks what he would like to order. She swallows her surprise that this younger man with light-golden-brown hair is the captain from the chateau the night of the attempted rape. He has a distinctive face, not so easily forgotten, with high cheekbones and a pointed chin, and a nose, slightly Roman in design, that reaches almost to his lips. She suddenly remembers the state of her dress when they first met and how he saw her with her skirt up and her bare legs. She feels her cheeks aflame.

The general has put his glasses over eyes sunk too deeply into his head, and he reads again from the menu. When he is finished relating what he wants, the captain turns to Josephine. He repeats the general's order, and she writes unsteadily. Though pleasant enough, he does not appear to have recognised her. She is much changed anyway. Her hair is up and under a cap. She is clean, her face not bruised and bleeding.

She takes the orders from the rest of the men and is relieved when she is once more in the kitchen with the chef. He is huffing, cursing at the task he is completing, and sweating profusely above steaming pans and burning fat.

"You look worse than me," he says. "Did you see a ghost?"

"No, but plenty of ghouls."

Chef roars with laughter, and Josephine hopes that the officers have not heard from their tables.

"You have turned around my mood. Who knew you had a sense of humour?"

He has lost his kitchen hand, and Benôit has not found someone yet to replace him. He has been irritable for days.

"Can I do something to help?" says Josephine.

She cuts up cabbage for a German dish he has never made before and that an officer has newly added to the menu, while he slices up some sausage. She does as he instructs her before Anja appears to ask for service help. The chef stops Josephine as she leaves.

"You're one of the better ones," he says.

Josephine serves another table, but her mind is on the captain.

"Who are those men?" whispers Josephine, when the girls steal a moment alone.

"I don't know," says Anja. "I haven't seen them before. Why do you ask?"

"The general is important," she says, hiding the fact she is curious about the captain only.

"They are always changing staff, sending them off for posts near the front line and replacing them with others. Hopefully, they will kill so many that we won't have to serve Germans at all."

Anja is hard and never hides what she thinks, not to Josephine. It gives her chills to hear this out loud. She could be arrested.

When it is time to bring the dishes and place one in front of the captain, her hands shaking this time, he barely glances her way. His nails are manicured, hands very white and smooth for a soldier.

Back in the kitchen, Chef passes her a little pastry as a thank-you for her help. There is another boy, arranged by Benôit, just arrived to help him.

"Sit down a minute," Chef says. "You need a rest. Something has clearly rattled you. I can hear the ghoul's mouth from here."

He has heard from Anja about the insult from the general. Though her unease is for several reasons, the general being only one of them. The shoes she borrowed from Anja are too small and hurt her feet.

"He is spouting his brilliance," says Josephine. "But I can't stop to rest. The general is impatient."

"He has complained that our service is slow," says Anja, hearing the conversation as she enters. "He has requested that his coffee be served immediately."

Chef raises one eyebrow and mutters something to himself as he pours the coffee that has already been made by one of his staff.

"How did you say the general wants his coffee?" asks Chef as Josephine waits nearby to take the tray.

"With extra cream," says Anja. "I will fetch the jugs for the table."

The chef spits in his cup. "There's his extra cream."

Anja and Josephine have to run to the storeroom behind the kitchen to put towels over their faces and howl with laughter. Josephine has not laughed so hard since Louvain. On reflection, she has not laughed at all.

Josephine takes the coffee to the general still with laughter in her smile. He makes her uneasy, and the captain looks at her curiously this time. She could swear he is reading her thoughts. Then she returns to the kitchen to laugh some more.

"What is going on?" says Benôit tersely, entering the back rooms. "You must stop making so much noise. I can hear you."

Josephine is sent on an errand for some supplies, and by the time she has restocked the larder and gone out to the restaurant to clear the last of the plates, the group with senior officers has gone.

Benôit has hired another girl, Renée, and she is lazy and turns up late, if she turns up at all, but despite that Benôit has kept her on.

"It is because she is the daughter of someone he knows," Anja tells Josephine, when there is no one else listening. "She is useless. She remembers nothing I tell her."

Josephine agrees, but there is something else that is bothering her.

"Have you seen Eugène?" says Josephine.

"Did he not tell you? He is working, making deliveries for people."

"For whom?"

"I don't know much, either," Anja says to the ceiling. "But he will be back soon."

"Maman is worried about him, where he goes. We haven't seen him for days."

Anja's expression softens all of a sudden, and she appears caring, as if she has just remembered that Josephine and Eugène are siblings. She has dark eyes and long, straight dark hair in one plait down her back.

"I will make sure he knows that," she says. "Tell your mother not to worry. He will be back soon. But it may be more convenient for him to stay with me sometimes."

Anja tucks Josephine's hair inside her cap and straightens her apron.

"Go!" she says with a smile. "There are hungry lions waiting."

Josephine casts her eyes over the faces to see if the captain is there today, then scolds herself for thinking about him. No one should want to see a German again, not even think about one.

9. THE WALK HOME

Josephine unties her apron, checks for stains to see if she can get another wear out of it, then stands on her toes to hang it on a hook inside the kitchen. She unpins her cap and places it in her satchel. The chef has already left, and his apprentice is finishing the washing. His previous one has been recruited to work in German factories, which he says pays better. Anja has said the conditions are terrible. That she has heard from people about the lies Germans say to send people east, the conditions the same as labour camps. They are rife with typhoid and dysentery.

Josephine's feet ache worse by the end of the day, and the seams of her blouse have cut uncomfortably into her armpits.

Benôit is at his desk, busily writing; he is there every day as she enters and is always the last to leave. It is rumoured that he lives in a room at the hotel, and it appears he has no family and no other life than the one at the hotel. She learned from Anja that before he was manager at Hotel Métropole, newly recruited after the occupation, he worked in another hotel in another city. Anja said he doesn't talk about his private life and advised to never question him about it if Josephine wishes to keep her job.

Anja is the source of much information.

Benôit stops what he is doing as she approaches the front desk to leave.

"Good night, Josephine," he says, but he nods in the direction to the side of her to make her turn.

"Fräulein Descharmes," says the captain, emerging from the shadows. "I wonder if I might walk you home." She is surprised he has remembered her name, then suspects Benôit has released the information, along with her coat that the captain holds out for her.

"I . . . Sir . . ." She glances at Benôit, who is back to focusing on his task, while she climbs into the sleeves with the captain's help.

"We have not been formally introduced," he continues, still addressing her in German. "My name is Captain Franz Mierzen, employed by the Imperial German Government, tasked with assisting the local police here and in other cities across Belgium, making sure order is maintained.

"I have learned from Monsieur Fallières that you often walk home in the dark."

She nods. "Yes, Captain, but I have a permit that allows me out at night."

Benôit shuffles some papers noisily.

"Of course," Franz says. "The permit is not in question. I am concerned about your safety, a woman on her own. Whatever it is you hear about Germans, we want to make sure our Belgians are safe most of all."

"I am responsible enough to take care of myself," she says, then regrets it. She is making a mess of her response. "I didn't mean to sound ungrateful—"

"I know what you are trying to say," he says. "It takes a little more than words to offend me. Come!"

She follows him outside and waits while he turns up the collar of his coat and peers out at the night sky from under the awning. She observes his smooth face and glittering eyes, illuminated under the lights of the hotel, and is caught off guard when his attention turns back to her. She feels self-conscious or perhaps in slight awe of him, or both. She looks down, aware of her skirt that has a small hole in it, normally covered by her long apron, and shoes that have soles almost worn down to her socks in places.

"Do you not have any gloves?" he says, changing to French now that they are alone.

Josephine digs into her coat pocket for the gloves she received from a Belgian charity. He watches as she wriggles her fingers into the wool, darned in places. She is conscious of the state of them, that he has noticed this, too.

"Do they pay you enough here to cover the things you need?"

She opens her mouth to say something, then closes it again. She nods. She might sound ungrateful if she tells the truth. They could replace her there within hours.

At first they walk without conversation, and he leads the way, seemingly familiar with the route she takes. The weather is starting to turn. The icy ground is beginning to melt in places. She catches herself from slipping as they leave the square.

He holds out one bended arm.

"Please . . ."

She hesitates, then threads her arm through his, creating as much distance between their bodies as she can.

"You are probably wondering if there is another reason I chose to walk with you. As expressed already, I don't like the idea of any woman unaccompanied, but it was for personal reasons also. I wanted the chance to talk about what happened in your cousins' house near Louvain."

She sinks a little.

A group of men pass with shovels, and narrow eyes that dart between the couple. She is aware of how this might look, the two of them together.

"I'm sorry about the soldier who assaulted you. I want you to know he was placed in prison for a period . . . Unfortunately, he is back in his unit, but I did everything in my power to keep him there for some time. We cannot allow such transgressions, and hopefully he has learned from it. I believe there are few like that."

Josephine wants to say that she has heard of other stories, other rapes, atrocities she can't bring herself to repeat. For several months after the days of trauma in Louvain, she had feared the sight of soldiers. She had lumped them as one destructive force, not as individuals. There was little evidence to suggest otherwise.

"I also want to say I am sorry I could not help you any further that night. I had a mission to complete. I deeply regret that we were unable to control the actions of some."

She nods, to stop herself from revealing her true thoughts. And she must be wary of excuses masked in apologies.

"Your French is very good," she says.

"I like the opportunity to use it. Though the general prefers we don't use it at all. How is your family settling in?"

"It is a change . . . My mother is trying to find employment. She has found two customers, but the work is low paying. There is not a lot of need for lace."

"She was busy in Louvain?"

"She once supplied needle lace for the queen's dressmakers," says Josephine. "However, the demand for such work has declined in recent years. Her customers dwindled because machine lace was cheaper. In Louvain, she sold lace-edged linen handkerchiefs and collars at the markets for tourists."

"Perhaps she should sell at the markets here."

"It will take some time for her to build up stock. It was all damaged in the fires." She takes a glance at him to see that he is frowning, that he is taking her words seriously. "Besides, there are no more tourists with handfuls of cash."

"Tell your mother to contact Madame Alland, the banker's wife, who has organised for women with lacemaking skills to receive donations of cotton from America. The charitable committee is selling lace to stores abroad."

"Thank you, I will tell Maman."

"You might also find at the markets that Germans pay handsomely for their wives, daughters, sisters, and mothers back home."

It is the first time she has considered the women back in Germany. What they think of their men and sons on foreign soil. Do they worry, or do they send them off with glee to take the spoils? Do they think about the husbands and children killed? She is tempted to ask with a sharp tongue. But she can't of course.

"She seems like a fine woman. I am glad I got the chance to meet her despite the circumstances. And you? Can you tell me something of you? Did you sew lace also?"

"I am the son my father always wanted," she says, and is surprised when he smiles at that, "or so he told me. I worked in our family printing and newspaper business. Helping with the press sometimes, but mostly I took photographs and developed them in our darkroom."

"You liked this work, yes?"

"Yes, very much." She remembers that her papa's camera was probably taken or destroyed. She fights the urge to tell him.

"And what about your brother?"

"He was an artist, and he drew illustrations for the magazines and brochures of our customers, and for other businesses also. He is having trouble finding work here. He . . ."

Franz has turned to look at her expectantly, and she wants to cross the line, reveal everything.

"Go ahead . . . Your brother?"

"Some Germans came to the door. They asked about my brother. You are sending men east to work in Germany, in factories. It is wrong what you . . . they do. Sending away men, some of them young, and separated from those they love. I have lost enough family. Besides, he is already working. He makes deliveries for people."

"Who for?"

"For farmers and others. Wherever he can get work."

It is unlikely to be true. She now wishes she hadn't mentioned this. They might investigate.

She is impulsive sometimes, and gullible, too, according to Eugène.

If I blow air in one ear, will Xavier feel it come out the other one? said Eugène, teasing. Always teasing.

If I box you in both ears, will you feel it in both of them? said Josephine. *Touché, Mouse!* said Eugène.

What did you expect, Gène? said Xavier. *Stop being such an ass. Besides, she is beating you at your own wicked games these days.*

"But I understand that this is war, that these things happen," she says, correcting herself, hoping she has not drawn unnecessary attention to her brother.

"If it is not full-time employment, he is still eligible to work in Germany."

He is silent for a moment.

"What sort of delivery vehicle does your brother use? Can he drive a motor vehicle?"

"Yes. He drove my father's delivery truck."

Franz has slowed down his steps to amble.

"We are looking for transporters to take goods around Belgium. It is an important job. We need the German men for other tasks. We have had to release many of our transporters to the Front. We need workers to replace them. Sometimes he might be away for a night or two, or perhaps more. Is that something he might do? If of course, he hasn't already registered as having another job."

"I will tell him about it," says Josephine, looking away so he does not see the excitement in her face. They have little, the cost of things doubling. Another job would make all the difference.

He picks up the pace to stop the cold from settling on their shoulders.

"Tell me something about your family," he says. "Your brothers."

"One was . . . is a priest, Xavier, who was imprisoned. We have not heard from him in months. Maman goes to the administration every week to see if they can find his name recorded, though they are not helpful. We tell her not to go so often."

"That must be hard on your mother."

"Papa was executed, if you remember my mother telling you, and Yves . . ." Guilt strikes like lightning when she is not expecting it. *Did I tell you I let go of his hand?*

He looks thoughtfully at the ground ahead.

"This war, Mademoiselle Descharmes . . . May I call you Josephine?"

She is startled by the question.

"Only when we are alone, of course," he clarifies.

This suggests there will be other times, and she feels heat rise to her cheeks at his familiarity. It seems too soon, too rushed.

"Then when it is just the two of us, please call me Franz."

I like him, she thinks, and wishes she didn't. *I tolerate him only,* she says with a stronger inner voice. People are dead. Their countries at war. They can't be friends.

"This war," he begins again, "was not planned this way. I can't explain things. I can't say whether I agree with its beginnings or I don't. I have had a life in the military for years, and my father before me. But I can say that I don't like what war does to people. We follow our duties, and we do things we would never even dream of doing in our civilian lives. I can apologise for the misery, that is all, and wish it didn't have to be this way."

She turns to sneak a look at him, to check his sincerity.

He is serious, and he pulls her arm tighter toward him, so her forearm is against his torso, as if to stress his point that he is genuine. She can feel the hardness of his chest. This is intimate and strange also, this confiding in a stranger, and something that would seem traitorous to some. Yet he is senior, and people do what he says. People admire him. She can tell from the way they looked to him across the table for answers, for leadership.

"Then why start a war?"

You can't say what is on your mind, you silly girl, said Papa. *You have to read people before you do. And if you still want to say something, at least anticipate the consequences.*

"That is not a question I can answer, not because I don't want to, it is because I have asked it, too."

He is honest. Too honest, she thinks, for the role he's been given.

Her house is now in view.

"Tell your brother to come and report to the administration tomorrow," he says, reverting to German once more, and in a voice of authority. "I will ensure he has regular work, and he is not sent away. He needs to ask for a Lieutenant Stuhl."

Approaching the door, he retrieves a pen and notebook from inside his coat pocket and writes several sentences.

"Tell your brother to give this to the lieutenant," he says, tearing out a page and handing it to him.

"*Adieu*, Josephine," he says abruptly, and he is gone.

She is not sure if she has displeased him. Perhaps her outspokenness that seemed to come from nowhere drove him quickly away. She has always said things she regrets. It is something she can't seem to change.

It takes a little more than words to offend me, said Franz.

The smell of roasting chicken is there to greet her as she enters, along with Eugène, who looks more haggard each time she sees him.

"Look, Josephine! I have a newspaper that details everything. It is from France. Their last campaign went nowhere. They have so many dead, more than they tell us. Here . . . right here it says they expected to finish the war by now, but it is becoming harder with so many allies joining the fight. It is all over the American news, too. The world is waking up!"

He looks wild as he talks, eyes wide and the smile so paper thin it might tear.

"Happy birthday, Gène!"

"Oh yes. My birthday," he says, slightly bewildered, as if he has not thought of it till then.

He bends down to hug her, and over his shoulder she sees the pleasure on Gisela's face as she brings the cake to place on the tablecloth she had edged in new lace. Josephine and her mother have been saving to ensure the birthday is special.

"Eugène, dearest," says Gisela, busy in the kitchen. It has been a while since Josephine has seen her manner light. "Get changed into clean clothes. I will wash these ones. Is Anja coming?"

"No. She has a stomach complaint," he says.

"That's a pity. She has been so good to us."

"I have some good news," says Josephine. "I met someone at work today who can give you a job."

She is glad her mother and brother haven't seen the captain walk her home. Consorting with Germans in public is frowned upon, even scorned by some. Only certain wealthy Belgians have the privilege of German friends: those who have their backing, who don't suffer the financial consequences as much, or who are to be feared by ordinary Belgians also.

"What kind of job?"

"In transport. You have to report to the German administration and ask for this man." She hands him the note.

"Work for the Germans?"

"Yes. As do I," she says, examining his sudden, horrified expression. "You said I should, too, remember?"

"Yes, of course." Though it appears his mind is racing to other things she cannot see.

After dinner, Josephine and Gisela present Eugène with a gift.

He commences to untie the strings, still distracted, still talking about news he has heard.

Once it is unwrapped, he stares at the art pad and pencils. His expression is one of pain, as if he might cry.

"Maman and I thought you would get back to drawing and painting again."

"Why did you waste your money?" he says accusingly.

"Your art, Eugène!" says Gisela. "You are so talented. We are thinking of you."

"There is no time for art," he says, agitated, pushing the gift across the table, as if it were the worst thing that could have happened. "You must be mad to think of anything but what is happening around us right now. What I have just read out to you from the news."

"Gène," Josephine says, to calm him down. "We didn't know. We thought you would like it."

"Return it and get your money back for more important things."

Gisela looks joyless again, which deflates Josephine more than Eugène's reaction.

"Very well," says Josephine, who has no intention of taking it back. It will be put away until he changes his mind. He is prone to changing his mind, sometimes in minutes.

"And this job?" says Eugène, seemingly oblivious to the effects he has caused. "What did he say about it again? Where might I be travelling to?"

10. THE GIFT

Anja and Josephine are placing the last of the silverware onto the table when there is commotion outside the hotel. Someone is shouting, and then there is the rumbling tread of many feet and a gunshot fired. The staff and guests rush to the front windows of the hotel to see, and even the chef has turned off the stove to inspect. Outside there is a man on the ground, and guards rush to surround him. At first it is thought he has been shot dead, but the firing was only to make him stop. Soldiers tie his hands behind him roughly, then drag him upright, his arms twisted behind him at an unnatural angle that is likely painful.

"What is happening?" Josephine asks Benôit, who has stepped up beside her. A crowd has gathered, though some slither away, fearful they might get caught up in the arrest.

"They have probably caught a spy," he says as if it is not something of importance.

The captive is yelling at them in French, and when he turns Josephine's way, she can see he is young, perhaps sixteen or seventeen. He spits on the feet of the soldier who is arresting him, and the boy is struck hard across the head with a baton so that he hangs like a puppet, unconscious, as he is carried away.

Anja has stepped up to the window, too.

"*Merde,*" she says under her breath.

"Do you know him?" says Josephine.

"He is the baker's son."

"What has he done?"

"Who knows? Nothing. In any case, the Germans will likely punish us all with another curfew."

Josephine can read from her frown that she is worried. That perhaps she has another answer.

There are loud, slow claps by one of the Germans dining there. "Everyone back to work! There is nothing to see."

"There is nothing to see here, world," says Anja, cynically, under her breath as they head back to the kitchen. "Just more people unjustly arrested!"

"Did you know him personally?" Josephine asks her.

She shakes her head.

"We missed you last night."

"What are you talking about?"

"For dinner. Gène's birthday."

"Oh," she says, scratching the side of her neck, which has reddened. "Yes, his birthday. I could not come. I was busy helping someone."

Either Anja or Eugène is lying.

Anja is pensive for much of the day.

During lunch there is no sign of Franz Mierzen, and Josephine is both disappointed and relieved. The captain has not been far from her thoughts. He is not just pleasing to look at and impeccably polite; he has awakened in her a yearning for something she has not felt before. Desire? Intimacy? She is not sure of her own feelings exactly. He seems unbreakable, just, even kind. It is also disconcerting, his ability to live outside the norms set during war, to speak to her as if they were on the same side.

After many hours of work, Josephine can finally go home, pleased to leave Chef, who is angry today, loudly clanging pots and yelling at the apprentice, who has not been cleaning the crockery thoroughly. At one point the previous day, the chef was so loud Benôit had to speak to him.

In the storeroom Josephine finds Anja writing in her diary. She closes it hastily as Josephine enters, and Anja places the book inside her bag.

As Josephine walks past the reception desk, Benôit passes her a cardboard box with a lid and tied with ribbon. He wears a curious smile. He smooths his moustache and raises his eyebrows before leaving her alone to open it.

She unties the ribbon and lifts the lid. Inside is a pair of dark-green reindeer gloves and a matching-coloured hat made with fine wool. There is no note, but she doesn't need one. She blushes and checks behind her to see that no one is watching, as if she had done something to be ashamed of.

Later when she is lying in bed, she rubs the soft leather against her face. She is unsure what this gift means. In the next room she hears her mother crying, and she puts the gifts back in the box, which she slides under the bed, guilty for the pleasure these give.

She knocks softly on Gisela's door, then enters to sit beside her mother, who is leaning back against the iron headboard. There are dark squares on the faded walls above her where photographs or pictures once sat.

Her mother looks gaunt and miserable. Josephine doesn't like that Gisela is alone so much of the time. Though she has started to receive scraps of sewing work through Anja and her contacts and has begun to attend church services again, there are still too many hours to dwell on things she can't alter.

"A husband, two sons gone, and one son who rarely comes home. Eugène worries me, Anja worries me. The pair of them living in sin, mysterious. What has happened to our family? Why did God choose us for this life, Josephine?"

"Maman, stop! God didn't choose us. We just got in the way of something evil. Do not worry about Gène. I will find out what is going on with him. Besides, it is a good thing he will start work soon. It will keep him occupied."

Gisela is shivering, and Josephine rubs her mother's cold hands in her own, then pulls extra covers up over her to keep her warm.

Gisela looks at her daughter with watery eyes. She is crumbling again; such turns can last for days.

"I love you, Maman. Things will get better."

Gisela looks away, as if she knows better and is fearful to say.

Franz Mierzen is dining at the restaurant again today. He has not been in for over a week. Anja is supposed to serve his table, but she has gone home ill, and without replacements this late, Josephine will be kept busy without a break.

She takes the order from Captain Mierzen, who is his usual charming self, though he does not acknowledge that he knows her. She wonders if he will be in trouble for fraternizing with a Belgian. She has heard of some local women who have begun affairs. Some are quite open about it. The idea of it amongst Belgians is widely despised. Some are talked about and ostracised, sometimes refused service at shops, even spat on, as Josephine once witnessed.

Women sleep with men they hate all the time, said Anja when one of the officers brought a Belgian widow in for lunch. *It is called prostitution. They have to survive.*

But what if she likes the German soldier? What if she has fallen for him?

Then she is a traitor. One can perform the same action, but there is a difference between survival and betrayal.

The conversation had taken place only days before Franz had walked her home. She is glad she has told no one about the gloves and hat, hidden in her bedroom.

Josephine approaches the captain's table to deliver their meals. She is aware that Franz is watching her shaking hands as she lays down the plate in front of him. The men in the group are sharing news and are good natured toward her at least. Benôit arrives to serve them wine, and she is relieved to disappear.

Franz has a casual ease, a silent laugh, and a way of showing he is interested without seeming nosy. The men stand and move to the cigar room for port wine and coffee.

She helps with some cleaning in the kitchen. When she returns to collect their crockery, Franz is gone. Josephine is strangely disappointed and guilty for it also. But as she is leaving, she discovers Franz waiting for her outside in the cold.

"You're not wearing your gloves and hat?"

She reddens and pulls a scarf around her neck.

"I'm sorry. I didn't mean to embarrass you."

"Thank you so much for the gift," she says.

"But you want to wait to pretend you bought them yourself?"

"I have thought of something else. I will say they were left at the restaurant and since no one ever came back to claim them, Monsieur Fallières said I could have them."

He is laughing silently again, his face stretching into a smile.

"So you are cunning as well as efficient, as well as being the son your father wanted."

She forces herself not to smile too widely in response. She remembers Anja's earlier words. Instead she turns away to scout for open shutters, for spies. Is pleased to find there are none.

"It is all right, Josephine. I understand. There are some things we must keep to ourselves but perhaps not for long. Germans are mixing with Belgians socially all the time. Time does not change the past, but it allows us the opportunity to change our hearts."

"That is from a poem, no?"

"No."

"Who said that?"

"Me," he says.

"It is something you wish for then. For everyone to forget what happened?"

"No. No I don't. I just don't believe we should wish for the things we can't undo. It stops us from building bridges, from healing, from living."

She nods, though she thinks of those who gossip, who are unlikely to ever heal or change their minds. Not that she can blame them, either.

Madame Sabine, the lady I am making some lace for, has a German neighbour, a soldier, said her mother nights ago. *He was seen going into her house often on Avenue Louise. And sometimes she entertains several of them at her home; other ladies were there, too. And these are supposedly fine Belgian women and widows. It is disgraceful. They have no morals.*

Josephine feels her loyalty pulled in several directions. Just feeling attracted to people, especially those she shouldn't, is complicated in war.

"Josephine, will you give me the pleasure of walking you home again?"

"Yes," she says, and he holds out his arm once more. He is difficult to read yet easy to talk to. Guarded but open, too, in some ways. He confuses her. He is not warm, but neither is he cold. He seems to know exactly what to say. And she does not know why he is interested in her.

"Thank you also for the job for my brother, Eugène."

"I heard it is working out well. He is efficient with deliveries so far."

Eugène had visited the administration the day after his birthday and was instantly awarded the transport job, issued a permit as well as a warning about the penalties he would face if he abused the position. He was told he must stick to the approved routes only. He must pick up the truck and return it to the headquarters. He has been paid decently for the work, and given food coupons also. Though it means even less time now that Eugène will see his mother.

"You turned twenty-four early this year, yes?" says Franz.

"You seem to know a lot about me."

"It is my business to know. To make sure people are where and who they say they are."

"You must be very busy then."

He presses his lips tightly together, slightly twisted, mouth curling upward on one side, and she is not sure if he finds her words amusing or not.

"Thank you again for finding my brother work."

He nods. "I would like to meet him sometime."

"I should like to meet your family also," she says, words spoken before she's had a chance to vet them.

He tells her about his childhood, about holidays by a lake, about his grandparents' house in the country, where he spent most of his childhood; his father was a military attaché in France, and his mother died when he was young. He has a sister who has small children. Josephine sees his vulnerability as he talks, a sense that he has missed out on things, that he would rather be somewhere else. Perhaps he is not as loyal to Germany as he appears, and she wonders then if he is always at the mercy of a rigid regime that sends their own to their unnecessary deaths: if he would rather be home or in another occupation.

"Do you wish you could see your family?"

She can see him thinking deeply about this as they pass under lamps in the street, allowing her time to study the straightness of his long, wide back and the silvery smooth flawless skin on his face and neck. Though some might call it haughty, she likes the way he turns his chin slightly upward and looks down his nose to speak to her.

"Yes," he says.

There is something else about him underneath the answer, something that gives more of him away, although it is too early in their friendship to ask and perhaps too absurd to think she should ever get the chance.

"It is a shame we are here, and then again in a strange way, it isn't," he says. "These relationships we make with people must all lead to something."

He turns to look at her, and she lowers her eyes from his gaze, feeling exposed. They have stopped at a corner, outside the city centre. At the next bend they will see her house. It is something they both seem to be delaying.

Her arm is still linked in his; she feels more at ease with their closeness this time.

"Why is it, Josephine, that you worked in a darkroom in Louvain, shut away? How is it that a pretty girl like you doesn't have a sweetheart? Or perhaps you do. Will you tell me?"

They are pieces from different puzzles that would require force and reshaping to make such a friendship work. Though the want is there for something more, to open up to him, to take away his mask, take away her own.

"I did have a fiancé once, but it seems I wasn't the only one in his affections. He is married to someone else now, I believe."

"Did that hurt you?"

"Yes and no. He was dull."

"He is probably boring his new wife to death then, who is likely shallow and making him miserable."

She turns to him to see if he is serious, since his tone suggests as much, then smiles when she observes his raised eyebrow and the slight twist of his mouth that shows he isn't.

"What happened, if you don't mind me asking?" says Franz.

She is wary of his interest, not that he might make use of the information in a negative way, but that he wants to cut her open like a peach, squeeze out information, expose her core. She is fearful of being vulnerable. *What does it really matter?* What is worse than war, than losing people she loved, loves still?

"My mother was convinced about him long before I was. It seemed to happen so fast, the engagement. I wasn't comfortable at first, but I didn't want to disappoint my mother, who was certain it was a good match."

"Did you love him?"

Not fully understanding what love was, having nothing to measure it against, she assumed she did. She loved her brothers and parents, but that was a different love. It is the kind that is there all the time, regardless of what she says and does, swaddling her, suffocating her also sometimes, but unquestioning nonetheless. A love she can't ever escape from even if she wanted to.

You will grow to love him, said Gisela. *You will build things with him. A family, a home.*

But what if I don't want that? There can't ever be love if I don't.

"No. I don't think so. My fiancé was ambitious, talked of taking me to live in Antwerp immediately after the wedding, separating me from my family, from my work with Papa. We wanted different things. Though I bawled when he broke it off and when there were rumours he was pursuing someone else. My tears were mostly because of the rejection, the shock of it . . . I got over it quickly, and then any sorrow turned to relief. And then I could go back to not worrying about a life away from everything I knew, from the life I was planning to build, from the business I wanted to help Papa build. Besides, Papa thought I was still too young for marriage."

Franz stops himself as if there is something else he is about to ask.

"Papa said very little when the engagement was broken," she continues. "Maman was humiliated, angry at the other parents. I can't help but think Papa was relieved. He seemed eager to teach me more things in the business. I could tell from that he didn't want to lose me. We were close."

I believe if there is hesitation, you weren't quite ready, said Maurice quietly. *You will learn from this. This experience will help you grow up and grow wiser.*

What if I don't want to grow up? What if I want to stay young forever?

You're exasperating sometimes, Josephine, he said with glassy eyes that sparkled, that suggested he was happy.

She cannot trust her voice at this point. It will likely break. She does not want this moment saddened with talk about her father. Not now.

"I lost interest in finding a husband after that."

"And that is it then for you?" he says teasingly. "All men are tainted?"

She shrugs her shoulder, offers a trace of a smile.

"I find my men are better in stories," she says. "Only the characters get hurt."

"Josephine," he says, his tone more serious. "I won't hurt you."

She looks away, wishing there were some diversion so she might not betray her own feelings right then.

"Are you cold?"

"No," she says, which is truthful because her heart is pounding, her body warming from their closeness. When she is near him, it is like standing near a furnace.

At the sound of several voices nearby, Josephine withdraws her arm. Some railroad men are coming their way, their faces, hands, and clothes lacquered with coal dust, casting murderous glances toward Franz, who is used to it, their conversation pausing as they pass.

This is wrong, she thinks. *Papa would think this wrong, too.*

Then why is she still standing here?

"Josephine," he says, his voice low and the accent to her name oddly soothing. "I wish this were somewhere else. Not war."

She had liked other men, boys, and had even thought she loved her fiancé, but sentiment didn't linger like it did then. She wants to tell

Franz things, her feelings, things she would never tell another soul. She wants more than a frivolous conversation; she wants to know him, find out what he understands, what he has seen.

When she lifts her eyes, she can see the same in him. He is a mirror of her own men, performing with expectations, for duty, for honour, for country.

"I wish that, too," she says.

She turns to go, fearful she will embarrass herself with words she shouldn't say, that she might reveal a needful side. He catches her hand, and she is frozen and afraid suddenly. These are no times for anything that might lead to romance. To be walking so brazenly with Franz in the first place is reckless. He is German and off limits.

"You should go," she says. "I'll be all right from here." Though what it is she is preventing, and what it is she is afraid of, has not been declared by either of them. But it is there, the want, unsaid. She knows this to be true.

"Franz, why . . ." She cannot bring herself to finish the question, does not want to sound presumptuous.

"Why you?" he says. "Is that what you want to know? Why my attentions are turned to you?"

She nods.

"Because after I first saw you, I thought about you often. And then when we met at the restaurant, I was certain it was no coincidence. I suspected you felt the same way. I have questioned myself many times, and each time I come up with the same answer. I want to see you. I want to see what becomes of us."

It was true. She had felt something also when she saw him at the restaurant. He was handsome, important, and she was curious. He had saved her life. Though she wonders, if he had left that day and never returned, how quickly she would have forgotten about him.

"I have feelings for you, Josephine. You must know that."

They are so close, touching. She suspects he can feel her pulse quicken. He looks at her, waiting for something. *For what?* She wants to tell him she feels the same way, but she cannot find the will.

The sound of cannon fire in the distance breaks the spell, a timely warning they are both at war. He drops her hand and steps away, formal once more.

"Have a good night," he says. He turns to go and then stops.

"Josephine, I cannot see how anyone would not want to marry you."

She watches him go, her heart beating faster, and she thinks of the women in her books. She feels a stirring within, though she doesn't understand what it means. He is a soldier, an enemy of Belgium. He is Boche!

11. POLICING

Today is Sunday. There is a parade with much German pomp in the city beginning at the Gare du Nord, and the smaller children run along the side of the streets excitedly. Soldiers are performing the march to celebrate a victory. In the Grand Place a German band toots and bellows their foreign tunes. Many older men attend in their frock coats and top hats, women in their finest dresses, and children with bows, ties, and blackened shoes. All this is expected. It is part of the charade. There are only a few younger men, since many are dead, injured, in prison, or sent away to work, or perhaps don't want anything to do with German victory if they can get away with it.

Franz Mierzen parades on his horse with several other men. Josephine is excited to see him. His group stops to the left of the podium. He scans the crowd, and Josephine is not sure if he has seen her. She resists the urge to raise her hand to wave.

He has walked her home on several more occasions since, but most days he is away on special assignments, sometimes outside Brussels, which he does not wish to discuss. Once when she asked him questions, he was brusque then distant, and she has not tried again. He is not always talkative, but attentive and courteous, sharing something of his past. When he comes to the restaurant during the day, it is usually a sign he will be waiting for her on the way home, and it is all she can think about while she works.

The mayor is telling Belgians that the German military needs their full cooperation. He says food supplies are running short, and he asks for donations to help the soldiers with their recuperation.

"Ours or theirs?" Josephine says into her hand.

Anja smirks and leans in close, so only Josephine can hear. "All those who want to starve for the good of Germany, step forward!"

The mayor is also talking about respect of the laws that are now in place, that the German General Government of Brussels has the capacity to imprison any dissidents. He also admires Belgian people, though even he can't make any of this sound believable, for he is not looking at the crowd in front of him when he parrots this.

Someone coughs several times, hoarsely and loudly from somewhere in the crowd, drowning out the tiresome talk of strength and unity, which everyone knows is a guise for oppression. The ill-timed interruption does not go unnoticed by several German officials standing at the front, whose eyes roam the crowd for the perpetrator. Josephine cannot see who it is, standing at the very back of the crowd. Josephine sneaks a bite of a waffle, which the Germans have provided as part of the celebration. They taste slightly chalky, using what substitute ingredients the street vendors can provide, and with little to no sugar. Though half as nice is better than nothing at all. A bribe of some kind perhaps, which will not make any difference with everyone wise to the bribes and measures to keep them content, and rhetoric merely babble.

"However, there are incidents where people are disrespectful, and the government would like to see more courtesy." The mayor pauses as he works up the courage to continue. "There are consequences for those who don't," he says, his puppet position being merely to repeat what the government of Germany has told him to say.

Josephine knows the event the burgomaster is talking about, as words spread like pollen here. The Sunday earlier a woman refused to get on a tram carrying several Germans. She announced through the doorway that she will never share a vehicle "with such monsters." The

Germans who heard this did not take issue at the time, but it seems likely they had reported the incident since. The woman is one of the lucky ones not detained on the spot. Josephine has also heard of a man who had too much beer and started gloating about how the Germans will be annihilated eventually. He was herded off to prison, and some say he has gone to a labour camp in the east. Josephine has heard from several sources now that conditions are extremely poor in the camps, the work hours long, the rations meagre.

The German soldiers, who are standing stiffly, arms by their sides, are then given the order to march to their new field barracks out of town. They are leaving for another battle that the mayor also advises will change the outcome of the war. According to German newspapers this is a common point.

"The hat suits you. And I like your new shoes," says Anja as the crowd disperses to another tune from the German band. Josephine is pleased with her boots, and her feet no longer ache throughout the day. "Though any extravagant purchases, you can probably ill afford. There are other, more important things."

Josephine's cheeks redden, her gloves hidden away in her bag. She does not like that she is being made to feel guilty for something she needed.

"The hat didn't cost me anything, and the shoes were inexpensive and purchased from a peddler. The others were too small and falling to pieces." She does not look at Anja when she says this. They were another gift from Franz, but no one can know this.

Anja touches her arm to make her look up. "I'm sorry. I should not have said anything. You needed them. Of course you did."

Anja is dark around the eyes today, and Josephine notices that she is edgy, looking around her. Something else is bothering her. Josephine suspects that her moment of ill will was not all about the shoes.

"Are you all right?"

"I'm fine," Anja says. "Have you seen Eugène? He came back yesterday. He has two days' break."

"Yes, he came and stayed last night, but he was gone by the time I woke up this morning."

From Anja's small nod it seems she is confirming what she already knows. Anja knows everything, the elusive pair so tight and secretive.

I like the job, Eugène said the previous night.

Where do you go?

I have to deliver goods, medicines, cartons of tinned food, sacks of potatoes to various parts of Belgium. To villages, the German outposts, hospitals, and right up to the border. Though my supplies are only for the officers. The ranks don't get the same special treatment.

Don't you get stopped by sentries at each of the towns?

Sometimes, but I have a special pass to say I work for the Germans. It seems the captain you met wields some power. I hear his name mentioned often. I have even seen him in Antwerp recently.

What was he doing? Josephine asked quickly, perhaps too quickly. She looked at her nails to suggest it was only mildly interesting.

I saw him visiting a private residence.

Just to talk?

I don't know, said Eugène, shrugging, turning a suspicious glance toward his sister. *Why are you so interested? Germans visit private residences all the time. Belgians are always entertaining Germans to gain special favours.*

Josephine bit her bottom lip.

That must be tiring for you, Eugène, so much travel, said Gisela.

He didn't hear her. He was already thinking of something else. He is always plotting things inside his head, always something that takes him away from discussions. It used to be that he was designing his next painting or drawing, now it is something else.

Josephine, can you come home with Anja after work on Monday? You are on the same shift that day, no? He had said this to Josephine in private when Gisela had left the room.

Why so secretive, Gène?

Because it has to be.

Last time Eugène was secretive with Xavier, bad things happened, and she had a sense that whatever it is, it is dangerous.

All right.

At least she might finally learn something more of Eugène.

Benôit has asked Josephine to deliver some pastries to a widow on the other side of the city centre.

"She is an Englishwoman, by the name of Lady Vivienne. She was married to a Belgian who is no longer with us. A German officer has instructed she receive a gift."

"Who is the officer?"

"Oh, you are such a curious girl! Did your mother never tell you to stop being so inquisitive?" Though he says this grinning.

"Yes, she did. Many times, in fact."

"It is one of the officers who frequents here, who is also an admirer."

"Oh!"

Josephine likes the idea of walking outside in the sunshine, a break from the busy restaurant, and since Franz is not expected there today. It is even better that she has special permission to do so, that she has a valid excuse to travel.

She is halfway down Avenue Louise when she sees Franz on horseback directing some soldiers on foot to follow him. When Josephine arrives at the end of the street, she loses sight of them. She is about to turn back to look for the house number for the delivery when she hears a shout. She follows the sound, curious to see what is unfolding, stumbling at one point on the cobblestone and scuffing her shoes.

She stops suddenly at another corner when she spies the group she is searching for, and steps back carefully out of sight. The foot soldiers are dragging a man and a woman from the house while Franz remains mounted and watching. Two small children are following, crying and wailing. The event is distressing, and memories of Louvain return. Bad things are still happening, hidden cleverly by an illusion of goodwill.

A soldier, frustrated by the chaos, raises his pistol and strikes the male prisoner after he pleads to let his wife stay for the children. Josephine cannot think of a crime that deserves this. The man falls over, and the woman cries out and drops beside him to see if he is all right.

Franz strikes the assaulting soldier with his horsewhip as punishment. He orders another soldier to help the injured prisoner up.

Two other soldiers come out of the doorway, and they carry two wooden crates. Franz dismounts to inspect. He lifts the lid of one, withdraws a rifle from inside, then instructs several of the soldiers to take the cases away.

The man is led away in the other direction, south of the city, and Franz tells the crying woman and children to return inside. Though Josephine can't hear the words very well, his actions are clear.

There are signs up all over the city demanding the surrender of guns, or the penalty of execution will apply. Josephine wonders what possessed the family to do such a dangerous thing, to store these items. To put their own lives in danger.

Franz is back on his horse and galloping in her direction, and she pulls back to duck behind a private gate.

She should hate him, yet the smuggling of guns must surely lead to more violence and death. Josephine has seen enough of death. She will never forgive or forget the people who murdered her family and what she witnessed in Louvain, but she can hope that Franz and others like him will prevent a rebellion and save the lives of innocent Belgian civilians. Franz is not like the drunken brutes, those vicious soldiers in Louvain and the other towns and villages; more stories emerged for several months after the invasion. Xavier once said that people can be good or bad in every situation, that it is a choice, not an order.

Lady Vivienne's house is in an expensive area where it is said that several German officers live also. The building is charming and grand, over four floors, with its arcade entrance, Juliet balconies, and pediments beneath the top eave with scrolls and garlands.

A maid answers the door.

"Who is there, Elise?" says someone else behind her, before Josephine has announced herself.

A woman appears, tall and lovely, fair hair pulled high on her head and little pearl earrings. Josephine recognises her from the restaurant, often accompanied by an officer. She looks at the box, and Josephine notices with dismay that one corner of it has been crushed during her haste to hide.

"Oh, I know your face. You work at the restaurant."

"Yes," says Josephine. "These are from an officer. Monsieur Fallières has asked me to bring this to you."

The woman pauses to examine her, appearing more interested in Josephine than the package being passed to her. Lady Vivienne wears a beautiful silk dress striped cornflower blue and white and with lace around the décolletage that looks as fine as her mother's work.

The maid has been sent back to the kitchen, and Vivienne instructs Josephine to wait a moment. She takes a piece of paper out of the little bureau near the door and proceeds to write a note. When she is finished, she folds it carefully, then seals it in an envelope.

"Please give this to Monsieur Fallières."

Josephine takes another look at her and wonders what the connection is with Benôit, and why the mysterious officer couldn't have delivered it in person. Something about this unsettles her, though not enough to forget to make mention of her mother's lace skills.

"My mother was a lace maker in Louvain. She is exceptionally good if ever you are in need of such work."

Vivienne looks Josephine up and down curiously before she smiles.

"Tell your mother to come and see me. If she is as good as you say, I would be delighted to use her services."

Josephine commences to walk back and is thinking about what she saw Franz do, only now she is just as curious about the woman, who is beautiful and wealthy and seems unscarred by war.

She has been gone longer than she should and quickens her pace.

Benôit looks at the envelope Josephine hands him on her return, but he says nothing about the time she has taken.

"A note for you also, my dear," he says, passing her a folded piece of paper.

She waits for Benôit to walk away before reading it.

> *Called away urgently. I will be gone for at least a fortnight. Just in case you were thinking of me.*
> *F*

12. THE NEWSPAPER

The new girls arrive for the evening shift as Anja and Josephine hang up their aprons.

"*Au revoir, mesdemoiselles,*" says Benôit with a little bow. "Go straight home," he says, with a sidelong glance, as if he knows they are up to something.

"What is it that you are showing me?" Josephine asks once they are outside, and squinting at the sun that burns weakly through a smoke-screen to the west. The night before, the rumblings of battle fire in the distance had woken her several times.

"Something Eugène has found in his travels. Important things that could help change the course of the war."

Anja steers her in the direction of the canal, toward an industrial area and ramshackle housing. She has never seen Anja's house before, but from past and brief descriptions, she was under the impression that her family had money.

"Course of the war? What do you mean?"

"Just wait. You will understand."

"But . . ."

"Hush! Don't say anything."

Ahead are two German soldiers who look around their own age, and Josephine feels her insides twist and her legs go weak. One of the soldiers is whistling and stops suddenly when he sees the two girls. His face seems to brighten, and he whispers to the other one.

"Papers!" says one, as they approach, obviously wishing to sound more superior than he is.

Josephine is about to say the first thing that comes into her head, that she is just enjoying a walk with her friend, when Anja interrupts.

"Sir, I am very ill. I think I might—"

She turns to retch on the pavement. Josephine rubs her friend's back and looks at the faces of the soldiers, who watch Anja carefully. One of them finally looks away, embarrassed or disgusted maybe.

The other persists and takes Josephine's identity paper, then Anja stands up to retrieve hers also from her bag, but with a certain amount of drama: her stomach clutched, her face contorted.

"Where are you going?" says the first soldier.

"My friend is helping me home," she says weakly.

The papers are examined, and a conversation between the guards ensues about their photographs, that they hardly look like the same people, "much thinner," and a chortle by the first, before the second, the more serious of the two, nods for them to pass.

"Be quick about it!" says the soldier to their backs.

After walking a short distance from the guards, the girls fight back smiles because there is so much relief, and they are pleased with the results of their deception.

"Come," says Anja more urgently. "This way."

They cross a deserted square where Anja points to stains on the cement, reporting of an execution she witnessed and describing Belgian bodies she had once seen floating in the canal.

Josephine is unsettled by this reveal, reminded of the fate that befell her father.

"Oh, I'm sorry," says Anja, quick to notice. "That was very insensitive of me."

Anja puts the key into a large arched oaken door. A business sign that was on the front has been partially torn down.

"This was my grandparents' business once. They had a grain store beside it, then it was sold and converted into something else. I live here now."

The road is level with the middle floor of a townhouse, which was part of the warehouse next door. Above a kitchenette is a window at the back of the room overlooking the canal and a pathway separating them. A low bed sits under stairs leading up to an attic. There is an armchair that is losing its stuffing, a table, an oil lamp on the floor, half a dozen chairs, and a bicycle. Off to one side is a curtained bedroom that has a window to the canal also, and a bathroom beside it. Another set of stairs just near the doorway leads down to a basement. The house is dark and old, mould creeping in from the corners, and there is a smell of mice.

Josephine can hear someone moving around downstairs.

"Down here," Anja says.

At the bottom of the stairs, under a single bulb of yellow light, Eugène is lifting items out of large crates.

"Josephine, you will not believe what we have," he announces.

On a large table in the centre sits a typewriter and a small printing machine. Beside it are jars of ink and a stack of paper. There are other items also scattered around the floor. Josephine sees a tripod, too; chemicals for developing photographs; and machine oil.

"Do you believe this? I found this on my travels. The Germans had closed all the printing firms, but someone I knew told me of a warehouse where they have taken many confiscated items."

He is excited, deliriously so. Eugène has always had a big personality, with extremes of moods. Sometimes she has felt crowded just standing next to him. Now is one of those moments, and she bites at her fingers nervously.

"There is more. We have many people working underground. People who deliver things, clothes, armaments, everything. This job is a godsend, Mouse. I get to deliver messages, learn about what's going on. It was Anja and her connections who put me on to people. All across Belgium there are people working for us—"

"Gène, stop!" says Josephine, raising her hands. "You're going too fast. Why all this? What has this to do with me? What messages?"

Anja places her hand on Eugène's arm, and he turns to look at her. He is clearly besotted. There is no doubt now that they are lovers.

"My name is Anja," she tells Josephine. "However, the surname you know me as isn't mine. I escaped from Namur during the hostilities when they burned and looted their way through our town. They took my father away. I don't know where. I was caught with a gun at my house, and I can tell you that it was our intention to kill every German that crossed over our threshold that day. They took me away and placed me on an overcrowded prisoner transport headed east. But I escaped. I found sanctuary in a village and met up with others also hiding, and someone then sent me to sympathisers they thought could help me. People were kind. People were being hidden everywhere. We went to the house of Princess Marie de Croÿ and her brother, Réginald."

"They work for the underground?" Josephine asks incredulously.

"Yes! Believe it! They took me in and gave me a false identity. Marie took the photo herself. I repaid both her and her brother by taking several Allied soldiers that they had hidden there and helped them escape across the border. And now we create identities for others also, people who need to leave Belgium, injured soldiers captured.

"There are many of us now around Belgium offering safe houses for people who want to escape. We are mostly women since our men are often watched or sent away to work. Princess Marie knew someone in Brussels who would find me employment. It was she who gave me a letter of introduction to Monsieur Fallières."

"Why there? Why at that restaurant?"

"Isn't it obvious? She believed Brussels was the best place to spy. It is full of important Germans. They talk. They say things. The more beer and wine we put in their glasses, the more we learn. You should open your ears more, too. They talk about much with alcohol: the truth about German casualties, failed battles, not what they report to us."

"Is Monsieur Fallières involved in any of this?"

"No," says Anja.

"The safe houses are for Belgians, people of interest," says Eugène. "People who they are suspicious of, those in danger."

"And you have been doing this underground work for months without telling me?" says Josephine.

"Yes," he says. "I didn't want you involved. Not just for your safety, and Maman's, but because I wasn't sure if you would be good at keeping secrets. You have always shown on your face what you are thinking."

"You should have told me at least," says Josephine. "And Maman worries so much about you. She thinks you work too hard. God forbid if she learned the truth."

"Then you understand why we can't tell her anything."

"We organise fake identities, photographs, fake certificates and references, and then we help those in hiding move from house to house, and eventually to the Dutch border," says Anja. "Some I have guided myself. I have taken two already by foot to safe houses, and to smugglers who make the final leg of the journey, some who negotiate with sentries. But it costs money to get them there, to pay the smugglers also. Most of our earnings go to keeping the people fed and clothed, to paying the fees. Eugène's money now has been a blessing, thanks to you."

Josephine thinks of Franz and how he got this job for her brother to stop him from being sent east. Her deceit she feels is double edged.

"Josephine, I need you to help us with the work, especially during the times when I'm away, but more importantly there is this . . ." He takes her hand, leads her to a box on the floor. Inside she can see there is a camera. She lifts it out to examine it.

"You want me to help make the false identities?" she says.

"I thought you would be pleased to take photographs again."

"Where would I take them?"

"Sometimes here, sometimes outside of Brussels at two of our safe houses."

"But I work, Gène. How am I to find the time?"

"It is perhaps only two or three afternoons or evenings a week. But it is not the only important work here . . . We are planning to publish our own small newspaper to inform people about what is happening here and outside of Belgium, then distributing it across the country."

He is grinning like a cat that got the cream, expecting some kind of reward.

"A newspaper?"

He nods, waiting for a better response.

"Where will this information come from?" says Josephine.

"We occasionally get Dutch, French, and German newspapers, which have the truth about what is going on. We are purposely being kept ignorant. We need you to translate some of the information from German news being smuggled in, as well as French and Dutch, and to type up the information we don't read here in the censored Belgian ones. It is like all the skills you have were created for this moment. It does not seem like a coincidence."

His words are persuasive, but Josephine no longer believes in fate, and neither, she feels, does Eugène if he were honest. She is too worried about the very real present, of people being sent to prison for the offences of harbouring deserters or Allied soldiers. There are posters warning of execution of those who help them.

"Who will we be delivering this publication to? How do we distribute?"

"We have already been sending letters to churches and shop owners who we know are loyal. For my job, I have to drive to the outposts of Ninove, de Lennick, and de Hal, close to several of our safe houses, as well as to Antwerp and as far as Bruges. This will give me the opportunity to make other deliveries. I have been given an unlimited pass to leave the city and enter others."

All thanks to Franz. She thinks of him again, and the trusted position he has given her brother. What he would think. *What does it matter?* They are not on the same side.

"We need you," says Anja.

"Why? Because many of you have already been caught?"

Anja looks away sadly.

"It is true. We have lost some. But we have grown smarter, more organised, we can sense who to trust. They don't suspect Eugène with the goods he carries. They wouldn't dream to think there are copies of newspapers hidden."

"I am also helping myself to the German stores when they aren't looking," says Eugène.

"You are stealing?"

"You can't steal something that is already ours."

It is too much. Too dangerous.

"No, I can't do this," Josephine says, shaking her head. "It is against their law to print anything without it being censored, to take photographs, to play music they don't agree with . . . I can't be part of it, Gène. If you want to, go ahead! It would not be fair on Maman if we were caught. Hasn't she lost enough?"

"I thought you'd be pleased to fight back," he says, sounding offended. "Give something back."

What did I take? She thinks of Yves. Perhaps Eugène will never let it go.

"We need you," says her brother, his tone softer, more convincing. He can be charming when he wants something. She is not fooled. Not anymore.

"But what if you are revealed, what if one of us is taken to prison and interrogated? Maman heard from someone after church service how they torture people to extract information."

Eugène is shaking his head.

"You will not have to worry. Everyone that carries the publication or has offered a safe house has sworn not to reveal what they do. We know these people."

"Do you, Gène? Do you really?"

He blinks several times. He is rarely ever challenged.

This life she is living isn't perfect, but they all have work. They are making the best of it until better times come. And now there is Franz, who has made their situation more tolerable.

"And guns, you say? Are you stealing those as well?"

"Yes, but only to use if we are attacked."

Josephine tells them about the man caught with cases of guns, though she doesn't mention Franz.

"Some are not as careful. Not like us. We are not out to hurt anyone. We are doing this to save lives."

Despite her scepticism, his words are beginning to take effect.

"Whose place is this then?" says Josephine, presuming they may have lied about other things.

"The building does belong to my grandparents, who used to lease it out, but it hasn't been used for many years. It is my home now, since my house was burned down in Namur."

"I'm sorry you had to go through that, too," says Josephine. "But I . . . What excuse do I have to come this far if I am stopped? And what would I tell Maman?"

"It is a risk, but you can always return home if you think you are being followed. Take a different route sometimes. Catch the tram. It is what *I* do. I drop the vehicle back to the administration; then I walk almost to Maman's place before I walk back here. I am careful. You just have to deviate if you see someone you haven't seen before, someone that might be spying."

"So, you believe there are spies then?"

"Of course! This is war. We are still enemies."

"There are many of us," says Anja, interrupting when she sees that Josephine is looking less convinced. "We are not alone."

Josephine turns to survey the supplies, and then the printing machine. She runs her hand over the enamel front. It is small, simple to operate, unlike her father's. She had watched her father repair machines, had been fascinated with them. When the press was running, her father used to say it was in time with his heart; he had put so much of it into the business.

"Does everything work?" She taps the keys on the typewriter.

"So far."

"Supplies cost money," she says. "We are going to need more paper than what you have here if you want to produce an issue each week."

"There are other Belgians who are part of this, as I told you," says Eugène. "They have agreed to finance the news and our work here."

"And what about Maman? She won't approve."

"In time I think she would agree. For now, tell her you are working late and staying at Anja's sometimes so you can walk safely home with someone."

"And will this news publication have a name?"

"*La Vérité*, which is what we call our safe house here. Underneath the title we will type Cardinal Mercier's words: 'Patriotism and Endurance.'"

"I will have to think about it," she says, the mention of the cardinal not offering as much reassurance as he'd probably hoped. Cardinal Mercier was placed under house arrest for being outspoken.

"Come upstairs," says Anja. "Have some coffee. We'll talk more up there."

"I should go," says Josephine, and she gives Anja a little hug. "Maman will be missing me."

Eugène has walked her to the door.

"What we are doing is huge, Josephine," he says softly. "It is dangerous, I'll admit that. But it is necessary, too. I can't do it without you."

"Does Anja know how manipulative you are yet?" says Josephine, half in jest.

"She can't resist my charm, Mouse," he says with a mischievous grin.

"Is that what you call it? Charm?"

He places his hands on his sister's shoulders.

"You stand up for yourself," he says. "I've admired that about you, even though I have never said it."

She drops her head so he can't see how this affects her.

"I am too easily rattled," he says. "I get caught up in the moment, as Papa would say. I am certain it would have been you taking over the family business, despite Maman's protestations that she wanted you to be a lady, a lace maker, a wife."

"I'm sorry I've been away so much. But what I do is for us: for you, Maman, Yves, Xavier, and Papa. For our future. For a Belgian future."

"I'm so scared for all of us, Gène," she says. "I'm not going to lie. I want to get through this and then for us to have a life again on the other side, and much like the one we had before."

"We must first show our loyalty to the Crown, to a united Belgium."

"Since when did you care about a united Belgium? You've changed."

"We all have to, Josephine."

"I understand about uniting everyone, but even Cardinal Mercier says we must respect the rules."

"He also says we can't forget our patriotic duty. When this is over, we will rebuild," he says. "Things will never be the same because *we* will never be the same. But whatever future we wish for, we must fight for also. We can't just stand by and say nothing. When all this is over, don't you want to say we did something?"

It feels like entrapment. She puts the tip of her thumb in her teeth, closes her mind to Franz.

She nods.

FLANDERS

1915

13. DARKNESS

How long has it been?

Arthur is edging toward wakefulness, voices around him, the tinny sound of shoveling, to push him finally into light.

Six weeks, he calculates. It is easy to lose track of dates, of days. Arthur's feet ache, and there is the putrid taste of chloride of lime in his mouth from the drinking water and the smell of cordite always in his nostrils. They are learning as they go, systems in place for a short war, they originally thought. He has had a bout of dysentery despite attempts at sanitization. He has been to the doctor several times, been given some medicine, which helps, though only to sleep. During the day he must persevere with it, ignore it. He laughs inwardly. It is easier said than done.

He estimates that he is perhaps just miles from where Jack fell near the border of France and Belgium, from where his body has not been recovered.

There was nothing. There are hundreds unaccounted for, the sergeant had told him abruptly when he enquired. The officer didn't have time for enquiries, rushing between errands at the time. Then perhaps a change of heart from the look on Arthur's face, a man close to his own age, from the shared unspoken sympathy between fathers. The sergeant's own son on his way to Gallipoli.

Jack Shine . . . was last in the Battle of Ypres, did you say?

Yes.

I'll find out. Give me a day or so.

He did, but it wasn't much clearer. The fields have been awash with bodies since. They have taken away as many of the dead as they could find. While the mud has claimed others, many more can't be identified. He knows this is possible. He has seen firsthand how a shell can strip away flesh, how deeply the earth can claim her men.

It is not the ending a father wishes for a son. *Is it too much to ask for? To know his final resting place?* He pleads silently in the darkness, where the horrors of war are constantly replayed.

It is time to leave again, and the men with a few days of rest after several weeks of battle seem ready to get it over with. There are few complaints, cigarettes handed around, cups of rum sometimes for Dutch courage at the start of battle. And there is always one who is generous with his expensive care package. Some of the soldiers, mostly the commissioned officers, receive packages from Harrods, from loved ones. Several women's groups have been knitting scarves and gloves, and Arthur is grateful for these most nights. He received one small food package, with a fruitcake from Harriet, which he suspects was more the work of Alice. They may not have been close, but she was always organised, thoughtful, often donating to the poor, arranging goods for charities. There is a card, written in handwriting he doesn't recognise, most likely from the store: *Stay strong, we are right behind you.* Though they aren't at all, he thinks with irony. They are far away, tucked into their soft beds with white linen, and crystal decanters, and their petty worries. It isn't with bitterness, just a sense of realism.

Arthur cuts pieces of the cake and passes them around between muddy hands. Someone gives him cigarettes in exchange. He hadn't smoked before. Hadn't seen the benefit. Now he does. They slow his breathing, calm his nerves. He needs every bit of help right now.

He has struck up a friendship with another private, a conversation at least.

"I thought you'd be one to enter with a commission," says Jimmy. "You sound like a toff." He is a nice enough lad, young, always smiling. It is hard not to smile back despite the conditions.

"I was at a private school, but the wrong kind, of course," Arthur says, drawing from his cigarette. He doesn't say he had turned down the rank of corporal, that he had willingly started at the bottom. For what purpose? For Jack. For atonement. For the things he missed. For the loss of a son he might still have if he had done things differently. Though war was an opportunity now to pay.

"I did, however, complete some military training."

"So, a wife back home then?" Jimmy asks.

"Yes," he says.

"I don't have one. I wish I did."

Thank God, thinks Arthur. *You are just a boy.*

"My dear old grannie's at home frettin' like mad. Mum and Da went years ago. It was this or the docks, and now I can send home a quid and she won't be working as hard."

"What does she do?"

"She's a housekeeper for them rich folks."

Arthur thinks of Mary. He is one of "them," he supposes.

"Anyway, I miss her," Jimmy says, looking slightly lost for a moment.

Arthur is moved by people's stories. Feels connected to him instantly.

"I'm sure she'll be proud," says Arthur.

Jimmy smiles, then shrugs and pretends it doesn't bother him either way. But the glance in the distance toward the guns, he is thinking about it. He is thinking of the time he will see his grandmother again, *if* he will see her again.

"Changed my mind a bit. The docks or the mines aren't looking half-bad now. Lost a mate the other day. Not sure this war's good for any."

"Well, you're good for me. I'm in good company at least."

And Jimmy is back to smiling, bright-blue eyes and large mouth and teeth, boyish, ginger freckles on his nose, fair. An impish face.

"How old are you?" Arthur asks.

"Old enough."

Arthur raises his eyebrows and Jimmy leans in.

"I'm seventeen, but they don't know that."

"You're a good lad," says Arthur. "And very brave."

The boy is endearing, his strength inspiring.

War, Arthur ponders, is a great leveller. Less than a year ago, he was in his accounting office, looking over the Thames, wondering whether Harriet had remembered to tell Mary about the glazier due to fix the upstairs window. Now he is here in a field, sleeping under the stars en route to another battlefield where there is more of the same, only maybe the soup will be slightly different, the rations smaller, and the terrain a little more worn. But the same feelings. The rain, the sun, the cold, the lack of sleep. The praying, too, which he does nightly now. He prays for Jack, the other men, and Harriet, too. He prays for her often, hoping that she is through her grief, that he will come back to her. That they can start again. *Though what can we start? We haven't finished with what we had.* Jack had ended it too abruptly. *Perhaps it is over,* he thinks, then stops himself. He is fighting for her, too.

"What do you think of this?" says Jimmy, poised to read him something he has written. Arthur nods him on and listens to his short fiction story about men in the army, though real enough, and the animals he befriends and a horse that wins the day, a layer of fantasy.

"Very funny," says Arthur. "You're not half-talented."

Jimmy is smiling at that.

"You can keep it. I've got lots more in here," he says, tapping his head.

"That's very kind of you, thank you," Arthur says, folding it and placing it inside his coat pocket.

After dinner, the rest of the group pulls out in darkness. They follow a winding path through the remains of a village, dodging crumbling ruins. Several people are camped around a fire under the shelter of suspended limestone that might fall at any minute. They aren't stopping here, thankfully. They continue, heading up a short rise to a clump of trees, a small forest that has by some miracle survived the fires, the rest of the earth surrounding it scorched, and an acridity that is surely decomposing flesh. The partial moon lays a white pathway across the tall grasses by the woods, dark enough to contain the enemy. They are to stay alert, which is easier said than done on barely any sleep.

"Walk stealthily or you won't be walking at all," their commander says.

The night is cold but beautiful, the march tiring, straps digging into his shoulders from a weighty pack. And soon they are camped again under stars. Then to sleep on a patch of damp grass below a hooting owl. Never before has he slept so well and so short.

On the horizon there are fires and explosions; it is someone else's battle until the baton change. Until it is his.

He is woken before dawn to march single file through the communication trenches until they reach the front line. Hunched trench diggers pass back the other way, the less weary of the group nodding their acknowledgements, their spirits low, faces muddied, but several still smiling their encouragement, one patting him on the shoulder as he passes. Tomorrow he may be dead, injured, lying somewhere, calling for help. Jack was right. It is hard to keep friendships. It is pointless to nurture them.

The next day it is straight into battle again. Though he is used to it now, even a little fatalistic. It is only after several days of rest that it grows hardest to go over. Those brief days of rest, of knowing they are going back, make one a little weaker. They have tasted an ounce of peace.

He has seen as many quaint villages and fields as he wishes since they left base southwest of Ypres twelve days ago, but there is joy at least that there is no rain on the horizon. Glorious sunshine into the second day, and the smell of summer coming, new wildflowers growing in the cracks in the earth, life still surging forward despite the war, in spite of it even.

The men are restless, and Arthur leans against the wall in the dugout. A cool wind blows above the trench while the sun directly above him burns worry lines into his upturned face. Twenty-four hours of combat have rendered him devoid of emotion. Life beyond the trench walls at that moment seems irrelevant. Every part of him submits to exhaustion.

The guns are silent for now, but there are more orders for another offensive the following morning. It is fire again at sunrise. Across from him, another soldier sits head tilted backward against the wall, escaping for peace inside sleep, unflinching as a fly crawls across his face; he'd spent much of his initial rest time plucking out louse eggs from the seams of his trousers. Jimmy sits down a way, cleaning his gun, and he reminds Arthur of Jack, a young boy always busy, always looking for something to do, always looking for ways to escape.

Jimmy is nothing like Jack, he then rethinks. Jack had everything he ever wanted. *Or did he?* It is a question now burning. *Did I give him enough?* If he'd had more time, he could have done more. They only had nineteen years. Nothing really. Gone in the blink of an eye.

Jimmy looks up suddenly, caught in Arthur's trancelike gaze before grinning. Despite having gone over the top twice now, the boy remains pure, himself, highlighting to Arthur his own failings. Arthur had stopped seeing joy anywhere.

"Arthur Shine!"

"Here!" he says. He shields his eyes from the light to see who is standing in front of him, then notices the letter the other man holds out. He recognises the handwriting, fondly, the calligraphy beautiful and fine, like Harriet. He slides the letter out, can almost smell her, the scent of her, soft and sweet like her violet perfume. He knows the smell even if it isn't on the paper. It is the thought of her, the sight of her writing that conjures the smell, that tricks his brain. How he would do anything to be lying next to her right now, studying her face in her sleep, feeling the warmth of her breaths.

Before Jack, Harriet had miscarried twice. She had wanted to start a family immediately. They were so grateful for Jack, and relieved: every step he took, every word, a gift. Though Arthur loved him, he had loved the joy a baby gave Harriet almost as much. Every joy she had was his joy. And then something changed. A gradual shift over seasons, aging, life more complex, a son growing up and gone elsewhere. A quiet house again, just the two of them. He wonders how long they might have gone on like that.

He reads the letter, feels an odd sense of release but also despair, if that were even possible given that he has been up close with despair for months. She loves him, she says. She wishes him well, wants him to look after himself.

I'm sorry, Arthur. I'll be staying with Mummy indefinitely. It is easier here. I realised how much I missed living in the country.

Pretty grey stone, filigree banisters, the finest of everything, and a sea of rolling green from every vantage at her parents' house.

Anyway, I hope you make it through all right. I wish you all the best. Remember I love you, Artie. Perhaps we can meet when you get back. Discuss things a little more, work out what's what. I'll have my lawyer settle a few things . . .

She is leaving him is what she is saying, is what she won't say exactly, the tone of her words light, uncommitted. How she might treat a casual acquaintance at a garden party.

I have taken Pippin. He likes it here. More space to run around.

It is Harriet but it isn't also. Not the Harriet he remembers from those first years.

It is better for me here. I already feel my health returning. We have made a little plot in the grounds and buried a few special things of Jack's, and Mummy had a plaque . . . You can visit when you return.

It is better she is there at least being looked after. He will try and sort it out when he returns on leave in several months. He planned to have a big celebration, invite her family, old friends. Make life about joyful things again, not tragedy. Though now, the letter, he doesn't know.

Goodbye, Artie. Both you and Jack are in my prayers.

He stares at the last line. Arthur is already dead to her perhaps.

She was unemotional when he told her over the telephone that he was leaving. There was nothing remotely loving in her voice; nothing to suggest she would miss him, no pleading for him to stay. He feels betrayed and melancholy all of a sudden, something precious taken away. He is alone, he thinks, no family, siblings. Everything, his life, is beginning to look meaningless. A business, a wife, a house, a son. All of them past now. *How did it get to this?*

"Are you all right?" asks Jimmy.

"Oh! Yes, yes . . . Just my wife . . . She worries."

Jimmy nods as if he understands.

And then it is over the top, and Jimmy is gone this time for good. Another telegram to England. And he, Arthur, is alive. *Why is that?* He has got better at fighting, has used his bayonet. Has taken a bullet to his helmet, some shrapnel in his back, and a chip off his hip, and only in need of a field hospital. Even God doesn't want him.

On the way back, Jimmy passes eyes closed on the stretcher, peaceful, looks untouched except for the gaping wound at the join of his neck. Arthur asks the stretcher bearer to wait. Takes out the short story of Jimmy's and folds it small enough to tuck in Jimmy's shirt pocket, the body still warm, he feels. They will send the story to his grandmother, where it should be.

At least they have a body. Someone can mourn.

Arthur sits near a tree, his head against the wide trunk covered in ivy, and cries so no one can see him. Cries for Harriet, cries for Jimmy, cries for Jack. Soon there won't be anyone left to cry at all.

Damn this war!

BRUSSELS

1915

14. THE HOTEL ROOM

Lying is harder than Josephine imagined. She wishes she could tell her mother everything, but Gisela has enough worries. When she visited the administration last time, they were so annoyed with her questions, with her "pestering," they told her not to come back or else they will put her in prison. She has joined a group of lace makers, but there is not enough work to go around, and payment is sporadic or slow to come.

That morning they have only a piece of dark bread each for breakfast, the only bread available at the bakery, which is so dry that Josephine has to chew it many times before she can swallow. What they wouldn't do for a piece of brioche with jam, a poached egg with cheese and fresh cream. Though Gisela does the best with what they have. The previous evening, she had dredged up rutabagas from somewhere and boiled them with small portions of dried salted beef for dinner. Today, while Josephine is at work, Gisela will line up early at the grocers to see what is available. If it weren't for Josephine's wages, and a part of Eugène's—since some of his goes elsewhere, unknown to Gisela—they would have to line up for rations and hope for the best. Some in Brussels, those with wealth, are still able to afford the high cost of butter, coffee, and tea.

In the past, Josephine and the other staff have taken home some of the hotel kitchen leftovers or the food that is about to spoil, not good enough for German plates. Even officers can no longer be choosy. In recent days, the chef has been unable to give the staff anything with supplies so short.

Josephine walks to La Vérité after a long day of work to recommence the job she started in the basement ten days earlier. When she had clamped the stencil and poured ink onto the roller for the first time, she could almost hear her father telling her how much. She felt him beside her in those moments. They are able to do their clandestine work—typing and printing articles, developing film, and creating documents for the fugitives—because of all that he taught them. He would have done this, too, she thinks. He would have approved and participated. *All roads lead to this.* It is this thought that drives her on, that forces her to work harder, faster, even when her eyes are stinging with exhaustion, even when she can barely stand, to later crawl into bed for a few hours of sleep before she is back at the hotel.

The news is distributed to farmers, priests, cafés, factories, and grocers, all those who have their own small army of supporters who seek a copy. The baker's son who was sent to camp was one such person working in an underground smuggling network.

Upon arrival, Eugène tells her about a Belgian accused of attempting to kill German soldiers stationed at checkpoints between the towns. They are helping him cross the border the following evening. Eugène is busy working on a new identity for him while Anja has gone to collect him from La Justice. All the safe houses have names now, La Paix, another one. For any messages that are passed, Eugène has developed a code for the time of smuggling, for goods that are needed, for the names of all operatives.

"Is he guilty?" asks Josephine.

"It depends which country he is standing in," says Eugène. "In Belgium, according to the law, he would be killed for his actions, but he is no longer guilty once he crosses the border, which is why we must help all insurgents to get out. They are fearless heroes. Josephine, you must not speak their names at all if you learn of them, even to Anja at work, do you understand? The walls are listening."

"Of course," she says.

"Tomorrow we are sending the Belgian over the border with our next issue," he says. "It must be completed tonight. We must give a complete picture of everything that has been happening here, the arrests, and every minor injustice witnessed. Here is an article Anja wrote about Namur and the arrest of her father. We must feed these to the world."

It will be a long night.

The next day at work, Josephine tries to cover her tiredness. She is losing patience with Renée, who is doing her best at doing nothing, pretending she is straightening the utensils on the table when she is gazing out at the street. The girl has to be reminded to do things, and sometimes Josephine can't help but snap at her. Benôit has noticed the situation, too.

"*Sainte mère!*" he says under his breath, exasperated. "If she spent as much time performing the task as pretending, the work would be done."

Josephine is not sure why he hasn't fired her. He clearly doesn't want her there. He has been so ruthless in the past. Others have been let go for less. It has become obvious to Josephine that he is obligated to keep her, and this ruffles his large, burly feathers. Renée has a sour face, which is not good for business. She doesn't fold the serviettes edge to edge, and sometimes she leaves her long, fair hairs on the table, the remainder escaping untidily from beneath her cap. She has had two complaints by patrons.

Anja thinks she is a spy for the Germans, though that does not make a lot of sense since, apart from the staff and a small percentage of Belgians, there are mostly Germans in the hotel and restaurant. Still, Josephine thinks to be careful around her.

Josephine is nearly at the end of the working day. It has been two weeks since she has seen Franz. With him away, she does not have to lie to him should he catch her walking toward La Vérité. But it hasn't stopped her thinking about him and wishing he were here.

Benôit enters the kitchen, where she has just returned several plates, and asks her to follow him to the lobby. She wonders what she could have done wrong, whether there has been a complaint.

"I need you to take this tray to the top floor."

Josephine gazes confusedly at the room number written, at the covered plate of food and tea in a silver pot.

"But I am not part of room service. I'm not allowed in the hotel."

"Captain Mierzen has personally requested it," says Benôit formally, giving nothing away. "You can go up the service stairs after you hang up your apron. You are finished in the restaurant for the day."

She has never been to one of the hotel rooms before. She has never even been to the room of a man. She wonders if he is alone.

"I would rather you not make mention of this task to your friend."

She knows he refers to Anja. Josephine nods and begins to walk away.

"And by the way, you have ink on your hands," he remarks as she passes. "Make sure they are clean by tomorrow."

Josephine has been attempting to hide her hands all day. Though she uses turpentine and bleach on her skin until it is raw, there are still traces some days.

"Monsieur Fallières says I can leave early today," she tells Anja. "I have a headache."

It is only when Anja raises her eyes to examine her that Josephine wishes she hadn't compounded the lie.

"Will you be fine to work tomorrow night?"

"Of course," Josephine says.

"Eugène is back then also."

Josephine enters the lobby, and as she heads to the far wall to climb the stairs, she sneaks a look behind her to see that no one else is watching. She is to walk to the second floor. Halfway up she passes a housemaid coming down the other way carrying a mop and bucket. The girl appears startled by the sight of her.

The walls are listening.

Josephine balances the tray on one hand and knocks softly on the door with the other. Franz calls for her to enter.

Inside the room, the curtains are drawn open and the sun is shining onto the forest-green rug. Through the window she can see the top of Saint Catherine's and the clock on the bell tower. In the far distance a stretch of pastel blue is interrupted by swirling purple smoke. These things are taken in briefly, for there is a pair of pale eyes watching her keenly.

Franz stands politely and guides her to a little wooden table on the far wall opposite a four-poster bed with a shimmery deep-green cover patterned with gold leaves. On the table is an ashtray with the stubs of cigarettes, though she has never seen him smoke. There is also a sweet scent in the room.

"You can place the tray here and then take a seat."

She sets it down and sits opposite him.

"How was your day?" Franz asks.

"You have asked me personally to perform this task?"

Franz smiles. "That is a strange sort of greeting."

Josephine reddens. "I'm sorry . . ." She looks to escape in the tranquil waterfall art above them. It is foreign to see him again after even a short time apart. It does not take long to become strangers again.

"You don't have to be nervous."

Though these words do little to calm her nerves. He leans casually against the back of his chair. He wears civilian clothing: a white shirt open at the collar and pressed beige pants, and his shoes are black and so shiny she can see the reflection of the chandelier.

"I wanted to speak to you in private. This seemed the only way . . . I put in a request for information on your brother, Xavier Descharmes. I have word that he is alive, that he was taken to a prison camp. That he is in the records, on several transfers."

"Truly?" she says, eyes wide with excitement.

"Yes," he says, mirroring her response.

Josephine touches her chest and tears spring to her eyes.

"You have no idea what you have done."

"I have some idea now," he says, still with amusement in his tone.

"That is so wonderful. I can't wait to tell Maman. She will be so happy."

"I have yet to hear back about the details and length of his conviction. That is proving more difficult. They were chaotic times. Many people on both sides have not been accounted for."

She nods, though she is still imagining her mother's face when she hears the news. Josephine wants to jump up and down, sing out the window that Xavier is alive.

"Josephine, you are smiling. You should do that more."

She looks down, a rush of blood through her heart. She realises how dowdy she must look in her white blouse and faded skirt.

"Will you join me for tea?"

She nods. "Thank you."

He lowers his head as he pours from the pot. She has her hands folded securely in her lap as she examines the white line at the part of his light-brown hair, the high bridge of his nose, and the lips that are usually sealed into wide lines unless he is speaking. Now his lips are slightly apart, a hint of a smile showing his top row of small teeth fighting for space, the two either side of the middle ones jutting forward slightly.

"I know what it is like to not know what has happened to someone. I have lost friends, people I grew up with, trained with at military college."

"In Belgium, did you lose them?"

"In France. They were lost at the Battle of Marne. A disastrous decision that lacked careful planning. We were too eager to get there."

"Will you have to go to battle?" The thought only just occurring then.

"If the war goes on for a lot longer, who's to say? I am prepared to serve."

"Do you miss being home?"

"Yes," he says after some deliberation. "I miss my grandparents, sister, and nieces. You are very thin, Josephine. I hope you don't mind me saying. Do you have enough food?"

"No one has enough food. Prices are high. Most days we have bread, and other days what vegetables and meat morsels Maman can buy from the market. The money I get paid hardly meets the rise in prices, but we are more fortunate than some."

It is silent for a period as they finish their tea, and then he looks at her, waiting for something. She examines the bottom of her cup without really seeing it, before looking toward the window. He affects her. Words and sentences jumble in her head.

"You have a nice view," she says to fill in the awkward silence.

He stands to walk to the open window that overlooks the square. It is her cue to do the same to see the people passing below.

She is level with the patch of white-gold skin in the hollow of his neck. A cold breeze on warm skin and she is thinking of his body just inches away. She turns toward a different view to hide her discomfort. She can sense him watching her, and without warning he is touching her hair, gentle hands pulling the pins that hold her cap. Then hands on her shoulders, burning through her clothing, warm breath at the nape of her neck. She closes her eyes to wait for his lips to connect to her skin.

There is a knock at the door.

"Stay," he whispers.

He is gone in a second. She stays watching the people walk below as she listens to an exchange that is brief, male, official. When she turns, the door is already closed.

Whoever was there she didn't see.

He is reading a note that has been handed to him.

"I have to leave," he says abruptly, like a cold splash to douse the flames that still burn through her body.

His gaze is distant, the cold look of a stranger, preoccupied with bigger worries. She is a waitress again, a prisoner in her own country, and he is someone else, someone who lives far away in her imagination.

"Thank you for the refreshments," she says. He picks up her cap, discarded on the floor, and hands it to her as she passes through the doorway.

She cannot bring herself to look at him. In the corridor, she is free to breathe deeply again, but there is a warmth in her belly that she has not felt before.

Josephine hasn't noticed the housemaid who has caught her smiling. Josephine nods a greeting; however, the maid does not return the gesture, purposely looking away.

Her mother is overcome with shock at the news of Xavier and has to sit down. Gisela weeps silently and crosses herself.

"I knew it. I felt him here," she says, clutching the front of her blouse.

Her breathing is laboured, and Josephine worries the news has affected her heart.

"We have to wait, Maman. Nothing is certain. It may be some time before we find out everything."

But her mother speaks of nothing else, what clothes she hopes to sew him when he returns, what items she will buy to make his favourite food.

Both women sleep better with the news, her mother still excited the following morning.

Franz is nowhere to be seen at the restaurant the following day. Josephine is both relieved that she doesn't have to face him after their moments together and disappointed, too, that she can't thank him for the gift.

A parcel of food had arrived at their home that morning. Inside were sausages, kohlrabi, butter, milk, salt, and coffee.

"Do you know anything about this?" Gisela had asked.

"I believe that it is from the manager of the restaurant," she said.

Gisela is not ready for the whole truth.

15. LOST

Arthur sleeps wedged into the wall of the trench. A drizzle of rain is enough to be a bother, but a choice of shelter is nonexistent. He puts his woollen coat over his head, and despite everything he sleeps so deeply until someone has to shake him several times to wake. It is time for watch. Sentry duty.

Once at his post, he stares at the blackness, low clouds that wash out any definition, imagines the distant Germans, their sentry staring back. The hiss of a flare precedes a burst of red and yellow in the sky that lights up the cratered grey-brown wasteland, and several enemy rifles fire at ghosts. Their side responds as if in conversation.

Just when he thinks he might sink back into his hole in the wall again, he is told it is time to move out. After walking fifteen miles northwest, he can see bursts of fire from another battlefield, two sets of firing lines just ahead.

He has had plenty of time to think on Harriet's letter, torture himself with words she hasn't spoken directly, that he knows are there. He has pored over it a dozen more times, hoping he had read it wrongly. Perhaps her time away is only temporary and another letter is on the way to say she misses him. But it is there in the things she doesn't say, an absence of intimacy. He has lost her.

The Belgian roads are hard on his feet and knees, and his water can is empty. A mile from their destination, there is a strange, pungent smell that attempts to claw its way into the back of his throat.

"Something's happening," shouts their lieutenant. "We need to go back."

The platoon is restless. Something doesn't feel right. They approach a wagon with a horse lying down still tethered. In the back lies a couple, their faces burned, their tongues hanging out. Several of the men, including Arthur, run a few yards forward to check others lying on the road. There are at least a dozen dead Canadian and Algerian infantrymen, one with green froth around his mouth.

"What is it?" says Arthur.

Someone shouts and points. In the distance he can see what these people had been running from, though they had been caught in it, too late. Another wave is coming. A greenish-white vaporous wall is edging ominously toward them, and the group of soldiers turns to scatter. As he runs to escape the gas, Arthur pulls at the straps of his haversack for the cloth veil soaked in sodium hyposulphate, losing some of the contents of his knapsack, his eating tin bouncing off into a ditch and something else, maybe the rest of his medical kit. He can't stop to check with the killing cloud on his heels. He discards his ammunition belt and sack as he reaches the nearby canal, his eyes now stinging, and he puts one foot on the edge of the embankment, then crouches to slide the rest of the way into waist-deep water, filthy, muddied with floating things: tobacco packets, paper, an empty tin, and torn pieces of cloth from soldiers' backs.

Arthur places his face just below the surface. The burning in his eyes is unbearable now, his eyelids on fire. The water is doing little to take away the pain, and tentacles of gas still linger over the canal. He rubs his eyes, then blinks them open. There is burning at the back of his throat, and he submerges again, swallowing a mouthful of water as he does. He bursts from the water coughing and spluttering. He has a choking feeling, as though his throat is closing, and imagines for himself the same fate as the dead men on the road.

He panics, scrambling blindly up the side of the embankment, unaware which side he is on and running several yards. The sounds of firing and then a whistling, and he braces for an onslaught of firepower, the earth then crashing in around him. He is thrown several feet. There are explosions farther away, a different target; he rolls over to rise on all fours, crawling across the earth, which rumbles under his hands and farther upward through bones. It is hell, he is sure of it. Life now muffled with the shrill of crickets in both ears. He stands to walk.

Arthur raises his heavy eyelids a fraction, his vision blurred. Squinting in all directions, he attempts to draw from memory the sodden stretch of wasteland and wooded valley that he came through. The cloud of gas has diminished, or he has strayed far enough from the path of the breeze, he can't be sure, and he heads toward the light that filters through a woodlands in the distance, tripping over himself and the bumps on the ground. It is unfamiliar territory.

Across a shallow swell of fog that hides the ground, he attempts to walk again, his foot landing awkwardly in a rutted track. He slips, hip smacking the slimy grey clay, elbow cracked on something solid. His hands find the coarseness of a knapsack, useful to lever his weight to stand; then at once he discerns the body attached. A dead man lies front down almost buried in the mud, his head twisted unnaturally, chin resting backward, one eye looking over the shoulder, the other a gaping exit wound.

Arthur hasn't stayed to find out if the soldier is one of his. He has scrambled once more to right himself, his feet sinking and his clothes now lacquered with claggy mud. A random shot flies over his head, and he ducks, waits a moment to ready for more, then on hands and knees crawls the last yards to the woods.

Bullets whizz past his ears as he stands to walk, then run, the sounds of war following him through the hazy line of poplars. A large explosion overhead, and suddenly the trees above him are on fire, raining burning leaves. He runs again and out the other side through the mist that swirls and rises thickly from the ground.

Ahead he can make out the barbed wire where others have failed to cross, men snagged garishly like scarecrows. He can see the lights glint off the bayonets of the enemy. He can even make out their faces, and then another shell and he is flying once more through the air, landing this time at a strange angle and winded badly. English voices sound vaguely in the distance. Arthur attempts to rise, but a rush of pain travels upward from his ankle, and he falls sideways.

"Over here," he calls, his own voice clearer, his hearing slowly restoring.

"One of ours," someone shouts back in English, and then more shots are fired and no more voices.

He drags himself on his good side, his left lower leg completely unusable, though he is unsure of exactly the point of injury since the pain extends all the way to his hip. Then dragging himself through sloshy earth, he reaches a dip in the ground, a shallow crater, and slides inside. He reaches down to touch his leg, feels that there is some kind of mess now near the end of it, buried in a mass of bloodied, torn, and ragged cloth. He straightens so that he can lie out fully on his back to rest, too exhausted now to contemplate his injuries further.

Arthur is unaware how long he stays there, drifting between wakefulness and sleep, dreaming of the fire once more with Jack, and Harriet, too, this time, burned to ash now in his nightmares.

He wakes to late afternoon and heavy rain upon his face, lying drenched in a pool of water. This haven from rifle fire is quickly becoming a small drowning pit should he fall back into unconsciousness.

To move his throbbing head too suddenly is worse than the pain in his leg, the burning sensation in his chest, and his stinging eyes. He drags himself inch by inch along the ground, teeth gritted against his suffering. *Did Jack suffer?* Too quick, it seems, if Private Penney is right.

Through the fog that sits permanently in his eyes, a low structure—a farmhouse, he thinks—lies ahead, across a stretch of land that seems impossibly far to cover. He stops, exhausted, then moves again, hand against something solid, a barrier or fence. He believes he is now behind enemy lines.

Must keep going.

Arthur climbs over the low fence and hauls himself the final yards to reach the house, to discover it is only the remains of one. He is surrounded by misshapen, jagged pieces of building that have stubbornly refused to yield. There is no roof to protect him from the rain, but a barrier against rifle fire at least. He may not die after all.

He can see dimly in the distance a crimson sunset sinking into ruin, and watches till its flame is extinguished.

He is so thirsty.

His eyelids are almost swollen closed.

16. DISTRACTIONS

"A French plane has been downed near the city just outside the military zone," says a woman who has come for lunch, perspiring and breathless from rushing to the hotel with the news, dampness showing in her armpits. "You can see the smoke from here."

"Can I help you, madame?" says Josephine.

"Yes, if you could take my arm," she says, and Josephine grasps the fleshy excess just above her elbow. "It has been a frightfully long walk. And all this smoke is terrible for my lungs. The tram didn't come today. Nothing works properly anymore." The last said a little quieter.

She leans her weight on Josephine until they reach the table with several women and an elderly gentleman of means.

The crash is all the news that is going around the hotel. Whispers and people pretending to be concerned while they overcrowd their cake forks with sponge and cream. Another Allied life gone.

Josephine stays with the woman a moment and waits for her to be comfortably seated. The customer flicks out her fan to wave it at her face.

"I'm terribly sorry you are feeling this way," says Josephine.

"Oh, never pity me. You look very tired, my dear. It is you I pity, working here," she says, then more quietly, "with all those Boche."

Josephine nods politely, giving nothing away, then is pleased to move on. She yawns when no one is watching. She had worked with Anja late into the night.

Benôit is snappy, and Chef acts like a growling bear. They have had to shrink their menu with supply lines blocked, and Chef has had to come up with other things at the last minute, all with Benôit nipping at his ankles. Chef has had to fatten up the sauces with whatever he can find. They are down two staff also, and all the tables are booked.

Franz is back in the restaurant today. At his table of ten is Lady Vivienne, who has been here several times in recent weeks as a guest of various groups. The German officers pay her much attention. She looks beautiful with her hair up and a hairpin with purple feathers and a jewel. She wears fine, long gloves, which she removes so gracefully. She appears not to recognise Josephine, their former exchange brief, as she places an entrée before her. Josephine wonders if it was Franz who organised the pastries to be delivered to Lady Vivienne, and with each passing minute that she observes the pair, it seems more likely. There was a smell of sweet perfume in his room. Could it have been hers?

There is talk about the lady in the kitchen. Renée suggests that she is not English, that there is Russian in her accent, and that she is likely selling her body. According to Renée, who is a purveyor of rumours, her husband was a diplomat of some note. Chef thinks she is related to royalty. Anja says that she is probably just a war widow who has lost her husband and to stop speculating. Josephine says nothing, but thoughts of Lady Vivienne run wild with all these possibilities, and envy creeps in when Franz bends his head low so that the woman in question can whisper something in his ear. It is as if there were no one at the table but them at certain moments. When Josephine moves near to serve their lunch, they pause their conversation and make pleasantries with others.

She has not stopped thinking about the hotel room, about Franz, about their closeness, about the way he has exposed some of his heart. But in the back of her mind, she thinks that he is toying with her. Could he only want her as a mistress? And what of the information on her brother? Does it come with a price?

Franz is reserved today, charming, pleasant enough, though she has watched him plenty to know that he has much on his mind. It has something to do with Lady Vivienne, she thinks. Perhaps he is enamoured with her, and unable to relax so close to her. She is older than he by a good number of years yet still very handsome, with perfectly placed features, and poised, and wearing the most beautiful dress of pale aubergine satin, tiny pearl buttons from the waist to the neck edged with lace, sleeves gathered fashionably at the shoulder. Josephine has now convinced herself that the pastries were from Franz, and Benôit did not wish to tell her the truth. To spare her feelings perhaps? *How much does he know?* She is also convinced that Benôit sees everything.

"Josephine," hisses Benôit. "You have to move quickly. You are distracted today. Eyes on the task!"

She rushes to the table with desserts, flushed and soaking in feelings of envy and other people's surly moods before tripping on a crease in the rug.

The bowls slide off the tray she carries and crash to the carpet, pieces of cake and cream splatter.

One of the officers stands up, a dollop of cream on his trouser leg. And there is some on the sleeve of his uniform as well.

"I'm very sorry," she says to the table, since she cannot bring herself to look at the faces.

Chef has run from the kitchen to see what has happened and then turns away to send out the apprentice with a damp cloth. Benôit apologises, then is horrified to find Franz crouched on the floor beside Josephine, helping to place items back on the tray.

"Oh no, no, sir!" says Benôit. "Please let us fix this."

Returned to the kitchen, Josephine fights back tears. She is sure to be fired. When she looks up at Chef, he is red in the face, holding back laughter before he then explodes.

"The look on his face . . . ," says Chef.

Benôit has entered and seen Chef. Did Josephine see Benôit smile, too? He claps his hands and tells them to get back to work. The officer has been cleaned up. Benôit says he will personally take the new desserts that Chef is preparing and Josephine is to serve another table. He says nothing specifically to Josephine about the incident and does not appear angry. Perhaps she won't be fired after all.

Josephine is disappointed to see Franz leave with Lady Vivienne on his arm. He is smiling now and relaxed, and his dining companion is paying much attention to him. Josephine wishes she did not have to see it. She wishes she didn't feel such jealousy, too. As she resets the table for the evening seating, she can see the pair strolling casually together across the Place.

Who cares? He is Boche! she imagines Eugène saying.

Franz is waiting for her on Hainaut Boulevard along her route home. There is a drizzle of rain, and he holds an umbrella.

He pulls the umbrella low between them so they are forced close and seemingly separated from the rest of the world.

"I have been eager to talk to you. I wanted to say something to you about the hotel room . . . I hope you weren't offended by my behaviour that day."

Josephine isn't sure how she should respond. She has thought of those brief moments more often than she cares to admit. She shakes her head.

"I wasn't sure if I would see you this evening," she says, diverting the conversation.

"Why is that?"

She shrugs. "I thought you would be busy with Lady Vivienne."

She is unable to cage her curiosity, but she regrets the comment immediately.

"Vivienne is a friend," he says, as if he is discarding information of no value.

They walk in silence. Several teenagers, who are sitting on the ground ahead, jump up at the sight of them to run away.

He takes her hand, and she looks at their fingers together, hers sitting limply, awkwardly, growing warm. She looks away, embarrassed.

Does he do this with Lady Vivienne, too?

"She seems nice," she says, though it sounds unconvincing even to her ears.

"She is a very informed woman. Many enjoy her wit and her company."

"My mother makes lace for her. Did you know she has a daughter?"

Grace is around the age of ten, according to Gisela.

"Yes, I did," he says with a faraway look in his eyes, as if he isn't particularly interested in the topic of Lady Vivienne.

"How did you meet her then?" he asks.

"Delivering the pastries last month that you requested for her."

"That *I* requested?" he says, slowing.

"Yes, I was sent there with some pastries. I thought they were from you."

"I sent her nothing. Who told you this?"

It is clear from such genuine surprise that he knows nothing about it. She regrets saying her suspicion out loud.

"I cannot remember now. It was a busy afternoon." She has lied to Franz and she suspects he knows it. "I must have got the wrong name." She does not wish to reveal the assumption was solely hers.

He is quiet for the remainder of the walk and steps away from her to close the umbrella. His eyes look more blue than grey under a sky that has grown clear during their journey, snatches of sunlight now lapping at puddles.

"There is another thing I must tell you, though I have put this off in case it is untrue. I need to wait for confirmation, but I believe that Xavier may already be released."

"When?"

"I am not sure. We have to wait."

Eugène has returned to La Vérité after time away with work. He sits cross-legged on the bed under the stairs, reading a French newspaper that is a week old. Something stale from the canal rides the waft of warm air through the window.

"Who told you about Xavier?" says Eugène, jumping up to confront her as she enters. He has learned the latest news from Anja, whom Josephine has already told. He appears jubilant, but it is his natural state to be sceptical also.

"The captain who comes into the hotel, who lives there," says Josephine.

Eugène's eyes dart between the girls curiously.

"The same one who revealed to Josephine earlier that Xavier was still alive," says Anja. "The one who got you the job . . . He has taken a liking to your sister."

Josephine examines Anja to see if she has seen something else, if she knows of the visit to the hotel room, but she is reading English news, mouthing the words silently, learning some of them, and appearing only lightly interested in the subject of Franz.

"What does he do exactly?"

"Another Boche who thinks he is more important than he is," says Anja, nonchalant. "He is one of the Germans who searches for people. I have seen him knock on doors and arrest people . . . They will send him away to war soon enough."

Josephine has no idea how Anja has the time to learn so much.

"Well, perhaps you can ask him about other people, too," he says to Josephine. "There are many missing from Louvain."

"No, Eugène," says Anja for Josephine. "We cannot ask these people for favours."

"I don't know him that well," Josephine says. In that moment she is almost as fearful of her brother's reaction as she is of the guards that patrol the city.

"Then maybe just listen to everything he says. He may reveal something that we don't already know."

She presses her lips together and nods to agree. Eugène turns his attention quickly back to the newspaper. He taps his finger on an article.

"Here is the report about the passenger boat returning from America that was sunk by a German U-boat, killing innocent citizens earlier this month. The world will surely wake up now. It is no longer a war between soldiers. It is a war that everyone must join. That is something we must write about for *La Vérité.*"

There is a knock on the door. Eugène stands up suddenly, indicating to Josephine to follow him down the stairs. From the lower floor, the pair listens to Anja exchange brief words with someone at the door and close it again. She calls them back up.

"Who was it?"

"It was one of our messengers. They have French infantrymen that have come across the border. We need to move them somewhere safely. They will need identities. We should know more tomorrow."

"Hurry, Josephine!" says Eugène. "Back downstairs! We must finish the printing. There is a lot more work to come."

She steps downward into her secret life, into another lie.

17. FOUND

Arthur imagines soft, melodic laughter, Harriet beside a brook, holding hands, touching discreetly, aware of others who may be watching, her face flushed from laughter and love.

A few random shots ring out across the silence. Through narrow incisions for eyes, stuck down with mud and the residual effects of the gas, he sees faintly the silver-speckled sky. The rain is gone, thankfully, though it is perhaps the least of his troubles. There is a shooting nerve pain in his side that distracts him from his other woes. He reaches down again to feel his lower leg, at the torn trouser, where metal fragments have penetrated the bone.

He is on his back again and lying still, his breathing more even today. Every movement of his limb has been painful, every turn of his head, every shift of his eyes. There is nothing he can do but wait to be rescued or to die. The latter more likely.

More voices, this time foreign. He is, he estimates, a mere one hundred yards from a resting area filled with Germans. Their jovial voices carry in the night, and the sounds of celebration after a successful battle.

His lips are dry and cracked, and his face is sore to touch. He has lost his pack, and his clothes are bloodied and torn. He must look a sight, and the thought of it, of him, riddled with wounds, makes him smile. It is hysteria, he thinks, for the pain is still awful and suddenly more so. He moans then. There is nothing really to smile about.

One more day here, if no one comes, he will try and get back. He will drag himself across the mire, a place from which few return. He tells himself this, whispers to himself for courage. They were warned about shrapnel, about poison gas, though nothing prepares one for the burning pain of both.

And then he has fallen asleep again and more dreams, this time of water, of swimming, of diving deeply into crushed ice.

He wakes shivering. A sound outside has stirred him awake: gravelled footsteps and whispers. Someone nearby. A German scouting party perhaps or maybe the Allies risking a daring attempt to rescue him. He awaits his fate. Being caught by Germans perhaps an improvement on death. He calls out feebly. At least they might take him to their hospital. Or they will shoot him on the spot, put him out of his misery.

Through crannied eyes he can see faces, ghoulish shapes at first, against a flare that hisses in an arch in the sky behind them, and then a small woman and her husband, aged, he thinks, come into focus. They speak to him in French, a different dialect that he doesn't understand.

"I'm English," he says in French. "I must get back to my unit."

Hands reach down for his shoulders, and they drag him across the ground, the jostling reigniting the intense pain in his leg.

"Please, stop!" he says breathlessly.

They ignore his pleas and continue dragging his dead weight. Then arms underneath him, the man, he thinks, lifting him to stand and both of them supporting him almost upright, half carried, half dragged. He cries out when the dangling, useless foot of his bad leg bumps against the ground.

"To farm," says the woman in sort of English then. "Safe."

A shot rings out, and the two people don't flinch, even though Arthur starts and raises his hands a fraction, instinctively. He is being collected and taken straight to the German line. He sees them everywhere in his head, helmets pointed, moustaches huge, images he has of them, of ones he has seen that follow him ominously into dreams.

He feels the air around him change, cleaner, and the path is smoother, and they are walking toward the morning sun scarcely risen, that hangs above a distant line of trees.

Arthur feels afraid, taken farther and farther from the Allied line, and he goes to protest, but the searing agony in his leg is back with a vengeance. His eyes still closed, teeth grinding, the wound on his leg opens again, hot liquid trickling down to his foot. Every jolt, shift, twist is felt until he passes out.

Someone touches his face with coarse fabric. He is on a bed of straw in a barn, propped up with a pillow. It is an abbey-like building, broken, shelled. He can smell and hear the shuffling and muted sounds of farm creatures huddled at one end out of the rain that now peppers the roof as it prepares for more.

"Medical come soon," she says. "You stay here."

"I don't understand," he says feebly. "Where am I?"

The woman passes him a canteen.

He opens the lid and puts it to his lips greedily, then chokes, his throat constricted. He tries again, sips this time. His throat is on fire. He has soiled himself, he thinks, though it is difficult to tell, his clothes wet, greased in oily water, then rolled and battered in mud.

He falls into sleep again. Dreams are clouded this time, as if his mind is fading, as if he is attempting to distance himself from them. He is woken again to soft trilling and shuffles in the ceiling. And he waits in his semi-darkened state, light, and shadows behind his eyelids. It is evening again, he thinks, the lights turning grey. It is close to two days since he saw the other men in his company, the same time since he has eaten.

Footsteps outside.

"You are English?" says an approaching man, low and soft in a strong French accent.

"Yes," he says, though he is barely audible.

"I will treat you," he says. "My name is Xavier." He turns to talk to someone else behind him, directing them in French.

"You are a doctor?"

"I completed a medical degree, yes."

"Are you taking me back to my unit?"

"I'm afraid not. Not yet at least. You are in a poor state. We need to attend to your injuries first."

"Where am I?"

"Belgium, just north of the military zone."

Arthur twists his mouth, close to weeping, though all he can produce are whimpers, his eyes no longer forming tears.

"It is all right," says Xavier, touching his arm warmly. "You are safe for now. I have two people here with me. We are secretly working for the Allies. We have taken other soldiers before and led them to the northern border. It's what we do."

"How soon for that, do you think?"

"Not too soon," Xavier says with a soft laugh in the back of his throat.

Xavier has his hand on Arthur's forehead, and he can hear packets being torn farther away, the dragging of something on gravelled ground, a bag, or a box.

"How bad am I?"

"You are extremely ill. But you are one of the lucky ones."

"Lucky ones," Arthur repeats. He is entering delirium, he thinks, because he has the urge to laugh again.

"At least you were found. What is your name?"

"Arthur Shine."

"Well, Arthur Shine, we are going to treat you with some medicine and then move you somewhere else. If it makes you feel any better, you will join some of your allies. Two Frenchmen we have in hiding."

Something cold is pressed to his chest and held there a few moments. A splashing of water and a cold cloth is placed over his forehead and eyes, at first painful, then soothing. Someone else is cutting away the lower half of his trouser leg with scissors.

"There was a gas attack, no?" says Xavier.

"Yes," he says a little clearer, his lips moistened. "Am I going blind? My vision is blurred."

"I will have to examine your eyes more thoroughly later. We will know better in a day or two. Your chest sounds mostly clear, a slight crackle. But you have a leg fracture and wound that requires urgent treatment. You have to know that your condition is serious."

Arthur nods. He feels emotional, the soft voice of the doctor so soothing. The truth that rolls off his tongue. Life and death so simply put. He wants to touch this man, though all he can think of now is sleep.

Someone is sponging the wound on his leg. Then something else, movement, a request in French, and someone else close to him who smells like antiseptic. Another cloth is placed over his face, and he resists at first, the chemicals burning also.

"Breathe . . . not too hard," instructs Xavier.

He feels slightly woozy, the headache still there but the other pains in his body unplaced now. He is semi-conscious, at first barely aware of the doctor who is plucking metal from his leg, then the pulling and stretching to straighten the limb, and jolts of stabbing pain that cause his body to jolt.

"Bite this," says a woman in accented English. A thick-wadded cloth is in his face.

He feels hands over his leg, soft and light across his skin, then another hand under the leg and another to reach in and scrape the bone. Arthur winces.

"This is not going to be easy, my friend," says Xavier.

Before Arthur has time to respond, an assistant stuffs the cloth into his mouth, then prying hands reach once more into his wound. He screams into the cloth, his sounds muffled this time. It takes two of them to hold down the top half while the doctor puts something over the leg then binds it.

Arthur listens to the doctor and his assistants discussing his fever, which may be something he has brought with him from the trenches. His leg isn't good. He may lose it if it becomes infected, which is highly likely. He could possibly die. All of these things he no longer cares about, just the pain, wishing it would go away. Whatever it takes to remove the agony. Take the leg if they must.

He passes out. When he wakes, unaware of time, there is a bandage over his eyes and around the back of his head.

"We have disinfected the wound on your leg, wrapped it in bandages, and set it in splints," says Xavier. "The bandages will have to be changed every day. Our biggest concern is infection."

An ocean of hurt in his head, throughout his body. He prays for an end to it.

What point is there to go on?

"Every point," says a voice, and he realises he has said his thought aloud.

He is lifted by people, all of them he assumes, and carefully placed on a stretcher. He is carried on this a short way, then lifted onto a horse-driven vehicle of some kind, animals pacing impatiently, backward then forward.

"We're going to place things over you to hide you. You can't speak. Don't open your mouth, don't make a sound until we tell you."

And then the light that he can vaguely see through his eyelids is gone completely as covers are piled upon him, and it is dark.

The jouncing is making him sick again and feeding a headache that is already unbearable. He feels nauseous. An eternity in darkness.

The rugs are finally dragged away, and light again around him and then more lifting. Some men nearby are having a conversation. He is placed on a squeaky, narrow bed, reclined slightly against a pillow and a wall.

"You are safe here for a few days," says Xavier.

"Where are we?"

"Just on the outskirts of Brussels."

He is so far away from his company.

"Water?" someone asks.

A cup is handed to him, and his own hand is guided to his mouth. His arms are heavy, weighed down with sickness. Water on his lips only, his throat filled with razors.

"My eyes . . . ," he whispers.

"They are damaged; however, it is possibly only temporary. It is hard to tell. This is something new I haven't dealt with, though I will speak to others. We can only bathe them for the moment and give you painkillers."

Xavier's hand rests on Arthur's arm.

"I have to be elsewhere, but we will meet again."

There are others in the room, French voices. There is a strong scent of hot, salty water that makes his nose twitch, and his stomach stirs. A spoon is put against his lips, and he opens his mouth obediently to sip back its contents. And then he is sick.

18. THE MISSION

At La Vérité, Josephine has already created several new identities for Allied soldiers hidden in safe houses, and Eugène has used his artistic skills to create a stencil simulating an official seal. Tomorrow, her work will become more dangerous, and she is feeling anxious.

Despite hearing news in the underground of a German defeat, there seems no end to occupation. Work at the hotel is constant, and to feed the officers as well as the men in the field, supplies have had to be ordered from America and Holland. Produce sold to shops and restaurants in Germany has been sequestered by the military.

"Your little German friend has a lot of work to do," says Benôit one day, catching her looking out the window, thinking of Franz. The manager has a sixth sense. "There are many people he has to catch."

"What do you mean?"

"There are some who sabotage the Germans' buildings here, and also the smuggling of people, which I hear them constantly complaining about."

"Oh," she says, wondering if her underground work is written across her face.

"Anyway, I'm sure he will return," he says. "Don't worry too much."

Josephine shrugs her shoulders to pretend Franz is of no consequence, and she sees that Benôit is looking at her hands, which are pink and raw. They are constantly in developing and bleaching agents, turpentine, and ink.

"You should get some cream for your skin," he says.

She nods and disappears quickly to avoid any questions.

The gravelly, pitted path crunches loudly under Josephine's bike wheels. Several chickens squawk and scatter in various directions as she approaches her destination just outside Brussels. She has followed Eugène's instructions, deviating along a narrow pathway that vehicles cannot travel.

It was here where war boots have trampled and littered the ground with uprooted trees left to rot beside the creek that runs through the village. This is another village where people were slaughtered. The remaining trees stand defiant with knowledge of the crimes that occurred, overhead boughs bending down inquisitively toward her, their leaves chattering their secrets of the dead. A feeling of panic sends a shiver up Josephine's back at the memory of Louvain. She can see tiny pockmarks in the skeletal remains of a wagon, turned on its side, violently it seems, stripped of most of its wooden body, likely to be used for heating. People still live here, but many were forced to move away, their houses razed. A house on the corner had been burned down to one level and gutted.

The small, pale stone cottage she seeks sits alone and back from the road. A rectangular, unremarkable construction that does not beckon to those who travel by. Windows boarded behind a dying tree with antler-shaped boughs.

Josephine pauses on the road, her skirt released from being tucked underneath her. She pulls the written instructions from her pocket to check the address, then searches behind her to make sure she hasn't been followed. She walks her bike the remaining distance along an uneven pathway to the front door.

She leans the bicycle against the wall and looks behind her to the clouds of smoke that billow in the south before inspecting the perimeter of the structure. She was told that there are soldiers inside this safe house to be photographed for Belgian papers. Once the identity documents are completed, Eugène will then collect the men. He has given instructions for her to deliver clothes and food as well. It is silent from within, windows partially boarded at the back as well.

She takes the camera and other packages out of the basket to place everything around the side of the house until she knows it is safe, until they trade their code. The only thing she carries is a small prayer book wrapped in brown paper. She knocks lightly and hears a rustling from within.

"A delivery for Monsieur Poisson," she says.

A man opens the door a fraction, one suspicious eye looking her up and down.

"You are delivering my book, no?"

"Yes."

He opens the door wider.

She retrieves the items from the side and steps into the house. The French soldier's hands are bandaged almost to the tips of his fingers, his hair appears singed, and there are burn holes in his blue woollen uniform. The stench of fetid wounds and battle sweat is overpowering. The house has been used to harbour injured soldiers for months. It is cold and damp and dim. Another soldier sits on a chair, wearing only grubby blue trousers, his torso bandaged. His eyes roam wearily over her and the goods she brings.

The third man lies on his back on a bed, one lower leg heavily bandaged, another dressing around his eyes, and his hairless, narrow chest speckled with nicks. He is lying under the only shaft of light that has entered the room. It takes Josephine a moment to realise that the faint clicking she hears is his teeth chattering. The first soldier picks up a blanket that has fallen on the floor beside the bed and places it back over the man.

The other French soldier in the corner continues to watch her, wide-eyed and numbly.

"What are your injuries?" she asks the first soldier.

"I have lost most of the skin on my hands. Adam," he says, pointing to the other French infantryman, "had a large metal biscuit cut from his stomach."

Adam snorts a response like a laugh.

"The Englishman has a fever, gas burns, and a fractured leg. He has not spoken at all."

She views the man on the bed curiously before unwrapping the cloth with civilian clothing. "I am told these are close enough to your sizes. . ." She looks at the Englishman. "I am not sure if he can wear these."

"We will make them fit," says the first soldier. "If we think it is necessary."

"I can take a photo of the Englishman first, if you wish, though the bandage . . ."

"I'm not sure it is worth it, mademoiselle," says the same man quietly and matter-of-factly. "I expect he will be dead by morning."

The Englishman remains still. He has perhaps not heard anything, does not even realise she is there.

She passes the clothes to the first man, who has already begun to strip down.

Josephine turns away and listens as the second soldier helps his comrade undress. They share a whispered joke, something she does not understand.

"What is your name?"

"Josephine," she says.

Adam sings her name, and she is moved at the way they shirk the cards they have recently been dealt.

"You can turn now. We are both decent."

"As decent as we can be," says the second.

The men wear ill-fitting shirts and trousers, the legs of one too short, the shoes too large. It is the best they could do. People are donating the shirts off their backs. Supplies are limited. Fabric is expensive and hard to source.

"How do we look?"

"Very well," she says. But they do not at all. They look beaten.

She folds out the tripod at the rear of the house. The men stand against a wall for their photographs. Josephine tells them to smile a little, look like they are about to take a holiday.

They snicker.

As she is packing it up again, the men have already started eating the tins of food she has brought, but the Englishman remains lying in the same position.

"What is his name?"

"We weren't told, and he hasn't spoken."

She retrieves the camera again.

"Would you mind if I took photographs inside here?"

She has realised the significance of this, a record of these men and their circumstances. She sets up the camera once more and photographs the Englishman under the window. On the way home she takes another of a burned-out house, and then one of a wheelbarrow, with smoke on the horizon.

At La Vérité there is no one home. It is nice to have somewhere to herself.

In the basement she develops the film. It is not her best work, the lighting and contrast only just adequate in some. They will have to do. She hangs them up on a line of string to dry and studies the faces of the Frenchmen and the other with the bandage around his eyes. She hopes he survives.

Josephine has been gone a long time and is suddenly hungry and eager to reach home. She wears a hat pulled down low to hide her face from people who may see her from the windows. There are people sweeping the street, and another man in a tailored coat stands beside a barrow of coal. These are strange men she has never encountered, who appear too well dressed for their occupations. Eugène has told her to be suspicious of everyone. Next time she will take a tram, disembark at a different location, and walk from a new direction.

At home, her mother approaches her as she arrives.

"Where were you?"

"It was my day off! I went for a long walk by the canal and then stopped by to see Anja," she says, certain that she wears the lie on her face. "You were gone already to Lady Vivienne's by the time I woke this morning."

But Gisela is not overly concerned about where her daughter went. She is excited about something else.

"I delivered the lace to Lady Vivienne this morning. I have told her all about us. She very much wants to meet with you properly. I think it is good to have wealthy Belgian allies, Josephine. She has invited us to supper this evening."

"This evening?"

"She says she has the evening free."

"I don't know, Maman," says Josephine. There is something about Vivienne that bothers her. Why the sudden interest in a lace maker? In her? What does Vivienne have the evening free from, Josephine wonders? Who does she entertain if she does not work? She appears a lady of leisure. It is a mystery, her connection with Franz, his confusion about the pastries, and there is an air of danger about her also. Though there is no sensible reason for Josephine to think this way. Vivienne is charming, and kind to her mother.

"What don't you know, Josephine?"

"Nothing," says Josephine. "Of course, I will come."

Because her mother is so tired from one visit across town, they catch the tram arriving a little closer.

It is Lady Vivienne herself who answers this time.

She is exquisite in a Chinese silk shawl with tassels, and she holds a ruched silk hat, her face flushed as if she has just come in from a walk. Josephine feels dowdy in a plain shirt and a skirt that has been worn close to death.

"I'm afraid that I have not seen my maid, Elise, for several days now, and it is hard to find a replacement of any calibre. Come! I've prepared some supper."

She leads them into a room at the front with its high ceiling and large Gothic windows that overlook the street. A deep-red carpet matches the thick velvet drapes, the walls patterned cream and gold.

"Please sit."

They take a seat facing the fireplace, and Lady Vivienne talks about the price of things, the inability to get the same quality of fabrics she is used to. Vivienne explains that her husband is dead, though she does not mention any detail, instead talking about her daughter, who is learning piano. Their life seems a world away from Josephine's. That people like Vivienne exist alongside people who are struggling to feed their families seems unfair. They sip tea from white-and-blue china cups and nibble delicately at creamed cheese sandwiches, beside heavy gilded lamp bases holding up shades in multicoloured glass.

"Your mother is truly a find, Josephine," says Vivienne.

"Oh," says Gisela, pleased and humble. Her mother is grateful for anything these days, any crumbs.

"I have seen you run off your feet at the hotel, my dear," she says to Josephine. "And I must say that you are highly efficient."

Josephine nods to her hands, unused to such compliments. Benôit has commented little about her work. Only the fact that Josephine hasn't been fired has given her some indication that she is successful.

"My son's friend works there and introduced her," volunteers Gisela.

"How fortunate! What is her name?"

"Anja," says Gisela.

"Oh, here she is!" says Vivienne, looking away, seemingly losing interest now that her daughter has arrived. Grace is a small girl, fair like her mother.

"Come! Grace and I will show you our little flower garden," she says. Past the kitchen they enter a courtyard full of colour. Gisela has taken an interest in the child, who is keen to show her the flowers that have just bloomed.

"We share the same German friend," says Vivienne while Gisela is being distracted on the other side of the courtyard.

Josephine turns bright red.

"Don't worry. We all need friends."

"Look, Mama!" says the girl. "A little bird!" Vivienne gushes over the creature that has suddenly flitted away from the excited movements of Grace.

"Grace, darling, can you take Madame Descharmes to the picture room, to show her your drawings?"

Josephine moves to follow also.

"Stay, Josephine," says Vivienne, who watches through the back doorway until Gisela is deep inside the house.

"You have an admirer!" she says to Josephine.

Josephine looks away, disturbed that someone else should know this.

"You should make the most of it. It will make your life more comfortable. But be warned. Tread carefully. Make sure it is you who sets the rules, not him. Hold all your cards close to your chest. You would do well to heed my words."

Josephine is thinking about the men in the ramshackle house, their lives on the line. How deft she has learned to become at deceiving everyone. Josephine has decided that she doesn't like Vivienne; she is perhaps shallow and insincere.

The light is disappearing from the sky. It is time to leave, declares Gisela, joining them with Grace.

"Before you go, I must give you something, Josephine, if ever you wish to entertain."

Vivienne disappears up the stairs and returns with a box.

"Don't open it until you get home."

Then she leans in to give Josephine a kiss. "He likes this one," she whispers.

"What a remarkable woman," Gisela comments on the way home. "She has lost her husband, too, and yet she manages such a household on her own, without reliance on the Boche."

Josephine feels wretched, suspecting otherwise about their new friend. It is obvious that Vivienne and Franz have spent time together, and spoken about her. What has Franz told this woman? Does she laugh at how naive, how inexperienced Josephine is? Such thoughts preoccupy her until they reach home, by which time Josephine is not only resenting Vivienne but resenting Franz even more.

Josephine opens the box. Inside is the blue-and-white striped dress Vivienne was wearing the day Josephine delivered the pastries. They are roughly the same height, though Vivienne has a fuller figure. Josephine tries it on for her mother, who is quick to bring out her pins to make some adjustments.

"Oh, my darling," says Gisela. "That is so beautiful. She is so generous."

"Yes," says Josephine, keeping her concerns hidden.

There is no doubt Vivienne and Franz are linked, but what has Benôit to do with it? In any case, there is no one to discuss this with. To tell Eugène and Anja would mean to reveal a closer connection with Franz. To talk to Benôit would be alerting him to something that might be only in her mind. And Benôit is a mystery also.

19. WAITING

Arthur was aware of the conversation with the girl who came to take photographs, aware that she had brought food. Though the conversation seemed like something in a dream. He is lost in a murky haze. At moments he feels as if his whole body were on fire, and at other times, he is cold.

One of the Frenchmen asks him if he can eat something. Arthur doesn't respond. To speak requires too much effort; to shake his head, excruciating. Their low talking beside him is muffled by a sound like rushing water in his ears. He drifts into a brief and restless slumber before one of the men puts the edge of a cup against his lips, water seeping across his tongue. Most is spilled, his throat too dry, too painful still.

"What is going to happen to him?" says one of the soldiers.

"I don't know what their plans are. We have to wait for contact."

Then Arthur is finally under, away from the pain, dreaming he is somewhere else: at a fair, lots of people, Jack with a toffee apple, Harriet with one, too.

Sit up straight, Jack, and eat with your mouth closed.

Then hands on him, shaking, and he is stirred awake, carried from the brilliant colours of his dream and into darkness. He is unaware of time, how long he's been asleep.

"Can you stand?" says an unseen male.

Someone else is here, one large hand wrapped around his shoulder, activity within the house, the scraping of a stool, a squeaking water pump somewhere outside.

"We can't take him to the border," says another voice. "He will have to be treated here by the doctor when he returns."

"We can't just leave him here alone. We will have to take him somewhere else then," says the first male voice, speaking so fast it is difficult to keep up. "Do you know where this doctor is?"

"He said he would see us at the next safe house before we are taken to the border, to check our wounds," says one of the men.

Arthur is lifted and placed in the back of a truck.

"I will take you first and keep the Englishman with me," says the new arrival tasked with decisions, "until we can decide what to do."

There is some discussion, talk of locations, names and places he hasn't heard of, and then there is more rough bouncing and the groan of an engine, and with every bump Arthur thinks he might die, or wishes he would, because movement of his leg is unbearable, his neck stiff, hands curled into fists.

The truck turns and jolts over lumpy fields and up and down hills before they enter a track or road that is smoother.

"It is a detour to avoid the outposts," the driver explains to someone who has queried. "It is part of my job to know where the Germans are located. I take them things."

They stop, doors open. Arthur is lifted again, swaddled like a baby, and he can sense the night air on his face that feels flushed and swollen.

Then into another building and laid down on a bed, the feeling of falling and blankets placed over him. Another cup of water put to his lips, and there is light inside; he can see yellow through a thick wad of gauze.

"My name is Eugène and this is Anja. We were hoping to send you to the border, but you will stay here to recover."

"Where's here?" he whispers, hoarsely.

"La Vérité."

He has no idea where that is. A town he hasn't heard of. Then they are discussing him, but it is too quiet to hear, and he is falling again into crashing waves that drag him out to sea.

20. THE SURPRISE

"Mouse," Eugène whispers.

He has entered her room and woken her up.

"Get dressed! You have to come straightaway."

"Where to?"

"It is a surprise. Get up, quickly!"

She hates lying to her mother, saying she is working, and sooner or later Gisela will wonder where the supposed extra pay is being spent.

Eugène wears a black coat to blend into the night. He looks like he is up to no good with his cap pulled down low over his pale face. She is led outside to his bicycle and a cold gust of wind.

"What are we doing?"

"You will see. Jump on!"

"You are mad!"

"Just a little."

"I will have to tell Maman."

"Not yet. I'll have you back soon, but I'm not so sure you will want to come back when you learn what it is."

Her excitement grows. It is not like Eugène to be so happy. Whatever it is it must be good. She remembers when they were children. He would shake her awake at midnight, dragging her out protesting from a child's coma. Though the moment she saw whom it was, she would know that something adventurous and thrilling was about to happen, Eugène always with something new to do. Waking up at midnight often meant cycling through Louvain under a full moon, chased by their shadows.

Josephine climbs up on the handlebars like she did as a child, and he pedals fast, the weight of her no issue. Eugène is tall and wiry, skinny arms that look like they cannot carry weight, but he has always surprised her with his strength.

A loud conversation by sentries travels their way. Someone's wife has written complaining of the milk that is becoming scarce, how dire it is becoming in some German towns, and it seems their conversation has only just started.

Eugène decides to go a different way that eventually leads to the canal; then he rides close to the edge to scare her a little, the water looking brown and deadly under dim yellow globes.

She climbs off once they are stopped at the door of La Vérité.

"Gène, what is happening?" she says, disappointed they are here again and not somewhere else. "Why the secrecy?"

"You will know in a minute. Stop talking."

He pulls Josephine along by the arm as she hesitates.

"You have to promise you won't scream."

"Gène! What is it? You're making me nervous."

Anja opens the door and steps back to let them enter. Xavier is waiting inside, dark hair grown to cover his ears like Eugène's, a short beard and moustache.

Josephine runs and wraps her arms around Xavier's waist before then crying into his shoulder.

"Hello, Mouse!" says Xavier.

There are so many questions she wants to ask, but nothing sensible is forming just yet. He has a slight scar on his upper lip and hair that has grown around it. There are other differences, too. Lines are chiselled into his cheeks and around his eyes, and there are scars on the backs of coarse hands.

Xavier repeats again what he has told Eugène and Anja already. They rounded up all the priests and paraded them around like animals. A number across Germany had been executed or sent to a prison in northern Germany, each accused of being a franc-tireur. He was transferred to two different camps and was then sent to build a road in Germany. Then to another camp and then eventually brought back and released. He has paid for whatever the Germans think he did.

"Preaching the word of God is encouraging people to bear arms apparently," he says wryly. He scratches his stubble thoughtfully.

"And you, Mouse, I have heard all about you and your bravery."

"Gène said something nice about me?" she says, sounding dubious, as if they are back in Louvain again and they are joking around the table, talking nonsense, and there is no occupation, no war.

"Yes, from Gène!"

She looks at Eugène, whose eyes have melted also.

"Josephine," says Xavier. "It is so good to see you! Everyone looks different, faces changed, thinner. Everyone more serious now."

"How have you come to be here with Gène?" she asks.

"I made contact with people in the west who use the same safe houses that Gène and Anja use. I've been helping the injured soldiers in secret. Part of a group who help those trapped behind enemy lines."

"When were you let out?"

"About two months ago. Our home . . . Well, you know there was no one there nor at the gutted printing house. I tried our cousins' house also, but when I couldn't find you, I went to the towns and villages along the military zone that had been ravaged to see if I could help the injured, put all my skills to good use. I had the belief that you were somewhere safe. I never lost that . . ."

"Eugène has told me about Papa," he says more gravely. "He is constantly in my prayers now. How is Maman?"

"She is not yet herself," says Josephine. "I am not sure she will ever get over what happened, but I think seeing you will make a difference."

"I am looking forward to seeing her."

"Xavier has been granted a pass between the cities and the military zone," Eugène tells Josephine.

"Yes," Xavier says. "The Germans asked for my services to treat their soldiers as well as Allied prisoners when they learned I had been trained in medicine. The job has also allowed me sanctioned access to travel between the war-ravaged areas and the cities. And with this I help smuggle the Allied troops through networks to get them out of Belgium. It was doing this work that led me to Eugène. And that's how I met Arthur also."

"Who's Arthur?" At the same time Josephine hears a bed creak in the other room.

"He is an English soldier," says Anja. "He is here resting."

"He must be the man I couldn't photograph?"

"His leg is damaged and infected, and a gas attack has affected his sight," says Xavier, then lowering his voice. "He is severely ill."

From where she is sitting, Josephine can peer through the gap in the curtains to the bedroom at the rear of the floor, to see the shape of feet under a sheet.

"Josephine," says Eugène, "we will all have to help nurse him back to health before he is taken to the border. Anja will do most of it. But when you are here . . ."

Josephine nods.

"I will have to tell Maman you are here before you see her. Her heart might not take it if you arrive unannounced."

"Yes, I want you to break it to her. I also want to clean myself up before she sees me. I imagine she will still scold me for my unruly beard."

"She never scolded you for anything! Always Gène or me or Yves."

"True," says Eugène.

"And will you be joining a church here?" she asks.

"No," says Xavier. "It is still my calling, but the church is on hold at the moment. I am led in a different direction for now. Bodies to save first, not souls."

"A wise choice, Brother," banters Eugène. "You would be wasting your time on the latter right now."

"For the first time, I would have to agree with you," says Xavier playfully, like old times. "Though yours is first on my list when I return."

"Are you staying here in the city then?" asks Josephine.

"No, I am living outside Brussels, closer to the military zone. I am living in a worker's cottage and go where I am called to see someone sick or injured."

Gisela nibbles at a piece of heavy black bread at breakfast, its only purpose to be filling. She isn't caring about food in that moment, her focus solely on the front door. She has been feeling poorly, lethargic, and her asthma returned. But that morning she is alert, her ills put to one side.

Josephine answers the knock at the door.

As Xavier enters, Gisela wobbles slightly as she rises from the table, her breaths are shallow, and Josephine thinks she might fall or faint. Her mother pauses, watching him, drawing one hand up to rest on her chest, the space between them filled with deep affection. She nods with a look of satisfaction, tears moistening her eyes. She has been dreaming of this moment.

"My son," she says. Xavier comes in two strides before she collapses in his arms. Gisela can no longer hold back her relief, sobbing quietly, which screams loudly into Josephine's heart.

"I have prayed and prayed for this day," says Gisela. "I have not stopped. I never lost faith. I knew it."

Xavier takes both of his mother's hands in his.

"I'm sorry my absence caused you so much pain."

He explains what happened to him, tells her that he is helping the sick, though he doesn't mention the German soldiers nor the Allied soldiers he helps to escape Belgium.

Xavier gives his mother some money, too, which she tries to refuse.

"You must grow strong again," she says. "You need more meat on your bones."

She is right, but he is rugged and brown and seemingly healthier than Josephine remembers him also, despite the fact that he has often gone days without food.

"Maman," he says. "I move around a lot and may not always be able to call in that often . . ."

"I know, my boy," she says. "My prayers were answered. That is all I needed to know."

21. CAUGHT

There is a haze across the city, dust sticking to the air. Josephine puts a scarf over her mouth as she walks to work.

"Did you hear the crash last night?" says Anja as she arrives.

Josephine had heard explosions, and she and her mother had run out to see tongues of fire flicking angrily at the heavens.

"Yes. What happened?"

"The zeppelin sheds east of Brussels were blown up by an English aircraft. There will be some angry Germans around today."

"Did they get away?"

"People seem to think so."

Josephine is relieved.

"Franz is back," Benôit reports to Josephine nonchalantly, face deadpan as if he is telling her news that is trite. She turns away to hide her look of pleasure, and for most of the day, she watches the doorway, hoping he will come there to dine.

"Don't look so desperate," says Benôit in passing. "It doesn't become you."

Josephine bites her lip and lowers her head, self-consciously, yet there is something about Benôit that is also benign. The more she knows him, the less frightening he seems.

Franz is busy, she tells herself. *Or he is tired of me,* says another tiny voice when there is no show of him at the restaurant. At the end of the working day, two streets away from her house, Franz is waiting for her. Josephine feels a surge of excitement at the sight of him, though she is reticent, too, that tiny voice returning to tell her that a deeper relationship is all in her mind, and maybe too dangerous to consider.

She steps toward him, unsurely, but he closes the divide quickly as if he can't wait, reaching to curl his arm comfortably around her own.

"I have to be honest with you, Josephine," he says. "I have thought much about you while I was away. Did you hear from your brother Xavier? I checked again and they confirmed he was released."

"Yes," she says, careful about how much she tells him. "We have seen him. Thank you."

"I promise you I will work to make sure that once the war is done, your family will have a good life again," he says. "I am quite certain Belgium will go back to how it was." He looks at his watch. "I wish I could stay longer with you, but you are probably aware of what happened yesterday?"

"Yes. Is it your job to investigate the damage?"

"It is," he says.

They near Josephine's home, where they stand apart for several seconds. Franz takes her hand and bends down to kiss it, then leans forward to kiss her lightly on the lips.

"Goodbye, Josephine."

She watches him leave and looks up to the window to see there is a neighbour watching, shaking her head.

Eugène is standing near the window as she enters, surprising her.

"So it is true! Anja's suspicion was correct."

"What, Eugène?" asks Gisela, walking toward them from the kitchen.

"She just shared a kiss with a Boche! With that German captain who is chasing after her."

"Who?" says Gisela, looking between the pair.

Josephine is shaking with the feeling that she has committed some terrible crime. Perhaps she has.

"The captain who came to my rescue that night," says Josephine.

"You are such a little fool!" says Eugène. "You are naive about men, Josephine. About this war, about whom to trust. The captain is not your friend."

"Stop it, Eugène!" says Gisela, while examining her daughter's face for the truth.

"You are selling your soul to the devil," he continues, ignoring their mother. "How do you know that he is not using you to get information? It was supposed to be the other way around, but you have told us nothing about what he does, where he goes. This is betrayal!"

Josephine looks down at her feet with feelings of shame and confusion but most of all the urge to slap her brother hard across the face, their relationship doomed always to be fiery, his mood that changes with the wind.

"Shh," says Gisela. "We have neighbours who we barely know that would give us up for food and favours if it came to it. Oh dear, Josephine, what have you done?"

"He knows something!" says Eugène.

"No, he knows nothing, Gène!" defends Josephine, blinking back tears.

Gisela is seeing the effect her son's words are having.

"Eugène, do not be so hard! Give her a chance to explain."

"You never even thanked him for the job!" says Josephine. "You would have been sent away. You would have ultimately been forced to go."

Eugène pinches his lips together in anger, preparing something else to say.

"Perhaps she is right," says Gisela. "Perhaps you should be thanking her, and this captain. She is doing what we all are doing. Surviving, not making enemies, making friends."

"I have an idea. Ask your friend where he goes, who he sees. Sleep with him if you have to. Make use of him."

"Eugène!" says Gisela, horrified at the way he is speaking. "That is enough!"

"I already saw it in your face, Josephine," he says, his anger still coursing through the veins that are now raised at his temples. "You have fallen for him. Even now, even after everything we've been through, you betray us by cosying up to Boche. Papa would be ashamed of you."

The mention of her father ignites anger, and she suddenly cannot take any more. She has had enough of people telling her how to think, how to feel.

"Do not think for one moment that I don't fight with my conscience! But yes, I will admit I have feelings for him. I also believe he protects us."

"So it's true then," he says, following her as she tries to leave the room, pecking at her like an angry gull. "You are sleeping with him for favours. And you have probably undone all our work, led him to our operations."

Josephine turns toward him to raise her fist, then pulls it away again in frustration.

"Who do you think enabled our work?" she says. "Without him you would never have had the chance to do the things you do. You would never have found the press or been able to travel wherever you wish."

His mouth is open wide now as if waiting for words to enter, ones he can't think of.

"Eugène?" says Gisela, her attention diverted onto him. "What operations?"

Josephine shakes her head at him, then throws open the door to leave. She needs to calm down, walk off her anger. Eugène calls after her in the street, but she ignores him. She walks toward the city centre, her head clouded with images of Franz and her family, trying to fit them

213

together somehow. Doubt creeps in. She knows so little about his work. Should she trust him?

She wishes she could talk to her mother about Franz, but Josephine suspects that it will be too painful for Gisela. She saw the look of horror on her mother's face when Eugène revealed what he saw. All Germans are the same in Gisela's head.

With some trepidation she heads toward someone who might understand, who might be able to tell her something more. Though twice she nearly turns back before approaching the entrance.

Josephine knocks on Vivienne's front door and cautiously looks around the street as she waits. A maid she hasn't seen before opens the door, looks her up and down, seemingly begrudging the interruption. Josephine crosses her arms protectively. It may be a risk to be here, to trust her, yet Vivienne is the only person she knows who might share some truths about Franz. And who, from their previous discussion, will not judge her by her friends.

Grace has seen her at the door and runs excitedly to see her, and Josephine is now glad she came. If for nothing else but the reaction from the little girl whom Josephine suspects rarely, if ever, mixes with other children.

"Oh, you poor dear," says Vivienne in a maternal way, approaching her in the drawing room. She sits down beside her on the sofa and takes both her hands. She is a vision of perfection as usual. "You have been crying. Someone has upset you.

"Grace, go tell . . . oh, what's the new girl's name . . . ?"

"Maud," says Grace.

". . . to bring some tea and biscuits." She turns back to Josephine. "I'm struggling to keep service staff. Elise never returned to work. Now it seems this new one must have lied about her experience . . . But tell me, what has happened?"

Josephine reveals her brother's outburst over Franz, tells her about her mother now knowing. Then, with Vivienne's sympathetic expression and her hand on Josephine's knee, other things tumble out: the fights growing up, their family losses, even the broken engagement. Vivienne nods at everything. Though Josephine is careful to say nothing else about Eugène, and about their secret work.

"Ah, I see," she says. "Yes, brothers can be a little protective and bossy. I'm glad you have come to see me. Life has dealt us a bad hand, but you just have to search the rest of the pack to find the good ones. I miss my husband very much. I miss my old life. I have lost friends because I am close with Germans. However, when I receive criticism, I let it slide away. Only you can know whether you are truly doing something wrong. No one else can tell you that. It is no one's business but yours."

"But how does one know if they are doing right anymore? Whom to trust?"

Vivienne laughs, stands up to walk over to the window, and strikes a match to light a cigarette she has taken from a small wooden box on the table.

"I have many friends, and the only way I can pay for things is from German money. I will give you some advice. Tell your brother that you are in complete control of things. Don't let anyone walk over you. From this day forward, make sure every decision is one you fully support or one you have made yourself. The men are forced away for work, and the choices for women are limited, and those choices we must bear. But that doesn't mean we can't shape them on our terms. We have to fight in spirit, endure in ways we might never have agreed with in times past. Persist until we are free, until our whole truth is eventually heard."

She looks back at Josephine from the window.

"If we don't outlast them, we are all just remnants of irrelevant history, our stories never told."

Under the light she is lovely and sad, and from her sombre words and a frown that wilts her visage, there is something more to her that Josephine hadn't perceived before. She has dark and deep thoughts that boil just beneath the surface that she must always contain. She hides secrets she wishes she didn't have. Perhaps Josephine has been wrong about her. Vivienne is far more complex than she seemed.

"You don't seem very confident, my dear, and perhaps you never have been," says Vivienne before Josephine has a chance to query what she said earlier. "That, I think, is the problem. It is what I saw the first time I met you.

"But you have something, Josephine," she says, tilting her head and smiling mischievously, her façade restored. "Obviously, something to attract a handsome captain."

"Oh yes, you are very pretty," says Grace, who had crept back in to listen. Josephine wonders just how much the girl sees and knows, and it seems strange that she is involved in such adult conversations.

"Can you tell me something of him, Vivienne?" There is no need to say his name.

"I know that he is part of the military police, that he seems a decent man and is highly regarded," she says, then shrugs her shoulders. "I don't think there are any dark secrets there. He is probably one of the few who doesn't have any, though it is only my opinion."

It is what Josephine was hoping to hear.

"Now back to you," she says, appearing keen to change the subject. "You need to stand up to people more. You are no longer the timid sister. You work, you pay your way, you have attracted the eye of someone important and influential. You must maintain that. But above all, you must make the most of what you have."

With the cigarette still in her fingers, and smoke swirling about Josephine's face, she pulls out the hair ties in Josephine's hair and combs out the plaits with her fingers.

"Tell your mother to come and see me. Tell her I have more work for her. That will smooth Gisela over at least. Don't worry about your brother. It is your mother's peace of mind that you should worry about.

Invite Captain Mierzen over to meet her. People are never as frightening in person.

"Maud, bring me a brush!" she calls, then hardly waits for a response. "Maud! . . . That girl is so slow! Oh, never mind. Grace, go ask Maud to hurry with the tea."

Grace is gone and back quickly while Vivienne works on Josephine's hair, curling it between her fingers and pinning it at the top of her head. Maud returns with the tray and sets it down. Grace bounces up and down, applauding her mother's hair creation.

"Now go look!" says Vivienne.

Josephine stands in front of the giant mirror in the drawing room. She likes it, her light-brown hair silken under Vivienne's expensive lamps, and styled the way that Vivienne wears her own. Though the person she sees wears it awkwardly. Her mother has always plaited it, dictated how she was to wear it. For the most part because Josephine didn't really care.

"Oh, that is pretty, Mama!" says Grace, clapping her hands.

"You look older, Josephine," says Vivienne. "You look like the grown-up you are. My last piece of advice is to not let your mother anywhere near your hair."

Josephine smiles timidly and reaches over to hold Grace's hand.

"But on a more serious side. The captain can make life better here, and the price you pay is a pittance compared with the benefits. Use the gifts you've been given to survive this war, my dear, if you want to take care of the people you love."

Josephine thinks of those last words all the way home, trying to fit them into the context of her own life, of her relationship with Franz. She should be less timid in the relationship. Be more like Vivienne perhaps. Offer him things.

What things exactly? Those things that no one ever says specifically.

When she arrives home, Gisela is waiting. Josephine passes on the message from Vivienne about more work.

"Well, it seems she's done a slightly better job. Your hair is very lovely, Josephine."

"Maman, maybe if I invite Captain Mierzen over, you will feel a little better about him."

"Eugène has told me everything," she says solemnly. "What he does. What you and Anja do."

"Oh goodness, Maman!" she says, unsure if that was wise. It will give her mother plenty more to worry about. "He told you what exactly?"

"About the underground, the news, the people hidden. I now understand why he is worried. I can't believe I didn't suspect anything."

"I'm sorry we didn't tell you, Maman."

"Please promise me . . . if something doesn't feel right that you will walk away. I know your brother can be very persuasive. That the people around him can get caught up in his mania at times. You, however, are still so innocent of things."

"I am no longer a child, Maman. You should stop worrying so much."

"Those two things don't necessarily go hand in hand. I will always worry about my children. Now more than ever."

"We will be careful, I promise."

"I have to be honest," says Gisela. "Eugène's news was more shocking than the fact you are being courted by a German."

"I know what I am doing. I will never give anything away that would get any of us in trouble. I have always been good at keeping secrets."

"Yes, you have," she says, nodding. "I had no idea of anything you were doing. I have lost my touch. I have been grieving still, my mind not always functioning as it should."

She looks frail on the couch, and Josephine sits close and reaches to clutch her hand.

"Maman, you have to trust me. Franz . . . The captain has promised to look after us, and I believe him."

And it doesn't matter whether anyone does or doesn't approve.

"What would your papa say?"

Papa, I am sick to death of Maman, said Josephine months before the invasion. *She is controlling everything, where I work, where I go.*

Don't be too hard on your mother. She is thinking of your future.

She is always angry and protective.

Be grateful that she is. It means she cares.

"He would say, do what your heart tells you," says Josephine.

"No," says Gisela. "He would say, use your head before your heart. Use both."

She is right. Gisela knew her husband better than anyone.

22. ANGELS IN THE DARK

Arthur wakes with the taste of chemicals on his tongue. Endless days of chills and sweats in a bed that is damp and squeaky.

He can smell rain, hear its first heavy drops. It reignites a yearning for England, for Pippin, who would bark to alert him of rain clouds approaching, sensing a storm well before it fell upon them. Pippin's warm body against his shin and his loud sighs when he lowered his silky head to the floor to patiently watch his master.

On the previous day, drilled full of painkillers and while in a slightly more lucid moment, Arthur asked Xavier to describe his life and family in Louvain. He had talked about the sister, Josephine, who gives the illusion of being timid, who is clever and quick, though unworldly, too. His father and youngest brother, dead, and the other brother, Eugène, loose, like a wheel that comes off its wagon and continues to roll, passionate but unbearably so at times. His mother, whose self-assurance has been stolen by grief. Arthur knits all these people and events together to gain a clearer picture of the home he has landed in, to form a human map with which to navigate.

The whistling of a kettle, like that of an incoming shell, makes him turn sharply toward the sound.

There is a conversation in French outside the room, in voices too low and fast, making it difficult to understand.

"We'll see by morning . . . We can't do anything else."

Then he is sleeping on and off, and there is darkness through his eyelids, through the bandage. His world is orange during the day and black at night.

In the distance he can hear someone singing a tune and the sound of a truck lurching, the clank of metal, the roar of an engine. The night before, he had heard an orchestra of explosions.

For the first time in weeks, he doesn't care what the next day brings. He has no plans, nowhere to be, not really. Only if he counts Pippin, if and when he comes home, and Mary. He is thankful at least he will not die completely alone on the battlefield, drowned in a crater.

Then it is daylight, and orange again. There is a window in the room that he turns to, where it is brightest. He has listened to larks and then crows to pass the time, and the sound of water trickling, and imagines a heavily shaded creek somewhere close. He feels cold and hot again, feelings of wanting to be ill, sometimes vivid colours behind his eyes.

A church bell chimes somewhere in the distance. *A death knell it seems.* He is on his knees at death's door. *It isn't long now.*

He wakes again, jostled slightly into semi-darkness, pulled from his melancholic dreams into wakefulness. Someone has replaced the towel under him. There is the sound of washing in a sink. Angels come in at any time with glasses of water, soup, and clean sheets. Xavier, Eugène, and Anja are here and gone so many times he loses track of where they are.

Josephine's name comes up often. ". . . German with her, kissing . . ." He grows more alert.

"The German has probably had us followed," says Eugène. "It is how they knew about the safe house."

"You can't know that for sure, Gène," says Xavier. "People have been given up before. She has told him nothing. I trust her to be careful."

"I agree," says Anja. "There are snitches everywhere, and they are more likely to be some of the locals who are sympathetic, who want attention taken away from them."

"She likes him, Gène," says Xavier. "He has helped Josephine, Maman, and you also." Xavier always the softest voice, the one whom people stop to listen to. "I don't believe it is anything more serious than that. But, Anja, you have to be extremely cautious anyway. Take no risks this time. If you think someone is observing you, abandon the mission."

Eugène agrees in the language of grunts.

They are lovers, Eugène and Anja; that much Arthur has learned from listening to their conversations, to listening to them upstairs in their bedroom, on floorboards that creak and bend with movement. Things he doesn't care to hear. The conversation continues. They are talking about places he has never heard of. He is drifting again, floating.

He sleeps.

Soft footsteps enter his room. A chair is pulled to the side of him.

"Have this?" a girl says, puts a tablet on his tongue and a glass of water to his lips. He swallows, relieved to put his heavy head back down again.

"Who are you?" She is someone different.

"Josephine. Xavier has shown me what to do. I have to check your eyes and leg. Tell me if I hurt you."

Small hands, gentle and soft like feathers, first around his eyes, and then she unwinds the bandage on his leg, applying ointment, then rebinding it again. She smells like freshly laundered linen. She is slower, steady, and careful like Xavier. Not as rough as Eugène or as fast as Anja. Though he is too tired to take in fully what is happening, the fatigue just as bad as the disease sometimes.

He sleeps.

There is a strange lightness in the room, his bandages gone, the roof of his mouth raw, tongue dry. He sits up at the edge of the bed, swaying slightly, and perceives the long nightshirt he has been placed in. When he looks up again, he can see the room, a chair, a window, an open curtain to another world outside. Though these things aren't as clear as they should be. As if he is living half in shadow. Perhaps they all are.

He blinks several times. There is colour. His vision is clouded as if someone has poured milk in his eyes. He touches his face, the bandage around his eyes is gone, skin rough and peeling on his face.

There are no more voices from outside the room but the churning and vibrations of a machine beneath him, and the sound of paper being sorted. And he can smell metal, machinery.

He pulls himself upright using the iron headboard, and he wobbles on one leg.

Xavier has left him a walking stick near the bed in anticipation, always thoughtful.

He puts much of his weight on the stick, then proceeds with one-footed shuffles across the floor to the entranceway. He leans his head on the door frame a moment to overcome a slight motion sickness.

Outside the room he blinks again. He sees the table they sit around, where people come to discuss things, and the small kitchen and the bathroom. There are items being shuffled and moved downstairs. The place is run down, a factory manager's house at one stage, though the factory has closed, and people have not lived here for years it seems. There is a smell like Yorkshire peat.

He enters the bathroom and for the first time in a long time relieves himself in the box-shaped lavatory, pleased that he is no longer using the pot beneath his bed with help. When he is finished, he moves to the basin and the mirror above it. He can see himself, an indistinct view at least, fur around his face, and the brown of his eyes set in pink-red pools. He turns on the tap that squeaks out drips, uses scentless oily soap, and splashes cool water on his face. The headache only dull, the light a touch painful on his eyes still, though he can live with it.

Josephine is waiting for him when he comes out of the bathroom. "Oh, it's you!" she says. "I heard something."

He is momentarily stunned by her sudden appearance.

"Oh, you do not understand me," she says, searching futilely for English words.

"Sorry if I frightened you," he says in French before heading to a chair to sit down gingerly, one leg stretched out stiffly. He imagines that he is probably more monstrous than what he could see in the mirror. "I understand you perfectly."

"You should be lying down. You should not be moving your leg."

"I couldn't lie there a minute longer. I had to get up."

She looks at him curiously, then nods.

"It is wonderful that you are," she says. "We weren't sure . . ."

He looks at her to see why she has stopped.

"If I would live? Yes, I heard it all. All the speculation." His voice sounds croaky and alien to him.

"I'm sorry if we talk too much," she says. "I'm Josephine."

"Yes, I guessed." He has heard much about her, and he has heard much spoken about himself also. "You are the first face that I can see with some measure of clarity."

"How much can you see?"

"Like I am sitting in a waning mist."

"Let me get you something to eat. Can you eat?"

A sudden realisation that he is weak with hunger, and he wets his lips. "Yes, I believe so. Thank you."

She moves away from him to the kitchen. Pours something in a saucepan and turns on the gas.

"How long have I been here?"

"Over a fortnight. You have been very ill."

He closes his eyes to rest them, then opens them up again to squint at his nails, overgrown, jagged. Behind him there are sounds from the kitchen, soft ones, the girl so used to performing everything secretively.

She sets down a bowl with brown soup, the origin of which he can't discern, and a spoon. Back a second time with a glass of water. He knocks the bowl with his elbow, liquid spilling.

"Damn!" he hisses.

"Do you want me to help you?"

"No!" he says in frustration.

Jack, don't be so clumsy!

She moves away to the kitchen and then returns to wipe the table. He clears his throat. "I'm sorry, I didn't mean to—"

"Don't worry about that."

The soup is lukewarm, though it is good enough, his stomach knotted slightly, not so welcoming of food. He has another mouthful, notices a pile of papers on the other end of the table.

"Is that what you do here?"

He tries to focus, words coming clear, then disappearing again.

"What is that? *La Vérité.* 'The truth,' isn't it?"

"Yes. We don't hear very much of it here, so it is our job to get it out there to Belgians."

"What is the truth?"

"That people are dying here, that we are forced to live on Boche time, we can't sing our Belgian songs, and we have to pay thousands of francs in tax to the Germans so they can buy more supplies for their soldiers to kill our own men and allies. That people are dying in prison. We live in fear here all the time, wondering if we should or shouldn't speak to people, if they are likely to repeat what we say."

He reflects a moment on the conversation between Eugène and Anja and wonders also what it is that this German captain, that he has heard so much about, wants.

He is just a peacock, Eugène, said Anja. *He will be gone soon enough.*

Even from the little Arthur knows about her, Josephine does not seem like someone who misunderstands people or will put anyone in jeopardy for that matter. He can see the colours of her better and snatches of detail when she comes into focus, his eyes adjusting each time he blinks. Her eyes are round ponds of Atlantic blue, dark lips against pale, translucent skin, and brows a shade darker than her walnut-brown hair. Her eyes rove from his face to his hands, watching everything.

"I'm sorry you have to live like that," he says.

"No, I am sorry that so many have to die to win our country back," she says.

There is more she could say, but she is holding back, guarded with her tongue, yet her expression appears open, trusting.

"You are a waitress, I hear."

"Yes. Though I was told yesterday that the manager is reducing my hours and my pay. It has not been as busy there in recent days. Some of the Germans have moved out and down to the Front. They are losing men. And there are not enough Belgians with money to fill seats."

"And your German friend, will he be sent away, too?"

She appears startled and shifts uncomfortably. She has closed the book to her thoughts. She wasn't expecting the question.

"Well, I suppose we should be happy that there will be fewer Germans to bother your family," he says awkwardly, then realises he should not have mentioned her friend. It means she knows that people are talking about her. He is not thinking clearly.

"Yes and no. I need the work. We need the money. We have been fortunate so far with all of us working, but food and heating are so expensive."

A pain again behind the eyes, and he feels nauseous, puts down the spoon before he has finished the soup.

"I think I might lie down again."

She stands to help him. He is trembling, cold, his leg starting to ache again. He brushes sweat from his forehead.

"It is too much too soon perhaps. Here," she says, her long, wiry arm around his waist to help him stand up and lead him back to bed.

She covers Arthur with a coarse blanket, lifts his head gently to plump up the pillow. She tucks in the blanket tightly around him, like he would for Jack when he was small, puts her cool hand on his forehead. She takes it away too quickly. He wishes she would keep it there. She returns with a cool washcloth and lays it carefully across his forehead. He feels for the first time in months a strange sort of fatalistic peace. That he is in the hands of better people than he could have hoped to know.

She leaves then to climb down the stairs to the floor below, and he falls asleep to the rhythmic clicking of a print machine, drifting peacefully in and out, woken up again when she comes back up.

He hears the dying hiss as she extinguishes the lantern's flame and the front door gently latch, and nothing of her after that. He pictures her stepping into the night, wrapping a scarf around her head and knotting it beneath her chin.

The wind rushes up against the window and recedes back like waves on a beach, where he is back in his childhood home and he can hear his parents in the kitchen. He remembers the warm, doughy smell that followed his mother, though it isn't his mother this time. It is a vague blurry picture of Josephine, how he would imagine her in his mother's kitchen.

Xavier arrives several nights later, and he is surprised to see Arthur sitting up at the table, leg outstretched. He has dressed in a shirt that was left for him and a pair of trousers, one side split up to the knee. Xavier examines Arthur's eyes while the patient studies those of the doctor, whose once undistinguishable multicoloured orbs are a deep and patterned imperfect blue. Xavier's face matches his voice: soft and even, and approachable. He is a man who finds peace even in chaos. Arthur envies him.

"You look better today, Arthur," Xavier says. He places a firm hand on his patient's shoulder, the very goodness of him spreading warmth. If there were any tears to weep, Arthur would for the care this man has given him.

"You have all been so good to me."

"I have brought some flour and eggs so we can start to fatten you up for the trip home."

"It seems everyone wants me gone."

Xavier smiles at his humour.

"Seriously though," says Arthur. "I am feeling much better. When can I leave?"

"Certainly not yet. I know that you are keen to return, but it will take time for you to heal. You will feel some effects from the infection for some time to come, and you will need two working legs for the journey. I should tell you that I thought you were close to losing one of them. It is also common to succumb to the infection of such injuries. So do not try and move around too quickly. You need to rest as much as possible."

"I am grateful for everything. I'm probably not the only one wanting to rush out of Belgium. I'll wait my turn."

"It is an odd situation out there," Xavier says. "Belgians wanting to get out but some, who left before the Germans arrived, came back so they didn't lose their homes that the Germans had threatened to take."

"What about you? Will you go eventually?"

"No, Arthur. This will always be my home."

"And what of the others? Do you want the rest of your family to go?"

"Eugène's work here is his passion now. He will be hard to convince. I will, however, work on my mother, who has recently learned what we are doing here. I have yet to speak to her about it, but I am doubtful she will go unless we all do."

Arthur has had time alone to study the place, to hobble around the middle floor with his walking stick while the others were gone, to stare at the photographs that are pinned up on the walls, the landscapes, the rooms, windows. There is even a picture of him lying on a bed, light across him from a crack in the window boards, hauntingly, his face in part shadow. The faces of the Frenchmen who were there, smiling with their bodies patched with bandages. He was moved by the sight of them.

Xavier speaks only briefly about his experience in the camp and the digging for hours in snow to repair tracks and help fix roads. Though he is not complaining.

"There was also disease that spread. Then we were returned in cramped conditions on a train with supplies, and by the time we arrived, more were dead in the carriage."

Arthur blinks a few times to moisten his eyes.

"How are your eyes now without the bandages?"

"They still sting somewhat when I look toward the light, but my vision is almost clear."

"Good. We should probably make up an identity for you, in case you have to present one unexpectedly during the coming weeks of your recuperation. Any name you prefer?"

Jack.

"Whatever you think."

"Would you like a drink?" Xavier asks. "I saw some whiskey in one of the boxes Eugène brought back from the German stores."

"So, it is still all right for a priest to drink a little stolen goods."

Xavier raises his eyebrows. "Do you want that drink or not?"

"Of course," says Arthur, a trail of soft chuckles leaving the room. Xavier returns with a bottle and two glasses, and the men share a drink and companionship he had almost confined to a life in his past.

"Tell me about yourself, Arthur. Who is Arthur? What does he do?"

He has already spoken briefly, intermittently between the bouts of nausea and pain, about Harriet, though he hasn't volunteered anything about Jack. It is a memory that he has held closely to his chest, protectively, afraid to expose it to others. He can't say why exactly. Perhaps once it is released it is gone to someone else. He no longer controls it. He has lost the rights. *Though for what purpose?* He can't think of one now. First it caused a deep ache to speak about it, and now the memory cordoned off and guarded. It is wasted on him. Others would do better with such a story.

"Do you have any children, Arthur?"

Jack.

Father.

"I had a son," he says, and the memory is released then, all of it in gory detail, the agony, the joy, the fear, they are Xavier's now to do with as he pleases. And the release for Arthur, the weight gone from his heart, the burden shared.

23. THE PROMISE

A smoke haze on the horizon to the west reminds all of Belgium how close they are to the moving line of fire. It is a helpless feeling, pathetic even for some, to have one's future dependent on the deaths of men.

Long, twisted fingers of pink and grey clouds fan out from the crest of a red-gold sun. Josephine studies the patterns in the sky, turns them into objects, like she and Yves used to do together. Though she doesn't ponder for long today. Franz will be here soon.

It was Belgium's National Day yesterday, and though it is against the rules to celebrate it, the church was packed with people singing "La Marseillaise" and their anthem, "La Brabançonne." And no one was arrested. Gisela is in slightly better spirits, at least enough for Josephine to approach her.

"Maman, Franz and I are spending the morning together," says Josephine. "He has some free time. He is coming here in one hour."

Gisela clucks her tongue and raises her eyes, looking perhaps for some divine intervention, a habit that she did not leave behind in Louvain.

"You could have told me earlier."

Josephine only now has worked up the courage.

They have been meeting for the past month, usually twice, sometimes three times a week at specific times when Franz is free of commitments. He rarely dines in the restaurant anymore and has not invited her to his room since, but gives her warning at least on the days he waits for her by leaving a private message at the front desk. She does not know how she would juggle her time with La Vérité otherwise, if their rendezvous were more frequent or spontaneous like they began.

Their connection has grown stronger during their walks, arms linked, hands held when no one is near, a brief and stolen kiss, and hints of a future together after war. Yet there are other times, especially this past week, when Franz is formal, angry lines between his brows, as if he fights with certain thoughts in his head, resisting any banter. Josephine worries that his interest is waning, and she has thought often of Vivienne's advice about survival. She wonders now how they would cope without his help.

"That is disappointing," says Gisela. "More for you than me. I support you, you know that, but you are putting your hands too close to the fire. Perhaps you should be listening to your brother this time."

Eugène knows little more, thinks Josephine.

"My brother, as you know," she says with emphasis on the second word, "has suggested I whore myself to procure some intelligence."

Gisela clucks again. "Eugène always says things to be provocative. You know that. It is part of his nature. He doesn't mean most of what he says."

"It is part of my nature to read people, and better than Gène."

Gisela looks hurt, and Josephine's heart is pliable once more.

"Maman," she says more tenderly. "Franz has done so much for us. He is looking after us. As you know, he has even had our electricity reconnected."

"And what does he want in return?"

"Nothing."

"I doubt that." She turns away, mouth twisting in frustration.

Josephine is almost tempted to reveal her suspicions about Lady Vivienne and her alliances with German officers, but she stops herself.

It would change Gisela's attitude toward her, and Josephine, despite her suspicions, feels protective of everyone.

"He wants to meet you."

Gisela has picked up a piece of lacework, pretending to examine it under the light from the window.

"We do not have to take turns standing in the soup line," adds Josephine. "And, Maman, he stopped his own man from rape. Have you forgotten?"

Gisela puts her stitching down and stares out the window. She has finished with the argument. She has nothing more to say.

Josephine changes into the dress that Vivienne gave her, then proceeds to style her own hair, on top like Vivienne's, though not with the same detail.

Gisela eyes her daughter as she enters downstairs.

"You should not draw too much attention to yourself."

Josephine turns away to bite her lips. She is nervous, but she doesn't wish her mother to see this, to know she tears herself in two with doubts. She must do what she has to for them both to survive this war.

"Where is he taking you?"

"Nowhere special. We are just going for a walk to have morning tea, then to the steps of Saint Michael and Saint Gudula."

"Perhaps you can say a prayer for yourself, for better choices."

Her mother has to get everything off her chest if Josephine is ever to get out of there.

"Maman," she says. "I can make up my own mind about people. I believe that Franz is acting honourably. And I would not put any of us in danger. I do not even talk about Gène, and he never asks. He has not asked me anything suspicious."

"You should at least be chaperoned."

Josephine turns to face her mother to see her green-blue eyes dampened with tears. She has endured more than she should have.

"If that makes you feel better, then come with us," she says, sighing. Perhaps it is best.

Gisela blinks a few times and looks away.

"I would, but I am not feeling very well. Besides, it would take me too long to get ready." Josephine knows the real reason: Gisela does not want to be seen in the company of a German.

Short knocks and Josephine stands well back from the door to allow her mother to answer. Josephine touches her hair one more time nervously, though there is nothing to fix, and she fights the urge to bite her fingernails, instead nestling her hands together in her skirt.

Franz is in full uniform, and he nods formally in her direction as he steps through the doorway. His eyes drop fleetingly to the neckline, then the skirt of her dress, and she detects a minor furrowing of brows before his expression is quickly restrained. He takes a brief glance around the room, then turns to Gisela.

"Madame Descharmes," he says in perfect French, bowing his head respectfully. "It is a pleasure to meet you."

Gisela nods in acknowledgement and forces a tense smile.

"The manager of this house has disappeared, but I can assure you that your electricity will remain connected."

"Thank you, Captain."

"Josephine," he says. "We cannot delay. We only have the morning." He smiles and holds out his bended arm for Josephine to take, and they commence to walk.

"Captain Mierzen," says Gisela, interrupting their departure, "she is my only daughter. What are your plans for her?"

Josephine looks down and then away to close her eyes, to mouth words that no one can see.

"Plans for her?"

"Where do you see yourself in her life?"

Franz looks bemused.

"I have to be honest with you. I am just trying to get everyone through these times."

"Oh, come now, Captain Mierzen. All men have some sort of plan for the women they seek the company of."

"Madame," says Franz, "I very much like your daughter, and I seek only to look after her wherever possible. And I imagine her values are much like your own."

"Maman, we have to go," says Josephine. "Perhaps we can talk about this another time."

Gisela attempts to smile, her lips wrapping around her teeth, wounds too deep to be fixed with simple words.

"I am sorry about my mother," says Josephine when they are some way from her house. "She worries."

"As she should," he says. The even tone of his voice suggests he is completely unperturbed, yet his eyes dart elsewhere as he speaks, as if he can't trust himself to look at her.

They are on the tram, and people are whispering, pretending it is about something else, though it is about them, a Belgian woman and an officer. She is closest to the window and looks out to the pavement, to watch the people scurry about like mice avoiding traps, and to avoid the judgmental glances from within the vehicle.

Franz holds her close as they ascend the stairs of the church to the terrace that looks out above the city. She studies him, his profile, pointed chin, perhaps slightly too long, though it does little to mar his face, his pupils shrunken to reveal the palest of grey in a ring of dark blue.

Some people who were planning to walk up the stairs have seen him, then retreated. Franz squints into the sun, pretending he hasn't noticed. He must be used to it, she thinks, being a pariah here. Knives in his back the moment he is turned.

"I will take you for refreshments now if you wish?"

"In your hotel room?"

"Not that I had planned," he says, a moment of confusion.

"Perhaps it is better there."

He thinks, watches some people below, then looks back to her. "You are obviously uncomfortable with the stares today."

She looks down.

"Of course, whatever makes you comfortable," he says.

You are naive about men, Josephine, said Eugène.

She is happy, is she not, in his company? Though the time alone in his hotel room scares her.

Use the gifts you've been given to survive this war, my dear, if you want to take care of the people you love, said Vivienne, drowning out the words of her brother.

She is not as naive as everyone thinks. She knows what she is doing, she tells herself as they enter the lobby, enduring curious stares. Benôit is somewhere in the restaurant and fortunately unaware. She is envious that Franz does not have to worry about such things as reputation.

He checks what refreshment she favours, then asks her to wait in the lobby while he instructs that their order be brought directly to his room. She steps up the centre marble stairway, legs resisting slightly, a nervous trickle of sweat between her small breasts. Once inside his hotel room, they sit at the table by the window, their conversation light at first. He shows her some pictures of his family. He asks about her mother's health.

"She clearly worries about you," he says.

"She is not yet over the loss of my brother and father. It will be some time before she can find forgiveness."

It is the problem then, the wall between them. The nation that caused their deaths. She knows he is aware of this as well; he has lowered his eyes and frowns in concentration. There is a knock at the door, and it is some relief for both of them. She does not want to make this about the past.

Coffee in a silver pot and a selection of petit fours are served at the table by a girl whose shoulders roll forward, head hangs over her chest like there is a weight around her neck, and eyes watch Josephine suspiciously under heavy lids. Josephine can sense the disfavour, knows she will be labelled and loathed for being alone in the room with a man, especially a German. Gossip that does more harm than good.

When they have finished their refreshment, they move to the sofa and sit there quietly a moment, separated by several feet of plush green cushion. She struggles to find the words as he takes her hand in his and examines it together with his, compares the skin, tenderly.

He leans over to kiss her, somewhat awkwardly, and she puts her hands gently on his chest without any pressure. The touch of her hands arouses a reaction, his arms reaching behind her back to draw her closer. She can hardly breathe, and she is trembling slightly, and then he releases her. She thinks of Vivienne, of what she believes he wants. She releases several of the buttons on the bodice of her dress.

"Oh God, oh no!" he says, standing up and moving to the window, his back to her.

She looks down at her open dress at the cotton chemise beneath and remarries the buttons to their holes, fumbling, trembling from the shock of his reaction.

"What is wrong?" she asks.

"Is that what you think I want?"

She can feel her skin burning red. "I've displeased you," she says, holding back a flood of tears.

"No, but you have mistaken me for someone I'm not."

She flees then out the door, leaving it open, to rush down the hallway. He is calling her name, but she is already down the stairs. Near the front entrance, she passes Benôit, who calls after her; she is crying now, distraught, and ashamed.

Pigeons scatter as she runs, and people stare. She is nearly blinded by her tears, her thoughts in fragments. She is humiliated, stupid. She is all those names that Eugène has called her.

Then she is nearing a corner to stop and take a breath, stitch in her side. She wraps her arms around herself, grips her upper arms. Her hair has come unwound, loose around her shoulders. She knows if she goes home in such a state, Gisela will not leave her alone until she learns the truth.

She proceeds then more slowly before happening upon a group—three girls and a boy of an age several years younger than Josephine—loitering at the entrance to an alley she has to pass through. Something about their presence bothers her. They seem very aware of her: eyes slyly directed her way, then back to whisper amongst themselves, one girl giving some kind of instruction with her hand.

Josephine walks steadily past them and recognises one of the house-maids from Franz's hotel room floor. Several times, the girl has appeared sullen and discourteous toward her.

"Traitor!" says the girl.

Josephine ignores them, hurries her walk, but they follow her.

"You are whoring yourself to the enemy. You don't deserve to be a Belgian."

"Leave me!" says Josephine in a firm voice.

The boy steps on her skirt, making her stumble, then she rights herself and begins to walk faster. They are on her tail, and one of the girls pushes her so hard that Josephine falls on her knees and hands, blackened and grazed. When she tries to stand up, she is pushed down again. She sits to one side, her leg tucked beneath her, watching them closely to gauge when she can make her escape. She observes them all clearly now and recognises them from the square where some of the younger Belgians go to meet when there are no guards around.

"What do you want?" says Josephine. "Is it money?" She pulls out her coin purse from a pocket in her skirt, and they grab it off her greedily, two vultures going through the contents. She moves to stand.

"Stay," says the ringleader as they form a tight circle.

"Whore!" shrills one of the girls.

"Help me, please!" Josephine says to a couple walking past, who pick up their pace, pretending they can't see.

"No one wants to help a traitor," says the girl. "You should be ashamed of yourself!"

With horror, she realises that this is not a robbery, and the serving girl has something silver hidden in her grasp. When she sees Josephine looking to her hand, she shouts, "Grab her, hold her arms down." The other three seize her.

A woman Josephine can't see calls out for them to stop. The boy barks at the woman to leave them or they will cut her up, too.

"We have to be quick!" says the boy, turning back to their crime.

"I am Belgian," says Josephine, wrestling hard to free herself, twisting her body, as they grip tight to her arms and force her to lie down. "We are on the same side!"

The head girl spits at her.

Josephine kicks out wildly.

The boy then holds on to her legs, and Josephine manages to free her hand to scratch him across the face.

They tussle again as she is wrestled onto her side, her face scraping across the cobbles, and her arms are forced behind her and wrists bound with rope. She is turned onto her back, her shoulders pinned backward to the road, the weight of her own body on arms twisted awkwardly beneath her. She calls out for help before a cloth soaked in something foul is forced into her mouth to silence her. The cloth shoved so far in that she gags.

Scissors hover dangerously near her eyes, held by the girl in charge, while someone presses their weight against Josephine's head to keep it steady. She feels the tugs of her hair as pieces of it are then savagely snipped away. She groans from the pain of her arms and her head being crushed into the road. She is unable to move.

The sound of a gunshot and the group jumps away from her and scatters.

"I have seen your faces," Franz yells as they flee. "You will all be found and put in prison."

There are people watching, and he shouts at them. "Anyone who knows those weasels and anyone who has idly watched this happen will be arrested also."

As expected, people scurry away. Franz puts the gun back into his belt and crouches down beside her. He cuts away the bindings with the scissors the girl has dropped in flight, then gently lifts Josephine to sit up. She attempts to rub the hurt from her arms.

"Is anything broken?"

She shakes her head. She doesn't think so. He pulls her to stand, and she lays her head against his chest. Part of her hair has been cut away, one side of her face grazed, arms aching from being pressed against the cobbles, the taste of blood in her mouth.

He has wrapped his arm around her protectively.

"There is nothing to see here," he shouts to people peeping through their shutters. She is thankful she does not have to look at their faces, at their judgment.

He hugs her to him for the walk home, and she is teary and limping, her leg badly bruised and scratched also. The skirt of her dress torn and covered in grime.

"We will find them, and they will be punished, all of them!"

Though she doesn't want that. She doesn't really know what she wants anymore.

"Josephine, I want us to be together so you are never hurt like this and you will always be under my protection. I want to take care of you. It doesn't matter if we live here or in Germany after the war. All I know is that I want you. You have to know that. You are not Vivienne, who was forced to take care of herself. Do not think you have to do what she does. You are safe with me. Your family, too."

She is sobbing now, from the shock of the day, from his words.

"Josephine," he says a little quieter, kissing the top of her head. "I love you."

Her face against his chest still, she wants to stay there. She had forgotten the feeling of what it was like to be safe.

But love, she is not sure about his love. She is not sure she is capable of it, her heart broken into pieces, her head unable to forget why she is here in the first place. Love will make a bigger mess of things.

24. BACK INTO THE LIVING

It is strangely lonely even with all these people. Arthur is a spectator to this beehive, and sometimes he just listens from behind his bedroom curtain. Feet up and down the stairs, bodies in and out the doors. Rushed conversations. Maps on the table. Machines tapping, clicking, and churning. He has no purpose. Feels conspicuous by it. Is glad there is a curtain to separate him sometimes so his inadequacy, his illness, these feelings are hidden.

It can't be helped.

As well as the constant ache in his leg, he still suffers mild fevers and insomnia, and is dizzy when he rises too quickly.

I am walking much better. Feeling much better, Arthur said to Xavier as he examined the jagged scar on his lower leg. *It has been two months.*

Be patient, Arthur!

Conversations about Josephine and the German have almost stopped between the lovers. Any mentions of the captain are not laced with as much bile from Eugène anymore. Arthur has learned that the captain has been called away to fight and will be leaving soon. Eugène will have one less thing to worry about. And the mentions of Josephine have taken more solemn tones recently. When her name comes up, Anja talks softly, gently. Eugène says nothing, grunts sometimes about something Josephine has to do, has done. They've had more important things to worry about. There is talk of arrests instead, talk of exposure. They are discussing much about that.

"We are going away for a couple of days," says Anja. "I have to go south again, pick someone up, deliver clothes, and Eugène has to take the newspapers west in the truck and obtain more supplies."

Arthur nods. He misses Xavier, who is now busy working in a hospital in Brussels by day while still caring for those in hiding at night, called out after hours, sometimes visiting with his mother, sometimes here.

Arthur has had plenty of time to contemplate things. This life is not his, and his old one in England would be only fragments of what it was. He seems to be drifting in a timeless state, in a sea of shadows. He must leave. He must get better quickly, return to battle. Feel worthy again and place his life in the hands of fate once more.

Josephine enters, footsteps light and fast, and Arthur watches her shut the door, then peer out through the gaps in the curtains to the street.

"Is everything all right?"

"Yes," she says, turning to view him at the table. "Just making sure I wasn't followed."

"Oh!" he says. "What happened to you?"

The side of her face is bruised, black and yellow, and her hair is different. It finishes level with her chin.

"I was set upon a few days ago."

"A robbery?"

"Yes," she says.

"Did they take much?"

She looks troubled, dark under the eyes, worry wrapped around her shoulders. He senses she doesn't wish to talk about it.

"Your photographs are very good," he says, changing the subject.

She nods, though her thoughts are far away.

"Your brother Xavier thinks you are very talented."

Her attention shifts to Arthur. Something has struck a chord with her, and she is suddenly interested in what he has to say. Xavier is her weakness, he suspects, someone who can reach her where others can't.

"You are much better, no?" she asks.

"Yes, thanks to Anja and Eugène and you, and Xavier of course, who is a saint."

"Oh, he was not always saintly. Before he was a priest, before he studied medicine, he had a wicked sense of humour."

She moves to the kitchen, and Arthur stands up, feels the need to be as busy as she is.

"I will tell you a story," she says, "but you mustn't let on that you know."

She puts butter in a saucepan, stirs it to melt.

"I can cook my own," Arthur says, "if you would rather."

"It is fine. Go to the table and rest."

He sits back down and watches her crack an egg into the pan. She wears a long skirt in dark blue and a cream-coloured blouse with a high neck and sleeves that cover the length of her arms. The only flesh exposed is on her face and hands, though he can see the shape of her narrow body. Her movements are quick and deliberate, bobbing from task to task like a finch.

His stomach rumbles at the smell of cooking.

"Xavier used to play pranks on Gène all the time because he knew he would get a reaction. Harmless things boys do, and I was on the receiving end of those also from time to time. As you might have seen, Gène can become moody and explosive. Xavier once went out and collected all the frogs he could find over days and put them in Gène's bed sheets. What do you English say . . . All hell broke loose?"

He smiles as she brings the fried egg to the table with a piece of white bread, which is rare, and she sits across to watch him, elbows on the table, face in her hands.

"Thank you for this. You have access to good food."

She looks away briefly, bites her top lip.

"Are you eating?"

"No," she says. "I should probably get back."

He is disappointed, eyes downward on his egg so his feelings can't be seen.

"I could stay a little while," she says.

"If you need to leave, I will understand. It isn't safe out there." His eyes stray to the bruise on her face.

She glances out the window, then back again. "I will keep you company for a little while. I am sorry we are all so busy, Arthur. You must be bored out of your mind stuck in here. I should try and find some playing cards. Maybe next time."

He was never one for cards.

She is suddenly curious about him. "It shouldn't be too long before you are home?"

"Yes," he says.

"You are probably keen to return to your family and country."

He nods. "I am." *I had a son.* She mustn't know that.

She is looking at Arthur with her darkest of blue eyes, and he feels that he knows her already. Xavier has spoken so much about his family.

"Do you have any brothers or sisters?"

"No," he says, placing down his knife and fork. "I believe my mother wanted more children."

"Your parents?"

"Dead. My father worked in a colliery. Worked hard, shortened his own life in an attempt to lengthen mine. We had a strange, strained relationship at times as fathers and sons sometimes do."

"Do you miss them?" she says.

245

"I suppose I did, or do . . . I never really think about it. We all just get on with things. All make do." No one has ever asked him. Odd that he has never even thought about missing his own father. Though he knows how good he was, how simple he made their life, so that they didn't want for anything. He can sense that Josephine is genuinely interested, and he has a need to tell her things.

"My mother went first, early, so memories of her are less clear, but the ones I have are of someone dedicated and kind. My father was distant in manner, yet he was a good man, modest. He never wanted any reward for fatherhood, for sacrifice. He did not think he did anything remarkable, or anything that warranted a lot of praise. I went to an independent school, my parents sacrificing a lot so I would make it through the world, to surpass them if I could, as any parent wants . . ." Arthur stops because there is an emotional lump swelling at the back of his throat. He is thinking of sacrifice, of a long life for his son, and how he would gladly swap his life for Jack's.

"You have gone quite pale, Monsieur Shine," says Josephine.

"Call me Arthur," he says, panic now lodged in his chest. "I have eaten too fast perhaps."

He closes his eyes.

"Are you sure you're all right? Can I get you something?"

A sense of doom sneaks up on him when he least expects it, makes him feel cold and renders him speechless for several moments. She is unsure what to do, perched close for an instruction of some kind.

"This war works against men in more ways than battle," he says, opening his eyes, the sensation passing. "Please forgive my turn."

"I am sorry. I shouldn't keep you talking. I should go. Anja is back tomorrow, and I will be working at the hotel for a couple of days, so I won't be here until the end of the week."

He regrets the things he cannot control, the thoughts, dark sometimes. Memories that come back to shut him down.

He nods, and she is gone, though not completely. She has left something of herself behind, a small fire that brightens and warms a corner of his soul. She has brought out something in him also. A curiosity, a desire to be better. He had wanted her to know things. *Why?* They are passing ships. Like in war, friendships should be avoided. Yet this was unavoidable, this meeting. He knows it to be true.

The sound of distant rumbling and machines running somewhere shakes him out of deep thoughts. He is ready to sleep now, his mind strangely devoid of noise.

25. GOODBYE

Gisela coughs into her handkerchief, and her whole body shakes from the assault on her lungs. These sudden sharp expulsions throughout the night kept Josephine awake. The previous evening she entered her mother's bedroom with a bowl of steaming water and oils that Xavier had left her with. She had rubbed her mother's back until she fell asleep. Then this morning, after more rest, Gisela is brighter.

"It is the change in weather," she says.

If you are any worse, Maman, Xavier had said previously, *you will have to go to hospital.*

"I have weathered these before. It will pass."

She does not remember her mother this frail.

Josephine brushes her chin-length hair and dons her cap. The haircut at least prevents her mother from plaiting it, though Gisela does not appear to care about her daughter's appearance lately. She makes no comment about Josephine's dress, no move to tidy her collar, check for stains, tuck away an errant strand of hair. She looks frail and small, sinking into her body in the chair by the window.

Gisela has some of her handiwork for Josephine to deliver to Vivienne before she starts work at the hotel today.

"I would go myself, but I don't think I will make it."

"Of course, Maman," she says, placing a shawl around the older woman's shoulders. Gisela is constantly cold despite the mild weather.

Franz is leaving for the Front tomorrow. His police job has been handed to someone else in the meantime. In some way it is a relief that she does not have to worry so much about playing different people: one for the restaurant, one for her evenings at La Vérité, and one for Franz. If he were a spy and using her, he would ask questions that are suspicious. His questions are always harmless: How is your mother? Do you have enough bread? And then talk of him, his past, her past, and more recently their future. There is nothing to suspect he is spying on her. Besides, they are lovers now, of sorts, secretly betrothed. Yet when they aren't together, their betrothal seems more imaginary. As with one of her stories, she can close the book at any time, and Franz is left between the pages. *Am I only playing a part?* She is not sure. Reality is growing harder to define.

She has seen Eugène several times at La Vérité since he caught her and Franz, but he has timed his visits to Gisela when Josephine wasn't there. Knowing her brother as well as she does, she is doubtful that his suspicions have gone away, and he is unlikely to forget. He was a little softer after the assault, but she cannot see him remaining this way.

He is ashamed of his outburst, said Anja when they were alone. *I have spoken to him about it. I have convinced him that Franz is harmless, that he is smitten. I have seen it myself. Though you should know my thoughts on that, and thankfully you do not feel the same.*

No, of course not, said Josephine, her torment hidden.

"Oh my goodness. Your face, your hair!" Vivienne says, turning her around to examine it from the back.

Josephine explains the reason, the people who were arrested because of it. Though she has not forgiven them, she has found no joy in their arrest, no sense of justice. People do extreme things in war; they have to fight for everything.

Vivienne has asked her to stay a minute. She opens the brown paper that Gisela has wrapped her dress in. It was made with striped yellow silk that Vivienne provided her, sewn completely by Gisela's fine hand. There is wide cream lace frill on the rounded neckline and an overskirt of chiffon, small lace-edged sleeves, and a wide satin sash just below the bust.

"She is so talented, your mother," says Vivienne, who puts it up against herself to look in the mirror.

Josephine has thought much about the last incident in the hotel room, confined it to a moment of naivety and confusion. It seems that Vivienne is the only one who will understand, who can be trusted with spicy titbits and trivialities that seem vacuous against the work that Josephine does in secret.

Josephine waits for Grace to bounce from the room to get something before telling Vivienne about her rejection. Vivienne's laugh is high and sweet. She finds much amusement in Josephine's painful description of her assertiveness.

"Why, it is not rejection at all, you silly girl! He wants you pure, isn't it obvious? He would not promise you things if he didn't mean them. He does not strike me as fickle or untruthful. Quite the opposite."

Vivienne smiles as if she always knows a little more than anyone else. *What does he tell her?* Josephine wonders, enviously.

"You should feel pleased with yourself. That you have won a heart without other demands."

Vivienne's eyes wander over the younger woman enquiringly, a hint of envy in her small frown.

"Anyway, it's too late now. You are beholden."

He is as much beholden to me as I am to him!

"And by the way, your hair looks very pretty that length. Wait here while I fetch some makeup for your face, so you do not frighten the patrons."

She feels a little better leaving Vivienne's, not so alone, not such a fool. Vivienne gives her that at least. Though still, there is much about her that Josephine doesn't know.

Anja is not at work today since they no longer share a shift.

It is probably because we talk too much, Anja speculated after they were told. *I feel that people don't like Belgians growing close, in case they are colluding.*

Josephine is stuck with Renée, who has grown more annoying, if that were possible. She is haughty and bossy despite the fact she knows so little about anything. Benôit has noticed it, too, a look of disgust toward her every time her back is turned.

Both girls are in the kitchen, waiting for plates that Chef is creating. The restaurant is quiet today, one table only.

Do you know who Renée's father is? Anja said. *He is a German soldier whose wife's family lives here. That is why we can't touch her, but more that we can't trust her, either.*

Renée makes a joke about a Belgian woman being arrested, about how prison will solve her weight problem, while Josephine bites her tongue and Chef pretends not to hear. She has already made a joke about the bruise, mostly concealed now, on Josephine's face, which she ignored also.

Chef has beaten some cream with sugar to serve with the fruit that he is cutting into slices. Renée stretches out a fleshy finger on the end of one short, pink arm to scoop up some cream that she pokes between her rubbery lips.

"Don't do that," says Josephine.

Renée laughs in response, as if she were a child, as if it were a game.

"Only Monsieur Fallières can tell me what to do," she says, walking away shielded by her self-importance. "Though he doesn't because he knows he can't."

When she is gone, Chef thumps the bench hard with the pestle, crushing nuts as if they were the fingers that have stolen the cream.

"*Sacrebleu!* That one is cursed!" he says.

Franz is waiting for her outside the hotel.

"I have a surprise."

He is also the surprise. He had told her he would call on her that evening at her home to say goodbye. She looks beyond to where he is pointing, to an automobile parked out front.

"Is that yours?"

"For an hour or so, then I have to return it."

"When are you leaving Brussels?"

"Later tonight. Which is why I'm taking you to the river, so we can have some moments of privacy before I leave. And then I can drive you straight home from there."

They stop at a grassy bend in the river, where it is quiet, away from city eyes. He has medicine for her mother that he promised, after he heard that she was sick.

Franz looks ordinary, boyish, not a soldier at all without the armour of a uniform. She likes him better this way.

He places a blanket on the ground, and they sit to watch the ducks that dip and dive, and they shade their eyes from the swaying streak of gold that bounces off the water.

"How long will you be gone?" she asks.

"I'm not sure exactly. They expect the exercise to go for three months or longer. But I am not that far away by train, and there may be opportunities to return during then."

He is difficult to read: a serious face, a thought, a frown, and then he looks away and then back again. In an hour he will be gone to war, and she may not see him again.

"It is dangerous," she says, plucking wilted yellow wildflowers. People die in war. Yves. Her father. What would he say if he could see her now? She blinks the thought away, but the ache of loss remains.

"Did you bring what I asked?" he says.

She produces the small photograph, taken back in Louvain. He examines the image.

"You are laughing in this one," he says, placing it in his shirt pocket.

"Don't sound so surprised," she says, in jest. "I wasn't always so stern."

He takes her hand, squeezes it. Suddenly the world is seen through tears, and she is in his arms, and he is kissing her eyes. There is desire, the touch of a hand, the sweet smell of his neck, her face full of sun before it falls from the sky. Then his lips on hers and she can hardly draw breath, and she is lowered onto the grass until he pulls away to lie on his back. They are side by side, warm arms together.

"We will get through this," he says to the sky, as if he is convincing himself. He is perhaps nervous about battle.

Then the hour is quickly over with, and they are back in the car, and she is thrust out of desire and back into the dark streets where people glare.

She envies Anja and Eugène, the spontaneity, the way they don't need to hide or fear their relationship at least. A wayward kiss on the eyelids, Anja climbing on top of him when they are seated, and the touch of a private part flirtatiously when they don't think someone is looking. That is not her relationship with Franz, and it is not that which bothers her. It is the way she can shift her feelings back and forth too easily. Is it love to want someone, a better life, but not think of them when one is alone? Not dwell on a future with them at all.

"I will write to you twice a week," he says.

The euphoria she was feeling leaves with him, and only guilt and shame remain. She cares about him, yet why does this not feel like love?

How will I know I'm in love, Papa?

You will know because every time you see him, your eyes will light up, your heart will feel like it might burst through your chest, and your head will feel like it is floating.

26. FATE AND FEELINGS

Anja is missing and Eugène is in a state. It has been three days since anyone has seen her. Xavier has gone to check the last sightings of her at the safe house; the elderly couple who lives there said she had left them late. She had called in to make sure they were all right, then had gone on to the next location with clothes. Xavier said he went there, too, to the house, but it was vacant, no signs of a disturbance, though he found clothing dumped in a corner. He thought he had been followed at one point, had retraced his steps, then tried again. There were men working on the side of the road last time he was there, and this time there was no sign of them. The group has agreed to suspend operations unless it is urgent.

"Did you say anything to *that German*, anything at all?" says Eugène.

"You know I wouldn't," says Josephine defensively. Arthur can see that her hands are trembling slightly.

"Think!" says Eugène. "Did you mention anything about where you go, what you do?"

She touches her temples with one set of fingertips, squeezes her eyes as if she is remembering, doubting herself almost. Arthur hates the inquisition.

"Did you?" Eugène says closer to her ear.

"No!"

"Try to remember everything!"

He is leaving her little room to think.

"That's enough, Gène!" says Xavier, who leads him to the table, pushes him gently to sit down. "Be calm! You will drive yourself mad."

Josephine walks over to Eugène, grips his arms with her hands so that he will look in her face.

"Eugène, I have told him nothing about us, about La Vérité. I have not been to the other safe house for some time. I have checked that no one follows me here. Even the street sweepers, if they look my way, I turn back, wait, then go a different way. You have to trust me."

Arthur is amazed at the patience of both Xavier and Josephine. They are used to their brother's moods, grown immune to them almost, and rehearsed on how they treat him.

He drops his head into his hands, and Arthur can feel the wretchedness from where he stands. Eugène is wounded, helpless.

"You need to keep a level head, Gène, until we find out more," says Xavier, who can be persuasive without being loud like his brother.

They have thrown blankets over the curtain rails to block out any light inside.

"We have to think on this carefully," says Xavier. "Perhaps she knew she was being followed and is waiting to come back here."

"Someone would have got word to us," says Eugène. "If it is the de Croÿs, they would have made contact by now. They were the ones who first helped Anja when she escaped at the beginning of the war. If she had gone there, she would have sent word to us by now. The de Croÿs have many connections."

"Has the manager said anything about Anja not turning up?" Eugène asks.

"He was angry that she didn't show," says Josephine. "He made a fuss, though only in front of me, and Chef."

"And the message in an envelope that I left you at the hotel the day that Anja didn't return?" says Eugène. "Did anyone find it?"

"No one remembers any message."

"Someone is lying then. Perhaps the girl that Anja couldn't stand, Renée, has been spying on the both of you," says Eugène. "Perhaps she is in with Franz."

"We can't just jump to conclusions," says Xavier. "We have to be wary of her and others, but there is more to this perhaps than the obvious. Someone must have seen Anja."

"Could she have taken someone to the border?" says Arthur.

"You said the clothes were there, but no soldiers, Xavier," says Josephine. "She may have taken the men directly to the border that night."

"She would not have done that," says Eugène. "They did not have their identity documents yet. That was the message I sent to Josephine. To come to La Vérité to pick up the camera. All in code."

"We must begin a search," says Xavier. "Gène can call into those houses on his transport routes, and I will visit the ones he can't."

"It will be too dangerous for you," says Josephine, imagining him caught and sent back to prison.

Xavier takes both his sister's hands. "I am careful. Do not worry. You need to be here for Maman and Arthur and others who might be brought here in an emergency. You are more likely to be missed than anyone. I will tell the hospital I am needed at the border field station.

"Gène," says Xavier. "You need to just do your job for a while for the Germans. Don't deviate outside the route. And watch your back, Josephine, when you are coming here. Continue printing if you wish, but distribution will have to stop for now. If anyone looks at you, if there is anything minor that looks suspicious, go home again."

Despair and helplessness plague the canal house. Xavier and Eugène failed to find anything that could lead them to Anja. She has been missing for three weeks, and there has been further bad news since. Shortly after her disappearance, an English nurse by the name of Edith Cavell, Marie de Croÿ, and others supporting the cause were arrested. No one knows what will happen to them, whether their incarceration is permanent and what they will be charged with. It seems likely that Anja has been imprisoned, too. But there is no way to find this out. Eugène has exhausted all avenues, and not knowing is driving him mad.

"We are operational again," announced Eugène a week earlier, bringing people that Arthur had never seen in the time he has been there. "Our network is growing. We will continue to distribute our news and hide our allies. The smugglers are establishing new crossings."

Sometimes Eugène flies into a rage over the smallest thing, from a mistake on the printing to someone who has pulled out of the network with fears for their family. Though the root cause is that he misses Anja, that he is angry with himself more than anyone. Arthur listens to him pace and torture himself upstairs, sometimes muttering to no one, crying occasionally. Then in the middle of the night, he might fly downstairs, as if he has just remembered something, and exit the door and not be back for hours. Arthur has tried to coach him about his concerns, but he doesn't seem to hear, his demons speaking louder.

It used to be that no one frequented the safe houses unless to deliver an item, person, or urgent message. Now strangers are calling in often. Eugène has lost some caution.

Clack, clack . . . ding.

Arthur wakes to noises downstairs. He had not heard anyone come in during the night. She walks with such a soft step. He welcomes the interruption. No one has visited him for days. Eugène is away again, Xavier is with his contacts down south, and Josephine has taken on half of Anja's shifts at the hotel.

He would have liked Jack to meet her, meet all these people. He can imagine his son would have got on well with all of them. It is strange, he thinks, how he measures people in Jack's eyes. He wishes he had done that before. Perhaps it is where he went wrong, that he didn't always see things from Jack's perspective.

Arthur rises, presses his weight down on his bad leg, then reaches for his walking stick. He has seen himself in the small mirror in the bathroom, eyes hollow, face gaunt, skin pasty, but almost back to whole. He steps carefully down the stairs, supported by the rusting metal banister.

Josephine is typing, the gold globe above her forms a halo around her hair. She looks up as he approaches.

"I'm sorry if I woke you," she says, pretty and poised, and unsuited, he feels, to death and espionage, and undeserving of the dust of drama that constantly settles on her shoulders.

"No, you didn't wake me," says Arthur. "I just can't sleep. What is that you're typing this time?"

"Summaries of news from Holland and Germany." She has stopped and turned to talk to him.

"Are you worried about Anja?" he says.

"A little," she says, lips pressed together, thinking. "But she is tough. Wherever she is, I expect her to be all right. She is a master of lies, a true escape artist. She is smart, too," she says, smiling with a memory that has just surfaced, before her face falls again. "I'm worried about Xavier more at present. I don't want to lose him again. He is pulled in so many different directions. And Gène, too. I am worried he will do something rash."

"Is there anything I can help you with here?"

"No," she says. "Just rest up. Gène hopes to take you safely across the border soon. It must be frustrating, the waiting, the changes every time we think we are ahead of the game. As you know the Germans have caught many people escaping, those outside our line."

There is much talk about that. With the electrified fencing and the increase in patrols along the border, it has become more difficult.

"I am willing to wait a while longer. I don't want to put you and your brothers in any danger."

She looks at him, studies his face intensely. He is concerned at how he looks, what she thinks of him. *Why should it matter?*

"I'd like to help at least, in other ways," he says.

"Anja used to translate some of the English articles, which I'm afraid I'm not very good at."

"Perhaps I can help you when you get more of them."

"Have you ever used a French typewriter?"

"I can learn, but perhaps it will be quicker initially if I read the English news aloud while you type."

"Yes, I like that idea," she says. "I could use some help elsewhere, too."

She gives him the task of tying up the newspapers into bundles of certain numbers she has on a list and writing a name, a code, on the front of them.

"And what of your German friend?" he says.

"You have heard much about him, I presume," she says, looking down at the keys on the machine that might rescue her from further questions.

"Yes, I did hear something in passing. Nothing of much substance, only that you have a friend." He omits the coarseness of Eugène's past conversations with Anja.

"I know it upsets Gène," she says. "You don't have to cover for him. He would have said a lot more than that."

She is too perceptive. He shouldn't have expected less.

"We grew quite close, or so I thought," she says, leaning forward to check something on the page, a mark that she frowns at. "I haven't heard from him since he left weeks ago. It is nothing." Though the last sentence is something she is telling herself, he thinks.

"Letters sometimes take a while to get through," he says.

She types the last sentence on the page, then winds the paper out. She moves to stand beside him at the worktable.

"I know about your son. Xavier told me," she says directly, and he can see something of her brother Xavier in the shape of her mouth, in the soft, round eyes that search for truth.

He nods. She probably knows about Harriet, too, then.

"Jack is his name," he says.

"Can you tell me a bit about him?"

Arthur stops what he is doing, too, arms crossed and leaning against the table.

He can hear Jack's laugh somewhere in his mind. He can see into his own broken heart for just a second, to see that there are good memories in there also, that he had willfully forgotten, the question opening the door wider to a place where Jack is more alive. Arthur thinks of all the marvelous things his son did, the paintings, the cheer, the desire to haphazardly make the world his own.

Even the small church service he arranged following the telegram was impersonal, a platitude about loss and salvation, a word of kindness from the vicar followed by hand holding and pats on the shoulder for courage. It was more about Arthur's loss and Harriet's than about Jack and the years he gave them. He should have said something; thrown away his bitterness about the loss for more than a brief moment, been more resilient, told stories, relived the years.

Josephine is gazing at him, searchingly, innocently. She is too young for so much tragedy. Like Jack, too young. But her yearning to understand a world that he had almost given up on gives him new life. *Is it selfish to want that?*

"He was quite the character," he says. "He was always in trouble. Always looking to do the wrong thing, but not in a truly awful way."

She laughs then, looks away to the floor, pondering, as if she can sense him, too; as if she can see what Arthur does.

"I didn't know about parenting a son who wants to do his own thing, who wants to challenge the order of whatever came before them, of authority. No one prepares you for parenthood, certainly not the fact there is a fair chance they will be nothing like you. He was bright and always had lots of friends. He loved sports, life, girls. I only had one girl, and that was Harriet," he says, watching to see what she makes of it, her curious expression encouraging.

He is sinking deeper now, lost in his own memories, staring at the nib of a pen that he realises he is still holding, something physical to affix his thoughts to.

"Fun wasn't something I wanted for Jack. I wanted more for him. I wanted, no, I expected him to take over the accountancy practice, but he didn't want that. He didn't know what he wanted. When he was expelled from the same boarding school I had been to, I thought military was the best. He loved it, too, it seems. He excelled, like he was born to it. I supposed I'd got it right in one way. Just my timing was bad it seems. War came, and he was gone. Didn't even tell us he had left the country. And there you have it, nineteen years old, a bright, young spark gone, and the war barely started.

"I'm rambling . . . ," says Arthur, looking up to see that she has tears in her eyes.

She reaches out to squeeze his hand tight and hold it there. He is first surprised then momentarily spellbound by the gesture.

She draws her hand away again, wipes her eyes, and turns back to her work.

The moment is gone, though the effects are still there. A friendship sealed.

27. WORD OF FRANZ

Lady Vivienne has invited them for morning tea. She examines the sample that Gisela has brought her, then is shocked by the sound of the older woman's cough. Gisela insisted she come, which Vivienne has now asserted wasn't a good idea.

"You should be home in bed . . . Maud!" she says, the girl standing nearby. "Bring Madame Descharmes some lemon water with a spoonful of honey."

Maud glances at Gisela peevishly before exiting the room, without the sense of urgency that Josephine is expecting from someone in her position, leaving the group to discuss the war, the usual things, the length of it, the cost of food. Vivienne talks about the deprivations, though Josephine can't see any evidence of it here.

"My housemaid managed to get some butter and eggs, but I had to pay three times the price."

On the coffee table in front of them are small cakes with icing, and a heavy sponge rolled with jam. Vivienne's daughter enters, following the scent of sugar.

"Grace," she says. "Only one, darling."

Grace struggles to decide which one to take before settling back on the seat closest to Josephine.

"It is terrible about the recent arrests," says Gisela. "Why they would even think to imprison a nurse who treats their soldiers."

Did Vivienne flinch?

"I am sure it is just a misunderstanding," says Vivienne brusquely, "and they will release the women and others they have taken in for questioning."

Vivienne appears lost for a moment, eyes searching for distraction, before she reaches for her teacup. Gisela is poised to speak again.

"Has the general been in this week?" says Vivienne, before Gisela can comment further.

"No," says Josephine. "I've not seen him for at least a fortnight." Prior to that Josephine had seen him there with several different women.

"Hmm," she says, pretending she is not interested. Josephine can see that she is bothered by something, perhaps the fact that she has not received an invitation recently.

She taps Josephine on the knee with one narrow white hand.

"I have received a letter from our friend Franz."

Josephine is not expecting to hear his name, and her eyes dart to Gisela, whose teacup touches her saucer with slightly more force than is necessary.

"He is bearing up, but he is in amongst it, poor dearest. Have you heard from him?"

I will write to you twice a week. He had said that to Josephine, though it may have been just words in the moment. Perhaps she is not the only one he has said that to.

"No," says Josephine. She keeps her gaze steady, tries not to appear curious or shocked to hear his name.

It makes Josephine sad to think of Franz injured, if he is even still alive. But if she is honest with herself, she has not thought of him in the loving way she'd hoped.

Gisela clears her throat, then sips the lemon water that is thrust into her hands, Maud not born to serve. From somewhere else originally, from better circumstances by the attitude, thinks Josephine. Such talk is making her mother nervous. She had a slight change of heart about Vivienne when she learned from elsewhere about the officers she entertains, when she saw one leave her house.

She runs with the hounds and hides with the hares, said Gisela.

Though Vivienne's illicit activities are still not bad enough for Gisela to turn down her business.

"Now, Grace, do play us some of the piano you've been learning recently," Vivienne says, and turns to the ladies proudly. "I've been teaching her myself. Her piano teacher was caught stealing from another residence recently. He has been taken to prison."

Both Vivienne's guests feign a degree of surprise at the news, since it is commonplace now, the arrests.

Elated by the request, Grace springs to position herself on the piano stool and commences to play. She hits several wrong notes of a tune that is barely recognisable, the sound jarring like the sharpening of a knife against stone, and Gisela grits her teeth. Josephine crosses one arm in front of her with which to lean her other elbow, biting hard on the tip of her thumb.

Josephine can tell that Vivienne is not listening, her head tilted in thought to look out the window with an air of despair. She closes her eyes, frowning a moment. Josephine has not considered that Vivienne's troubles might be worse than her own in some ways. She has presented an illusion of a gilded life, of one that is free. But she isn't. Josephine can see that clearer every time she visits. She is altered. Her hair isn't perfect today; Maud has made a mess of it. And Vivienne doesn't seem to care.

Then they move to sit on the back terrace to catch a ray of warmth, and Grace plucks the last of the sweet-scented lilies before they fade.

Halfway through a conversation Vivienne appears to think of something, excuses herself, and enters the back door.

"I'll be back," says Josephine to her mother as she commences to follow furtively. She pads down the hallway softly, listens to the murmurs of a conversation between Grace and Gisela behind her, sees the trail of Vivienne's skirt creep around the corner and into the drawing room.

Josephine stands back from the doorway to spy on Vivienne near the piano. She peers through the gap in the door to watch their host lift the lid of the instrument, place something inside it, then walk to the window, her face in both her hands.

28. NEWS OF ANJA

Xavier looks solemn as he takes off his hat. He has brought with him a boy, Arthur speculates a few years younger than Jack. Eugène and Arthur stand up to greet them.

"Gène," he says. "This boy is part of the underground. He is the one who helped bring two Allied soldiers for Anja to collect from the safe house that day. He was there the same day as Anja. He lives in the village nearby. He saw what happened—"

"You saw Anja?" says Eugène, interrupting him and addressing only the boy.

"Gène . . . ," says Xavier, trying to finish.

"They came, several men, and we saw them from the windows," says the boy. "We had to hide, my parents and grandparents. We watched from the windows."

"Who's they?"

"Soldiers."

"This was at the house for the injured, no?" says Eugène to clarify, leaning intimidatingly close to the boy.

"They shot the soldiers and some others from the village; then they took her, the girl, they tried to—"

"She was arrested?" says Eugène. "She was taken to prison?"

The boy has grown nervous, looking at Xavier and back to Eugène.

"Gène," says Xavier, stepping forward to take his arm. "Anja was shot."

Eugène yanks away his arm and steps closer to the boy, who moves his head slightly backward.

"What did you see exactly?"

Arthur can see the answer even if Eugène can't. He is fighting the truth like Arthur did once. They have rounded up so many this past month. They had seized an underground newspaper. Edith Cavell, it is said, had helped many of the Allied soldiers she was treating escape across the border. That much they had learned so far. She will likely be charged with aiding them.

"Gène," says Xavier, "I will go and check the house."

"Where is she now?"

"They buried her beside the house with two others."

Eugène grits his teeth and turns to punch a wall several times, blood on his knuckles, and emits a cry that is more like a howl, deep and guttural.

Arthur and Xavier have moved to stop him from harming himself, Xavier taking him in his arms, Eugène's head now on his shoulder, sobbing, his body shaking. Arthur turns away from this private moment between brothers.

"I have to see for myself," says Eugène, finally pulling away.

"Let me go instead," says Xavier.

"I won't be dropping the vehicle back until tomorrow. I'm going there now. Please, Xav, don't try and stop me."

The two men face each other.

"Then I'm going with you," says Xavier.

Arthur knows it is dangerous. Even worse for everyone if they are both caught, but it seems that Eugène will not back down.

"I will come with you, too," says Arthur. "We are safer in numbers. I am good with a gun if need be."

Arthur is finally walking without a stick, spending time stepping up and down the stairs to exercise.

Arthur, Xavier, and the boy are in the back of the truck. Arthur carries a gun, given by Eugène, which the brothers believe won't be necessary. Eugène has been this way before. There are no sentries along the route. But being stopped is a secondary concern, Eugène's mind on Anja, on seeing the truth for himself.

As they enter the village, Eugène lets the boy out to run home, then drives down a rise and up again. He turns into a track to a small farmhouse, a sad, sagging silhouette against the starlit blue. The boy reported that Germans have been back here several times, interviewed people in the village. He had waited until there was no more sign of them before he made the trip to Xavier's house.

The house sits once more abandoned, according to the boy. Illuminated under the light of a small torch, there is a raised mound of earth beside the house just as the boy described. Eugène gently pushes his brother out of the way. There is no anger this time, just a determination to get it over with. To know. His pain contained for now.

They have no shovels, and the three men dig out the cool, damp earth with their hands.

"Here," says Eugène, finding something. Though it is not Anja, it is the body of a soldier, then another one found quickly after that.

Lastly, another face emerges from the soil, grey and green, and smoothed of dirt, her mouth stretched into a hideous caricature of the girl she was before: long, shiny dark hair, eyes of liquid brown. Xavier's arm slips around his younger brother's shoulders, with little hesitation, like he has done this many times before, to whisper words of comfort that Arthur knows will not be remembered. Not for days. It's how grief works to begin with. It suspends all rational thought. It waits insidiously behind the pretence of normalcy, then ambushes its prey when they least expect it, often at their weakest.

Arthur steps away to allow them some privacy and to wait for the sounds of a broken heart. Instead Eugène is silent. Xavier, too.

"It isn't her," says Eugène flatly, his voice steady, his grief on hold.

Xavier steps besides Arthur, breathing out a sigh. He shakes his head.

"No, it isn't Anja."

29. AN END

Franz has been gone over two months, and Anja just as long. It is over a year since the Descharmes family first arrived in Brussels. Leaves of gold that have caught the wind from the north swirl around Josephine as she hurries toward work. The air in the restaurant recently seems stale and starved of joie de vivre. Not that any of the staff ever felt it, since that privilege is only for the elite. Instead, it is more sombre, meetings are serious, quiet voices low in the cigar room, armchairs pushed together so conversations can't be overheard. Fewer Belgians are coming to socialise, and officers, back from their planning in the field, march through with boots now crusted with sludge, their jackets seasoned with old sweat and French dust, and shirt cuffs edged with grime.

Benôit has had to change the menu again to suit whatever raw goods are available. If not for the imported goods, there would not be enough for their fancy plates, though people back in Germany are also feeling the restriction of food from the naval blockade. Chef's big hands and grunts of perseverance continue to conjure up splendid dishes, according to the diners, but with servings smaller.

Benôit keeps a share of food for all staff now, aware that the cost of living is higher than the pay. He is altered, more on edge, spending time fussing through papers he seems to have lost control of on his desk, looking up suddenly when Josephine walks in, as if he has been caught doing something he shouldn't. He never once questioned her about the day she ran from Franz's hotel room, as if he had already learned about it elsewhere.

You must stop daydreaming, said Benôit one time when she was looking from the window, thinking about Anja, wishing she were there. *There is still so much work to do!* Though even he seemed somewhere else in his thoughts when he spoke.

It is raining heavily and loudly, awnings filling up with water and threatening to spill over onto passersby. The autumn nights are growing colder, and Josephine is worn and tired and hungry. She has nothing to take home again today, and without Franz, they may not have enough coal to get them through the winter. Lady Vivienne is very generous with her payments, and they can sometimes afford items that others cannot, but it does not always keep Gisela from the soup queue.

Several people stand huddled under a shelter, faces deep inside an open newspaper that one man holds up, words of horror, of disgust uttered at something they have read. She moves a little quicker to get home. Eugène will surely know what it is.

"Where is Gène?" Josephine asks. "I thought he was coming."

Gisela puts the plates down on the table heavily.

"He will be here soon," she says, flour on her apron and across her face.

She hugs her mother. A surge of love for Gisela, her reliability, the way she carries on, children first, always. It is hard on her with her husband gone, the two of them once sewn together and weaving children into the home they created for all of them. Josephine is grateful she is there to come home to every day.

"What is that for?" asks Gisela, flushed and light and pretending not to be affected by the spontaneous affection that is rare from her daughter, whose attentions were always on her father.

"Just that I love you," she says.

"Did you hear?" says Eugène, entering in a rush, whipping up the curtains beside the door. "They have executed Edith Cavell and another."

"Surely not!" Josephine says, the two women pulling apart, the gentle moment vanishing. "People are killed for protecting others. It is war but it is not. It is greed and evil. There are no words but these."

"It has something to do with Anja missing, too, I am certain," says Eugène. "They were likely arrested at the same time."

They have had to cancel some of the resistance line, disconnect some of the houses they use, Xavier now working at the Brussels hospital most of the time.

Eugène is poring over every word in another underground newspaper.

"It is a scandal. It is surely against the law to execute someone who treats all wounded, who does not care what side they fight for! Your captain's replacement has had a hand in her arrest, no doubt."

Josephine looks away, tensing. Something has just come back to her, a moment that seemed irrelevant at the time. And may be irrelevant still. She won't mention it to Eugène, who is looking for every excuse to lay some blame.

You are very close to Anja, yes? Franz had said once.

He would have seen them whispering to one another much of the time, smiling at each other across the room, a secret between them.

Yes. She is a good friend.

Though now she thinks about the question. Harmless or leading? And Renée. Josephine remembers the disinterest in her face, the apparent lack of guile, the annoyance at being asked something when she was busy picking her nails, busy doing nothing. Or could it be that she is neither ignorant nor innocent, but a clever actress?

After the question, Franz had changed the subject then, and no mention of Anja after that. Then he was gone and so was Anja. There are too many people gone, dead, missing.

"You must be careful, Josephine," says Gisela when they are alone. "This roundup of people. It is too dangerous."

Josephine agrees. The stakes are now higher, the fact that they execute women in full view of the world without apology.

Another day of work, still filling Anja's absence. Josephine is tired from being pulled in so many directions. She hurries inside the house, eager for solace from her mother. She has come to depend on her being there.

Gisela sits at the table with her head lowered.

"Maman?"

Her mother raises her head, eyes filled with tears.

"What is wrong?" says Josephine, hastening to her side.

"We can't forget about them." Josephine can see that Gisela is holding a photograph of Yves and Maurice.

"We won't, Maman. Ever!"

She helps her mother stand and leads her to the bedroom. She is listless, exhausted from her grieving. As Josephine assists her mother into her night attire, she sees the folds of skin where Gisela carried the four of them, the gold chain and cross around her neck that was handed down from her own mother. She has developed a stoop since she came, and her cough is harsh this evening; it brews and crackles in her chest.

From the medicine box, Josephine takes some of the tablets Xavier has brought to help her sleep. She crushes them in water, then helps her mother sip the liquid. Gisela then slips beneath the covers and rolls away with a faint groan to face the wall. Comfort, Josephine hopes, might come to her in dreams.

She looks around the room, which has a layer of dust, Gisela too weary, too distant from this new life to notice. This place is like a mausoleum now, the city oppressive. Gisela must leave. They both must. Josephine has often thought about the idea, but for thoughts of Franz, of love that should not happen. There is nothing really keeping her. Xavier and Eugène must make their own choices. She must get her mother out of here. And Arthur, what of him? He is eager to be home, to fight again. Parting with him, she imagines, will not be easy. She has grown to like his company.

30. A FLAME IN THE WIND

Eugène has taken the last of the newspapers and loaded them into the back of the car, hidden under a shipment of rain capes.

The weather is dire. Rain in sheets day after day as if it will never cease. It drips monotonously through the ceiling into a metal bucket, and dampness coats Arthur's clothes, bed, furniture, and paper, too, which he has left near a heater to stop pages sticking together. He has used up all the kerosene.

The rain blows sideways, pushing Josephine through the doorway, pellets of water swirling in after her.

"Here," says Arthur, rushing to assist her, closing the door against a heavy squall. "Let me help you."

He takes off his coat to place around her shoulders.

"Is Gène here?" she says, looking up toward the attic.

"No, you've just missed him. He is back tomorrow," he says.

She is thinking, small creases between her eyebrows.

"I'm sure he is fine," says Arthur.

"It's not that . . ."

"Heavens, you look terrible. What has happened?" Her eyes are red and swollen. She has been crying. "Are you all right?"

"Maman is worsening. Xavier thinks she might have pneumonia, but she has refused to go to the hospital. She is stubborn. He is watching her tonight." From her bag she pulls out a wedge of cheese, a potato, and some oats. "Xavier brought things back and said to bring you these.

"And these, too?" she says, holding out a pair of secondhand trousers while studying the ones he wears that show his ankles.

"What is he trying to say, do you think?"

"That you look ridiculous," she says with a trace of humour.

"I'm sorry about your mother," he says.

She is shivering, her fingernails turning blue.

"I should keep moving to stay warm."

She enters the basement, sounds of clatter. She is tidying, looking for things to do.

"Are you hungry?" Arthur calls down the stairs.

She comes back up, wraps the coat tighter around her body.

"A little."

She grips a piece of cheese with long, bony fingers and nibbles at it. When she is finished eating, she stands near the window in the kitchen to watch the rain on the canal. He has done that enough times himself. It gets boring here. He has begun to write a short history of his time in the war so far, to pass the hours.

"Are you lonely?" she asks.

"Yes," he says. He was almost going to lie.

Her hair appears lighter where she stands, wavy and sitting just above her shoulders now. He had learned the story surrounding her assault though never felt comfortable asking her about it. She turns from the window with tears streaming down her face.

"What is it? Are you all right?"

"Maman's heart is broken again, and she is struggling to get out of bed. It happens sometimes, because of Papa and Yves . . . She tries to put the tragedy out of her mind, and then her grief comes back so suddenly, as often as this stupid rain!"

She perches on the edge of the bed nearby, arms crossed.

"It must be hard on her," he says. "And on you. It is a lot for you to deal with."

She bows her head, tears falling uncontrollably. He sits down next to her, wraps his arms around her to comfort her, and she sinks into his body. She is small and cold against him, face against his chest. She sobs, and he rubs her back until she stops, her body limp with sleep. He lays her down gently on the bed and covers her with a blanket.

"Stay," she whispers, stirring. He lies down next to her, and she nestles into him again and falls back asleep, the drips through the ceiling not so grating now, more rhythmic; and he is falling, too, downward into darkness and then into the colour of dreams.

Hours later he wakes. The bed sinks in the middle so that they are pinned together. Evening has slipped away while they were sleeping, and night has entered the room and brought with it lightning and sounds of thunder. He turns to look at her face, to wait for the strike of light again to see her. When it comes, he is surprised to find she is awake watching him.

She shifts slightly, to rest against him once more. She tells him things, her voice deeper, louder in the tight space between them. She is in Louvain; she is with Yves; she has dropped his hand. She is there the moment her father was killed. She relives it more for her sake but that he might know, too, that Arthur might absorb some of it. And then she asks about him, and it is Arthur's turn, and his voice sounds like someone else's, so unused to retelling his life he has become. All of it almost, the parts at least that no one else has heard. Stories of Jack, the first time he held him, the first time Jack saw his father, the surprise on his son's face, the smile, the fists squeezed in excitement at every discovery. These things he has talked about with no one, not even Harriet. And Josephine asks for more, she wants to know his thoughts, reach inside his head to understand why he is the way he is, why he thinks the way he thinks. He shares his life, his love for Harriet even—the day they met, the times he loved her and the times he didn't. All of it rolling out of him in the space between that is warmed by hot breaths and words until they have both run out of them.

She is clinging to him now, her fingers gripping onto the folds of his shirt. They are stronger together suddenly, loss and history shared.

There is gentle rain that surrounds them like a blanket, the thunder distant now, far south. Her breathing slows again, and he follows her into sleep.

The morning light from the canal window stirs them awake, pries them apart gently, though not completely.

She finds his hand under the covers, slides her fingers into his so they are joined, as if they have always been this way.

"What's the time?" she says, struck by a thought.

He has a pocket watch somewhere that he finds in the folds of the bed sheets.

"I have to go home and dress for work," she says. She sits on the edge of the bed, her back to him. He memorises the shape of her as she stretches her arms above her head. She turns her head, hair messy and beautiful.

She is at the door and looks back.

"Thank you," she says.

He stays where he is, afraid to break what they shared, a hum in his ears from the sudden silence she has left him with.

31. MURDER IN PLAIN SIGHT

Josephine steps on clouds toward Place De Brouckère, a smile lurking at the edge of her mouth, at memories and words that spilled unburdened. There is a strange sensation in her stomach, a twinge that borders on an ache at the thought of her closeness with Arthur, at their building relationship that was left unspoken between them, yet she is certain he feels something, too.

She was home before her mother woke but not before Xavier, whose curious smile made her look away. She has nothing to be ashamed of.

"How is Maman?" she said.

"She is better this morning. I have told her to stay in bed for the day. I will come back to check on her in a couple of hours and tonight . . . if you need to be somewhere else."

She looked at him quickly and away. "No, I am here tonight."

He kissed her on the cheek and reached for the door handle.

"Nothing happened, by the way," she said.

Xavier shrugged and smiled. "You are old enough to do what you want." He turned to go, then stopped. "He is a good man."

God won't judge me? she wanted to ask playfully like she often does about other things. But it seemed childish to talk of it so, to make that time seem smaller than it was.

She notices that the air has become tense as she passes conversations in the lobby of the hotel, and more that continue inside the restaurant.

"A nurse, how do you execute a nurse who looked after German soldiers, all soldiers . . ."

Everyone is talking about the execution. Josephine is guilty of things, too, executable offences. Thoughts of her neck in a rope, of men pointing guns at her heart. She has grown cold again, shaken from a tree in a heavy wind, the moments of the night discarded like withering leaves.

Benôit has been distracted for much of the morning. Something has rattled him, perhaps this news. It is a quarter past twelve, and there are only two tables booked for the whole day. Several tables have cancelled. One table is for a group of Belgians and another for Lady Vivienne. She has booked it herself and invited several elites, officers, to join her. Though only one guest has come so far, and he sits alone to wait for her. Something doesn't feel right.

Vivienne arrives in the yellow silk dress. She wears a round hat with a jewel and ribbon to match the dress colour, and a pearl brooch pinned to the front of her bodice. She is stunning. Blond hair pulled up to show her neck. More makeup today, more colour brushed onto her cheeks. After a period of time, when her other guests fail to show, they place their orders.

Josephine serves the entrée, and Vivienne glances her way, smiles sympathetically as she would to a beggar or a child.

In the kitchen Renée is sitting down since it is quiet. She pulls something from her pocket, a small envelope addressed to Josephine.

"What is this?" says Josephine.

"Something I found in another pocket. I forgot I put it there."

Josephine opens the letter, the note from Eugène about meeting Anja at the house with the camera, the day she had gone missing. It is written in code. Renée would not have understood it if she had been clever enough to open and seal it again.

Josephine is angry, thoughts of that afternoon with Franz.

She grabs Renée's arm roughly, and she squeaks like a child's toy.

"Why didn't you give me this?"

"Let me go! You are crazy! I forgot about it. I just told you."

"You held on to it on purpose, didn't you, you little witch?"

"Ow!" she shrieks.

"Josephine!" says Chef.

Josephine lets her go.

"I'm telling Monsieur Fallières," Renée spits. "You will be fired now."

We can't trust her, Anja said.

"Girls, stop fighting!" says Benôit, who doesn't make eye contact when he says this, his head elsewhere. He can't be bothered today.

"Renée, you are serving now. Get to it!"

She looks smugly at Josephine as she struts out of the kitchen.

"I want you to make a delivery for me," says Benôit, pulling her aside so that they are alone and reaching beneath his collar to pull out a small key that hangs on a chain. Josephine looks at it strangely. She had been expecting terse words instead. "There is a locked drawer at the bottom of my bureau. I want you to take the file from there and pass it on to your brother. No one else can see."

"Brother?" she says, confused.

"Eugène. This is especially important, do you understand?" Sweat trickles down the sides of his face, and he is breathing with some difficulty.

"Are you all right? Do you need a doctor?"

Before he has answered her question and passed the key, he is suddenly distracted. Another officer has walked in through the doors of the restaurant, and Benôit rushes in his direction. He steps toward the newcomer seemingly to block his path. The lieutenant pushes past him.

"Sir, Lieutenant!" says Benôit, following him. "There is a table over here that is free."

The German ignores him and strides toward Vivienne's table before Benôit can catch him. Vivienne looks up as the officer approaches, startled by the urgency in his step. Her companion, his back to all, is still chuckling at something she has just said. Her expression has gone from playful to grim, and the other officer at her table turns to see what ails her, his smile falling also. She rises from her chair.

"You will have to come with me, madame," says the lieutenant.

She remains poised and undaunted, her expression betraying nothing but her own sense of worth with her head high. Vivienne's hand at her side disappears into the folds of her skirt. The next motion of her arm is swift and fluid, the colour of gunmetal, and over in a second. Josephine jumps at the crack that splits the air, the burst of yellow gunfire, aimed at the lieutenant.

Benôit rushes forward, then pauses, mouth open. Vivienne has stopped him with a look, this moment a fragment of apologetic love by both of them. A moment that is shattered by a second shot fired by the guest she may have been charming into the bedroom. Vivienne's body jolts, and her head is thrown slightly backward, pain contorting her immaculate face, as she falls to the ground.

"No, no, no!" says Benôit, who is blind to everything around him except Vivienne. She lies on her side, a red, gaping stain creeping across her bodice and Gisela's lace, blood on her tongue.

Josephine has pulled a cloth from a table, cutlery clattering then bouncing onto the carpet. She presses the cloth against the wound, Benôit on the other side. Vivienne is ashen, colour drawn from her face and seeping out through the hole in her chest.

"Our daughter . . . ," she rasps, her further attempts at speech futile as she chokes on her own blood.

"It is all right, my darling," says Benôit. "She will be safe."

There are guards coming now, running across the square, Josephine can see from the window.

"Josephine, the file," Benôit says, his voice shaking, yanking the chain with the key from around his neck and handing it to her. "Get my daughter!"

"And take her where?"

He looks at Josephine in a daze, cheeks wet with tears.

"Wherever she is safe. Go, please!" These last words almost silent, hopeless. He turns to watch Vivienne take her last breaths.

Josephine runs to the desk. She can hear their running boots, these men that make the choices over who should live. She puts the key in the lock, though her hands are trembling, and the key bounces out of her hand. There are shouts outside the hotel, directions, orders, telling everyone to leave. She picks up the key, stabs at the keyhole, and turns it quickly then. Inside is a grey file tied with string. She places it inside the bodice of her apron, ties the strings tightly around her waist to stop it from slipping through.

She rushes across the lobby and up the service stairs and pauses when she is out of sight, her back against the wall, listening, waiting. Guards run through the lobby, and once they reach the hotel, she bounds toward the front doors and out into a crowd of people gathered to stare through the windows of the restaurant at the bloodied body, at the man who weeps over it. Josephine then slows to walk across the square, so as not to draw attention. More soldiers run past her toward the hotel.

As she reaches the church, she crosses herself, something she has not done much of in the past. She cannot erase from her thoughts the face of Vivienne dying, and Benôit, his heart breaking, with an expression of such tenderness that she had never seen him wear before. It is tragic, all of it. She cries from the shock, from the loss. More loss. And what of Grace? Was it all planned? Did Vivienne carry a gun to keep herself safe, or was she warned something would happen, that the lieutenant would be there to arrest her? Whatever it was she perhaps knew she'd be dead regardless. She'd known it the last time Josephine had visited.

She had worn her fate on her face, read only by those who may have known her well. An icy wind traverses the streets with brutal precision, lifting her skirt above her ankles, telling her to hurry.

She stops at the end of Avenue Louise. Soldiers are exiting Vivienne's house already. She turns to look in a shop window and watches them march past behind her in the reflection. She approaches the house, the front door wide open and papers lying scattered on the doorstep. She steps carefully into the entrance hall, alert to sounds. Furniture is over-turned. They have been through the drawers, paintings pulled down, a hurricane of angry Germans leaving their destructive signature. She slinks up the stairs, her legs shaking. She still has the file. If she is caught with it . . . She dreads to think what will happen.

Grace is not in her room, nor in any other. Cupboard doors are open, cavities searched, bedcovers strewn across the floor, mattresses shredded. Then it is back down the stairs and out to the courtyard.

Grace is nowhere to be found. Josephine leaves the house, frustrated by failure. Two men in hats stand on a corner, talking.

"Have you seen the little girl who lives here?"

They shake their heads.

She hurries toward home. She can't trust anyone. She must get far away from Vivienne's in case the guards come back, fearful that the men are spies. Farther on, more men she doesn't recognise are watching her. Shutters in the windows are closed to the drama, occupants hearing the activity and fearing repercussions.

At home, Josephine closes the door behind her and breathes out all that has happened. She would collapse on the floor if there were not more to do. She flicks a switch on the wall, and light hisses into the nooks. Her mother is in her bedroom. She can hear her sleeping wheeze coming from the floor above. Despite that she is unwell, Gisela has been up at some point, a plate of sandwiches on the table for Josephine's supper. Her stomach rejects the sight of it, Vivienne's blood on her sleeves.

Josephine unties the string around the folder and flicks through some text on pages until she reaches a map. Numbers are scratched along the dotted line of war above towns and villages of France, along with arrows suggesting a movement of troops. Though she can't make sense of other notes. The other pages in the file are correspondence and urgent requisitions by German officials for more ammunition and men.

Josephine tries to imagine how Vivienne acquired them, stolen while her lovers slept perhaps. Creeping around in her satin dressing gown, under the soft light of a candle, sifting through satchels. How brave she was, how strong was Benôit to stomach her work. How brave of both of them.

Then something else, a paper, a short, handwritten note from a month ago advising that they had located one of the underground houses used to hide Allies and dissenters of German orders. There are no details, and it is not addressed to anyone by name and unsigned. But it is dated the day before Anja was last seen. Could authorities have gone there to catch the men and wait for her? But who found it and who reported her? She is grateful that Anja's address was listed falsely, and likely the reason the canal house has not been uncovered.

She remembers Benôit's anger, the scene he made when Anja wasn't there. He knew. He was frightened. But she, Josephine, could be saved perhaps by Renée's stupidity. And then Franz waiting also. These events stopped her from receiving the same fate as Anja.

She rebinds the file. She will take it to Eugène and Xavier. Benôit knows of them, Eugène at least, which still causes her confusion, the link between them and Benôit, Benôit and Vivienne. How blind or stupid must she have been? How clever must they be?

Josephine puts wood that Gisela has acquired from somewhere into the fireplace, builds up the flame. She brings a bucket of soap and water close to the heat, takes off her clothes, and scrubs the blood from the sleeves of her shirt and the mud from the hem of her skirt. She lays them to dry near the hearth, then, wearing only her chemise, leans back in the armchair to stare at Yves on the mantelshelf. The heat and tension have made her weary and her eyes close involuntarily. She searches for Arthur for comfort somewhere in her clouded thoughts, but before she finds him, she is deeply asleep.

Josephine wakes suddenly, some hours later, her legs burning hot from the fire. She tries to picture the item that Vivienne had hidden in the piano. *What was it?* Was it the contents of the file or something else?

She changes back into her clothes and steps upstairs. Her mother is propped up on her pillow, breathing more soundly. In Josephine's room, she hides the file between the mattress and springs of her bed, tucks her hair into a beret to pull it low over her ears, and climbs into her coat. The click of the door echoes loudly down the street.

Several cavalrymen clip-clop across the top of the street, and she waits crouched like a cat in the shadows until they are distant.

At Vivienne's, nothing has moved, the place in darkness and furniture and paper still scattered. She draws the heavy brocade curtains closed, then turns on the lamp that is closest to the piano. She reaches deeply beneath its lid to feel around before her hand lands on something odd. She shines her torch inside to see that a book is taped to the wall inside. She peels it away and closes the lid. When she hears a noise, Josephine turns off the lamp, then forms a crack in the curtains to peer at the street. A peddler is dragging a trolley in the dark, muttering, and he disappears into the darkness at the end of the street.

Josephine turns on the lamp again and scours the pages of a journal. Every few days is written an officer's name and the time of the appointment. She can fill in the reasons.

We have to fight in spirit, endure in ways we might never have agreed with in times past, Vivienne said.

Franz Mierzen is there, mentioned twice, and then there are pages and pages where he isn't. From the day that Franz started walking her home, he does not appear again. It can only mean that he was telling the truth. He had stopped seeing Vivienne, his heart then with someone

286

else. She flicks through the pages carelessly then until something catches her eye and she turns back again. Franz's name appears once more, two days before he left for the Front. He had gone to say goodbye, or was there something more?

From that date her appointments are irregular. Many of the officers were being sent away. Houses on Avenue Louise vacated. Then at the back is a pile of letters. She opens one, and it is a letter from a lover, a heartfelt note that expresses longing for another time. She recognises Benôit's handwriting. It is too personal, about the time they had spent together, queries about their daughter, where they will take her when this is over. She feels guilty, closes the pages, as if she were spying on a deeply personal moment through a keyhole.

They had come from somewhere else, started their secret work. They are not who they say they are. That is now obvious.

Then another letter there, too, from Franz, and dated a month after he left for the Front. She grabs it greedily to read, learns how hard it has been and that he wishes Vivienne well and will call on her when he returns. She closes the letter and puts the diary back in the piano. She has seen enough to know that letters are getting through, confirming that she was an idea, a passing fancy for Franz, nothing more. Josephine is disappointed by his betrayal but strangely unmoved also. It is proof that she is perhaps a fool after all.

She closes the piano lid, sad now that the owner won't be back, that there is another child somewhere without her parents. There are no hard feelings toward Vivienne because of Franz. She feels liberated from the spell that he had cast.

There is a bump in the darkness from somewhere above her. She stops to listen. Something scrapes then slides along the floor.

She climbs the stairs to the top floor to investigate, careful not to make a sound. In the room at the end of the hallway, someone is opening drawers, shuffling things. She thinks of Vivienne's gowns, her trinkets, which might be a temptation to some. She turns to leave before she comes face to face with the looter. Her heart won't stand it, she thinks. It is enough for one day.

Then comes another sound, whimpering, from the same room, from someone young. Someone like Grace.

Josephine walks quickly to push open the door. Inside, the curtains are drawn closed and lamplight fills the room. She can see the boards that have been lifted and left beside the cavity between the floor and the ceiling below, a perfect hiding place for someone light and small.

Grace sits on her mother's large bed, forlorn, hair untidily around her head, eyes swollen. The little girl rushes into Josephine's arms.

Josephine squeezes her tightly against her chest with one arm, the other hand gently stroking her hair back from her forehead.

"I will take you to my house," Josephine says. "You are safe now."

"Did Mama send you?"

Josephine pauses.

"Yes," she says. "But we have to get to my house quickly, and you must keep a tight hold of my hand."

The little girl sniffs back tears and nods.

32. TIME TO LEAVE

"Here," says Josephine, passing Eugène the grey folder of Benôit's. She has just arrived at La Vérité and revealed what happened at the hotel. "You need to read what this contains," she says.

Eugène does not open it straightaway, because his hawklike eyes are fixed to his sister as she begins to detail the incident at the restaurant. He holds the folder like it is something sacred, looking down at it occasionally, aware of the sacrifices Benôit and Vivienne made because of it.

While she continues to speak, he opens the folder and spreads the contents across the table. Eugène bends over to study the documents, drawing up pieces of information through the forefinger he uses to scroll down each of the pages. He straightens and paces around the table, agitated by the extra news that has just been relayed about the child, whom Gisela is now taking care of, and running his hands through his wild mane when something is said that makes him uneasy.

"Some others from the line pulled out shortly before Anja went missing," he says, breaking into her recount as something more important enters his head. "I believe that people were frightened. I believe that someone gave up Anja and Vivienne to save themselves. Who knows who else they've betrayed?"

Eugène shuffles through the pages, then stops on one in particular, unable to contain a frenzied look of excitement that adheres to the page he gives to Arthur.

"It seems this is Germany's next offensive! Here, Arthur, look!"

Arthur examines the *X*s and the names of towns and numbers employed beside them on a roughly drawn map. The next page he is passed has details of ammunition and other supplies required, and correspondence concerning the issues they are facing with some of their equipment.

"Do you see, Arthur?" he says.

"Yes, I do." They are in possession of vital intelligence for the Allies.

"I believe that Vivienne stole these things from the officers she entertained," says Josephine, confirming what they already seem to know.

"You knew about Benôit, didn't you?" she says to Eugène, some stoniness in her tone and hurt that Arthur recognises, too. "He was feeding you information about the Germans, studying and listening at the hotel like Anja."

"Yes," he says. "Eventually I learned about his involvement. Anja had hidden his involvement from me, too, until she was unable to hide it any longer. I know that she was introduced to Benôit by Marie de Croÿ and that there was information coming through them and others that I wasn't aware of. I have never met Vivienne, but Anja had learned much about her from Benôit."

"You should have told me, Gène."

"You should have told me about Franz from the beginning."

"It was nothing that would have affected the operation."

"You don't know that for certain, do you? Anja is missing. Someone knew."

There is a look between them, a standoff. Arthur hasn't been around these people long enough to understand all the complicated tensions in their relationship. He is about to say something, to step in the middle, when Eugène gets in first with some kind of truce.

"Mouse, you didn't need to know. It served no purpose, and Benôit told Anja from the very beginning that she was not to reveal him. He was the one who convinced me recently that he thought your relationship with Franz was innocent. So that is past now. I've moved on."

She does not look convinced.

"If you want to know the whole truth, Benôit thought you were extraordinary. He was very protective of you. Didn't like it that we had involved you at all. But his assignment was simply to obtain information, intelligence, to get it back to France and Britain. He was not part of the smuggling operation . . . It did not seem necessary to involve you any further. The fewer who knew about Benôit and Vivienne the better. Though I can tell you now that they worked as spies for France and were in direct contact with Princess Marie until she was arrested, when things have been slowly unravelling."

She looks down, seemingly exhausted from the information, from the complicated lines, from the things she is constantly trying to understand.

"So, Anja wasn't only listening to conversations then. She was transferring the information from Vivienne and Benôit."

"She did hear many things from officers in the restaurant but nothing as significant as the intelligence that came from the pair of them."

"Do you know anything of Benôit?" she asks. "Could they have taken him to Tir National? Could they execute him, too? Could they be such brutes?"

"You know that they can. He is probably in prison, awaiting a trial. He is probably being questioned as we speak."

Or tortured, thinks Arthur, and fears for Josephine's safety suddenly stab at him.

"It is getting dangerous, Eugène. For you, for everyone," says Arthur.

"I agree," says Eugène. "The restrictions, the borders will be too tight soon. People have more reasons to fear and therefore more reasons to talk. We will have to find other ways out of the country."

Eugène trawls once more through the stolen documents.

"I'm thinking that we get Maman out with Grace," says Josephine.

"Yes, yes," says Eugène. "Of course. Soon. But we must do something with this first." He closes the file and waves it in the air. "We have another English soldier at another house nearby. Arthur, we should get you both out tonight with this file while we can. This advance by the Germans is only days from now. There is no time to waste."

Arthur is stunned for a moment. Not by the thought of leaving, which was always going to happen, just by the speed of the decision.

"Tonight?" he says. He looks at Josephine, who looks away. There is something about leaving these people behind, people Arthur has grown close to, that makes the idea of returning home strangely foreign.

"Are you sure it is safe, Gène?" says Josephine.

"Of course," he says.

"I can't take you all the way to the smuggler," says Eugène to Arthur. "I have orders from the *Kommandantur* to transport items urgently to the Front, only this time I have to collect passengers as well. I can drive you part of the way to Aalst late this afternoon, but I will need someone else to lead you to the smuggler from there and negotiate on your behalf."

"I can take them," says Josephine. "I know where Karl's house is, and you brought him here once, before Arthur came. He knows me."

"I don't think that is a good idea, Mouse. I will find someone else."

"You will have trouble finding someone at such short notice. I know how to get there."

"The English will be given maps," says Eugène. "Perhaps they can find their own way."

"You know these smugglers hate dealing directly with foreigners," she says.

Eugène eventually agrees, though Arthur silently objects. He doesn't like this plan that might put Josephine in danger.

Eugène has gone to collect the vehicle and the other Englishman, Gordon. Arthur has packed a water bottle and knife. A pouch of tobacco, a can of peaches, and money will be used by the smuggler to bribe a sentry. The smuggler is to keep half the money for himself. Arthur leaves the bag ready by the door, then goes downstairs to help Josephine finish their work.

Josephine has cropped the photo that Eugène has already developed and is fixing it to the identity document for the new Englishman, should he be stopped. She passes it to Arthur to complete.

He leans in close, nose to the page, and gently dabs the ink across the stencil to forge an official seal. He has been filling in for Eugène recently, making himself more useful.

"Your mother has shown some improvement, I hear," he says to Josephine, who is watching closely.

"Yes, a little."

He looks up at her, and she doesn't move away. There is something there still from the other night, something unfinished.

"I am sorry to hear about your friend," he says, and turns back to his work.

"I did not know Vivienne very well, but we had been growing closer. I am sad for her, for Benôit, for Grace, their daughter. Maman is still in shock about it."

He peels the stencil away.

"You will soon be home," she says as he stands up and waves the document to dry. "That is something to look forward to." He glances at his pocket watch, the glass cracked, Harriet's initials engraved on the back of it; it was the only personal item that survived his last battle. Eugène will be here any moment.

"Yes," he says. He hands over the document for her to inspect.

"It is perfect, as usual."

"You must pass on my thanks to Xavier for all his help," he says. She is not meeting his eyes. She is unhappy. He wants to ask her things, to know that there was something between them, that he didn't imagine it. "I'm sorry I can't say goodbye to him in person. I hope that we can all meet again one day. I must repay you all. Perhaps after the war . . ."

There are too many words he wants to say. He wants to tell her that he is afraid to leave her, to lose the friendship they had begun. That it seems cruel in a way to part now.

"You will go back to fight, I imagine."

"Yes, I must . . . Josephine, are you sure you need to do this tonight? We will make our own way. I am used to reading maps."

"Quite sure," she says.

He nods.

"Arthur—" she says.

The sound of Eugène coming through the front door and another voice, too.

"I will miss you," she says.

"I will miss you, too."

He pulls her toward him, and there is no resistance. She tilts her face upward, and he bends down to kiss her cool lips. She is trembling.

Eugène is calling them. Telling them to hurry.

Josephine, Arthur, and Gordon study the house at the end of the path-way. The group has walked for several hours northward after parting with Eugène. He will meet Josephine the following evening at the same place he had left them.

"Are you sure it is this one?" asks Gordon.

"There is ivy in a plant box by the door," says Josephine. "It is the latest marker for this line. You both need to stay well back from the door."

"What did she say?" says Gordon, who speaks no French. Arthur has had to translate most of their conversations.

A woman answers, scarf around her hair and stains across her apron. Behind her, two children jump up on their knees on their bed to see who it is. A baby on a rug caws in front of the fire, and a bloodied rabbit lies interrupted on the kitchen table at the back of the room.

Josephine asks for Karl.

"He won't be back tonight," she says, looking over Josephine's shoulder at the two men in the shadows.

"I have two soldiers with me that need to get to the border tonight."

"You'll have to take them to his brother, Herbert, who lives farther north of here. Though I cannot guarantee he'll take you tonight. We need more notice for such things."

"This is urgent," says Josephine, retrieving a map from her coat pocket. "Can you show me on the map where he is?"

The woman looks again behind Josephine. "Come inside. You are letting the cold in." She nods to Josephine. "Only you."

Josephine disappears behind a closed door.

"How do you know this girl we are following will take us to the right place?" asks Gordon.

"I trust her. I know her."

"Or love is blind perhaps."

"What?" scoffs Arthur. "No. She and her brothers are good people."

"I've seen the way you look at her and she at you."

"How did you end up here, in Belgium?" says Arthur, changing the subject, annoyed by the other man's candour.

"I was captured and taken to the hospital, and the nurse there gave me instructions to a safe house. Then I was introduced to Eugène, who arrived there a few days later. He told me he would get me out."

The two men briefly discuss their units and commanders until the door opens and Josephine is released.

Arthur shines a torch on the map where she has marked another smuggler's house.

"I can take you there. It is at least two hours away."

"Perhaps we can find this ourselves now, Josephine. You should go back," says Arthur.

It means two or more hours to the next house and then a long way back for Josephine.

"No," she says. "It is better if I talk and make the trade. The smugglers are suspicious of any foreigners unless they are accompanied. Besides, I have no work to get up for tomorrow. The restaurant is closed temporarily."

It is quiet for most of the journey. Josephine walks ahead, painted in shades of blue under a sky that is star filled and a moon that is half. Nightjars shriek their warnings, and foxes poke their noses out of bracken to inspect the scent. Only once when the group heard human voices did they have to stay low to the ground, Josephine's hand touching Arthur's in the dark as they waited for the sounds to pass and disappear. The trek is longer than anticipated, his leg aching past midnight. The air is wet and cold, and the hours trudge by before they find the house. They are wearied, though fear has kept them focused.

The man who opens the door appears angry. They have woken up the house from its peaceful rural slumber. Herbert reluctantly lets them inside the house, lit by a single lantern and mostly in darkness. From the shadows there are voices, and an adolescent boy steps into the room. Herbert's eyes dart between each of them, small dark beads that don't blink. Josephine explains their situation in Dutch. When Herbert doesn't say anything, she retrieves from Arthur the pack that contains the tobacco and tinned fruit for the sentries and the banknotes that are to be split between them and the smuggler.

Herbert stares at the contents of the open pack, then nods. He examines the items that she empties onto the table, then responds in a curt tone, gesticulating, pointing to his son and the roof. Though Arthur can't understand the actual words, it is clear the loot that Josephine presents is not favourable.

"He wants more," says Josephine to the two men. "He said he wants all the notes as well. He said it is becoming too dangerous. He has been able to bribe a German who guards the electric fence and lets them cross at a gate. But he said the guard will expect more for two people, and Herbert's own rate has gone up, he tells us. He also said things might have changed again. He has had to create new routes twice already to find Germans he knows. The risks are higher now, and we must pay for it."

Arthur repeats the words for Gordon.

"What does that mean for us?" asks Gordon, stepping forward. "Tell the greedy bastards they have no choice."

Herbert picks up his rifle, sensing the combative tone, and the son, who seemed placid, steps bravely past his father, preventing the Englishman from coming any closer.

"Stay," says Josephine impatiently to Gordon.

She has never dealt with smugglers before. She is out of her depth, yet at the same time, Arthur is impressed that she is taking charge. They talk some more to revise the terms, and she briefly looks at the floor to think before she turns to relay the changes.

She will stay at the house and wait for Herbert's return. All the money they have must go to the sentries. Herbert will then return with her to Brussels in his wagon to collect more money for himself. In other words, Josephine is offering herself as a guarantee until Herbert gets back.

Arthur doesn't like the sound of these terms. He does not like the cutthroat look of Herbert.

"It is the only way," says Gordon. "We are running out of night hours. We should just go now. Leave her to it. It is a risk she has chosen."

Arthur calls her away to speak to her quietly.

"Are you sure you are safe?"

"Yes. He just wants more money. He has a family to support. Everyone is struggling, even more so here. His farm is no longer profitable. The Germans took almost everything in those first weeks, and then the smoke of the battles destroyed his last harvest."

"I—"

She puts her small, cold hand against his cheek, then steps up to kiss him on the lips, uncaring that Gordon is watching. Arthur feels his heart hammering.

"You must go," she whispers. "I will not forget you."

He hugs her, afraid to let her go.

"I am alive because of all of you. I wish I could say more—"

"Hurry," says Gordon.

They pull apart, and he turns once to see the silhouette of Josephine in the doorway. Leaving is much harder than he thought.

Arthur stays at the rear as they weave through fir trees, and the cold pine air brushes the hair from his face and cools his neck. Herbert, wiry, on bowed legs, grunts and waves his fist forward, indicating for them to walk faster when they start to slow.

After hours of walking, Arthur is bone weary, teeth clenched to bear the ache in his limb, as they wade across a knee-deep waterway to reach the other side. Halfway up the embankment, almost at their destination, Herbert lies down on his stomach and gestures for the others to do the same. The grass is cold and damp as they slither to the top. Arthur can see two guards at the gate and hear their muffled banter.

"Do you know them?" he whispers in French.

Herbert doesn't answer but puts his hand up to stop him from talking. Minutes go by while a brilliant crimson band appears where the land meets the sky.

Then one of the guards walks away along the fence line.

Herbert is over the top, and he approaches the remaining sentry, who raises his gun then lowers it again. They know each other. They talk in low voices; then the two Englishmen are waved forward. The guard eyes them carefully, one hand rested on the gun at his side. Herbert gives him the tobacco and food, but there is no exchange of money.

"Where is the money?" Arthur says to Herbert. "Give him the money!"

The smuggler shakes his head. Either he doesn't understand or he is pretending not to, perhaps not trusting that Josephine will get him more money. Arthur suspects the latter.

"More," says the German soldier in English. "Jewellery?"

It seems they have to negotiate themselves. Herbert has nothing to lose but two dead Englishmen that Josephine won't know about. He can tell her it was successful.

Herbert nods to Arthur, who takes off his wedding ring and hands it over. The sentry doesn't inspect it but puts it straight into his pocket.

Gordon moves forward toward the gate.

"Wait!" barks the guard, his rifle in front of him. "From you."

"Oh, for the love of Christ!" says Gordon indignantly. "I have nothing!"

"Money!" says Arthur angrily to Herbert. "Give him the money. Some of it at least."

The sentry speaks in a raised voice, and Herbert is saying things heatedly to the fugitives. The guard then raises his gun to point at Arthur, but before he can act, Gordon has already plunged a knife into the German's neck, pushing it harder until the soldier sinks to his knees. The guard manages to fire off his rifle into the air then falls dead.

Herbert raises his gun to point it at Gordon. Arthur has anticipated the reaction, grabbing the barrel of the rifle with two hands and pushing the smaller man back on the ground, twisting the weapon so that it then lies pressed across the smuggler's neck and into his windpipe.

Herbert pushes back harder, rising upward, teeth gritted now and face red with rage. He is stronger than he appears, and Arthur feels himself weakening. The smuggler jerks back suddenly. Gordon is stabbing at the side of Herbert's chest, both men splattered with his blood. It pours from the smuggler's mouth and wounds, and he turns over to crawl a few feet before dropping to the ground, making guttural noises. Arthur can't stand the suffering, the sound of a man drowning from the blood in his lungs. He picks up the German's rifle and shoots the dying man in the head.

They can hear shouting farther along the border. Other sentries are now alerted.

"Hurry!" says Gordon.

Arthur thinks of Josephine at the house, waiting. What will happen to her if Herbert doesn't return?

He takes out the folder from inside his clothing and hands it to Gordon, who has retrieved the tobacco from the German's coat pocket in the meantime.

"What is this?" he says.

"It is information that the War Office will want. About the next German offensive. It needs to get to them urgently."

"But you have to bring it!"

"You must go!" Arthur says.

"You have to come. Good God, man! This is your chance!"

Arthur can hear voices closer alongside the electrified fence, which he has heard can fry someone instantly. He looks at Herbert, regrets these moments, and wishes he hadn't accepted the terms. It might have been different.

"Good luck!" says Arthur, their faces bathed now in a pink-gold sunrise. Arthur catches the disbelief again of the other before he turns and glides across the border, the gate left open enticingly. Though not enough to change Arthur's mind.

The Germans who investigate will not be looking for the culprit in Belgium. They would not think someone mad enough to stay.

Arthur slings the rifle over his shoulder and scampers over the embankment.

There is someone else to fight for now.

33. YVES'S BIRTHDAY

There is chaos in the sky, clouds of thick purple smoke that hide the sun and blow low above the town. Explosions sound in the distance.

The French soldier Josephine photographs is standing inside a lit building on the edge of the city. He is ill, with beads of sweat across his head, his hands trembling from battleground sickness. Xavier has told Josephine that he is concerned that the soldier's foot will become gangrenous. He might have to amputate before the man can leave the country. The woman inside the safe house is packing her bags. She believes it is only a matter of time before she is caught and is leaving for Antwerp to stay with her sister. This will be the last time she offers sanctuary to someone who wants to escape. She must think of her family. Josephine can't blame her. There have been moments lately she has questioned her own involvement, whether in the end her family and others will suffer because of it. She admires Eugène's passion for their cause, but she is wary of his devotion to it and of being caught. The number of people they can trust is shrinking.

Arthur had come back for her after the skirmish at the border and told the son of Herbert that his father had been killed by German sentries. The son, used to deceit and the double deals of his father, wasn't convinced. The boy had threatened them both at first, pointed his rifle, while Josephine translated the false narrative. Only an offer of compensation eased the tense situation in those moments and potentially solved what could be disastrous for their line. They needed the other smugglers and could not afford to make them enemies.

Josephine was grateful to Arthur for returning, relieved, in a selfish way, to see him again. He had held her hand for much of the journey back, and he has filled her thoughts in the days since. She has shown him everything about printing, about photography, and finds more reasons to be at La Vérité. He interprets the English news to her in his halting French, and while she types, she is aware that he is watching her, the energy between them like tiny sparks on tinder that never have enough time and air to build.

The previous night Arthur had walked her to the end of the street from La Vérité before pausing in the shadows uncertainly. He drew her to him, kissed her forehead. She had then rested her head against the warmth of his chest, snuggled within his woollen arms until she tore herself away. One of them had to make the first move before they were missed.

Josephine has not had much time to be with Arthur alone, though even when her brothers are there, she can sense a simmering of possibilities beneath their exchanges. She had not thought of Franz in the same ways she does Arthur. Not with hope and desire and yearning. It is Arthur's face she sees at night, his arms she imagines around her, his body.

They are stealing only minutes. And for what? Where will this take them? She must be realistic, accepting it might be all they will ever have. He will be gone soon, tomorrow, a week from now, a month.

Once she has taken the photograph, Josephine helps the Frenchman back to the bed. The woman has left him the crust of a loaf of bread and a glass of pear juice. It is all she can spare. He is too ill to be hungry. Eugène will bring him to another safe house the following day.

Josephine sits with him awhile, puts a washcloth across his head. He is dying, she is sure of it, and is reluctant to leave in case he dies alone. He may not last the day. He reaches in his pocket to pull out his wallet and hand it to her.

"Can you read the letter inside?"

She opens a piece of paper folded into four, soiled and opened so many times the paper is curled and cut at the seams. It was tucked inside next to a photo of a woman and two small children.

"Dear Papa," she reads from the letter, written by a noticeably young hand. "We are sending our prayers and hope to see you soon. Love, Olive."

The man nods, and she replaces the letter as she found it. She hates this part of it, the finding of notes or photographs left behind by the dead or dying who have not made it to cross the border. They have to bury them in Belgium. It is not the first time they have lost people. Arthur was nearly one of those, which is why she believes he works hardest for those who are injured. A payback for his own life that was saved. Josephine feels so close to all these people, knows what it is to lose hope, to lose those close to her.

She pats his hand.

"You will be fine," she says to the dying man. "You will see your family again."

"In heaven, not too soon hopefully," he says drowsily, before she has lost him to sleep where he twitches from bad dreams.

Xavier and Arthur have been helping carry men from the hospitals before they are shipped to the east. It is dangerous work. They had paused again for a couple of weeks after the disaster at the border, now the queue to leave is growing long.

Arthur has been wonderful company, and when she is not working with him, she is thinking of him also. He has taken over the print room entirely, and he is strong enough to carry some of the injured who are resting there.

Arriving home, Josephine is greeted with the smell of baking. Eugène has brought Gisela flour, eggs, and sugar, and she is making a cake to celebrate Yves's birthday. Her mother appears content today. Her heart seems stronger. It seems that the demands of Grace and her losses have given Gisela more purpose, and she has put some of her own sad thoughts on hold.

Grace has lost the bounce in her step. She was told that her mother is dead, and her father is in prison. They told her much of the truth, but she is too young to understand all of it. They have warned her to be careful she does not talk about her parents with anyone. Josephine is worried about sending her across the border to an orphanage where she will know no one.

"It gives me joy to bake something again," Gisela says. "No tears today. I know they are watching."

She smiles at Josephine, who gives her mother a hug.

"Besides, it keeps Grace busy, too."

Josephine has been unable to convince her mother to leave. The last attempted smuggling was almost a complete disaster, and she is not sure her mother, with the persistent cough in her chest, could make such a trip. Eugène had to smooth things over with Herbert's family, with money, though there is no certainty they can trust them.

Eugène pores closely over a newspaper like a bloodhound with a scent. He has always been eccentric, but this has manifested into something more intense. Josephine wonders if his underground work is now an addiction rather than a purpose.

"Benôit has been sent to a prison in Liège for the crime of espionage," he says. "There is no word on a trial or the details. But if they are aware of his connection to Vivienne, then it is prison in the east, at the very least."

Josephine is thankful that Grace is upstairs in the room they share.

"Can we visit him?" says Gisela. "Perhaps take his daughter."

"Only if you want to be followed from that point, Maman." Eugène puts the paper down in disgust. "I will be looking for somewhere else to operate a safe house, where you, Josephine, and Grace can move to also."

"Why, Eugène?" says Gisela.

"There are too many who know the house on the canal. And now some that carry a grudge against us also."

Xavier and Arthur enter, bringing a bottle of wine Xavier was given as a gift and more candles since the electricity is once again off.

Arthur wears a bright-white shirt that Josephine has lovingly laundered, and his face is cleanly shaven. She thinks how handsome he is, square shoulders, neck long, and eyes of brown that burn gold from the candles. Introductions are made, questions are asked by Gisela. Small talk, talk of family.

Xavier opens the bottle and pours when they are seated around the table.

"To Yves and Papa and all the people who couldn't make it," says Eugène, raising his glass.

"*Santé!*" says Gisela. Clink, clink.

A look between Arthur and Josephine, connected briefly by glass. She can see something far ahead: bright, airy hallways; meadows; warmth.

In bed Josephine can hear Eugène breathing heavily and her mother's soft snores. And she is aware of Arthur, down on the bottom floor, who will sleep only hours before he retreats like a bat to his cave. Everything feels right and wrong at the same time. There is too much to worry about and no time for anything. War is stupid.

She wishes she were still working, still bringing in money. Jobs are scarce. The Métropole has not called her back, and she is frightened of enquiring there, of being conspicuous to Germans now.

Outside her window, she can see Arthur smoking a cigarette. She sees the tip of it burn and fade. She puts on her dressing gown and steps quietly down the stairs.

Xavier is on the couch, eyes closed. She opens the door to the rear patio and slides to sit beside Arthur on the bench. The waft of tobacco smoke tickles her nose.

"Would you like some?" he says quietly, handing her the cigarette, his features growing more distinguishable as her eyes adjust to the night.

She nods her head.

She takes the cigarette, draws on it, and hands it back. She doesn't much like smoking, but it is something to share, to be closer to Arthur.

"What is it that you want to do after the war?" he asks.

"I want to do what I did before."

"Photography?"

"Yes," she says, then shrugs because that is only part of it. The part with her father and Yves she can't have back.

"And you?"

"I have no idea," he says.

"None at all?"

He draws back deeply on his cigarette.

"Do you want to try and work things out with Harriet?" she asks tentatively.

He is thinking deeply.

"Jack was her life. She had no other, really. I was there to make it happen for them . . . Not that I am complaining. I can just see things better now. We needed each other until we didn't."

"I'm sorry," Josephine says. "It can't have been easy for either of you."

"She left me . . . after Jack, though I think it was over long before that, if I am honest with myself. She blames me for Jack's death, and she rightly has a point. I think back to the things I could have changed, where it was exactly that I let him down."

He reaches down to stub out the cigarette on a paving stone, then clasps her hand.

Josephine is thinking, piecing his life together, putting the facts in an order that she can visualise. She cannot say what it is like to lose

306

a child, though she has seen the ill effects on Gisela and knows well of loss, too. Grief pushed her through a maze of confusion and guilt, and she has found her way out again. Grief still follows, waits for her sometimes, but it is only a shadow of what it was, which crosses her path occasionally and disappears again.

"Arthur, you can spend your life telling yourself that you are responsible and what you could have, would have done. But it helps no one. If we start apologizing now for things that have happened, then we will be apologizing for the rest of our lives. We will drive ourselves mad. Everything we do, every step we take affects someone else, just as every step someone else takes affects us. And it is simply chance that puts us in the wrong and right places at any given time."

He is silent, his face so near to hers.

"And chance has brought us together, too," she says.

Something clatters lightly inside the house, and they separate suddenly, then giggle like children who have been caught in the pantry.

Inside, Xavier is in the kitchen with a glass of water. He says nothing as they enter.

"Do you mind if I have one of those?" Xavier says, indicating the cigarette packet.

"Of course not."

"I was thinking that perhaps you and Maman should leave here at the first chance we have," Xavier says to Josephine. "We should get you out of Belgium."

"Maman will never agree to it, Xavier," says Josephine. "And neither will Gène. He needs me here."

"There is no need for all of us to be in constant danger. We will make do without you."

"But I can't make do without you."

She reaches up to kiss him on the cheek and listens to their low voices as she climbs back up the stairs.

34. FALLING

Arthur is in the print room. Eugène has gone to bed on the top floor. He had come home exhausted from travelling, muttered the reasons, then dragged himself up the stairs in heavy boots. Arthur can hear him softly grunting and purring in his sleep.

Arthur uses the magnifying glass as he carefully forges signatures on permits for new members of their line to travel between cities. He likes the work, and the smell of it also. Everything in the room reminds him of Josephine. He enjoys watching her work, absorbed by her tasks, and sometimes unreachable. She has an oval face, eyes large and fanned by thick lashes, and features sculpted evenly. She is pretty, but this is not what draws him. It is her selfless support of her brothers, and the people around her, that is deeply attractive. It is that she is questioning, thoughtful, and clever, that there are many sides to her.

Arthur finds himself thinking about Josephine during the night. Sometimes he will sit below the window in the quiet hours, when the distant guns and machines have paused and sounds echo off the night walls. He feels young again, hopeful in the silence, daring to ponder a future that includes her somehow. Then he will scoff and shake his head and tell himself to stop imagining. It is not like him to speculate so much, to have abundant time to do so.

You should have left when you had the chance, returned to your regiment, he hears Harriet say wisely: a face for his conscience.

It wasn't that simple, he tells her inwardly.

She is not for you, Artie, he can hear her reply.

Josephine is late tonight. He worries whenever she is delayed. Relief when he hears a key in the door and the click of it gently closing, and he can breathe again now that she is here.

His heart quickens when he sees her commence the stairs, stepping down toward him. She wears a cardigan over a rust-coloured dress that finishes just above her ankles. She smiles at the sight of him. Her face is flushed, though he can't tell if it is the cold wind, which has been pushing against the windows upstairs for hours, or she is trying to contain the same excitement. The same kind he feels when he first sees her foot on the top stair. Either way, he doesn't care. He is glad she is there.

"Gène is asleep, I can hear."

"Yes."

"There is a dish, a stew, upstairs that Maman has sent with me. She is worried about Gène, worried he might forget to eat. She is worried about you, too. She feels she is contributing this way, she says. It is good when she is cooking or sewing, that is, when there is something to sew or cook with. Whenever Gène can bring something. And Grace, too, has given her purpose again."

"Tell your kind mother I said thank you."

"I will."

She moves nearer, leaning over his shoulder for a close look at his work, her face only inches from his own. He has the urge to turn and kiss her.

"That is very good. I am a little worried you might steal my position here at La Vérité."

"There is no danger of that. I am not as fast as you at typing, and I'm still a fledgling with my photographic skills, as you have seen . . . While I was waiting I wrote out in French for you several English articles."

"Thank you. What is the news?"

She takes off her cardigan, and he can see the dress better, the bodice fitting tightly to her small body. It is new or an old one at least that Gène has probably found her in his travels. He is thoughtful like that occasionally, on his better days, when he is not scheming or worrying. He has been anxious and jumpy with Anja gone, and worse still since the night the smuggler was killed.

That Englishman has ruined everything! Eugène said about Gordon. *Herbert's son could give us up for reward now if he were so inclined. It has cost us more money! Money that we now don't have for other supplies.*

Herbert was crooked! said Josephine. *He was keeping all the money as Arthur said.*

Eugène punched the air in front of him with his fist to stress his point. *You can't negotiate with smugglers at the border. It doesn't work like that!*

The situation allowed for nothing else, defended Arthur. *If Gordon hadn't acted so quickly, we might both have been killed. I am not sure things could have been done differently. Always decisions are made in the moment and seconds between life and death.*

"The paper is weeks old now, but some of it is relevant," says Arthur. "Another Allied destroyer sunk by the Turks, another zeppelin spotted over London. But this one I thought was important," he says, tapping the handwritten translation he has prepared. "There is much debate on the other side of the Atlantic as to foreign participation in the war. Several politicians refusing to acknowledge the Belgian experience."

She is shaking her head. "What about my experience? Is that exaggerated?"

"I think it would be a very good idea if you wrote about it for the newspaper. Doesn't have to be long. There is not much in this one yet. The whole back page is free if you wish."

"I am not the only one with a story. Other underground papers have printed plenty of accounts."

"You are allowed a voice, too."

She shrugs, hesitant, and he is worried he might have offended her, dredged up memories.

"One voice can speak for many," he says coaxingly. "I believe it is important that those across the borders get to hear yours."

"I'll try."

She wipes the printer rollers in preparation, then sits down to wind a stencil paper through the typewriter. He listens to her work behind him. It feels comforting to have her close, where he can keep a watchful eye, protect her if need be.

Arthur has finished most of his work and eyes it critically while drawing back on a cigarette. The tapping behind him is silent for a period; then Josephine winds the paper from the machine.

She places the typewritten page in front of him, and he picks it up to read. It is heartbreaking and honest, though it is not so much her story but a collection of thoughts, about broken families, missing family members, and her perspective on the war, how Belgians were betrayed and how they will be affected long after there is any end to the madness. It is about the soldiers she has helped treat, what they have suffered, what it will mean for the families they leave behind. He blinks rapidly and clears his throat of emotion as he stubs out his cigarette. He reads it again and turns to see she is sitting down facing him, waiting anxiously for his response.

"It is very good. It is beautiful."

"It felt a relief to write it, to put it into words on a page. You were right to suggest it."

"Perhaps the more we reveal, the more it is believed, and the only way the truth about the severity of this murderous conquest will not be diminished."

She nods.

"You are very brave, your brothers, others," he says. "Many would not do what you do."

"Maybe others are more smart than brave," she says, offering a small smile.

"Josephine, are you all right with all of this?" he says, looking at the work scattered across the room, at the huge responsibility she has been set.

She shrugs. "I try not to think too hard about it. There is no choice now."

"Your country will be very proud of you when this is all over. King Albert should award you each a medal."

She looks down, appearing uncomfortable with such a statement. It is not yet clear to him whether she is proud or not.

"I never really thought about my country before the war, about being patriotic, but it figures greatly in our minds," she says. "Patriotism is a new form of currency that enables some to exchange with those they despised before. But this currency that binds us is created with the blood of so many. Is it worth it? I question myself constantly and wish that I'd been more grateful about my simple life before, which seemed at the time so complicated. I would gladly go back to a divided Belgium; I, like everyone else, I expect, would gladly go back to how it was."

He is amazed at her wisdom and openness. She does not seem naive at all in many ways, perhaps with relationships, but certainly not at seeing a clear picture of the world. He is in awe and suspects she can read it in his face.

"And I will admit that I sometimes question whether we are truly making a difference, if we are simply helping the soldiers return across the border to ultimately die on the battlefield."

He nods and looks down at his hands.

"Then there are the connections I have made," she says. "The people I think about more than I should. People who have wrapped themselves around my heart."

He looks up. She is standing now, with eyes that are glistening and inviting.

He stands, steps tentatively toward her. He puts his arms around her and draws her to him. There is no resistance. He leans down, kisses her gently, and her hands reach around the back of his neck.

There is a clanking and a cursing as a pan is dragged across the stove upstairs. They move apart, and then laugh softly, faces flushed.

"It seems the gods still don't favour our togetherness," he says in jest.

"No, it is just the interruption by one of my brothers as usual, coming between me and any other life I wish for," she says playfully. "Eugène has obviously found Maman's dish of food."

He watches her move toward the printing machine to set the stencil. Arthur turns back to the desk, unable to concentrate on the next task now with her so close.

35. DANGEROUS LIAISONS

She lies in bed and presses her fingers against her lips, wondering how they feel to Arthur, what he thinks of her. Remembering the kiss from several nights ago makes her breathless and warm. She has only seen him twice since, and with others in the room, observing him surreptitiously with new eyes, with wonder and curiosity. Desire also. He had caught her watching him speak, examining his lips that are soft and full, and she had looked away startled at first then back again moments later to find his eyes still upon her, curious and searching.

She has never been so moved by anyone. There is an awareness of each other that is so strong it seems it is yelled across the table and visible to all who are there. She is almost afraid of her feelings, of her inexperience, of being alone with him. She has never been fully intimate, only kissing with her former betrothed in Louvain and Franz at the hotel and beside the river. They were uncomfortable moments in many ways. She could not sink into the idea of those men, could not block out misgivings when she was with each of them. She was playing a part, out of expectation more than anything. With Arthur, questions don't plague her. She can even dream about him without guilt or fear or regret. There is no sense of possible treachery. Her father would have liked him. She is sure of it.

These feelings have crept up on her, pushing those of Franz into the distance. Though not completely out of view. He is a cool breeze that enters occasionally to blow away warm thoughts of Arthur. Yet at these moments Franz is not Arthur's adversary and an enemy of Belgium, but another forgotten soldier, and certainly not a lover, despite their moment by the river. She thinks of him in the conditions she has heard about from Arthur and others and thinks more with pity than anything else.

She sinks into the mattress and stares at the walls in the dark, the walls that belong to someone else, that might one day be returned to them, reminding her that life is transient, and opportunities can disappear. She has come to a decision.

At breakfast, Gisela tells her daughter a story that she heard from someone at the marketplace. Two lovers were slain when they tried to escape Belgium together, and their bodies were burned, then buried where they were shot on the border. People take flowers to the grave when the guards aren't looking.

Josephine feels a chill at the back of her neck, tries not to read anything into this.

Grace is late to wake up. She looks radiant in her sleep, red cheeks, fair hair, gemstone eyes that shimmer green, hidden beneath closed lids. She was woken in the night with nightmares, and Josephine had comforted her with an untruth, that the monsters in her dreams aren't real.

Slivers of sunlight catch the dew on a patch of green. Josephine puts her hand to the cool glass on the window to the yard below.

The birthday fever that suspended them from reality hasn't lasted. Eugène will have to steal more food, with German stocks low, and he thinks the theft will be noticed. They have no money, and the previous day, besides enjoying the egg and flour bounty, they had stood in line for bread and potatoes.

"How long will you be?" Gisela asks as Josephine leaves.

"I don't know, Maman." She could say that she is working, but she is tired of lies. "I wish to spend some time with Arthur. He may be gone soon."

Josephine has been helping Arthur pack up some boxes as instructed by Eugène. It will mean they leave the printing machine behind. She is disappointed that they won't be working together, that they may not have many excuses to spend time alone.

"Do you want to go somewhere today?" she asks.

"Where?"

"To the park to walk, for fresh air."

"It is risky."

"Everything is risky."

They are both feeling carefree, perhaps a little giddy since somehow, without saying it aloud, they are together; they are bound.

It is Sunday, and her mother has told her that people are going to the church to sing "La Brabançonne" in protest again. Somewhere close by, German music plays, drowning out the distant sounds of war. It means the guards will be diverted, gravitating to the centre of Brussels, where most of the population is gathering.

You need to be more fearless, Mouse, said her papa, many years earlier. *More like your mother.*

36. BOUND

They take the tram north to the forest park. Arthur watches her walk ahead, light-brown hair with glints of honey, tendrils falling about her face.

She holds out her hand, which he engulfs with his own, and they step along the pathway, sun streaming in angles across her face, her long dress sailing behind her. They stop to study fish in a pond, and she is as still as a fountain statue, focused, and he can't remember Harriet ever being so still. He is talking about good things now, about life in better times. Josephine brings it out of him. There is never judgment in her eyes. She is not unlike Xavier, but she isn't like him, either. Their characters differ, Josephine fearful and careful, Xavier careful but fatalistic, and Eugène fearless, even godless sometimes, the way he talks of revenge.

Arthur wants Josephine, there is no denying it, but he can't have her. He has already told himself that. It is wrong. He has nothing to promise her. She could have anyone. She must not feel the same way about him, yet she says so in the kisses they share, in the looks she gives that are long with promise, and in the way she colours when she catches him staring. They are signs, though perhaps he misinterprets. He is older, out of touch maybe.

The air is cold in the shade. They amble for a period, watchful as guards walk past them on the way to somewhere else, strangely festive, as if there were no war. Arthur has blended in. Only days before, a zeppelin had passed overhead to bomb another town, and the mood was different.

Back at La Vérité she is close and not close enough, and his arms reach around low behind her, spontaneously, and he lifts her up in a bear hug to kiss her, and she tastes sweet and edible, and he has fallen like he told himself he wouldn't. She puts her lips on his forehead and holds them there, her hands on either side of his face, fingers searching and stroking curiously.

And he can't stand it anymore, what she does to him, the power she possesses. His lips on cool skin, and his hands touch her tenderly, caressing, until they are joined with passion, their hearts beating large as one. He can see no bad in the world, no life outside what they have in these moments in the space they share.

She is crying unexpectedly, and he realises that this is her first time, and guilt cuts him open, exposes his doubts once more. She laughs then, strangely, during the tears, then rolls on top of him and kisses him everywhere on his face to erase the frown, to clear his heart.

"I am hopelessly in love with you," he says under laughter, too, and she reaches for more.

In the fading light of afternoon, she has her chin on his chest, looking up at him expectantly, eyes patterned like opals when the light is directly on them.

"Where are you?" she says.

"Right here," he says, then with his large hand he cups her chin, thumb tracing the small white scar on her cheek. She turns her head to the side and closes her eyes to doze, her head gently rising and falling with his breathing, while he ponders their earlier conversation.

⊸

We should not waste a moment. Do you think? he asked.

You are thinking of your son, no? Josephine asked.

Yes. I am. I am thinking of his life, hardly lived. Only a few years younger . . . You must not waste a moment of it. Not you.

That is strange. You are thinking I'm too young for you then? It is something Papa would likely say, though only when he was walking past so he did not have to face my response.

The age, does it bother you really? said Arthur, cautiously.

I thought the English loved younger brides.

I believe your lot did, too.

True.

Well?

The truth is I don't care about age, she said. *You are a young man, no?*

She smiled widely. He wasn't used to it. It was beautiful, unguarded, so unlike her, too, from when they first met.

I'm sorry, it must sound odd to ask you these things, said Arthur. *But it is your life. Your time. I want to be part of it if you'll let me . . . The truth is that I'm altered, too. Today I don't feel the same as I did yesterday. They say a man can be born again if he believes it at the point that death is nigh.*

I say a man can be born again while he is very much alive, she said.

She climbs out of bed while he searches around the floor beside them for the match to light the lamp. It whooshes into life. He watches her wriggle into her petticoat and pull on her dress, tiny fabric buttons that she pushes through nimbly with fingers that he has kissed a hundred times. He could watch her for hours, though it is only seconds she has given him to take her all in.

"I will take the bicycle this time," she says.

"They will probably take that like they take the horses. Carts are being pulled by oxen if those are not taken also." He will worry about her until he sees her again. "Maybe I should walk you."

"No!" she says. "Enough risks for one day. I am safe and you are not."

"And if you are stopped?"

"I will think of something. I always do," she says. This answer doesn't make him feel better, niggles of doubt. She climbs on top of him to dispel it, arms around his neck and cool kisses on his hot skin.

"You will be here tomorrow?" he asks.

"Yes," she says, peeling away from him.

She is gone and he paces the floor, feeling buoyant and a sense of calm.

How did I find her? It is love. He knows it because his heart is beginning to repair. He can go on now.

He is startled. There is a sequence of knocks on the door. He is hoping it is Josephine returned.

Eugène has someone new with him, a Belgian, to break apart the stillness. Not that Eugène is unwelcome, nor that he didn't expect him back this morning, just that the energy of the stranger is intrusive. He is raking over the contents of Arthur's life with his eyes, pillaging the mood, examining the view of the canal, even the sheets on the bed that are crumpled. He seems to stay on them a moment.

Eugène doesn't seem to notice any of it.

"This is Cédric," says Eugène. "He has been sentenced to prison for refusing to work for the Germans. They have sent his father away already. He is staying here until we can get him to the border. I would normally take him closer, but some have abandoned us. They are too frightened now. And I do not trust the smuggler Karl because of what you did to his brother, Herbert."

"I can take him to the border if you wish," says Arthur, wanting to make up for it.

"We will both go," says Eugène, "when it is time. One of us must be there in case we need a decoy. There must always be two now, since the fiasco at the border with Gordon."

Eugène likes to remind him of this, of Josephine's involvement, too. Arthur nods.

"I need to go see Maman," says Eugène. "Remind her that if we are missing for many days to not go to the authorities. Will you be all right with him?"

"Of course," says Arthur, and Eugène is gone.

"Are you an English soldier?" Cédric asks, the question puerile.

"Yes," he says, turning to the stranger, suddenly aware there is a person there he must contend with. Life on the run, mutating. Another day. Another change.

37. A SOLDIER RETURNS

Josephine cycles fast, the cold wind in her hair.

German soldiers are coming her way. They look tired. They are grimy, they are back from war. A bandage on a hand. One is old enough to be her grandfather. He is probably a father, too. Her heart is strangely soft and free.

"Guten Tag!" she says.

One of the soldiers raises his hat, his other arm bound up to the elbow. He is tired of war, too. Leaves and litter bluster around her wheels. She lowers her head and tunnels through the wind.

She rolls her bike around the side of the house and enters through the back door, hangs up her coat and hat. The house feels warmer today, and she can hear murmurs coming from the other end of the hallway.

Josephine bounces into the front room, then falters. Franz and her mother rise from the sofa to greet her, and Gisela is first to speak.

"Captain Mierzen has brought us some coal," announces Gisela. There is no sign of Grace. A fire is in the grate and a basket of food on the table.

"Josephine," he says unsurely, as if he can't quite believe she is real. He is smiling his twisted smile that he makes to control his emotion. He is pleased to see her. It is obvious.

"I've just been telling Captain Mierzen that you went to the Parc du Cinquantenaire to listen to the band today. Did you see your brothers there?"

"Yes, Maman," she says, holding her mother's gaze, her message received. "It was very pleasant."

Josephine stares at the empty teacups between them on the coffee table, wills her eyes to meet his.

"You have had trouble with food, your mother was telling me," he says. "You lost your job."

"Yes," she says, images of Arthur in her vision, his name, she feels, emblazoned across her face.

"I heard about what happened to Vivienne. It was a terrible shock. I had no idea."

Didn't you? she wants to shout, memories of Vivienne and the hole in her chest. Is it that he is more shocked by her death or that she was a spy? No doubt he knows something.

Gisela is reluctant to leave them.

"Maman, can I talk to you, please?"

Gisela looks at her daughter, her face shifting between pleading and defiance. Josephine is aware that she does not like the German, that she would throw the coal and food back if she could.

Gisela stands up to follow her daughter into the laundry near the back door.

"I need to speak to him privately. You must leave us."

"I thought it was over between you."

Josephine swallows.

"Maman . . ."

"I will go," she says, her hands up in surrender. "But, Josephine, you need to ask him not to come. Especially now that Grace is here. You can't trust him. He is probably the one who got Vivienne killed. He is on the side that killed your father, that killed our Yves. Don't you forget that!"

Josephine stares at her back as she leaves.

Franz has his back to her, too, his hands behind him casually. He is looking at the photo of Yves on the mantelshelf.

He turns as she approaches.

"I did not expect you," she says, possibly the only honest thing she can find to say.

"You never wrote," he says.

"I would have replied if you'd written. If I'd known where to write."

"I wrote you many times."

Maman has not once asked about Franz. This thought flitters through her head and out again before landing, before reaching a truth.

"I can't explain why the letters didn't come," says Franz. "I wrote six times, each time waiting for yours."

She feels a thump to the chest as if she has been punched. Imagines the torturous conditions in the trenches, which Franz has just come back from.

"You have to believe me."

She steps to face the window, so she doesn't have to look at him. So he can't see that she believes him. Cause and effect, Xavier would say. He didn't write. She moved on. She can't go back. But if she were truly honest, she would have likely moved on anyway.

A pigeon swaggers along an architrave across the street, and Josephine's eyes follow his steps. *What now?* she asks him before he takes flight.

"Did you have anything to do with Vivienne being caught?"

"No, of course not! I have read the report. I would have brought her into headquarters myself for questioning had I known of her operations. It would not have happened with a staged arrest in public. It was a calamity . . . She was a spy, in case you weren't aware."

She believes him, though there are still things about Franz she would like to know.

"You visited her before you left," she says, turning now, a vision of where she wants this to go.

"Yes, to say goodbye. She was a friend . . . I have perhaps performed poorly in my role since I did not suspect her at all. Perhaps I am not particularly good at spotting deceit."

Josephine looks away, hoping that he cannot see hers.

He takes her hand, and she lets him for now.

"I meant what I told you before I left . . . I wish to take care of you."

He retrieves a crumpled, water-damaged photograph from his shirt pocket.

"I have kept you next to my heart."

Tears spring to her eyes. She had been so sure of him. And she is sure of him now. Though it is different. She is different.

"Josephine, what is wrong?"

"I'm sorry. I didn't hear from you . . . Your letters never came. I am in shock, that is all."

She can see it all then. His heart is pure. Her plans are thwarted. She does not know what to say. He has been to the Front, fighting. There are traces of the battle he has brought back, the burn marks on the backs of his hands, the dark circles around his eyes, the way his jacket no longer fits firmly to his body, the jagged part in his carelessly combed hair, the attention to himself less important. He has been through war. He puts his hand on her arm.

"I am sorry that I have arrived without warning. I didn't mean to shock you."

She steps away, frees herself from his hand that brands her guilt.

"Are you back here permanently?"

"For a little while, yes. They have asked me to find some people. It is a better job than the one I've been doing. I can't tell you how hard it is out there. How much of your past life is stripped from you. I've had time to ponder things that are more important."

She shakes her head.

"What is wrong?" he asks.

"I'm not sure it will work. You and I."

"What do you mean?" he says.

"I can't . . ." She is unable to think of the right words to say.

"Josephine, I have to go. I must return to the *Kommandantur*. I arrived only hours ago and stole some time to come here."

He perhaps does not want to hear what she has to say.

"I love you, Josephine."

There is something she feels still. Though it is more the feeling of being loved, not a feeling of being in love. She has tasted the latter and knows the difference.

He is gone, and Josephine sits down to stare at the wall, to find a way out of this. She is only vaguely aware of her mother, who has returned to sit next to her.

"Why, Maman?" Josephine asks wearily, when she is able to speak.

"It wasn't right." There is a break in her voice. "I'm sorry. But, Josephine, I never told you. The national committee who distributes charity food told me that they would no longer serve you, that you were banned from receiving any rations if you continued to consort with the German captain. Word had spread. Your reputation was at stake. I did what I thought—"

"Where are they?" says Josephine. She is not angry at her mother but at the committee for making a fool of her mother, likely in front of others.

Gisela shakes her head.

"I don't have them."

Gisela was always thorough with everything. The only trace of letters perhaps now ash in the grate.

"Why?"

"To protect you."

"From what exactly?"

"How can you know what it is to be a mother? To see all the bad around you that your children can't."

"Maybe it is that I have to work things out for myself sometimes. That I must make my own way, even my own mistakes."

"Though this was not any ordinary mistake," says Gisela grimly. "He is fighting our men. Have you forgotten that? What would your father think?"

Josephine looks at something on the floor, remembering.

"He would say to look for the stars in every dark situation. Don't turn away in ignorance. Don't ignore what is right in front of you. Take ownership of everything you do."

"Your father was an idealist. Where do you think you and Eugène get it from?"

Her mother smiles sadly.

"There is something about the captain I don't trust," Gisela says. "I have felt it from the beginning. I believe that there is something else that drives him, that he does not care for you the way you think."

"Perhaps it is that someone, even a German soldier, could like someone as plain as I am."

"Oh no, my darling. But you aren't at all. You are beautiful inside and out."

"I know why you burned the letters, Maman," she says. "But Papa and you would tell me to judge a man in isolation, to not put labels on people, to not blame the world for the ruthlessness of a few. It's how you brought me up. And Franz . . . he was kind and that is all. Could I have been swept away? I know my own heart. I know that it was not fully given to him, though I admit I liked the feeling of belonging to someone."

"Oh, my dear girl . . ."

She is weeping now. It is her way of an apology. It is rare for her to admit anything.

But we are not ourselves.

Franz is waiting for her as she leaves the next day, leaning on the fence at the end of the street. This place is too dangerous for her family. Xavier is right. They must leave.

He grips her arm and they walk for a while silently. She could lie and say she just needs some time to adjust to him being back, while she finds an opportunity to leave the city. Or she could tell him she doesn't love him. Would he accept it? Doubtful, but he deserves to know the truth.

"Can you tell me what is wrong? It is Vivienne, isn't it? You blame me for her death."

"No. I don't blame you for anything."

"Then it is that I am German."

She looks up at him, his face toward her, and she sees strangely a miserable future that can never be.

"Franz . . . I've met someone else."

She is shocked by the suddenness of her own words, by her own courage.

"I moved on when I didn't hear from you."

"It is very fast that you have found someone and moved on. Who?"

"It doesn't matter, does it?"

"It does to me," he says, still holding her arm.

"Franz . . ."

He releases her.

"It would never have worked," she says. "My family would never have accepted you."

"What does your family have to do with us?"

"Everything. We have lost so much to this stupid war, and you will always be a reminder of that."

"I thought you felt the same."

"I thought I did, too. But . . ." She has grown, she wants to say. She has broken out from the naivety she entered Brussels with.

"Answer me this," she says. "Would *your* father have been happy? I have heard what Germany thinks of us."

"It doesn't matter what he would have thought."

"I don't think I fit anywhere when I'm with you, that's the problem. I am either a prisoner of Germany or I am a traitor to Belgium."

"Love should override that."

"If there were love, I might agree."

Franz puts his head down, caresses the piping on the hat he carries, and then looks away into the distance. He nods to her, though he can no longer meet her eyes. He wants to disguise the hurt, avoid her pity.

Her shawl has dropped from her shoulders, and she pulls it around her to ward off the northern wind that whips around her neck.

He walks away and does not turn back.

He will understand, she tells herself, in time. He will love again and know the difference, too.

Time does not change the past, but it allows us the opportunity to change our hearts. His words that she hopes he will remember.

She can't go home straightaway. She wanders past *La boulangerie du peuple*, where she and her mother line up for their bread—more often made with potato or rice now—taunted by the smell of pastries ordered to be distributed separately to Germans and only those Belgians who can afford the high price of sugar and fruit. Farther on Josephine walks widely around a park where soldiers lay their heavy coats to air, close to the *Kommandantur*.

Then an odd feeling, cold creeping up her spine, as if she is being watched. She turns all of a sudden, and movement across the park catches her eye. A girl with dark hair, small build, pulls a scarf around her head. A man in a hat bends down to speak quietly in her ear. The girl gives a short nod, and they part hastily in opposite directions.

Anja!

Josephine stops to wait for a tram to pass, sees the girl's skirt swirl round a corner. She hurries to the end of the street to catch sight of her. Then down another. Then another. She looks around her, puzzled. The girl has vanished. Josephine shakes her head, shakes away her imaginings.

What am I doing? She is seeing things that aren't really there. Anja has been gone for months. She would be with Eugène now if she were here.

38. THE BELGIAN

Something is bothering Josephine today. She appears despondent and distant, her eyes unable to settle on any one thing for more than a few seconds, arms tightly crossed, and walking several times to the window. Arthur believed at first it was the presence of the fugitive Belgian whom she was not expecting to see. For two days the lovers have not had a chance to be alone in the house.

"Is everything all right?" he asks her when she is next to him in the kitchen, scraping the tea leaves that have already been used twice.

She nods dismissively, a gesture he thinks to prevent any further questioning.

The Belgian, Cédric, is sitting at the table, close-set eyes following the pair's every movement. He has a mouth that stretches from one side of his face to the other above a wide chin. He has spoken much since he arrived, but of things that are vacuous, filling the air with sound and not substance. He is tiring and repetitive, and alarmingly edgy. He said at one point he needed to get out, go for a walk.

"That isn't wise," says Arthur, even though it would be a relief to see him gone. "Not yet."

Cédric is restless, knee bouncing up and down when he sits, chewing the inside of his cheek: habits that are annoying. He is constantly looking at the door. Arthur is relieved that Josephine is here, though at the same time he doesn't like the way Cédric is looking at her, as if he wants to salt and pickle her, wetting his lips with his tongue in anticipation.

She tells Arthur she needs to package the printing accessories in preparation for their move. He follows her to the basement.

"He has been here before, no?" she says to him quietly.

"No," says Arthur, frowning. "Not while I was here."

"He looks familiar."

"Is that what is bothering you?"

Their attention is diverted by the squeaking of a vehicle pulling to a sudden stop outside. Arthur bounds upstairs, Josephine close behind him, to greet Eugène as he hastens through the door, highly agitated. With both hands he pushes the mop of curls back from his face and holds it there, his bottom lip bitten white, as he paces once in a circle. There is blood on his shirt and under his nails.

"It all happened so fast," he says, eyes across the floor, searchingly.

"What did?" says Arthur.

"I killed someone!" he says. "In the warehouse."

"Who?" they say in unison.

"A soldier," he says, speaking fast. "A German. He is in the back of the vehicle."

"You brought him here?" says Josephine, in disbelief. "But—"

"No," says Arthur. "That is good. Getting rid of the evidence. Is there any trace of his death, any blood?"

He shakes his head, attempting to free a trapped thought. "I don't know. I don't think so. I don't know. I had to leave quickly before someone else came."

"Are you sure no one else saw you?" says the Belgian.

"Of course I'm not sure." Voice raised, frustrated. "They are everywhere! Like gnats."

"Calm," says Arthur. "Sit down. We will think of something."

"I have to get the truck back before they notice I haven't returned."

"First then let's get the body," says Arthur. "Cédric, keep a lookout from the street! Eugène and I will bring it in."

In the back of the truck, the soldier lies, arms twisted around him, in some strange macabre self-embrace, legs splayed, thrown around erratically in the back of the truck, blood smeared across the floor and some against the wall.

Cédric has stepped forward to look at the body as they slide it out.

"Cédric!" says Arthur. "Eyes out and about."

Eugène and Arthur carry in the body, see the jagged cut across the throat, blood dripping onto the floor. Josephine returns with Arthur with a bucket of water and sheets from the bed to clean it out.

Arthur dumps the blood-sodden sheets inside and, returning to the vehicle, sees movement at the end of the street.

"Someone's coming," he warns.

A woman, a stranger, has entered the street and proceeds their way.

"Who is that?" says Cédric.

"I don't know but we need to hurry," says Eugène, jumping from the vehicle.

By the time the woman reaches them, they are almost finished. Josephine is wiping the last traces and furtively glances the woman's way before sweeping the used cloth behind her.

"Do you want some help, dear?" says the woman, peering inside at her.

"No, thank you," says Josephine.

"It stinks," she says. "Vinegar might help mask the smell of blood.

"Good day!" the stranger says without waiting for a response.

"I should follow her," says Cédric when she is far enough away.

"No," says Josephine. "I doubt she has seen anything, and she would not have given herself away if she was spying."

"You don't know that," barks Cédric.

"Do you want to draw more attention then?" says Josephine.

"I wasn't asking for your permission to leave, *chienne*!"

"You do as she says!" says Eugène, stepping menacingly toward him. "Or you can kiss your freedom goodbye!"

Cédric throws Josephine a hostile glance before storming inside the building, bumping into Arthur's shoulder as he passes.

There is a look and a nod between siblings: an appreciation of one another that has been missing for some time.

"I will get some chemicals and machine oil from the basement," says Arthur. "Wipe over the walls to mask the stench."

When they are finished, Eugène leaves to return the truck.

"I will be back shortly, and we will discuss what to do with the body," he says.

Later that evening, Xavier arrives bringing two loaves of bread and potatoes and pepper, the information thrown at him by Eugène as he walks through the door and is confronted by the body.

Xavier is thoughtful while he sets down the package of food.

"Why did you kill him?" says Xavier.

"He works in the German storehouse. He caught me stealing, putting food inside my coat. I reacted straightaway. It would have been over for us all. Arrested."

Xavier is nodding, agreeing.

"It is a pity people have to die," he says, but not in a voice that invokes any sympathy. "The bodies are piling up in Belgium."

"What should we do with him?" asks Eugène.

"Wait for dark, throw him in the canal with bricks to make him sink," says Xavier.

Cédric has torn a piece of bread from the basket Xavier has brought, stands above the body, eats with his mouth wide open.

Arthur looks at the stranger, disgusted by him, then back to the face of the German, who was his own age roughly. Feels something for the man whose only job was to guard the store.

"Eugène, do you think you were seen?" Xavier asks. "Was anyone else in the vicinity?"

"Not that I saw. But I expect he will be missed quickly."

"Hmm," says Xavier, which means it isn't good. He would use other words if it were.

39. ON THE RUN

Josephine wakes up suddenly. An image appears in her mind, a memory blurred and grainy like one of her first photograph experiments. She is picturing the profile of Cédric in the crowd, the day of the parade, his sly glances under the brim of a hat, the high step on his nose, a heavy chin. She caught only a glimpse of him, but these features grow more distinct in her mind. However, this memory of Cédric alone is not what causes her alarm. She is almost sure she has seen him with the same man accompanying the girl she thought was Anja near the German headquarters. She hurries out of bed to change her clothes. She must tell Arthur and Eugène.

Stark against the early morning, several urgent knocks at the front door force her to pause her task. She steps outside on the landing at the same time as her mother and looks back to check that Grace is still sleeping.

"You stay here," says Gisela from the other doorway. "I will find out who it is."

Josephine crouches at the top of the stairs, her head against the banister rails, listening.

There are voices.

"Frau Descharmes?"

"Yes," says Gisela.

"We would like to speak to your son, Eugène Descharmes."

"He isn't here. What is it that you want to speak to him about?"

"It is military business, madame, about a crime concerning security."

Josephine steps quietly to her bedroom, throws off her nightgown, and pulls a dress down over her head.

There is another man as well that speaks in French too quietly for her to hear.

She misses some of what her mother says in reply, but she is questioning them further, and Josephine can sense some frustration in the voice of the second inquisitor.

"It is important," says the first man with the loud German voice. "He is wanted in connection with a crime, a serious crime. If you are harbouring him, you must let us know. Who else is here with you?"

"No one," says Gisela. "My other son, Xavier, works at the hospital, saving your men, and my daughter has left to stand in the long queue for—"

Gisela coughs harshly, and a command is given to search the house.

There is a trunk at the end of the bed. It is musty when she lifts the lid. Old rugs and blankets. It is too small for them both to climb into. She wakes up Grace, puts a finger to her lips, and the little girl sits up and rubs her eyes. Josephine indicates for her to stand, leads her to the trunk. She understands. She has been tutored in hiding by Vivienne. She needs no coaxing to climb in. Josephine closes the lid gently and locks it with a key she hides under the dresser. Then she climbs out the window, onto the narrow ledge of their attic bedroom, and grabs hold of the shallow eave to hoist herself on top of the roof. She crawls carefully across to the chimney stack, where she perches.

Across from her a woman at a window appears to be watching her. Josephine puts her finger to her lips but there is no acknowledgement. She is not sure whether the woman has noticed her, if she can even see this far, or if she is pretending not to see.

Josephine can hear footsteps moving between the rooms. She sees the woman then move quickly away, and senses that someone is standing at her bedroom window, looking out.

The trunk is obvious, she thinks. They are sure to check it. It was a bad decision made in haste. She recognises that now.

"Captain, there is no one in the other rooms," she hears someone call below.

"Check again!" someone yells in response, the man's forceful voice close by the window and sailing outside and up to her. She trembles, knowing to whom that voice belongs. She closes her eyes, gripping tightly to the bricks, and listens for further movement by Franz. He seems to stay near the window for too long. Perhaps he is leaning out, looking below, even upward. Perhaps he knows. He is clever.

Then his soft, clipped steps cross the floor and the squeak of the hinge on the wardrobe. Then no sounds at all for what seems like a lifetime. She imagines he is examining the trunk, discovering it is locked, and about to break it open. He is someone who is too thorough to not look in something so obvious. She thinks of Grace, practised in hiding, used to fear. Josephine cannot do this, cannot put the little girl in harm's way. She makes a decision and releases the chimney to begin the climb back down to face him.

"To the street!" Franz shouts to others. The shock of his raised but familiar voice causes Josephine to lurch, her foot slipping partway down the tiles. She crawls backward and upward to reach out and once more wrap her arms around the chimney, fearful of falling now. Several sets of boots recede down the stairs, then silence.

She strains to hear, to check it is now all clear. Soft steps surprise her near the window again. She waits, breathing rapidly. Then those same steps toward the centre of the house and down the stairs.

Soldiers shout in the street below, and then sounds of men running and of horses galloping echo throughout the city.

Josephine stays there for minutes to wait for the noise to fade, then breathes out heavily, shaking with relief. She cranes her neck over the edge to search below for anyone watching. It appears to be clear, and she begins her descent more carefully, climbing over the side of the roof to reach her foot down blindly to find the ledge. It is twice as difficult, this journey in reverse. Any wrong move and she might slip and fall.

Gisela calls for her daughter, unaware of where she is hidden, then gasps in fright as Josephine appears outside the window to climb in. Her mother rushes to help her through.

Josephine unlocks the trunk and lifts the little girl out, brushes the hair out of Grace's eyes, and gives her a hug.

He would have looked here. Why didn't he?

"You did well," she says, the little girl's face solemn, her thoughts and fears deeply buried.

"It was your German friend," says Gisela. "It seems that he is no longer looking after you."

"They may now send people to watch the house," says Josephine.

"Then I will head toward the hospital," says Gisela, "to warn Xavier, and hopefully they will follow me, thinking I will lead them to Gène. You must leave through the back garden, and Grace will have to stay here."

"But Xavier . . ."

"He is strong, Josephine. He will be all right."

Her mother stands there, straight backed, unyielding in stance, as if she might stop an army. It was how she always appeared to Josephine. She has grown tall again with courage.

"Maman, you must be careful, too. I am not sure what will happen after today. No matter what comes, you must take care of yourself and Grace."

Gisela has tears in her eyes. Josephine kisses her quickly on the cheek, bends down to do the same to Grace. Her mother pushes her gently to hurry. There is no time for lingering goodbyes. She steps carefully from the back door, then climbs over the wire fencing to another property, snagging the sleeve on her cardigan and tearing through some skin. Scrawny chickens cluck next door, and she dodges them before climbing another fence and out the front garden of the house three doors down. She will have to go the long way round to the west then north of the city, then to La Vérité, in case there is someone spying on the direct route between houses.

Josephine looks behind her, then runs, the soles of her feet burning until she reaches the industrial outskirts of the city. Several soldiers walk across a square, gesticulating about something, sending an elderly man and woman away from the area, distracted at least.

By the time she reaches La Vérité, she has run out of breath.

"What is it?" says Arthur.

"Where is Gène?"

"He is on the way to your house. Come sit," he says, seeing her sudden distress. He stands to get her some water.

"The German police," says Josephine. "They came this morning. They want to speak to Gène."

"For what? Did they say?"

"They said for a crime concerning security, so we must presume it was the incident that he revealed yesterday."

"They probably became suspicious when their own guard went missing. But that is not our only problem. This place, we have to leave anyway. Eugène and I believe that Cédric was a rat. He was gone by the time we rose this morning. I've had my suspicions. He has been constantly looking for excuses to leave the house. We have to get away from here, get out of Belgium as soon as we can."

"I have to head back toward home. Find Gène."

"There is no time."

She knows he is right. She has to hope that Eugène watches their mother's house before he enters, that he sees the spies that she suspects by now have been installed to watch.

"But if the police are there because of the murder of the guard, how would they know for certain it was Gène?"

"I suspect it was Cédric," says Arthur.

"I have to tell you something. I have seen him before, talking to another man. I believe they both have some connection to the German government . . . But that isn't all. I thought I saw Anja, too, several days ago. And I think it was this second man who was with her."

"Anja still here? How certain are you of this?"

She shakes her head. Doubts creep in. The idea of the girl being Anja suddenly seems absurd. It is simply hope, looking for people who aren't there.

"They could well be linked, though I'm not sure how Anja fits into it. I trust your instinct, but perhaps don't mention anything to Eugène yet. There is too much risk the way things stand. Maybe when we are safely far away so he does not go out of his way to get himself arrested."

Any word of Anja might send Eugène over the edge. Arthur appears to know her brother well.

Arthur rushes around collecting things and pulling his suspender straps over his shoulders as he goes. He takes his cap off the wall and places it on his head. Hair uncombed, skin unshaven.

"What is happening with Xavier?" he says.

"Maman has gone to warn him."

"Cédric would have revealed every one of us. You can't go home. You all need to get out of Brussels."

Josephine thinks of Franz, and the son of Herbert the smuggler. Perhaps the money Eugène supplied him would never be enough.

"I know."

"Eugène has been talking about going north. If he doesn't return soon, then perhaps we should head that way toward the border," says Arthur.

In a bag he has placed a pistol, food that is left in the pantry. He pulls on a coat and gives her one to cover the thin dress and cardigan she is wearing. They must travel light.

"In case we are caught and interrogated, there must be no evidence," says Josephine.

She pulls out the ribbon from the typewriter and the photographs of men that she didn't end up using, faces staring out at her, strangers that came through here, that she will likely never see again. She walks out to the canal, looks along the walkway, then drops her equipment, film, and photographs, wrapped in linen, into the water. Arthur is inside, tearing up paper that they will scatter on the canal. As she stands to wipe her wet hands on her dress, she sees a man across the water with a set of binoculars turn away suddenly. It is only by instinct that she knows he is aware of her. She has seen him before. He is the man who sits at the fountain with his wife. He had stopped going there several months ago.

"Arthur, we have to go now," she says, back inside. "We are being watched."

"By whom?"

"Across the canal."

Arthur goes to the window to peer from behind the blanket.

"There is no one there now."

"If he is a spy, it means he will report that we are destroying things," says Josephine. "We must go! Hurry! We can't wait for Gène to return. We agreed once that if anything were to go wrong, if we were to lose contact with one another, we were to meet at my cousins' house on the road to Louvain, like we did once before. He would go there first, I am sure of it."

Lightning on the horizon southeast, where they are heading. They weave through the streets, moving close together like the lovers they are when they are looked at. Though they have to be mindful of their closeness also. It is not the time to appear too happy, too in love. They continue down the main thoroughfare to the Parc du Midi in the south.

In the southern forest they keep a lookout for Eugène, hoping they might see him on the way. They remain in a copse of trees to wait for dark before they continue travelling on the open road. In the silence of the night, they listen to the cannon fire in the distance that competes with the tune of a bird. Arthur leans against a tree, and Josephine sits between his legs inside the cavity of warmth he creates with his body. At dusk, they leave the forest.

A scattering of dim yellow lights across the lowlands guides them along the road to Louvain and toward the brick chateau that glows a shade of midnight. They enter through a barren arbour, pass the flower gardens now overgrown with weeds.

"You wait here," he tells Josephine. "I will make sure there is no one in the house."

"No, I'll come."

Below a window he lifts her up on his shoulders, and she grips his head with her thighs, her skirt ridden up her legs. She peers inside to the rooms that are still, dark, and silent. He lifts her down and holds her hand as they approach the front door. It has been broken and splintered, and swings open with just a gentle push.

Trails of muddy boot prints are mashed together in the hallways, where many have trodden and scratched the polished floors. Some of the curtains have been torn from the walls for bedding. There is rubbish strewn and the odour of men who have spent weeks in the field.

Every cupboard door in the kitchen has been opened, one torn off.

"They have left nothing for the rats," she says. She feels sad the invaders have destroyed the furnishings, that they continue to destroy her past.

She explores upstairs while Arthur collects splinters of wood. The top floor smells of urine, and the sheets are streaked with mud, the large mirror in her aunt's bedroom cracked. She can't sleep up here. The smell is too much, and there is now misery attached to these walls.

In the fireplace, Arthur has built a pyre with the broken chairs. In a drawer he has found some paper to start the fire. He curses and mutters, matchsticks damp from inside his bag, before finally striking a flame. He spends the next half hour keeping it alight. They lay their damp coats over the chairs near the fire to dry.

"Here," says Arthur, retrieving something from his bag. "You should eat."

She takes the tin of sardines and lifts one into her mouth, crushed into paste and gone, her stomach crying out for more.

Josephine stands by the window, watching the darkness.

"Come," he says, lying down on the couch, raising a blanket invitingly. "Get some rest, get warm." She puts her shoes together tidily near the fire to dry and climbs onto the couch beneath the tall windows.

His arms wrap around her, and they lie awake, afraid of sleep. Though she is drifting at times and seeing the cold eyes of Franz that turn warm then cold again.

She is restless until she hears Arthur's slow, rhythmic breaths, his heart against her back.

40. CHOICES

It is morning and Josephine is sleeping finally. Arthur's arm is dead underneath her head, and he lifts it gently away, then rises to step toward the window. Rain still drifts across the roof and out to the east with a heavy wind. The fire has burned out, the room perfumed with warm ash. He had imagined a time when he would have to leave, when something would have to change. Though he didn't expect it to be like this.

It is months now since he crossed the border to Belgium, and the comfortable life he had in England has been swept into the past. He wonders briefly about his choices. If he had left with Gordon, he would be on the other side of the border in a trench. He thinks of the poor souls there now, in deep ditches filling with water, frozen, hungry, awaiting their orders and fate. No amount of preparation can brace them for such an existence.

Rain patters on the grass and paints a pathway of silver to the houses, the size of peas, at the bottom of the valley. He checks the map again. *How long to wait here?*

Josephine wakes, and he brings her a glass of water. Her eyes are swollen slightly, though she still glows with youth. She does not smile immediately at the sight of people. It is not her nature to give smiles away at random. They are measured out carefully, which, when they come, makes them all the more special.

He sits on the couch as she rises, drawn to the light of the window like a moth, arms wrapped tightly around her own body from the cold.

"I'm thinking that we go north if your brothers don't come here by the end of the day. They might have gone that way already. They may have had no choice."

"No, they wouldn't leave without me, and I can't without any of them."

But what if we are captured? He cannot bring himself to say it.

She sits beside him, head against his shoulder. They have snatched a moment of tenderness that he is not sure they will see again between here and the other side of the border. Their relationship started in secret. He does not want it to die that way, too.

"Perhaps we will be all right here for a day or two," he says. "We could go down to the village for food."

"I hope Maman is safe. That they haven't arrested her."

"There is nothing to arrest her for." Though he knows that family members are unjustly held accountable, too, in many instances.

"Arthur," she says, "I want you to know that I love you. I didn't say it before, but I thought it and I expected you to feel my love, too."

"I did. I felt it. I feel it now."

The moment of tenderness is quashed by the sound of feet splashing noisily through sludge. They jump to the window to see Eugène bowling along the pathway to the house. Josephine rushes excitedly outside to meet him, uncaring of her bare feet in the cold and wet. Arthur watches the pair hug from the window as if they have been parted for months. Josephine's face is flushed with emotion. Despite the occasional domestic turbulence, they are tightly tethered, these siblings, this family a force together. It is something he never got to experience, such uninhibited affection. He is envious and in wonder at the same time. The image of closeness then gnaws at his insides, sends a chill up his spine. *I can't compete.*

"It isn't good," Eugène says once inside, door wedged shut again. "They have arrested several from our group. They have got a list of the houses. It was that stinking Belgian, though how he came to know us I don't know. Someone must have talked to the authorities, and they planted him then in the group."

"It makes sense," says Arthur. "He did not shut up when he was with me. Always questions."

"Xavier will bring us food later. They are after me. I know. Maman got a message to Xavier, and I thought to go to him when I saw strangers patrolling the street. Xavier said he will make sure he isn't watched. He is devising a plan to make it harder for them to follow if they do."

"And to the northern border?" says Arthur. "Can we not all go there?"

"No. Not at the moment. Since the sentry was killed, they have been crawling up and down the border. It is not wise. Not right now. We wait for Xavier. He thinks we should continue to the new safe house for now, until we get a later opportunity."

"He is coming with us, isn't he?" she asks.

"He is only bringing supplies, but he won't be leaving Brussels. Maman is not well enough. Grace will slow us down." He searches for movement outside the window. "He should be here soon."

It is late morning when Xavier finally comes, and he has brought sausage and beans. They break some of the wood from the chair to burn to cook, to boil water in the kettle for coffee, or something like it, at least, that they have in their pack.

Eugène is showing Xavier on a map the location of the house he has talked about. Xavier advises on the best route.

"Is Maman all right?" asks Josephine when they are finished.

"As well as to be expected. I have taken her and Grace to the home of one of the nursing assistants. They will stay there until things calm down. Maman has done nothing wrong. She is hopefully safe."

"No one is safe," says Josephine. "They can easily find her if they want to."

Xavier puts his hands together thoughtfully and nods. He is already aware of the risks.

"You three," says Xavier, "must leave this house by tonight. It is exposed. Germans travel through here all the time."

"Where will you go?" asks Josephine.

"I must return. Move Maman and Grace again if I have to. Hide until it is safe for us to leave."

"They must know about your involvement from Cédric," she says. "They will hunt you down."

"There is nothing I can change about that now."

Josephine looks stricken. Xavier will likely be arrested if he stays. Their plan had seemed safe from failure, but now it seems scattered.

Horses pound the mud outside, and Eugène drops the map to his thighs as Xavier rushes to the window.

"Soldiers!" Xavier announces.

Eugène retrieves his gun from inside his coat and walks to the window.

"No, Gène!" says Xavier. "No killing! We will talk to them. There are only two. It is Captain Mierzen. We know that he can be reasonable. You and Arthur just need to stay out of sight. It is you they want most. Hide and get ready to run to the woods."

Eugène and Arthur stand to walk to the room on the other side of the wall. The Germans kick apart the door, announcing they are not here to talk. Eugène disappears, but Arthur doesn't reach the other side of the wall in time, his gun still in his pack.

41. LIFE OR DEATH

Franz is pointing his gun at them. Josephine can see his eyes, dark flesh beneath and angry webs of red amongst the white. She knows before he even opens his mouth that he is wounded. And wounded animals are unpredictable.

The soldier he is with is similar in build and height and youth. There is something about this second man that frightens her even more. There is nothing at all in his stare but disgust for the people he sees, for Belgium. He carries a gun also, though it is something he does with more ease, as if he might casually release bullets on them all without a passing thought.

"Franz," says Josephine with a pleading look.

Franz twists his lips, the smile anything but amiable. It is cruel, his mouth, she thinks now, the look down his nose, arrogant.

"We are good people," she says. "Please, let us go."

"Are you, Mademoiselle Descharmes?" says Franz. "A man was murdered. A man following orders. He was a good person. Though it is not the only crime you and your brothers are guilty of."

"My sister has done nothing wrong," says Xavier.

Franz points his gun toward Xavier, who then raises his hands to gesture his compliance.

"Do not speak unless I direct you to," Franz says in a voice Josephine hasn't heard before, steely and unforgiving. "I want to hear from her only."

The other soldier has left the room down a hallway, in the opposite direction of the room where Eugène is hiding, his rifle gripped tight against his belly and pointing forward in anticipation. Josephine's heart pumps hard.

"Where is Eugène?" Franz says, continuing to address only Josephine.

"He is not here," she says.

"No!" he snaps, and she jumps. "You are buying him minutes only. He *will* be caught."

"Please—"

"You are guilty of much, too, mademoiselle," he says too calmly. "You will all be imprisoned and likely executed. Perhaps your mother also."

Josephine's body begins to shake with terror. She can feel his hatred, cold hands around her heart, threatening to freeze, then crush it into pieces.

Xavier squeezes her hand for support, to stop her from crumbling. She does not trust herself to speak further.

Franz turns to Arthur.

"What is your name?" he asks Arthur in English, clearly aware of his origins.

"Arthur Verhoeven," Arthur replies in French. Josephine suspects that the false name is pointless.

"You have a strange accent, Monsieur Verhoeven. I expect you are the Englishman I have been informed about."

Franz is finished with him quickly, returning his attention back onto her. It seems she is the motivation behind much of his fury. She can also see now how frightening he can be, how others must have felt when he visited them. She despises him also in this moment.

The other soldier has walked back into the living room where they are standing to cross toward the hallway on the other side. He will only have to take several more strides before he reaches Eugène hiding in one of the rooms off the hall.

"We will come with you peacefully," says Xavier, stepping forward to divert the attention from her.

The other soldier turns back to them and strikes Xavier on the side of the head with his rifle.

"He ordered you to stay silent!" shouts the soldier into Xavier's ear. He staggers sideways before righting himself, and Josephine rushes to his side.

"I told you that you must not talk, Monsieur Descharmes," says Franz.

"Please . . . Franz . . . ," she pleads. "Don't hurt him."

Arthur steps protectively close.

"Stay where you are!" commands Franz.

The other soldier walks toward Arthur as if he might strike him, too.

"No!" commands Franz to his subordinate. "Keep searching the rest of the house."

The soldier turns to inspect the rear of the property through the large window.

"There is something I imagine you wish to know," says Franz to Josephine. He pauses, though he is not waiting for her response. "Your friend from your . . . rebellion, your small army, whatever it is you call it. She was caught. Anja squawked the moment we said she would not be sent to prison if she gave us what we wanted."

"Franz," says Josephine, "I had to do what I did. It is war. We need to help our brothers."

He is amused by something as the second soldier proceeds to the hallway on the other side.

"She never mentioned your part in anything. Only your brother, her lover. She gave us him to save herself."

"Liar!" says Eugène, tearing down the hallway toward them. Josephine can see Eugène's face seconds before he fires into the soldier advancing in his direction. The German is hit in the forearm, but not before he has fired also. Eugène's body shudders as two bullets enter his chest and a third shatters the side of his head, blood splattering across the furniture and walls.

Eugène's body sinks into a pool of his own blood.

What I do is for us: for you, Maman, Yves, Xavier, and Papa. For our future. For a Belgian future, said Eugène.

"No!" wails Josephine as Arthur seizes hold of her.

The injured soldier grips his own arm to stop the blood and looks murderously at the rest of the group. Franz appears in a state of confusion, his hand unsteady as he raises his gun, glancing sideways at Eugène.

While both soldiers are momentarily rattled, Xavier charges at Franz, pushing him into the other man, and both soldiers fall hard against the large, low window, shattering the glass, which explodes in shards. Franz's gun is knocked from his hand.

"Run!" Xavier booms as the soldiers scramble to recover, and Arthur grabs Josephine's hand to pull her down the hallway to the kitchen, Xavier following. Firing behind them misses as the three flee through the back door and down some stairs and into the rain. Josephine slips on the sodden grass and rights herself, Arthur just ahead of her, only metres from the thick trunks of trees at the rear of the property.

Another firing and Josephine can hear Xavier groan behind her. She turns to see that he is facedown in the grass, bleeding from a bullet wound in the back of his leg, and runs toward him.

"No, Josephine!" Xavier warns.

She falters when she sees the German soldier's gun aimed directly at her.

Another shot is fired. She releases a scream and drops to the ground.

Arthur appears beside her as she raises her head fearfully. Blood trickles from the mouth of the soldier who murdered Eugène, as he stumbles toward them, his gun still clenched dangerously in his hand. A second shot, and only feet away, he falls forward and lies still.

Franz stands at the foot of the rear terrace steps, his arm still raised, gun pointing.

Xavier moans and rolls on his side. She touches his shoulder with her trembling hand, while Franz walks toward them, his weapon arm out unsteadily.

"Josephine," Franz says loudly above the rain, moving closer so they are barely metres apart, hair drenched and flattened to his forehead. "Do you think that I didn't know what you were doing, what you and your brothers were doing months ago?

"I stopped you from going to the house where Anja was that day. I wasn't sure if you were planning to, but I couldn't risk it, either. I had followed you many times before, once when you took a camera to photograph soldiers. I had kept your secret."

She stands up to face him. He has her full attention.

"And Vivienne?"

"I knew nothing about her. I was telling you the truth."

"You chose me to get to others," she says. "It was never about us."

"Not to start with," he says, attempting to blink away the heavy raindrops. "I knew the restaurant was connected to members of the underground. I suspected Benôit was involved. I needed a pair of eyes and ears. I was hoping you would lead me to the ringleaders."

Josephine sees that his hand is shaking. She can sense he has lost the coldness that he brought here. Franz looks to Arthur and Josephine in those brief moments; he sees something then, feels it perhaps, the connection, and she can see only his misery, not hate.

"My brother is dead in there . . . ," she cries. "You have taken someone else from me."

Franz shakes his head slightly, struggles to meet her gaze. He lowers his gun, seemingly defeated, though she can't be certain.

She takes another look at Xavier, his teeth clenched, clearly in pain. Arthur has wrapped his shirt around Xavier's leg as he lies sideways now on the ground.

"Go!" Franz calls to Arthur and Josephine. "Go south through the forest, cross the border near Villers-Sire-Nicole. Go to the church. The priest there will collect the mayor's son-in-law. He will look after you. He will find a way to get you to the Allies. He plays for both sides."

Josephine is not sure what to do. She turns to Xavier and his pleading eyes.

"Go!" he says. "Do what he told you."

She takes a final glance at Franz, who is no longer watching them.

"Run, Mouse!" says Xavier. "Have no fear!"

"I love you," she whimpers, stroking his face a final time.

There are sounds of horses and shouts in the distance. More soldiers are coming.

Arthur picks up his jacket and reaches for her hand to pry her away.

She runs with him then, through her tears.

42. THE BORDER

They stay in the forest till dark, then head south, their journey hampered by rain, fear, and grief.

Josephine stops suddenly at moments, crouches down and puts her head on her knees to sob. She can't go on, she says, and each time Arthur picks her up again, keeps her steady. She is wretched, following him blindly, her thoughts on those she has left behind, and those whom she will never see again.

They draw some water from a fountain in an abandoned village and find shelter late that night in the partially destroyed buildings that line the road. Josephine rests her head in Arthur's lap to sleep. He watches her until he dozes briefly, both waking when a deep rumble through the ground reminds them that they sit on the doorstep of war. Then when the sun has barely touched the day, they walk through swirls of mist and blackened trees, to find a man pushing a cart, collecting things from the chaos, indifferent to the danger that has sent his neighbours away. He points the way they should go.

Then farther on they see houses, close together, the faint sounds of wheels and commerce. On the other side of it is their supposed deliverance.

"I think we're nearly there," says Arthur.

Then across the border, they weave through a shallow wood, and just beyond it, a village under a crest of sun that dusts the roofs with gold. Like a coin he found as a boy. He thinks of that moment then, the same joy. Someone else is walking toward them, carrying bags full of moss. He knows the village they seek, gives the final directions.

The ground shakes angrily now from a battleground even closer. The noise from his nightmares too close, slight tremors in his fingers. He will fight the war again with greater plans beyond it, rage against an enemy with new purpose.

He steps down the incline and into sunshine, and turns to look up at Josephine, who remains in the shadows. She is looking above him, beyond him, her face passive, her eyes perhaps not landing on the future he sees.

"This way," he says, tipping his head toward the village. He holds out his hand to guide her down. She looks at his outstretched hand strangely, then back at him, her eyes like crystal, glinting but unseeing.

"I can't, Arthur," she says.

"What can't you do? I'll help you. Whatever it is."

"I can't come with you."

He blinks slowly, looks to the village and back again at where they stand, the line between the two wider all of a sudden.

"Josephine, I love you . . . please." He reaches for her again.

She turns her head as two rivers of tears begin to flow.

"I will take care of you," he says gently. "We will get through this."

Then she is looking at him pleadingly.

"Josephine, we will be free."

"Will we?"

There is a small voice somewhere telling him something else, creeping in again, the uncertainty, people dead. War not over.

"My mother . . . Xavier. I have to go back. They aren't free. No one is free, Arthur."

He looks down. He should have seen this.

"You can't go alone. I must come back with you then."

"No."

He steps back toward her on level ground, his hands trembling to reach her, and she meets him halfway. At the touch of her skin, he is on his knees.

"I can't . . . ," he says weakly, tears squeezing out the sides of eyes, closed to the truth.

He is nothing without her now.

She lowers to her knees also and cups his face.

"You can go on," she says. "You must go on. For Jack."

He pulls her toward him, places his cheek against hers, and breathes her in a moment. He is not sure if he can let her go. She peels herself away to stand. He watches her go, disappearing behind some trees. Part of him has broken free and floated away with her.

No, no, no!

He stands and runs after her.

"Josephine!" he calls softly.

She stops and turns, and he sees her tears.

"Please come with me," he says. He is terrified what might happen to her now, if she will be captured, and where they might take her. "I will take care of you, take you somewhere safe, then go back for your family myself."

They are standing yards apart. He is not game to come too close, afraid that she will run.

"Arthur, no . . . ," she says in a quavering voice.

He wants to touch her, kiss her again, but they are strangers now. He can see distance in her gaze; he can see her looking somewhere else, to a different journey.

"Arthur, you are a wonderful man," she says, her voice breaking. "I can think of no one else I'd rather spend my life with. But I must do this for Yves, for Gène, for Papa. I can't leave any of them. This is something I must do. Not you. You are needed somewhere else."

He is needed nowhere, he argues silently. But there is nothing more he can say. The fight is over. He has lost.

"I love you, Arthur. Always."

She turns again, and he listens to her footsteps disturb the fallen leaves.

"I will find you after this, after the war," he calls softly, but he is not sure she has heard. And he is not sure if it will ever be over.

She is gone, though her presence remains. He can see her clearly in his mind, stepping purposefully across the soft earth, the vibrancy of her gaze; he can feel her narrow hand in his own and her warm breaths against his skin, their hearts connected. They share the same warm sun, the same cold breeze.

He looks toward the west.

It seems too great, this life, to bear it alone.

The life that was so near, so perfect in his mind, is perhaps a figment after all.

43. INTO THE DARK

They have left under a light fall of snow. Josephine has slept for much of it, but there are no windows to see the day, to see the waxwings twitch their crests and tilt their heads sideways for red berries on winter twigs.

Look, another one, Papa! said Josephine, handing him a pair of binoculars. *Do they know we are here? . . . Be quiet, Yves! You will scare them away.*

They don't scare easy in their flock, said Maurice, squinting, mouth open. *They are watching us as closely as we are watching them.*

Though she has little interest in birds. Not now since her father is gone. Not since Louvain turned red with fire, then black.

She cannot sleep. Her head feels full of metal beads that bounce against her skull when the wheels hit a rut. Gisela still coughs, though not as harshly or as frequently. She tries to stifle it so as not to disturb Josephine, whose head rests in her lap.

There are old men, women, and several boys, not quite men, in the back of the truck, its engine groaning loudly over snow-covered roads that crunch under the weight of them. The coat she was given scratches at her neck, her bones beneath it frozen.

They bounce and shake, twelve of them, on the way to a German prison, where disease is rife, and a return is not guaranteed. They have not seen outside the vehicle for hours. The guards are worried that they might become infected by the sick.

A German soldier is a prisoner there, too. He was caught looking the other way when several people ran for the border. They say he was willfully blind to it, that he was not happy with the work. That he wanted to go home. He is going home now, just not the way he wanted.

Several of the Belgian boys tease him, and one kicks him in his thigh when he doesn't respond to their taunts.

"We should kill you," says one.

"And then you will be shot," says the German, though he is frightened, and shivering without a coat. Josephine feels sorry for him.

He is unexpectedly set upon and beaten.

"Stop it now!" Gisela bellows. "He is just a boy like you. You should be ashamed of yourselves."

The boys stop, one landing a final thump, before sheepishly moving back to their original positions. The boy who was set upon wipes his bloody mouth with the back of his hand, crawls to his earlier space. He sneaks a look at Gisela, seemingly humbled by her intervention. Josephine is proud of her mother, who was always fierce about injustice anywhere.

"We are all the same on the inside of this truck," she concludes aloud before grinding out a cough. She needs a doctor. She needs her son.

Josephine thinks of Xavier. Patched up hastily and shipped off on a train to someplace else. She saw Franz once more at their trial. He had looked at her, but she had looked away. He had given special permission for Xavier to talk to them briefly to say goodbye. She had learned from him then that Franz had taken him to the hospital, that he had even visited him once more after that, and he was returning to the Front the day after the trial. Grace had been sent to an orphanage, and Franz had said that after the war she would be sent to her English relatives. Franz had since learned more than they did about Benôit and Vivienne. Benôit, he also revealed, hanged himself in his prison cell so he did not give away the information interrogators were seeking.

"They are hoping we die before we get there," says someone in the truck Josephine can't see; her eyes are closed now.

Someone has brought some sausage and offers a small piece of it to Gisela to give to Josephine. Gisela pushes it in between her lips, but Josephine can't stand even the smell of it, and she is too tired to eat.

In Josephine's dreams, which are fraught with trauma, Arthur is standing in the doorway of their house in Louvain. He is calling her in. But sometimes Franz is there, too, watching them, his eyes shining like silver in sunlight, blinding her.

Did I cause this? Where they are now? All of them. If Franz had caught the line early, caught Benôit and Vivienne before she began her secret work, would everything be changed? He would not have needed her, not then have staged the pretence. These are the kinds of thoughts that swirl in her haze of illness.

The truck slips off the road and into deeper snow, and several prisoners are pulled roughly out through the large back doors to dig out the wheels. Guards curse. It isn't working. Everyone must get out to push it back onto the road, the effort too great for some.

Josephine can barely stand. There are pains in her back. She has no strength.

They are rewarded at least with mouthfuls of snow to give them momentary ease of their cracked lips.

The German boy whom the crowd had set upon makes a run for the edge of the track that falls away into hilly forest. Everyone stops what they are doing, shocked. Two of the four guards react quickly, firing on him at the same time as he reaches the edge. He falls with bullets in his back, and Gisela chokes down a sob.

"He was just a boy," she whispers to no one.

One of the guards is so angry about the loss of a prisoner that he kicks one of the other boys, none of whom are game to try the same.

An elderly gentleman puts his arm around Josephine and helps her climb inside, Gisela on the other side, helping her in. Josephine crawls into the dark, grateful again for her mother's lap.

The doors are shut. The engine roars loudly, blowing out the cold.

"Remember how Yves used to climb on top of your lap when he was small and suck his thumb?" says Gisela. "He didn't want anyone else. He was yours. He was always yours."

Josephine smiles inside, feels the weight of Yves almost, can smell his sweet hair.

Gisela strokes her daughter's head and hums a tune. Josephine is small again, her parents each with a hand.

A stabbing pain in her lower belly to remind her where she is, what is happening to her, what to fear. How much she has lost.

Memories are best left in the past.

44. THE DAY OF THE END

The tent door flaps aimlessly in wind. The dim light of the lantern shudders. Through the cavity Arthur can see the moonlit field that has a single, tall wooden stake, where he will be shot at dawn. He wonders if there is some rationale behind his placement so close to his execution, whether the stake reinforces the idea of good versus bad, as the symbolic line between the two.

He had come back from Belgium six months after he had left his unit. He had argued with the captain who had first applied the charge of desertion. He had not deserted, Arthur stated. He had helped their cause a different way.

But you had the opportunity to return, did you not?

It was a point that he could not counter with any solid argument. Gordon had told them that it was Arthur's choice to stay. Gordon had told them of a girl, of a life that appeared to his jurors as comfortable compared with the standards of soldiers in the trenches.

You are setting a bad example, how to avoid fighting for your country, said one of his accusers.

I was severely injured when I arrived there. I didn't run, I just thought that I was still needed, most of the country occupied.

And who were the people you were living with?

With members of a resistance organisation. We helped Allied soldiers escape.

Are you aware that you swore an oath to fight?

Yes, but—

Are you aware that we have a witness statement that claims you were able bodied for several months before you returned?

Yes, but by then it was harder to leave . . . I want to fight again for Britain—

It didn't matter. They needed to make an example. The war was looking hopeless. They could not allow men to have thoughts of fighting it elsewhere. They needed every man, and they would sacrifice one if that meant securing the loyalty of others.

Arthur had seen some misgivings on the faces of the men charged with assessing the account of his crimes. The officers had examined a pale man with soft golden-brown eyes, with an accent that every so often held a hint of the North. He did not freely speak or self-defend but answered all the questions without any apparent grievance. They had heard him admit to his crimes with a humble acceptance that was almost, if not for the seriousness of the offence, endearing. They had seen a man who appeared honest. And it was this honesty that saw them confused and to some degree pained to prescribe the punishment of death.

Though not all of them felt this way. Some of them, narrow eyed and with a keener understanding of the thoughts of certain men, saw him as an enemy of the Allies and deserving of death.

What sort of man are you, Shine, one such juror had asked, *who can admit to negligence of his own comrades-in-arms and then in the next breath profess to be innocent of malfeasance?*

One that knows the difference between the two, sir.

Not that it mattered to anyone. A crime was committed, a charge was laid, a sentence was passed, and it would be recorded for anyone, for no one. In a matter of hours, he would be in a box and buried unceremoniously in foreign soil.

A company of men crunch the dried earth in heavy boots as they pass the tent of shame, the faint jangling of their tin cups strung to packs. He can picture their faces, knows what lies ahead of them, knows that they are once more headed to uncertainty to draw the lottery of life and death.

Gordon stands just outside the doorway of the tent, glances furtively behind him, then steps inside. He is a young man, perhaps early thirties. Dashing if he had to describe him and likely to succeed in life if he makes it out of France alive.

"You are extremely humble, and I will never forget your help," Gordon tells him. "You should know that I never expected the powers to take it this far."

Arthur nods, but doesn't look at him; more in the hope he will leave him alone to his thoughts, for there is so little time left now to think.

"When I arrived back I made the mistake of telling them about you, made a passing comment about the girl. Wouldn't have mentioned her name even if I'd remembered it, you have to know that . . . They wrote it all down, of course, everything noted, though were seemingly uncaring since I'd brought back intelligence . . . You seemed more of a hero for a brief minute. To be honest I thought I'd never see you again. Then later . . . after . . . well, they called me in again, a more intense interrogation the second time."

He pauses. Arthur looks up to see that he is sincere.

"As you learned at the trial, the information you gave me in the file was false," Gordon continues. "Our men were led into an ambush. The map was staged, I'm assuming. Your contacts there were played . . . It didn't help your case in the end, as you know. I spoke in your favour during the trial. I'm still a bit stunned by the sentence. A short prison sentence maybe, not death . . . I'm sorry. Truly I am, Arthur."

Arthur nods tiredly, closes his eyes. Perhaps it's for the best. He's done some things he knows will not be forgiven. He has torn open torsos and filled them with lead and copper. He has seen these dead men that continue to live inside his mind.

"I have to go," says Gordon, "before someone sees me here."

Gordon bends down to him, pats him gently on the back, speaks softly, then is gone. Arthur lowers his head on his chest and drifts into sleep. There are no fires in the dream, as if this close to death there is nothing more to fear. His images are clear, of Josephine, Jack, and Harriet, the three of them vibrant and carefree; and of himself, at peace, his feet on soft sand before an ocean that shimmers and beckons. This place he does not wish to leave.

Father! No!

"Jack," he mumbles, then jolts awake, chills at the base of his neck, and something drops from his hand.

Through the doorway to his death, the sun bursts out from a cluster of feeble clouds on the horizon to lay one long yellow arm across the earth toward him. He looks down to follow the light to his feet and a small hunting knife on the ground beside his chair.

There's been a delay, I've heard, said Gordon. *You have at least an hour. It's all clear at the back. Forest mostly. Broken buildings. Take the rope with you so they don't see you were given a knife. It's your choice in the end, of course, but I know what I would do.*

He looks up quickly and around him. No sounds outside.

He tilts the chair, falls heavily on his shoulder. He strains the bindings to reach for the knife, clutches it firmly, then twists it toward the rope. The metal meets his hands twice, blood trickling down his fingers.

He thinks of Jack, who is gone, Harriet, too. There is nothing here for him but death.

The measure of a good man, he was told once, is the way he treats his friends and enemies, as if they are the same. But he would argue that the measure of a man means nothing in the end if he dies alone.

45. THE FUTURE

Eleanor

1938

The train hisses to a standstill. I take my small suitcase from the shelf above me. I have watched the fields and villages for hours. People, cars, horses, bikes. The air is clean after a shower of rain. A man is waiting on the station platform expectantly.

He sees me first, and his smile takes my breath away. Not that he is fine looking, which he is, but that he is so like the man in the photograph, my father.

The package that was handed me at the funeral contained two letters that were returned to a Gisela Verhoeven, who had written to my father. I opened the first of these to find a photograph of a very young child. Gisela had sent the letters secretly, the war still a year away from its conclusion, thinking that Arthur would receive the news via the English address that he had given to Xavier during his recuperation at La Vérité. Gisela had been sent to prison, serving a short time for no specific crime other than being aware of activities deemed criminal. She had no way to know my father wouldn't be at this address to receive the announcement that he was the father of the small boy in the photograph. The envelopes had been opened, and since the handwriting instructing the letters to be returned is in my mother's hand, I have to presume Harriet knew of the letters' contents.

"Hello, Eleanor," says Etienne.

He bends down to graze my cheek with his. He has a thick head of dark hair and light-brown eyes. He is dreadfully handsome, tall and broad shouldered, with his open-mouth smile, a small gap between his front teeth.

"I am so glad that we finally meet," he says in English, but with a heavy accent. He takes hold of my shoulders, then leans back slightly to inspect my face, as if to convince himself that I really exist, before stepping forward to hug me.

He is my half brother, the brother my mother decided to keep from me. To try and piece together my mother's thoughts, from a letter that she had of my father's—perhaps the only one that wasn't destroyed—was to understand the grief she had felt from losing my brother, Jack, in the war, for the misguided blame she had toward Arthur. A possessive nature that certainly was not always in my best interests. But to blame her for anything is wrong. For people work with what they know, from their own experiences, good and bad, and I know that she did this because she loved me, that she feared the loss of another child. That she had not fallen out of love with my father, but that she couldn't live with such a daily reminder of what she had lost.

My father wasn't told of my existence. That probably hurts more than anything else. Would that have changed what happened to him? Of course. Would it have changed my view of life? Absolutely.

There was no letter from the War Office correcting the news of his execution. I presume it looked better if they hadn't in fact lost him. Amongst the personal items that I had discovered while cleaning out my mother's past were my father's personal effects—found in his haversack on the battlefield and sent back from France—that my mother had kept hidden. Amongst them was her letter to say she'd left. She would have known about me by this stage of the pregnancy, yet she didn't mention me.

My mother's choice was to raise me by herself. She was pregnant at the time my brother, Jack, was killed, though she didn't know it then. However, she knew it by the time my father had signed up for war, by the time she left him. I imagine the pregnancy had been a part cure for her grief.

"I learned about my history very early," says Etienne casually, light jacket over an open-neck shirt. I can tell he is a man who is comfortable with himself, but without conceit, if I can judge this early. "My uncle Xavier wrote a book that tells much about what happened during those days."

We have walked to the car. He puts my suitcase in the trunk. And we climb into his cream-coloured drop-top coupe. On the floor of the automobile is a newspaper. It is in French. I try to read the headlines but fail.

"What is happening?"

"Oh, you have probably heard. The chancellor of Germany is growing his army, annexing his neighbours, and France is particularly worried like the rest of us. Adolf Hitler has already negated the Treaty of Versailles, as you would be aware, and placed troops along the Rhineland."

I had heard, though I had never taken a deep interest in news or politics.

"What does it mean?" I say.

"No one really knows. But people are talking all the time, thinking there might be another war."

"Surely not like the last one."

"We pray it is not."

"What happened to your uncle Xavier? At the funeral, I saw that he'd been injured."

"He was shot during the escape of our father and my mother, and then was sent to prison, where his leg became infected. While in prison it became so bad they had to remove it. And since he was useless for labour and not deemed a threat, they sent him back to Brussels. He seems to think that authorities thought he would die anyway . . . You will be seeing him again, too. He is very keen to meet you properly."

"He was a priest, you wrote?"

"Yes, he didn't go back to the priesthood, but he did much for the church in other ways. He helped with counselling people in grief. He set up a charity to help the families who had lost loved ones in war, and an orphanage near the church. He is a great man. You will love him."

I watch a family have a photograph taken in a park outside. Mother with a baby and two other children who stand up and lean against her. On the crest of a rise behind them is a church and tiers of gardens and narrow pear-shaped trees. The sun shines in through the window so that I have to shield my eyes with my hand. It is beautiful here and peaceful.

"You told me some things in your letter about my father and Josephine," I say. "It saddened me greatly, what happened. To learn that . . ."

He turns to look at me to see why I've stopped. I am choking on the words to stop me from crying, but some tears escape anyway.

"It is overwhelming. I know," he says. "Then to meet your half brother for the first time. I didn't really understand a lot of it until I was older. Papa didn't tell me some things. He didn't think it would benefit me to know all the details, only that he loved my mother and did not return to England when he had the chance because he wanted to be with her, to protect her. I know that it probably hurts to hear this, but he did not even know you existed until recently. He used to buy the English papers to keep up with news and look through the obituaries. He came across the obituary for your mother, and in it he learned there was a daughter whose father died in the Great War. Xavier offered to go to the funeral to learn the truth. He recognised straightaway that you were Papa's daughter."

I frown at my reflection in the glass. I feel a tinge of bitterness that comes in a rush sometimes, which I attempt to force back, because of my mother, her frailty.

"I'm really sorry for the lost years," he says. "Papa had escaped his early death, his execution. It may have seemed dishonourable, but the powers at the time, the men, had not seen a future when a daughter and a son would want to know their father, that what they saw as justice would deprive us of a past. He had escaped from where they were keeping him; then he was caught by Germans as he attempted to cross back into Belgium. He served out the remainder of the war in a German prison. Once released, he returned to Belgium to look for Josephine. Papa knew she had previously lived in Louvain and searched and found my grandmother Gisela in the broken town and Xavier and, to our father's shock, his baby son.

"I have tried often to think of my mother giving birth in prison, because of her participation in the resistance, and then having to hand me away to strangers. My mother died in my grandmother's arms in prison, not knowing where I was and what was to become of me.

"It was a German by the name of Franz who intervened shortly after that, who had me returned to Gisela. We were then sent back to Brussels. It was so hard on my grandmother . . . ," he says, voice breaking with emotion, though he controls it better than I could.

I know that Gisela suffered much, too, losing her husband and two sons and then her daughter.

"Who is this Franz? How did they know him?"

"My grandmother said he knew my mother, and while they were in prison, he argued for their release. He won the release of my grandmother but at a cost. He was demoted. He came to see *Grand-mère* once after the war, and they talked for hours. He stayed the night and then went back home the next day. Though that was the only time he came. They have exchanged a number of letters since."

"Where is he now?"

"Germany. He married. Has some children. Two, no . . . three. He is still in the military, I believe."

He slows down as we approach a narrow laneway.

"Over in that direction is Louvain. Some call it Leuven, the Dutch way. Don't get me started on the politics, and don't talk about it in front of *Grand-mère* whatever you do . . . Anyway we live in a village close by."

"What do you do?"

"I am a photographer. I have a studio in the town. A lot of people getting married."

"And my father?"

"Yes?"

"He is looking forward to seeing me?"

"Very much." His eyes glisten warmly.

I feel my stomach flutter. I had believed him dead for years. He is a traitor in England but not here. He is a hero, much loved, by the sounds of Etienne's letter.

"I'm sorry you didn't know. Papa couldn't come himself. You know why. It is why Uncle Xavier came instead."

"He left quickly," I say.

"He did not think it was the time. You were grieving."

Also in the package that Xavier gave me at the funeral was a photo of Josephine, Etienne's mother, the woman my father fell in love with.

"Was her death hard?"

He pulls over to a small cottage that has a stone fence. Behind it is a gentle drop to a shallow valley where sheep graze. It is quiet. There are few cars, but several people on bicycles and a horse and wagon.

"*Grand-mère* says that Maman was sick on the way to prison, mainly from the pregnancy. Then as it came close to birthing, she fell ill from tuberculosis. Could hardly breathe. She wrote a letter to me, hoping that I have a long and happy life, and several letters to Papa, who she was sure would come back."

He reaches over to hold my hand.

"He did not think he would be missed by Harriet. I know from Uncle Xav that she had left him . . . I—"

"You don't have to explain," I say.

"People do a lot of things we can't explain. My grandmother can take a dislike to someone for no reason at all." He says this smiling and sends me a wink. "She will like *you* though." He squeezes my hand for courage.

He is gentle with me, and I can't help but smile above the nerves.

"Did he, my father, ever remarry?"

"No. He works with me. He develops the film. In fact it was Papa who taught me the craft.

"There is a plaque above the door where Maman lived in Brussels. It is an engraving to honour my mother, Xavier, and my uncle Eugène, who was killed, as I mentioned in my letter, for all their underground work and all the lives they saved. I will take you there also while you are here."

Etienne jumps out quickly from the car to open the door for me. At the same time several people walk out the front door to greet us. One is Xavier, whom I have sort of met; one is an older woman, positively beaming with excitement; and the third is my father.

Arthur stands tall and narrow, hair so white against his tanned skin.

"Hello, Eleanor," he says, his voice rumbling softly. He takes out a handkerchief to dab at his wrinkled eyes; then he steps to pull me into an embrace that I have imagined a thousand times. My head against his chest, I sob uncontrollably. I had promised myself I wouldn't.

Gisela gave him her family name apparently. Though I only know him as Dad, which I have called him always, in my dreams.

AUTHOR'S NOTE AND ACKNOWLEDGMENTS

Often when I'm asked why I've chosen particular themes, I talk about a "connection" with places, events, or people that sparks an idea. For this book, the first connection was with sixteen-year-old Private Abraham Bevistein, from the Middlesex Regiment in WWI, who gave a false name and lied about his age when he signed up for war. His parents were heartbroken to learn he had enlisted. After being released from hospital after physical injury and suffering severe anxiety, he was returned to the field, only to be injured again in the following battle. Cleared for duty once more and ordered to the Front, he still felt unwell and wandered away from the trenches. He was swiftly arrested, taken to prison, and put on trial for the crime of desertion. In his final letter to his mother, from prison, he revealed he was "in a bit of trouble," perhaps not fully aware or stoically underplaying the gravity of his situation for his mother's sake. He was alone, without advocacy, and duly executed. Bevistein's mother was haunted by her son's death until her own.

Oftentimes these soldiers had been paralyzed by fear, disorientated by the noise and chaos of battle around them, or suffering a nervous breakdown or shell shock, the condition yet to be fully explored. This punishment for desertion was deemed circumstantially acceptable by a few at the time, but seems incredible to most of us today. Like Bevistein, many other soldiers were also shot for the same military crime, which had devastating and lasting effects on their families.

There were 346 British executions during WWI, 266 of those for the act of desertion. Other offences that resulted in execution ranged from the crime of murder to sleeping at post. The number of French executed for disobeying orders or "cowardice" and for other crimes was over 600. There were very few German executions, according to records; however, they were to make up those numbers with thousands of their own men executed during WWII for such actions. Punishments for similar offences were repeated across other countries during both wars. Thankfully in Britain, by the time of WWII the penalty of execution for such offences had been abolished.

To add further torment during the WWI period, pensions for British families of men who died in service were initially selective, and war widows of deserters didn't qualify. Only late in the war was this rule reversed. These widows weren't automatically eligible; it was up to each to make an individual claim. I can't imagine how hard it would have been for families forced to carry the stigma associated with such events, especially during this period of history, and reveal this "dishonour" publicly. In 2006, 306 of these British soldiers, executed for desertion or cowardice, were given a formal pardon by the British government, Bevistein being one of them.

My second connection was with the story about Leuven (formerly known by the French name of Louvain) in WWI and the burning down of its Catholic university library, which lost over two hundred thousand precious manuscripts and pieces of art. This led me to read in detail about Belgium's story of invasion, which seemed obscured by many other English-written texts regarding major events, tragedies, and acts of heroism from the WWI period. The Belgian experience was by no means a minor event. The invasion and occupation of Belgium saw over 5,521 civilians brutally killed during the initial conflict between 5 August and 21 October 1914, after the invading army broke through

Belgian forces. During that same period, over 15,000 private residences and public buildings were senselessly destroyed, mostly burned. Throughout the war, 277 civilians were executed for resistance participation and other offences against the German government, and 2,614 died from deportations, inadequate food, and disease from poor conditions. The casualty figures are most likely higher, as numbers quoted are only those reported. The injuries and rapes that also occurred should be counted among the atrocities committed as well.

Due to the occupation 1.5 million Belgians were displaced. Belgians lost loved ones, homes, and businesses. Personal items and equipment were seized, food shortages grew more dire as the war progressed, and lives and occupations were drastically rearranged to suit the rules of the occupiers. The university library was eventually rebuilt, only to be destroyed and rebuilt a second time after WWII.

Historians in recent times have revisited, investigated, and shared more of this evidence in detail, such as Larry Zuckerman with his book *The Rape of Belgium*, and John Horne and Alan Kramer with *German Atrocities, 1914: A History of Denial*. These thorough works were helpful to gain a clear picture of events that occurred, particularly in those early months of the war.

In my story, I mention several factual heroes of this time. Edith Cavell was executed for her participation in the resistance in Belgium, helping Allied soldiers escape into neutral territory. Princess Marie de Croÿ and her brother, Prince Réginald de Croÿ, also participated in this endeavour. Cavell was executed on 12 October 1915, alongside another member of the resistance, Philippe Baucq. Prince de Croÿ was implicated during their trial also but by then had already escaped to London. It was later estimated that Cavell helped around one thousand injured soldiers cross the "Frontier." Her work as a spy had long been suspected, but on the centenary of her death, Dame Stella Rimington, the former director general of MI5, revealed there was clear evidence that Cavell's organisation was involved in sending back secret intelligence to the Allies. Cardinal Désiré-Joseph Mercier, archbishop of Malines, is remembered for his pastoral letter *Patriotism and Endurance* opposing the invasion and deportations.

There were a number of underground publications that were courageously operated in secret. The most prolific distributor of news was *La Libre Belgique*, but amongst the other smaller publications was *La Vérité*, of which seven issues were printed and distributed during May and June of 1915.

There are also other books and reports that have assisted with this book's journey: *Six Weeks: The Short and Gallant Life of the British Officer in the First World War* by John Lewis-Stempel; *Storm of Steel* by Ernst Jünger; *Edith Cavell: Faith before the Firing Squad* by Catherine Butcher; *An English Governess in the Great War: The Secret Brussels Diary of Mary Thorp* by Sophie de Schaepdrijver and Tammy M. Proctor (Mary Thorp's diary from 1916); Britain's Bryce report about the "German outrages"; and *The German White Book*, which gave a heavily watered-down version of events, was later found to contain manipulated evidence, and had omitted witness accounts. As always, there are countless other articles, government reports, and personal letters I've collected over the years that have also contributed to my understanding for parts of the story and enabled this book.

As with all towns and cities, there are always structural changes to adapt to urban progress. The Anspach Monument and fountain mentioned is no longer in Place De Brouckère in Brussels, but is now located between the Quai aux Briques and the Quai au Bois à Brûler.

Much of my aim in the stories I write is to put human faces, be they fictional, to the many who lived through these events and imagine the experiences and reactions by innocent parties thrust into such situations. My thanks to Lake Union Publishing for allowing me to do this and to their team of editors, artists, producers, and marketers for their time and work on this book. Without you all, none of my book wishes would have come true!

ABOUT THE AUTHOR

Gemma Liviero is the author of the historical novels *In a Field of Blue*, *The Road Beyond Ruin*, *Broken Angels*, and *Pastel Orphans*, which was a finalist for the 2015 Next Generation Indie Book Awards. In addition to novel writing, her professional career includes copywriting, corporate writing, writing feature articles and editorials, and editing. She holds an advanced diploma of arts (writing) and has continued her studies in arts and other humanities. Gemma lives with her family in Queensland, Australia. Visit www.gemmaliviero.com for more information.